The Codi Cassidy Mystery Omnibus

VOLUME 1

Dan DeKoning

Contents

Acoustics
and
Alibis

CHAPTER ONE

My name is Codi Lynn Cassidy. I'm really excellent at three things: writing and playing music, getting into trouble, and daydreaming. At the time, I found myself attracted to the third since I didn't have my guitar with me, and I didn't feel in the mood for trouble. So, I decided to daydream. I snapped out of my reverie and focused on the scenery passing by the window of the old bus. I took a moment to glance at the GPS on the dashboard. After getting both values, I compared its arrival time to the time on the radio display. Then I calculated I had forty-seven minutes, give or take until we arrived in Quincey, New Mexico.

I looked at the driver, a tall hunk of a man, who currently entertained himself by singing to the radio while keeping the bus between the white lines.

"You want me to drive?" I asked.

He looked over at me and shook his head. "How many times have we had this discussion? There's no way you could handle this machine."

"I had to ask. You good for the next hour? If you need to pull over and take a rest, go ahead. We don't need to be there until this evening," I said.

Bozeman James dismissed me with a wave of his hand and turned his attention back to the road and the radio.

He was right, though. I couldn't drive the big bus. It was over thirty feet long and handled like a brick on wheels. Since I only stand two inches under five feet and can't tip the scale over one hundred pounds wearing my heaviest boots, it's not designed to be driven by a waif like me. I bought it from a retired musician who moved into a retirement community. Although I really didn't need something so large, since he was a good friend of my mom's, he made me an offer I truly couldn't refuse. I admit, there were times I regretted buying the rolling fortress, but those times were far and few between. Bozeman is a skilled tinkerer who keeps the old bus rolling with equal parts mechanical know-how, duct tape, and magic. We have an equal partnership, and we split the bus duties fifty-fifty. Bozeman drives the bus and handles the maintenance, and I keep it clean, and the tiny refrigerator and the adjoining pantry stocked. It's important that the bus feels like a home. We spend over three hundred days on the road, traveling from town to town, doing laps through every state west of the great plains. After all, I can't make a living as a roaming singer/songwriter and cowgirl poet if I don't roam.

Bozeman reached forward and turned the volume down on the radio. "You plan out the set list for tomorrow night?"

"Almost have it done. I need to talk to Sam before I firm it up. We'll see her tonight when we meet her for dinner. From what I gather, it'll be mostly covers, but I'm hoping to get a few originals in."

"How long we playing for? Our usual ninety minutes?"

"Need to shore that up, too. It's one of those gigs where we're playing a set through dinner, and we may do a separate set after dinner."

Bozeman shook his head. "C'mon, Codi, you know how I hate playing during dinner. People are more interested in those side conversations and eating than they are in paying any attention to us."

I understood exactly what Bozeman meant. A concert over dinner meant no attention paid to us, like we were nothing more than background noise. And usually, we got a cold plate of food ten minutes before the diners finished their meal. But it was a paying gig, and exposure, and if it's one thing I liked to do, it was getting good exposure. "I appreciate you hate them, and I normally wouldn't accept, but I'm doing it as a favor for a friend."

"Am I off track, or do you end up booking most of our gigs based on you doing favors for friends?" Bozeman asked.

I offered a smile as an answer, even though Bozeman didn't see my grin while he kept his eyes on the road. It was true. I booked a lot of shows based on leads from people in my circle, but that only accounted for just over fifty percent of the shows we did every year. The entertainment business was all about meeting people and collecting contacts and business cards, and you never knew who would be at a show. Lots of folks on the radio got there because they played a gig that some music producer or executive was at on happenstance.

"Hey, did I not get us at the Colorado State Fair last year? I didn't know anyone there," I said.

I glanced over and saw Bozeman trying to hide a smirk.

"Hey, I said most of the gigs, not all," Bozeman said. "I'm going to take a quick break after all. There's a wayside coming up."

A mile farther down the road, Bozeman pulled into a rest area and parked the bus between two idling semi-trucks.

"Are you getting out?" he asked as he unclasped his seatbelt and opened the door.

"I don't have to. I think I'll check on the kids."

Bozeman nodded, then disappeared through the door, and a glance through the window told me he needed to use the facilities in the worst way. Although we had a functioning bathroom on board, we visited public restrooms whenever possible, since Bozeman hated pumping out the gray water and black water tanks. I don't blame him for that, and every time it needs to be done, I suddenly have other important tasks I need to attend to.

I unbuckled, stepped into the kitchen, and rummaged around in a cabinet until I found the container of cat treats I wanted. Carefully, I shook three of the fish-shaped, salmon scented goodies into my palm, replaced the container, and started my search for Gibson.

Since we were on a bus, that meant limited places for Gibson to hang out. I looked around the small common area that contained the kitchen area. The area also held a small table, four chairs, and a built-in entertainment center that held a sound system and a television. Gibson was nowhere in sight. I walked down the hallway past the closed bathroom door, and the closed door to the room where we stored our performing gear. That left only two options.

I took a quick peek into Bozeman's room, and it took little

effort to see Gibson wasn't in there, either. Bozeman is a tidy man, almost to the point of annoyance. He made up the twin bed with military precision. He squirreled away all his clothing in the small closest or compartments in his room. The small space smelled a bit like lemon, so I guessed he must have deep-cleaned recently, which he did once a week without fail. His room, like mine, had a small dressing table with a folding office chair, and his table held a few sheets of manuscript paper and a coffee mug filled with pens. I stepped over, glanced at the paper, read his scrawl, and determined he was writing a tune about some girl named Jenny. I continued on my quest to find the cat.

Way in the bus's rear was my bedroom. My bedroom, like Bozeman's, was spartan and held only a bed, table, and chair. Unlike Bozeman's room, mine looked a little more lived in. My bed had a bookshelf headboard stuffed with paperbacks, and although I pulled the bed's comforter up, the bed still looked messy. The foot of the bed held the two shirts I had tried on that morning before I settled on the T-shirt I currently had on. My desk held a couple more paperbacks, my laptop, and my favorite hairbrush. I owned a coffee mug that was a twin to Bozeman's. Instead of having only pens like his, mine held a single pen, hair ties, paper clips, pocket change, a butterscotch candy, guitar picks, and other assorted items. Around every six weeks, the mug fills up, then I'm forced to dump out the contents and clean it out. It's always a surprise to me what I find. I shouldn't have that mug at all since sometimes Merle or Dolly get in there, look for treasures, and spread the stuff all over the bus. On the bed were two pillows stacked one on top of the other, and on the top of the highest pillow slept Gibson, my cat. As I entered the room, Gibson opened one eye, stretched out a paw, then yawned while I approached. The five-year-old tuxedo cat sat up when I opened my hand and offered the treats to him. They were Gibson's favorite, so he ate them right out of my palm.

"Who's a good boy?" I picked up Gibson, put him over one shoulder like I was burping a baby, and scratched his ears and rubbed his back. In response, he nuzzled my ear and purred. I met Gibson at a gas station outside of Provo, Utah. When I headed to use the restroom, I heard a mewing coming from a cardboard box, and when I opened the box, there was Gibson with his big green eyes. He was only a couple months old then, was undernourished, and was the most pitiful creature I had ever seen. Of course, I fell in love with him right away and adopted him on the spot. The bus rocked, which meant that Bozeman had returned, so I gave Gibson a kiss on the forehead and placed him back on his pillow and returned to the passenger seat.

"How is everyone?" Bozeman asked as he strapped in and turned over the engine.

"You were back too soon, so I only found Gibson."

"I guessed that already," Bozeman said.

"How could you tell?"

"The black fur on your left ear."

Instinctively, I tugged at my ear, then looked in my hand. Sure enough, there were three black strands of hair between my fingers. I brushed the fur on my jeans and returned to my duty of watching the world go by.

Bozeman swerved to avoid a tumbleweed, and a mile later, we passed the sign welcoming us to Quincey, New Mexico, which was founded in 1861. We passed block after block of one-story houses, then turned left on Main Street.

There was something that always appealed to me about small towns' main drags, but it was something I could never put my finger on. As we headed downtown, the buildings inched closer together, until businesses on entire blocks shared party walls. Had Quincey been a county seat, I'm certain there would've been a courthouse directly in the middle of the town. Since it wasn't, Main Street continued straight through the little burg. We drove past a movie theater that featured *Rear Window* on the marquee. The theater was next to the florist, followed by a clothing store, a hardware store, and a consignment shop. Sometimes I passed the time playing a game in my head where I had to spot certain businesses. Like a diner or a barber, or other establishments that were common to ninety percent of America's tiny towns. Today, though, I simply looked at the buildings as we passed them.

"Where are we supposed to park this beast?" Bozeman asked.

It was a valid question since Main Street barely handled the cars already parked along the road. As it was, I was nervous that Bozeman was going to knock off a side mirror or two as we passed cars.

"There's an empty lot behind the bakery. The GPS says the bakery is another two blocks up on the left. Turn left on Jefferson Street, and it will be right on the corner."

Bozeman found Jefferson, turned left, and took a quick left turn into the lot. There was a rusted sign that identified the lot as 'Smith's Motors', but other than the sign, there was no suggestion that a business had ever stood on the property. Bozeman parked the bus and shut it down. He stood and stretched. "Long ride. I'm glad that's over. When do we meet your friend?"

"We're supposed to meet her for dinner at seven, but since we're so early, I might try to see if I can find her. What are you going to do?"

Bozeman rubbed his chin. "Don't know. I could use some air, so I might take a walk, maybe work on some music."

I nodded, walked to my bedroom, and grabbed my copy of the bus keys, my wallet, and my favorite ball cap. Once I was ready, I said my goodbyes to Gibson and Bozeman and stepped out of the bus. I took a deep breath of New Mexico air, then walked back to Main Street. At the corner, I got a whiff of fresh baked bread from the bakery. My stomach rumbled, and I desired a loaf, but the locked door and the sign told me the store was closed. Dejected, I walked down the sidewalk and did window shopping as I passed a pharmacy, a used bookstore, and a confectioner's shop until I came to the hotel. I noticed a brass plate attached to the building, and I loved learning about history, so I stepped close and read the plaque aloud.

"The Quincey Inn. Established 1862 by John J., Quincey serviced the town along the stagecoach route from Texas to California. The hotel has hosted five presidents, and such notorious figures as Doc Holliday and Butch Cassidy. The Quincey Inn joined New Mexico Register of Historical Places in 1996."

My eyes had barely focused on the last word of the sign when I heard a shrill, excited laugh come from my right side, followed by my name being called.

"Codi Lynn Cassidy!"

I hadn't even turned toward the noise when I saw a flash of long brown hair and I fell into an embrace that knocked the breath from my body.

"Codi! I wasn't expecting to see you until later. I'm so happy you're here."

With some effort, I pulled away from the hug and looked into the beautiful brown eyes of Samantha Henry. "Hi Sam, it's great to see you too. You look great."

I wasn't lying. Sam looked great. Spectacular, actually. She was a good eight inches taller than me. She also had twenty pounds of muscle on me, and had a sparkle in her eyes that never died out, regardless of what she was going through in life.

"What are you doing here so soon?" Sam asked as she hooked her arm into mine and led me away from the hotel and back down the street in the direction I initially came.

"We left earlier than expected, and there wasn't much traffic, so here I am."

"I can't tell you how grateful I am that you came. You know, I never wanted to be on the committee, and I especially didn't want to be in charge of the entertainment. I was thinking of hiring one of the wedding DJs from one of the surrounding cities, but then I thought of you."

Once we got to the corner, Sam fished a set of keys out of her pocket and opened the bakery door. Immediately, the fabulous scent of baked bread enveloped me as she pulled me over the threshold and closed the door behind me. If there was a man-made scent as pleasant as the inside of a bakery, I was yet to find it. As Sam locked the door and set down her keys, I glanced at the display case. My salivary glands kicked into overdrive when I saw the arrangement of pies and muffins in the case. Clearly, I couldn't hide my gaze or my intentions.

"Would you like something?" Sam asked.

"I'd love a muffin. Preferably blueberry."

Sam went around the corner of the counter, took a muffin from the case, and handed it to me. By touch alone, I could tell that it was moist, and it looked like it came right out of a magazine. I took a bite and let out a moan. It was definitely the best muffin I had ever tasted.

"Good?" Sam asked.

I couldn't speak, so I just nodded. I couldn't imagine where she had gotten the blueberries from, but they were the largest, juiciest blueberries I'd ever eaten. She topped the muffin with just a touch of caramelized sugar that added another layer of sweetness and a crunch that added to the overall texture.

"Be right back. You enjoy that." Sam disappeared into the rear of the bakery while I finished the muffin. She appeared three minutes later carrying a sheet pan of pies that she placed on the counter.

"Would you like another muffin?" she asked.

"I'd love another, but I can't. You've seen how once I get started with something like that, I can't stop. The button on my jeans would burst open in an hour."

I dug around in my pocket for some cash. "What do I owe you for the muffin?"

"How about sixty cents?"

Her answer flabbergasted me. "Sixty cents? How do you make a profit selling a muffin for sixty cents?"

Sam smiled. "I won't make a profit on that one. The ingredients run around fifty-three cents, plus labor and whatnot. I usually charge three bucks for a muffin, but consider it the friend discount."

I wanted to argue, but I also didn't want to insult her generosity, so I handed her a dollar. "Thank you. It was wonderful. Keep the change."

Sam accepted the dollar and set it next to the cash register.

"What's with the pies?" I asked.

Sam took a stack of boxes from behind the counter and started boxing up the bakery. "Besides being in charge of entertainment, I'm also on the catering committee."

"Sounds like a lot of work."

Sam shrugged. "It's not too bad. I'm only supplying the bread and the dessert. Rob and Lisa McMurtry from the diner are taking care of the lion's share of the meal."

Sam slipped back around the counter and captured me in a hug again. "It's so good to see you, Codi. I almost didn't recognize you with that hair of yours, but I figured it had to be you."

Ah, yes. My hair. Growing up, I never did like my hair, unlike Sam's, which was a consistent, beautiful brown. Thanks to genetics, I started going gray in my mid-twenties. Since then, I had been dying it practically every color under the rainbow, and at the present time, it was a light blue. You would think that would be off-putting for a country singer. But since I currently had a pixie cut, and I normally wore my cowboy hat when I performed, people rarely noticed, and if they did, no one ever mentioned it.

"How did you find me? I haven't seen you in years."

"Social media. I keep tabs on you. When you broke the top forty and your song was on the radio all the time, I'd tell everyone I talked to you were a friend of mine, but of course, no one believed me." Sam laughed as she stepped back to her pies.

"How did you end up here? I thought you always wanted to be a big-time baker in Manhattan with your own cooking show," I said.

"You, of all people, should know how those dreams work out. I had a place in Atlanta for a few years, but I didn't like it. The bakery was making good money, but most of that was in wedding cakes, and those were something I never enjoyed making. Besides, how many bridezillas can one person deal with before they go nuts? Through some acquaintances I discovered this place was up for sale, so I took a chance, packed my bags, and headed west."

"I'm surprised a town this small would have its own bakery."

"That same thought occurred to me, but I went over the numbers with the previous owner before I took the plunge. I have a contract with the diner to supply their bread and pies. Every morning, I do a pretty good donut and bagel business, and I still make cakes for birthdays and weddings. I'm actually making just as much money as I was in Atlanta, but here, I know all of my customers and can appreciate the small-town life."

I knew what Sam meant about the small-town community. There was something special about a close-knit group of people that added value to everything. Going to work was much easier when the people you serviced were the people you knew. I even felt that way in my business, even though my small-town community had spread over a dozen states. It wasn't the distance, so much as the people, that, for me, gave it a small-town feel. Every time we put on a show, I recognized a few faces in the crowd.

"So, what are you working on? Can I give you a hand?" I asked.

Sam smiled. "Sure thing. I usually have a woman who works here with me, but she came down with the flu. How good are you at making pies and bread?"

It was my turn to smile. "Well, to be honest, I can bake a cake if I follow directions on the back of the box it came in, and I'm great at putting sliced bread into a toaster. Sometimes I even remember to plug the toaster in before I use it."

Sam motioned for me to follow her into the kitchen. The sight of the stainless-steel appliances, the multiple ovens, and huge bins of flour and sugar immediately overwhelmed me. I swear I saw a wire whisk that was half my height, and a mixing bowl I could probably swim in. I had been inside commercial kitchens before, but this was my first bakery. Once I got done looking around, Sam helped me into an apron and gave me a hairnet.

"You'll want to wear this instead of your cap. You'll never get all the flour off it. How are you with taking things out of the oven, letting them cool down, and then putting them into boxes?" she asked.

Now she was on par with my skill level in the kitchen. "I think I can handle that."

"Great. We've got one more batch to bake up and then we'll head on over to the diner for dinner. You've got a boyfriend, right? He's meeting us for dinner too?"

"He's not my boyfriend, he's my business partner," I said.

It was a common mistake that most people made. Everyone assumed that a man and a woman living on a bus together had to be involved romantically. But for us, it wasn't the case. I admit, Bozeman is a hunk, but he's not my type of hunk, and although we have a musical connection, we never even had a single spark of a romantic one. "I'll call him when we're ready to go over to eat. We're both really interested in hearing what this benefit is all about."

CHAPTER TWO

What's good here?" Bozeman asked as he set down the menu and looked around to check what other people were eating.

"It's Friday night, so it's the pot roast that usually brings folks in. Meatloaf is pretty good too. Burgers are always a safe bet," Sam said.

"What about the catfish?" I asked.

"I've never had it, but lots of people seem to enjoy that, too."

The server approached the table and dropped off glasses of water for the women and a beer for Bozeman. "Have you decided on what you want for dinner?" she asked with her pen hovering an inch above her order pad.

Sam took a quick drink and set down her glass. "Lisa, this is my friend Codi, and her partner, Bozeman. They're the musicians I booked for tomorrow night. Lisa and her husband, Rob, own this place and are doing the catering for the event."

"Pleased to meet you," Lisa said. She wiped her hand on her apron and shook with Codi and Bozeman. Lisa stood five-seven, and had a bright shock of red hair atop her head, and dimples in both cheeks.

"Likewise," I said.

Bozeman tipped his hat in his cowboy way. He preferred to stay in character when out in public.

Bozeman ordered the pot roast, I ordered the meatloaf with a side salad, no dressing, and Sam opted for a burger.

"Codi says we'll be playing during dinner?" Bozeman said after a long draw on his beer.

"For some of it, anyway," Sam said. "The plan is to get the ceremony kicked off. Then, the important folks in the room will be introduced, dinner will start, and we'd like you to play for around twenty minutes. After that, there will be some speeches from the mayor and a couple of others while dessert is served."

"What about after?" Bozeman asked.

"After the dinner, it becomes a little more informal, so you can play for as long as you want to, or rather, as long as the agreed fee lasts. It was four hundred, correct?"

I nodded. "I hate to charge you at all, but we've got to cover our expenses."

"Don't be silly, Codi. Of course you should charge for being here. Everyone who is providing a service is getting paid. It's not a benefit, it's more of an awareness campaign. That reminds me, here." Sam reached around and pulled an envelope from her back pocket. "Here's the cash."

I took the envelope, and without opening it, folded it and shoved it into the front pocket of my jeans. "Thanks. Tell us about the event. What's it about, a fundraiser or something, right?"

"Well, see that guy over there at the table by the window? Wearing jeans and a sport coat and talking like he's trying to draw attention to himself?"

Although Bozeman had a straight view, I had to turn almost all the way around to look at where Sam was pointing with her fork. Near the front window sat a party of five. The man sat in the center of the table, with his back to the window so he could look at everyone in the restaurant. Two people sat on either side of him, and the fellow in question was telling a story more loudly and more animated than the story probably dictated. From where I sat, if I concentrated, I barely heard his voice, but between the distance from him and the other conversations around me, I didn't make out the words. I turned back around to face the people at my table.

"That's Sherman Stier. He's our local real estate mogul. He owns a bunch of land outside of town, and he's trying to get support to build a golf course and resort out there. Those people he's with are potential investors he's brought in from Phoenix, Taos, and Albuquerque. They initially proposed this event to rebuild and rebrand Main Street and generate more tourist business for the town. You know, spiffy things up a little, make this town a stop for people looking to get off the interstate and get a taste of the good old days. The committee has been working on the plan for seven months."

"Who's on the committee?" Bozeman asked.

"Most of the business owners on Main Street, since we're the ones most affected by the increase in tourist traffic. Me, Rob and Lisa, the mayor, the owner of the Quincey Inn, and a few others. You'll meet most of them tomorrow night if you want to. Oh, and Sherman, of course. He's the chair of the committee."

"The mayor isn't the chair?" I asked. "Wouldn't that make the most sense?"

"No, she isn't. Everyone assumed she would be the chairperson, but she declined. She's got enough to worry about trying to run the town. To her credit, she's gotten us pretty far in the three years she's been mayor. Did you notice the potholes on Main Street when you drove in?"

Bozeman leaned forward in his chair. "I don't recall seeing any."

"That's because after probably a good twenty years of complaining, the new mayor got them all patched up. Even installed pretty cobblestone crosswalks at every intersection around downtown. She's also been working hard at getting the local schools updated, and the water quality improved."

"She sounds like a go-getter," I said.

Sam nodded. "Sure is. She would've been the perfect choice to lead the committee. Unfortunately, we're stuck with Sherman."

"Is he doing a terrible job?" I asked.

"Let's say he has a tendency to push things in directions that will benefit him the most."

"Like the golf course?" I asked.

Sam nodded. "Exactly like that. Although he claims that bringing people into his resort will be good for the town too. A rising tide and all that."

I spied Lisa approaching with a tray of food. Behind her trailed a tall, thin man in a chef's coat. While Lisa passed out our food, she introduced her husband. "Rob, this here is Codi and Bozeman. They're the singers for tomorrow."

Rob offered his hand. "Glad to meet you," he said. As Lisa finished food distribution, Rob simply stared at me. After a moment, he scratched his buzz-cut head and walked away.

Lisa's cheeks turned red from embarrassment. "You'll have to excuse him. He's a little shy around celebrities."

I spotted him rushing back from the kitchen with his phone in hand. "I'm not really a celebrity. And he can't be that shy. He's coming back."

Rob reached the table and turned his phone so I recognized the person on the screen. "Is this you?"

It only took me a glance to determine he had pulled up the video of my one hit song. It was an excellent song, but I always hated the video. The producer headed in a much different creative direction than I wanted to, but I was only a kid and didn't have a clue what was going on, so what did I know? "Yep, that's me."

Rob smiled widely. "I knew that was you the second I saw you. My gosh. I loved that video. Can I get a selfie with you? And maybe an autograph?"

In my peripheral vision, I saw Bozeman smirk. He wasn't big on being approached by fans, but I didn't mind. I always figured it was the fans who bought CDs and tickets and other merchandise. It was the fans who showed up at county fairs and other gigs. It was the fans who waited for the show in heat or cold or rain. I never turned a fan away. "Of course."

I stood and pushed away from the table, and I stepped closer to Rob and put my arm around him. Rob handed the phone to Lisa. Since there was a good foot's height difference between Rob and me, Lisa had to back up almost into the lap of the person at the table behind her. After a few photos, Lisa shooed Rob back to the kitchen.

"I'm so sorry about that," Lisa said.

"No worries, it happens all the time. I've got some promo photos on the bus. I'll sign one of those for him and give it to him at the event tomorrow," I said.

"That would make his day," Lisa said. "I'll leave you to dinner. If y'all need anything, just call."

I retook my seat and adjusted myself in front of the meatloaf and dug in. I was famished, despite the giant muffin I had eaten earlier.

"That happen often?" Sam asked. "Getting asked for pictures and autographs?"

"It all depends. Usually on show nights I'll get asked for a dozen or more, and occasionally someone will recognize me out in public and ask, but most people will leave me alone. I don't really mind, though. It's all a part of the business. The way you bake those muffins, people should ask for your autograph."

Sam laughed, put down her burger, and wiped her fingers on the napkin. "Well, I get asked for recipes now and then, but that's not quite the same thing."

"Sure, it is," I said. "You provide something that people love, and they want to share that experience. Do you ever give them the recipes?"

Sam leaned in until our foreheads almost touched. "Yes, but to be honest, it's not the complete recipe. I always leave out the secret ingredients, so their version never comes out quite like mine. Nothing to make the recipe fail, mind you, just something that will make their finished product just a little different from mine."

"That's really smart," I said. "Keeps them coming back for yours."

"My thoughts exactly."

Bozeman finished his meal, drained his beer, and stood. "Excuse me, ladies. I have some work to finish on the bus. It was nice to meet you, Sam. I look forward to seeing you again tomorrow." Bozeman winked at her, then walked toward the door.

"He likes you," I said.

"How can you tell?" Sam asked.

"We've been partners for a long time. I could tell just by how he wouldn't stop jabbering."

Sam took the last bite of her burger and washed it down. "Jabbering? I don't think he said over six sentences."

"Yeah, but that's a lot for him. He's the strong, silent type. You'll see more of his personality on the stage tomorrow night."

"Didn't he just leave you with the bill? Shouldn't the cowboy pay? Is chivalry dead?" Sam asked.

"Not in this case. Whether he pays, or I do, it comes from the same business account. So, consider it a company expense," I said.

"Ah, gotcha. That makes sense. You didn't eat your salad."

"Oh, yeah, thanks for the reminder." I pulled a plastic gallon-sized bag from my pocket, and discretely as possible, dumped the salad into the bag and sealed it up.

Sam looked at me like I had a third arm sprouting from my chin.

"It's for my pets," I explained as I set the salad next to the leg of my chair.

Sam looked like she didn't believe me.

I was about to offer a more in-depth explanation about the kids when someone slipped into Bozeman's chair.

"Hi," the man said. He was wearing a Toronto Blue Jays windbreaker and hat to match.

"Codi Cassidy, meet Dean Williams," Sam said. "Dean is our local historian."

"In training," Dean said as he shook my hand. "Fourth generation, actually. My great-grandfather started it, and it just got passed down from there."

"I would've figured you for a tourist," I said.

"Nah, I'm just a big baseball fan. Just got home last week from my yearly pilgrimage to baseball parks. This year I hit Toronto, Detroit, Cleveland, and Cincinnati. I'm trying to get to a game at every stadium. I'm about halfway there."

"That's interesting," I said.

"Are you in town for the big event?" Dean asked.

"She's the singer," Sam said.

"No kidding. I look forward to the show then. Hey, listen, can I take Sam away for a minute or two? Just some committee members' stuff."

I opened my mouth to reply, but Sam beat me to it. "That's rude. Whatever you can say to me, you can say in front of her. She's my friend."

Dean looked at me. "I meant no offense." He turned back to Sam. "It's not about her overhearing. It's just kind of busy in here, don't you think?"

I saw the almost imperceptible shift of his head toward the front table. Sam caught it too.

"Oh. I understand. Yes, it is loud in here. Let's go outside and talk for a moment. Codi, I'll be right back, okay?"

I smiled my best smile. "Of course. Take your time."

Dean took Sam by the hand and led the way, and I turned my head to watch them leave the diner. Then I shifted into Bozeman's seat, so I had a better view of the place. Like Bozeman, I always preferred a seat with my back to the wall so I could monitor everything going on around me. It wasn't a cowboy thing, but something my father had taught me.

Brian Cassidy, my father, was a detective for as long as I could remember. He worked for the Denver Police Department, and since I was an inquisitive kid, I always had questions about the cases he worked on. Although he would divulge no personal information, so I never knew the 'who', he always shared the tips and tricks he used to figure out who the criminal was. During that time, I also had a love of police procedurals on television. We would watch those together and he would tell me what would work in real life, and what would work only in Hollywood. By the time I got to my teens, we'd discuss his cases, and I would tell him what I would do if I were the detective. More often than not, I was on the right track of what clues to look for. By far, the biggest skill he taught me was the power of observation. He often said that I could learn more at a crime scene, just sitting in a chair and watching a suspect pool than I could with all the fancy DNA evidence shown on TV. He said that's where most shows got it wrong. The detective's job was narrowing the suspect list until it was down to just one, and it was the court's job to prove it.

My mom, Christina Cassidy, was where I got my love of music from. It was mom who taught me the guitar and the piano. She was the one who got me into music theory and songwriting, and it was she who first supported my first public appearance at my ninth-grade talent show. In the summer when school was out, mom would let me travel with her to local shows. I'd help set up her equipment, or change her guitar strings, or run lines for the amps. I learned from her all about stage presence and how to work with an audience, and how to create a set list to keep the crowd from being bored. Interestingly enough, she also taught me about the power of observation. She drilled into my head that when on stage, I always had to be aware of who was out there and what they were doing. You never knew if someone was going to cause trouble. And when trouble started, it was best to grab the guitar and head backstage if the venue had one, or head for the door if it didn't.

I didn't really know what she meant, but the more shows I went to, the more shows I spent sitting in the wings and watching the audience while listening to her. I could tell who was there to have fun, who had a little too much to drink, who was looking for love, and who was looking for trouble.

I learned a lot of lessons from both my parents, lessons that I still carried with me and worked to hone every time I was out in public or up on a stage.

What I learned while I was sitting alone at the diner waiting for Sam to return was that people didn't seem to care for Mr. Sherman Stier. As the locals entered or left the diner, they stopped at other tables to share handshakes with friends. I noticed several friendly slaps on the back, and a bunch of quick snippets of conversations, but none with Sherman. In fact, most people seemed to avoid his table altogether. That didn't seem quite right to me, and I wondered why, but since I had no one to ask, I held onto my question in my head.

I saw Lisa approaching the table, so I emptied my glass of water and put on a smile.

"I'm sorry to bother you, Ms. Codi. Sam called and said she'd be away for longer than expected, so she asked me to tell you not to wait for her."

"Okay. Thank you. If give me the bill, I'll settle up and be on my way then."

Lisa waved her hands back and forth as if trying to ward off a demon. "No. There's no charge. If Rob heard I made his favorite country star pay for dinner, I'd never hear the end of it. He'd bug me about it from now until judgment day."

I reached into my pocket for my wallet. "At least let me leave you a tip, then. The service was excellent."

Lisa begged that off as well. "No. Please. If you can remember that signed photo for Rob, and that will more than make up for a tip."

I put my wallet back. "Thank you so much, but please, the next time I'm here, I'll pay like any other customer."

Lisa nodded and left to check on the other tables. I grabbed my bagged salad and left the diner.

The diner was only two blocks from the bakery, so we had walked there. It was a beautiful New Mexico night. The stars were coming out, and the moon was bright. I would've loved to get out into the desert and away from the city lights to really appreciate the night sky, but I knew I had other things to do. As I walked to the bakery, I passed the historical museum, which was on the opposite side of the street. I noticed downstairs all the lights were out, but on the second floor, there was a light on. Although someone had drawn the curtains, I could see animated shadows pacing back and forth in front of the window, as if in a heated discussion. I couldn't help but wonder if that was Sam and Dean. Were they lovers having a quarrel? Was there something else going on? Either way, it wasn't my business.

It was just after seven the next morning, and I was sitting outside the bus on my favorite lawn chair with Merle on my lap. He was a playful fellow who enjoyed getting his belly scratched. From where I was sitting, I saw Sam come out of the bakery's back door and walk toward me with her head down. It was body language I remembered from long ago when we hung out together. Sam was feeling penitent. She stopped a couple feet in front of me, lifted her chin, and looked me in the eye.

"I'm sorry about leaving you alone in the diner last night. Dean and I had some … committee business to discuss."

I thought about letting her go on, and giving her the business about her ditching me, but honestly, I couldn't do it. I was never one to hold grudges, especially over something so minor. "It's okay. I understand."

Sam took a step closer. "That's a pretty cat."

At that moment, Merle did a circle in my lap, revealing his striped tail before settling back down.

Sam took two steps backward. "Is that a skunk?"

I lifted him up so she could see him better. "This is Merle. Don't worry, he can't spray. Come, say hello."

Sam didn't move.

"Come on, you chicken, he's okay. Come feed him a tomato and he'll be your friend forever." I reached for the salad bag at my feet, extracted a couple of cherry tomatoes, and held them for Sam to take.

Merle watched the transaction with great interest as Sam took the fruit from my hands and took a hesitant step closer. She held out a tomato, and Merle reached forward with his paws, grabbed it from her, and nibbled at it. A drop of tomato juice appeared on his chin, and I wiped it away without thinking about it.

"Why in the world do you have a pet skunk?" Sam asked.

"I rescued him from a vet when I had to take my cat in for a tooth removal. He was in the cage right next to Gibson, and they looked almost like twins, so I took them both home. Skunks are smart and sociable animals. You can scratch his belly if you like."

"Thanks, I'll pass on that. You have a cat and a skunk? Do they get along okay?" Sam gave Merle the second tomato, who had made quick work of the first one.

I nodded. "You should see them together. I think they think the other is part of their own species. For most of the time, they all get along fine."

"All?"

"See anything interesting under the front fender of the bus?"

Sam bent at the waist, looked for several seconds, and straightened. "Is that a raccoon?"

I nodded. "That's Dolly, the famous three-legged raccoon. She's part of the family, but you'll want to watch your wallet around her. Despite being down a paw, she's a formidable pickpocket. Willie and Waylon are somewhere around here, too. They're a couple of chipmunks who live in a nest in a rusted-out spot in the back of my bus."

"And you travel with this menagerie?"

"Yep, we're one big, happy family." I lifted Merle from my lap and set him on the ground. He nuzzled my leg with his nose, then went off to join Dolly under the bus. "What's the plan today?"

"I've got bread and a couple pies to bake for tonight, and then I have to be at the event early to set up."

"What time can I get into the venue? We have to set up and do a sound check."

"I'll be there around four, so you can come anytime you want after that. It's being held in the hall of the First Baptist Church, which is about five blocks from here. Go down to Adams, turn right, and you can't miss it from there. It's the only enormous church on that street. There's a small lot in the back, and I'll cone off some room for your bus so people don't park there."

"I appreciate that. You need any help?" I asked.

"You have nothing you need to do for your show?"

"Not really. We worked out the set list last night, and I'd like to go over it with you to see if there're any changes you'd like. Other than that, all I need to do is restring a guitar, but that won't take any more time than fifteen minutes," I said.

"Well, come along then. We'll talk about the music, and I'll make a baker out of you."

Somehow, I doubted that.

CHAPTER THREE

I got up from my chair, dumped the remains of the salad into the bowl Merle and Dolly were eating from, and followed Sam into the bakery. When I walked in the door, I expected to have to set things up from scratch to begin the day. To my surprise, there were already dozens of dinner rolls cooling on racks, and more rising.

"In about ten minutes, those pies can come out of the oven," Sam said as she donned an apron. "After you're finished with that, there's a blueberry muffin up front that needs eating, so I'd appreciate it if you would do something about that as well. Since you're helping me out, you can keep the dollar."

I didn't bother to hide my smile. "If you insist. What time did you get here?"

"About four. I open the doors at eight, so I always get here early to make the donuts and bagels. Once the morning rush is gone, I make the dinner breads and desserts for the diner, and slide in any special orders I have."

"You sound like you're always busy."

"A baker's life is never idle." Sam basted some melted butter over a sheet of unbaked rolls and slid them into the oven. "Probably just like yours, right?"

I thought about it. We spent the vast majority of our time on the road, just getting from one place to another. Bozeman and I both wrote songs and practiced playing music, both separately and together. But because of the simple nature of our business, we did those things anytime we wanted. The only real committed time we had to be anywhere was any time we contracted for. That time would range anywhere from one to four hours, including the time spent on sound checks and selling merchandise afterward. "No, I got the better end of the deal. I couldn't even imagine working as hard as you do."

Sam put her hands on her hips. "It's not that bad. I take every Sunday off, and Saturdays too in the winter. And all the major holidays, of course. Although, I do put in extra hours before Thanksgiving, Christmas, and Valentine's Day. As you can probably guess, I always have lots of orders for those. I don't mind, though. I wouldn't give up being a baker for anything, not even for being a famous country star like you. By the way, you've got flour on your nose, superstar."

I thought she was kidding, so I grabbed a stainless-steel mixing bowl and checked out my reflection. Son of a gun. "How did that get there? I didn't touch a thing yet."

Sam chuckled. "It's a workplace hazard. Trust me, that flour dust can get into places you wouldn't want me to mention."

I was about to tell her I needed no further information when the back door opened, and a woman entered. Physically, she looked to be in her late thirties or early forties, but the weariness on her face made her appear older. Aftereffects of a severe illness, I thought. Like Sam, she dressed in jeans and a T-shirt with the bakery's name emblazoned on it.

"Hey, Shanna. This is my friend, Codi Cassidy. Feeling better?"

"Hi Codi. Nice to meet you. Yes. Sorry I wasn't able to be here for the last few days. It was a struggle to even get out of bed. I wasn't even sure if I would be in today."

"I told you before, if you're sick, stay away. We certainly don't want you sneezing all over the pastries you're serving to customers. Shanna runs the front of the house for me, and I'm teaching her some of my tricks of the trade as well."

Shanna donned a fresh apron and disappeared to the front. I overheard some shuffling, and the cash register opening and closing. Shanna moved back and forth, grabbing bakery items for the display cases. The timer dinged, so I pulled four pies out of the oven and placed them gently on the cooling racks. All four were Dutch Apple, my second favorite pie, after only a fluffy Boston Creme.

"Better get that muffin before Shanna sells it," Sam said.

Taking Sam's advice, I rushed to the front, where I found the muffin sitting on a napkin next to the register.

"I sensed you coming," Shanna explained.

The bakery had three small wrought-iron tables common in old ice cream parlors, and each table sat two, so I took my muffin to one and sat down.

"Want something to drink with that?" Shanna asked.

"Water would be fine." I half expected to get a simple cup of water, but Shanna presented me with a chilled bottle. I opened the bottle, then took a swig. Chilled was fine, but I actually preferred my water at room temperature, but I wouldn't tell her that. "Thanks. Do you enjoy working here?" I removed the liner from the muffin, broke off a piece of the bottom, and ate it. It was just as delicious as I remembered from the day before.

"It's a great place, and I can't imagine working anywhere else. I got lucky. I just got back to town a couple of months ago after being away for a few years. You see, I had to escape from a… toxic relationship, so when I came home, I had to find work. Sam found out about my hard-luck story and asked me to work here. I really like it. I'm thinking of opening my very own bakery someday. Sam's been a godsend, and I don't know what I would've done without her." Shanna disappeared for a few minutes, then returned with a tray of donuts that she placed in the case.

While I worked on my muffin, I looked outside and saw Sherman Stier across the street with the four fellows he entertained for dinner the night before. Directly across from the bakery was a small artist's gallery. I saw it was closed since there was a big red 'closed' sign in the front window that I noticed from my seat. It seemed the group of men were more interested in the actual building than the shop inside. One turned down the corner and studied the building, as if he was accounting for each brick in the structure. At one point, he reached up, touched the stone, then looked at his fingers. After a few minutes, they regrouped, and Sherman pointed in my direction. Without stopping to look for traffic, the men marched across the street. I checked the clock on the wall over Shanna's shoulder. The bakery didn't open for another twenty minutes.

Sherman peered in the window, saw us inside, and rapped on the door. A bit of anger flashed through Shanna's hazel eyes, and she sighed heavily. She took a moment to compose herself before she opened the door a crack and slipped into her best professional voice. "I'm sorry, we don't open until eight."

Sherman pushed his way through the door, and aggressively stomped into the bakery like a lowland gorilla showing its dominance. "I'm not here for food. I'd like to talk to the owner."

Shanna took an involuntary step backward. "You know what her name is."

I tried to stay invisible and eat my muffin while Shanna fetched Sam from the back.

Sam came from the back, wiping her hands on a towel as she approached. "Can I help you?"

Sherman stepped forward with no introductions for his colleagues. "I'll come right down to it. We'd like to buy this building. As you've heard, there's a resort and golf community going up outside of town. We'd like to make sure we have a presence within town itself, and what better place to have it than right here on Main Street?"

"We've talked about this before, with the same answer. The bakery is not for sale." Sam said.

Sherman took another half-step closer to her. Apparently, he wasn't used to being turned down. "I'm not interested in the bakery, just the building. Everything is for sale. Just tell me your asking price, and we can get this deal done."

"And what am I supposed to do with the bakery? This is my livelihood."

"Surely you can move it to another part of town."

"No way. There's been a bakery at this location since they founded this town. I'm not moving."

"Well, I'm sure we would find you a position at the new resort. In management perhaps? Better hours, better pay, benefits, vacation time."

"No deal. Please leave. I have customers to serve soon."

Sherman leaned in close to Sam and whispered soft enough I had to strain to pick it up. "I will get this building. You and your precious bakery can't stop the wheels of progress." Sherman turned, left the building, and escorted his party down the street to the next target on his wish list.

Sam closed the door and locked it behind him.

"Nice guy," I said.

Sam shook her head. "He's a prince. He rolled into town about three years ago and started buying up properties like mad. At first, it wasn't a big deal because he seemed to go for tracts of lands that had for sale signs on them forever. He bought defunct farms and businesses and other properties like that outside of the city limits that no one else wanted. Within the last few months, he started focusing on properties in town. Clearly there's a plan there, but I can't guess what it is. All I understand is people aren't happy."

"Why?" I asked.

"Partially because he's an outsider. You get how small towns can be, right? Hard to fit in? I've been here for eight years, and it's only been within the last year or two that people have warmed up to me."

I wiped away the crumbs from my shirt. "The muffins probably help."

Sam laughed. "You're probably right. Yes, I'm an outsider, but I provide a service that the people want, so I'm sure that has helped. Stier, on the other hand, just pushed his way in, without trying to fit in, which hasn't endeared him to many people. The townsfolk here like what they've built and are resistant to any big changes."

A timer dinged in the back, so Sam excused herself. I took a moment to make sure I hadn't left a mess, and Shanna returned to stocking donuts.

Shanna took one last look to make sure everything was ready to open. Satisfied, she unlocked the door and turned on the neon sign that declared the bakery was ready for business, then stepped behind the display case. "I sure hope she doesn't sell this place. That would be bad for everyone. Especially me."

The door opened and an elderly woman entered, followed by a mom with two toddlers in tow.

"I'll get out of your way," I said. I stopped in the back and said goodbye to Sam, and headed out the back door and returned to my favorite lawn chair next to the bus. Curious about what they were up to, I looked for Merle and Dolly, but neither was in sight. Since skunks and raccoons are both nocturnal, I assumed they had settled in for a long day's nap. They normally spent the daytime in the special converted storage compartment beneath the bus they called home. I picked up a skitter, then saw two brown flashes of fur, so I assumed Willie and Waylon were out enjoying the day.

Bozeman's boots clunked down the bus steps, and he set up his chair next to mine.

"Have you been off with your friend?" Bozeman asked before he sipped a steaming mug of coffee.

"Yep. She's turning me into a baker."

Bozeman laughed. "That ain't gonna happen."

I grinned. He was right. I worked a six-string just fine but put me in front of a recipe card and I was hopeless.

"Does she have a husband or boyfriend you know of?"

I thought about that for a second. She hadn't said, and I hadn't asked, although I should have, if only to be polite.

"You'll have to find that out for yourself. You can ask her tonight. I wouldn't bother her now."

"What's going on, Codi? You got that look on your face, along with flour on your nose."

I wiped my face. "Which look is that?" I asked, although I already had the answer. This was a conversation we've had on more than one occasion, but since it was like a comedy routine we followed, I played my part.

"It looks like you're going to go out looking for trouble," Bozeman said.

"You know me. I don't have to go looking for trouble. It's there in the morning waiting for me when I wake up."

"You got one of your special feelings?"

"Yeah. There's something not quite right going on here, and I think Sam is right in the middle of it. She didn't outright say anything, but she's not the type to spill all her problems on anyone over a beer."

"Or it might be nothing."

"I considered that too. It could be the stress of the party tonight combined with working too hard. Honestly, I don't comprehend how she does it all."

"It's got to be tough on her, especially if she doesn't have a man."

I leaned over and slapped Bozeman's leg. "Slow down there, cowboy. I never said she didn't have a man. And although we like to wear our tall hats and dusty boots, this isn't the nineteenth century. Women are perfectly capable of living life without a man around."

Bozeman chuckled. "Yeah, I'd like to see you live your life without me."

I sent a sarcastic chuckle right back at him. "That's only because you drive the bus and carry all the heavy stuff, but even then, I could find someone else to that in half a heartbeat."

Bozeman was silent for a minute. "No, you couldn't."

I capitulated. "Yeah, you're probably right. Hey, do me a favor, will you? Keep an eye out for any funny business tonight, okay?"

"I always do." Bozeman pushed out of his chair and stretched. "I'm a might hungry. I think I'm going to head over yonder for something to eat."

As I smiled, I shook my head. Once Bozeman caught a scent, he was on it like a hound dog. Usually he caught his prey, since he was a good-looking man with his rugged looks, six-pack abs, and scruffy beard. I didn't know why women ever fell for his cowboy act, but he played the part well, and bless his heart for it.

"Bring me back a muffin if they have any," I yelled to him. Bozeman lifted a hand to acknowledge me, then slipped around the corner of the building.

I got out of my chair, checked on Merle and Dolly, and stepped onto the bus. I walked to the equipment storage room and pulled out my favorite guitar. After I rummaged around in a drawer for a fresh set of strings, I started into the pep talk I had with myself before every show. "Don't worry, everything will be fine. You and your guitar will be in tune, you'll get no amp feedback, and you won't forget any chords or lyrics. The show will flow as smooth as room temperature butter over a slice of fresh toast. Not a single thing will go wrong."

I used the same mantra before every show, and every single time I thought about changing that last line. It seemed often, things not only went wrong, but flew completely off the tracks.

A little after four in the afternoon, I made sure all the pets were aboard and Bozeman drove the bus the short distance to the church. I would've preferred to walk, but we would have had to make several trips lugging all our gear. As promised, there was an area in the church lot marked off by traffic cones, and I stacked them up while Bozeman parked the bus. As Bozeman started gathering the equipment we needed, I approached the church to determine where we were supposed to go.

A cinder block was leaning against the church's back door, holding it open. I considered that an invitation, so I passed through the entry and followed the hallway past several dark classrooms. At the end of the corridor, I had a choice of left or right, and I trusted my intuition, turned right, and within a few yards, came to the empty sanctuary. Since my intuition failed me, I backtracked and eventually entered the large space that doubled as a gymnasium and meeting space. The far end of the area contained a small, raised stage, and atop the stage was an upright piano and a drum set. I hoped no one planned to sit in with us.

"Can I help you?"

I turned around and found myself almost eye to eye with the man before me. He was short in stature, only two inches taller than me, and he wore dark jeans and a light green polo shirt.

I smiled and stuck out my hand. "Hello. I'm Codi Cassidy. I'm the singer for tonight."

The man eyed me for a few seconds without speaking a word. I'm pretty sure it was the blue hair that distracted him.

"I'm Pastor Tom Percy and I'm sorry if I startled you."

"You didn't. Sam told me she'd be here after four to set up."

"I'm here, I'm here," Sam said as she entered the room, lugging two large plastic bins filled with dinner rolls. "Sorry I'm a little late. Anyone else here yet?"

Pastor Tom took one bin from her and carried it to a table. "No. Just us and the singer."

There was something icy about his tone, but I didn't know why, and at the time I didn't care. "I can come back a little later," I said.

"No, you're good," Sam said.

"Am I on the stage tonight?" I asked, not wanting to assume anything.

"Yes. We can push the piano back a bit if it's in your way. We'll need to save a little room up front for the dignitary speeches," Sam said.

"Y'all can use my mic for that if you need to. I'll go grab my gear."

I excused myself and left the room. Because my sense of direction is just as bad as my intuition, I backtracked to the wrong hallway. I could tell I headed toward the church's main entrance instead of the back door based on the signs I passed. I figured I'd simply exit the building and walk around the outside instead of venturing through the labyrinth again. As I got closer, I heard two people arguing.

"I'm telling you; something has to be done about him." The man's voice echoed through the deserted hall. It sounded familiar, but I couldn't put a face to the voice.

"I agree with you. Keep your voice down. This is a church, and someone will hear you," came the reply. It was a woman speaking, one I hadn't met before.

The statements dropped to a whisper, so I could no longer hear the words, but I could tell by the cadence and the tone that it wasn't a pleasant conversation. I took another step, rounded a corner, and found the couple arguing just inside the front door. The woman stopped in mid-sentence when I approached, and they both looked at me. Both of their countenances switched from furrowed brows and frowns to bright eyes and smiles in an instant. I'd seen that reaction lots of times. They came from people who internally buried their current thoughts and moods, especially around strangers. They put on a smiling face in order to hide the conflict.

"Cassie, right?" the man said as he stepped forward and offered his hand. "Good to see you again."

"Codi," I said. I couldn't place him.

He could read the non-recognition in my face. "Dean Williams? Local historian? I met you at the diner last night?"

It clicked. He was the one who rushed Sam away from me.

"Dean. Blue Jays fan. Of course. And you are?"

A silver-haired woman stepped forward. "Reba Chestnut."

"Reba owns the bed-and-breakfast over on Third Street. It's a lovely place. You should stay when you get a chance."

"We're all booked up through Labor Day," Reba interjected. "Summer's our busy time."

Dean moved a step closer to Reba and held his fist to his mouth. "Not for long."

Reba threw him an icicle stare, then turned and rushed from the church.

Dean gave me an awkward chuckle. "You'll have to forgive her. She's stressed about the event tonight, although I don't know why. She's only in charge of the decorations. In her state, she can't take on much more. Where are you headed?"

"Um. I was going to the back parking lot, but I got turned around."

"Happens all the time if you're not used to this building. They didn't do the best job with the layout when they added on from the original church. Follow me, I'll take you."

Without waiting for a reply, Dean marched forward, and I got into step behind him. We passed the gymnasium, and within two minutes he was holding open the back door for me even though he didn't need to since the cinder block was still in place. Outside the bus, I saw a small pile of gear, and Bozeman was carrying an amplifier down the bus steps.

"How does it look?" he asked once I got within speaking range.

"Pretty typical. Small stage. Room is a converted gym, so we should be able to get by without the full sound system."

Bozeman nodded, then stepped back into the bus for more gear. While he was gone, I opened the storage compartment nearest the door and wrestled our portable luggage cart to the ground. I flipped up the handle and transferred the gear on the ground to it. The little cart wouldn't haul everything we'd need at once, but it would save effort and energy from lugging everything by hand.

Bozeman reappeared, toting one of his guitars. "Here, take this and I'll pull the cart."

We switched tasks, and I led Bozeman to the door, down the hall, and into the gym. He stopped just inside the door and looked around, saying nothing. From experience, I could tell he was mentally mapping out the space. I knew he was thinking of where the best speaker placement would be to get the best sound throughout the room. He also considered if we should bother setting up our lighting rig, and a million other trivial details. He even went to the level of determining the floor composition and what material they made the walls of. The man knew his acoustics.

Bozeman glanced at me, pulled the cart to the stage, and together we unloaded the gear. Bozeman's eyes looked over the gear for a moment, then he nodded and took the cart out for another load. While he was gone, I took an assessment of my own and decided the piano would indeed need to move. I jumped onto the stage and gave the piano a nudge, but it didn't move an inch. I looked at the casters, saw that they were unlocked, and I tried again. It wouldn't budge. It was clearly the heaviest piano ever made.

CHAPTER FOUR

T he locks are backward."

I turned around and spotted a short, plump man standing before me. He wore blue jeans, a checkered shirt that reminded me of a tablecloth, and a light brown sports coat with a carnation pinned to the lapel.

"Hanson Johns. I own the flower shop up the block." He thrust a meaty hand forward, and I shook it.

"Codi Cassidy. What did you say about the locks?"

"Someone installed them backward. Unlocked means locked, and the reverse."

I looked down and stepped on one lock, then the other. I already detected a noticeable difference in the way the large instrument handled.

"Let me help with that." Hanson stepped over and took a side. Together, we rolled it to the back wall and reset the locks. "You need a pianist tonight? I'm quite good." Without waiting for an answer, Hanson sat behind the piano and played a little Mozart for me. He was right, he played well.

"That was fantastic. Do you know any country songs?" I asked.

Hanson said nothing, but his reddening ears told me all I needed to know.

I smiled. "Tell you what, you learn some country tunes, and the next time we come through you can sit in with us, okay?"

I overheard someone clear his throat. I turned around and caught a look from Pastor Tom that told me he didn't seem happy. "Hanson, come on. We need your help."

Hanson blushed again and left the stage in a hurry.

Bozeman returned with a second load, dropped the gear off, and left again. Included in the pile sat my laptop, that played an essential role in our operation. I opened the laptop and placed it on top of the piano. The laptop contained all the programming for our show, and, other than my music, was the thing I had the most pride in. I had cobbled together a program that would run a lighting and sound system for any set list I selected. Besides lights and sound balances, it also provided the remaining members of the band.

We had backing tracks included in there for much of the music we performed. I had everything from fiddles, to slide guitars, to banjos, to our electronic drummer that I had affectionately named Ringo. Usually, some in the music circle frowned on the backing tracks, but I liked them because they gave the act a much richer sound than only the two of us provided. And I made it a point to mention that what the audience viewed on stage was the real deal. I sang, and Bozeman did background vocals, and we each played our instruments in real time. Usually, the first couple of numbers we did were acoustic ones, so the audience understood it was us doing the work. Once I brought in the backing tracks later, they didn't distract from the performance. I had set up most of the gig beforehand, but I had a few variables to plug into the program. I needed to turn off the lighting options and enter the rough dimensions of the room. The rest I'd adjust during the sound check.

When I turned around, I spotted Bozeman who had returned and seemed busy setting up the PA system we used on smaller gigs. He attached a cable and tossed the other end to me, which I caught on the fly and plugged into the laptop. Bozeman positioned the speakers while I followed him and ran the cables and electrical. After that, he got out his guitar and fussed with all his pedals. I set out the guitar and microphone stands, then the microphones, then hooked up the remaining cables to tie it all together.

Bozeman sat, tuning his guitar, and I checked the space for mine. "Where's my Martin?"

Bozeman looked up. "You tell me. I didn't see it in the locker, so I have no clue."

I slapped my hand against my forehead. "That's right. It's on my bed. I'll come right back. Are we missing anything else?"

Bozeman glanced around the area, shook his head no, then returned to his tuning.

I jumped from the stage and rushed out to the bus. My Martin laid right where I had put it when I restrung it. I slipped it into its case and closed it up. As I stepped from the bus, I noticed a delivery van parked three spots over. The back door stood open, and I saw Hanson removing a large box, which I assumed contained flowers or table centerpieces. Next to Hanson stood Rob, and I noticed Rob wasn't happy about something because he kept jabbing Hanson in the shoulder. From my position, I noticed the back of Hanson's neck redden. Hanson handed Rob the box, then removed one for himself. He used his hip to close the van door, and they both disappeared into the church.

I set my guitar case on the ground and reentered the bus. From a small file cabinet in the gear room, I took out a glossy promotional photo, scribbled a message and my signature on it, and left the bus.

When I returned to the gymnasium, I placed the photo on the piano next to the computer and opened my guitar case and checked the tuning. Once my guitar and the rest of the gear sounded up to my standards, I looked over at Bozeman.

"Ready for a sound check?" I asked.

In typical Bozeman fashion, he nodded and powered on all the equipment and made sure everything worked properly. He gave me the thumbs up, and I approached my microphone. "Hey everyone. We're going to do a quick sound check."

I did a four-count and together we launched into a Lee Ann Womack song. As I sang, I looked out at the audience, which comprised those setting up the room for the event. I saw Sam and Dean straightening tables and laying down tablecloths. Hanson placed floral arrangements on each table. Lisa and Rob arranged place settings, and Pastor Tom helped Reba put up red, white, and blue bunting on the walls to add a little more color to the spartan gym. There were other people I didn't know doing various chores, but I saw everything was coming together bit by bit.

Once Bozeman felt his gear was working fine, he stepped off the stage and stood in various areas of the room and watched me play. He came back, made minor adjustments to the speakers, and changed the volume on the PA, then returned to the far wall. He listened intently as I repeated a chorus and gave me the thumbs up. I stopped playing, turned on the computer, and started a backing track. Bozeman stayed at his location, then soon gave me a second thumbs up. I turned off the track and stepped back to the microphone.

"Thanks everyone. That'll do it for now."

It did not surprise me when I got a smattering of applause and a random 'woo-hoo' from someone I didn't recognize. I set my guitar on the stand and turned off the electronics until show time.

"Did everything sound okay?" I asked Bozeman when he returned to the stage.

"As good as it can. It's not the Ryman, but it'll do for this show."

I was about to respond when I sensed a loud crash. I looked up just in time to spot Sam racing out of the gym with Dean hot on her heels. The amazing thing was everyone else in the room went back to what they were doing, as if Sam's actions were a normal occurrence.

"I'll be right back," I said to Bozeman, then rushed out of the room without trying to look like I was rushing out of the room.

With haste, I exited the church and looked around the parking lot, but I spotted neither Sam nor Dean. I caught a commotion from the sidewalk, and even before I reached the end of the building, I heard voices.

"Sam, I'm telling you, we all agree. We have to do something about him before it's too late. We have to act. Now. As soon as possible," Dean said.

"And I'm telling you, I can't go along with you. That's not me."

"It's not me, either. Or Lisa, or Hanson, or any of the others. But there's no other choice. Do you really want to lose your bakery? That means everything to you."

There came a long pause, a perfect chance to step around the corner and announce my presence, but something held me back. I didn't want it to seem like I was eavesdropping, but on the other hand, I had an instinct to jump in feet first to protect my friend. I waited.

Sam's voice seemed quieter, yet more intense. "I won't lose my bakery. Ever. We'd better get back in there. We somehow need to make it through this sideshow of an evening. Then we can figure out what to do."

I took that as my cue. I felt like a kid listening in on my parents, and I didn't want to get caught, so I ran as fast as I could to the bus, threw open the door, and scrambled up the steps. As I caught my breath, I looked out a window and spotted Sam and Dean walking around the corner. Dean went on ahead while Sam stood and stared in my direction, and I wondered if they had caught me.

From the kitchen, I loaded a cooler with a half dozen bottles of water, caught my breath, and left the bus carrying the cooler. Sam stood still in her position. As I got closer, I saw her eyes glistening, as if she'd either just finished or just begun crying.

"What are you doing out here?" I asked in my most innocent voice.

Sam wiped her eyes with her palms. "Just getting some air." She looked like she wanted to say something else, but didn't. She stood there, unmoving, and I did the same, like a gunfighter standoff in the center of town at high noon. At last, her body relaxed, and she reached out and took the cooler from me. "Come on, let's get in there. It's going to be a wild night."

Bozeman and I sat at a table off to the side and tried to stay out of the way while people funneled into the room. The ceremony was supposed to start at seven on the dot, and a check on my phone told me it was already a quarter after the appointed hour. Mayor Mary Sweets sat front and center, but the seats on either side of her were empty. She seemed to be an amiable woman, in her early sixties, dressed in a navy-blue business suit and a simple string of pearls. The mayor talked to everyone who approached her, shook their hands, and smiled graciously. I'm sure had there been any babies in the area, she would have given out kisses like they were going out of style. When there was no one near her, I could tell she wasn't happy with the situation. She kept checking her watch, and her body language screamed that she didn't like to be kept waiting.

Sam looked nervous. She paced beside the door, and as people entered, she greeted everyone, directed them to their seat, and went back to pacing.

Everyone I met earlier in the day seemed on edge as well, but as the bartenders opened the wine bottles and filled the glasses, a quiet calm settled over the crowd.

It was seven-thirty when Sherman Stier and his party strolled into the room. Sam ushered them to the front table and dismissed herself. Sherman introduced the rest of his party to the mayor, and they all sat.

Pastor Tom appeared from nowhere and took the stage. I saw him walking toward my microphone, so I jumped up and turned it on before he got there. He nodded his appreciation, and I retook my seat.

"Welcome everyone, please rise and join me for a quick prayer before we get started. Heavenly Father…"

Like everyone else, I stood and listened to the words, but although I bowed my head, I kept my eyes open and I scanned the room. Although most of the attendees prayed as expected, a few didn't. Lisa and Rob McMurtry were both standing at the back. Lisa stood behind a pushcart loaded with pitchers of water, iced teas, and soda, and Rob was holding back the wait staff. With the delay, I hoped people liked lukewarm food.

Hanson busily fussed with a flower display at the table in front of him, and for some odd reason, Dean Williams was staring directly at me.

"… Amen." Pastor Tom finished and invited everyone to sit. "Before the meals are served, I'd like to invite the mayor up to say a few words. Mayor Mary?"

To polite applause, the pastor took a step back to make room for the mayor on stage.

"Thank you, Pastor Tom, and thank you to everyone for attending. When the Main Street Committee first approached me to bring more business into our town, I admit I thought it would be a great goal, but also an ambitious one. You and I know our little corner of New Mexico offers a lot to travelers, but how do we get that word out to those passing by on the interstate? I was so excited when the committee came to me with a well thought out plan that could actually grow business. It's time to introduce that committee now and have them say a few words about what they've each been working on. I'll start with the chair, Mr. Sherman Stier."

Polite applause rang through the space again. As Sherman walked to the stage, I glanced at Sam, who was in the process of an eye roll.

"Thank you, Mayor Mary." Sherman was taller than the microphone, and rather than adjust the stand higher, he bent over to make himself heard. "In any corporation, it's important to keep a close eye on the rock-bottom line, which fosters well-being with the investors. It's no different from a town. Imagine yourself all as investors in this town and imagine that you have a sea of customers passing us daily, going seventy miles an hour right past us. If you want to bring them in, you need a purpose, and you have to give them either value or an experience, and I know we can do both. By building a top-notch golf course surrounded by a resort, we'll give travelers a reason to come here. To relax. To enjoy all the amenities that this great town offers. Together, we can build a future."

As Sherman took his seat, I leaned over to Bozeman. "I wonder where he was all day. Committee comes in and sets everything up, and the chair shows up late without contributing a single thing?"

"You never know. Maybe he fronted the costs and had important meetings to attend."

I shrugged. Bozeman was right. I didn't know the entire story, nor did I need to. I was just a gig player, and I had already gotten paid, so all we needed to do was sing a few songs, then head out to the next town.

The mayor introduced each committee member one at a time. They stepped up and told the audience what their specific actions were to drive business for the town. Each member focused on a specific area. Dean Williams was putting together a regional history tour. Its goal was to highlight the contributions of the town and county toward westward expansion. Reba Chestnut, the bed-and-breakfast owner, introduced her daughter, Robin. Robin was developing a nighttime haunted tour. The McMurtrys were creating a cookbook featuring local favorite recipes. Sam and Hanson had created a booklet that included many Quincey businesses that she intended to hand out at wedding planning events around the area.

"Of course, we can't do this all alone. We need your help," Mayor Mary said as a part of her closing statement. "Although we have a lot of great ideas already started, there is room for more. There's a table at the entrance with note cards. Please jot down any ideas you have and drop them in the box on the table. If you wish to remain anonymous, that's fine, and if you want to volunteer to serve the community, add your name and phone number. We have another presentation planned for later in the evening, but for now, I know you've been waiting to eat, so let's get down to dinner."

The mayor got the largest applause of the night at that remark, and she laughed as she took her seat. From the rear of the room, Rob guided the servers to tables with the meals as Lisa dashed from person to person to fill glasses.

"Well, I guess we're up," I said to Bozeman. I took a moment to tuck a stray strand of hair under my hat and took my place at the microphone. "Hey everyone, my name is Codi Cassidy, and this is Bozeman James. Thank you for having us, and we hope you enjoy your dinner."

I gave Bozeman a nod, and we launched into our set. Since we were playing over dinner, we did an entire acoustic set without the backing tracks. As usual, people focused on the food and those around them rather than us. Sam could've hired a DJ or turned on a radio as background music, but I was still thankful she thought enough of me to book us for the gig. This part was the dinner. The after-dinner set was the one where we'd let loose and have fun.

After twenty minutes of tunes, I announced we were taking a break and Bozeman and I made our way to a table in the back. Within a couple minutes of sitting, Rob dropped off plates of food for us. It was standard event fare. Baked chicken, mashed potatoes and gravy, corn, and a dinner roll I recognized as one of Sam's. My stomach rumbled the second I picked up my fork. I was ready to dig in. Bozeman was already at it.

"That was pretty good. Are you going to play your hit song?" Rob asked as he stepped back.

"I usually save that one for the encore. Since we're not doing an encore tonight, it'll be the last song of the set."

"I have to wait that long?" Rob frowned, and his shoulders shrugged like a five-year-old being told they couldn't have a cookie.

"Of course. We have to give the audience something to look forward to. Don't want to play the big hit first, then have a bunch of people leave because they got what they came for."

"I guess that makes sense," Rob said.

"Oh, I've got an autographed photo for you. It's up there on the piano. Come pick it up after the show, okay?"

Rob's body language shifted in a moment, and he was upbeat and looked happy again. "I'll be back in a moment with some pie." I wished all my fans were so easy to please and were so quick to offer me pie.

Bozeman had cleaned his plate before I had eaten half of my meal.

"You not liking that?" Bozeman asked.

"Love it. I'm just waiting for dessert." I put my fork beside the plate and glanced at Bozeman. Based on the way he stared at my unfinished meal, I could tell he was still hungry. "Go ahead," I said.

Bozeman reached for my plate. At the last second, I snatched my dinner roll back and took a bite. It, like the muffin, was heavenly. I had just finished the roll when Rob reappeared and slid slices of Dutch apple pie before us. With eager anticipation, I slid my fork through the pie and took a bite. The crust was flaky, and the sweet crumble on top was the perfect complement to the tart apples inside. I moaned as I chewed and the flavors exploded, and I glanced at Bozeman, who had almost finished with his slice already.

Bozeman scraped the fork side against the plate's bottom to

get the remaining crumbs, ate it, and sat back. "I think I want to marry Sam."

I took a drink of water and smiled at him. "Silly man. I've known her longer, so she's mine. Don't worry though, I'll throw scraps out the back door to you."

Bozeman grinned. "Even better."

I finished my pie and looked toward the stage where the committee was still doing post-dinner presentations. As I sighed, I hoped the talking would be over soon. I was itching to play, and I was already thinking about getting on the road over to the next gig. I knew my mind shouldn't wander, but it often did during downtimes like these.

Bozeman nudged me in the ribs to knock me from my daydreaming and pointed to the stage, where Sam stood waving, trying to get my attention. I adjusted my hat, and we took to the stage for our second set. I grabbed my guitar and checked the computer while Bozeman made sure he switched all the electronics on. Then suddenly, it was showtime. We buzzed through a few country standards, a few modern songs, and slid in a couple of originals as well. The set was going swimmingly. I saw the audience was engaged, and they moved a few of the tables closest to the stage to create a dance floor. The chords were tight, and the sound was brilliant. From a performer's standpoint, it was a great show.

They pushed aside more tables when we played a number suitable for a Texas two-step. As I looked into the crowd, I estimated that many of the original two hundred people that were there for dinner had stayed for the show. There was the usual percentage of folks who didn't dance and would either listen to the music or chat with friends, but that was fine by me. I also noticed at one point, every member of the committee gathered near the back door and clustered in a tight circle. Sherman noticed it as well, so he broke off the side conversation with Mayor Mary and headed in a beeline for the group, pushing aside anyone who got into his path. From my position on the stage, he looked like a bull chasing a matador.

Hanson saw Sherman coming and must have informed the

group because most of them turned and looked. With the rest of the circle distracted by the oncoming problem, Hanson silently slipped out the service door. Lisa, who was standing next to Hanson, followed him out the door. Since I was in the middle of a Willie Nelson tune, I couldn't stop playing. Over the din, I also couldn't determine what they were discussing. I saw Sherman was using animated gestures wild enough to cause Sam and Rob, who were standing on either side of him, to take a step back.

I glanced at Bozeman to see if he saw the same thing I did. As I followed his sight line, it appeared he was more interested in a buxom brunette in a yellow sundress who was swaying in front of the stage.

I redirected my vision to the rear of the room and saw Sherman shove Sam. Sherman raised his hand and balled his fist, and Sam shrank to the ground. With great haste, Rob stepped in and grabbed Sherman's arm before Sherman could strike. Sherman tried to pull himself free but couldn't. Reba escorted Sam from the room while Rob and Dean held Sherman back from pursuing her. Rob and Dean held Sherman for a full minute, then Sherman put up his hands in surrender and the men let him go. Dean rushed from the room, Sherman started pacing back and forth, and Rob came forward to find the mayor.

Mayor Mary was in the center of the dance floor being spun around by a cowboy when Rob cut in. Rather than dance, Rob leaned in and whispered something in her ear. She said something back I couldn't hear. Rob nodded, and they both left the room through the main door. I finished the song, then grabbed my water bottle to take a drink as I looked again at the back. Sherman was gone.

I stepped aside and let Bozeman sing a couple of his originals, then I took the lead again. I was ready to begin my big single when I saw the mayor return to the room, followed by the town's police chief. Close behind the steps of the chief was a deputy. In the back of the room, the committee filed back into the room, followed by another deputy.

The chief stepped onto the stage and tipped his hat at me. "Sorry, ma'am. I need to interrupt the show."

I took a couple of steps to the right, and he took my place in front of the mic. "Attention everyone. There's been an incident, and we ask everyone here to sit tight until you're questioned by myself or a deputy. As soon as we get your contact information, you're free to leave unless we ask you to stay. When you go, exit from the side door only. For now, please find a seat and be patient with us. Thank you."

"What's going on?" I asked.

The chief took off his hat and ran a handkerchief across his brow. "Someone murdered Sherman Stier."

CHAPTER FIVE

The concert came to an abrupt end, and not in the usual cheerful way. Although the chief wouldn't allow us to leave, he granted Bozeman and me permission to pack up our gear. I assumed the chief had us included in the suspect pool simply by being in the building at the time of the murder, but I didn't fret about it. Being on stage in front of a few hundred people was always an iron-clad alibi. Well, not always, but that's a different story.

I was shutting down the laptop and disconnecting its cables when I felt a tap on the shoulder. I did a quick pivot, expecting Rob wanting his autographed picture. Instead, when I turned, Sam stood there.

"Are you okay, Sam?" She didn't look okay. Her face appeared pale, her hair looked messy, and her frown almost extended down to her shoulders. She still carried the sparkle in her eyes, but even it seemed muted.

"Codi, I... I think I'm in big trouble."

"What? Why? Come over here and sit down." I pulled out the piano bench and Sam took a hesitant step forward and sat down. She looked down at her feet and refused to look up at me. Sam's eyes watered and she quietly began crying. Instinctively, I reached out to pat her on the shoulder, then noticed her shirt had little dark red dots over the front of it. I pulled my hand away.

"Sam, why is there blood on your shirt?"

She didn't answer right away. I looked into the room. Several law enforcement officers were collecting contact information from the guests. Way in the back, they had the committee sequestered to a few tables. Rob, Dean, and Hanson huddled in a tight circle talking to each other. Reba worked on drinking a bottle of wine, seemingly by herself. Her indulgence was probably against advice, considering how she looked around the room anytime she refilled her glass. Pastor Tom ministered to Lisa, who seemed to be in the middle of a full-on breakdown. Shanna sat off to the side, not talking to anyone. I hadn't even known she was at the event, but based on the apron and hairnet she wore, I guessed she had been a part of the kitchen staff for the evening.

Sam showed no signs of slowing down, so I left her for a moment to round up a handful of napkins. When I returned, she took the napkins and dried her eyes. I sat patiently by her side and waited for her to compose herself. I estimated the number of people in the room and guessed it would be at least an hour before I would go anywhere.

After a few minutes, she finally stopped crying, dried her eyes for a last time, and blew her nose. She looked around for somewhere to put her used napkins, and finding none, she balled them up and stuffed them into the front pocket of her jeans.

"Thanks. I needed that," Sam said. Her voice, still quiet, sounded stronger.

"Sam, what's going on?" I asked.

"Codi, I didn't do it. I didn't kill him."

"I believe you." Then again, what was I going to say? I didn't honestly know if she had done it or not. It's hard to be a witness for people if they're not in the same room as you. Besides, her shirt looked like a Jackson Pollock painting.

"Sam. Talk to me. What happened?"

Sam looked up for a brief second, then down at the floor. "We had some words. He's been trying to rattle my cage for over a month, trying to force me to sell my bakery, and tonight he did it again. I called him a jerk, and he pushed me, and we moved into the kitchen. The next thing I know, he's dead. Please believe me. I didn't do it."

"All you did was call him a name, and he pushed you for that?" I asked.

Sam nodded.

I'm not sure if I accepted that or not. In my line of work, I've seen my share of tough men. But usually, the rich ones seemed a little more careful about displaying random acts of violence, especially in a room filled with witnesses. If something set

Sherman off, I doubt if it was being called a jerk. After all, there are a lot of worse things to be called. But again, I didn't know him, either. He might be one of those guys who flew off the handle at the least bit of provocation.

"The police are here. They can help you," I said.

"No. It has to be you. You can do it. Remember back at Greenway High when the school mascot got stolen, and you found him and figured out who kidnapped him?"

That brought back memories. I made the front page of the school newspaper and page five of the *Denver Post* local section when I cracked that mystery. It brought a smile as I remembered how proud my dad was of me. It was the first adventure of Codi Cassidy, Girl Detective.

Someone had sheep-napped Ramsey the Ram the week before homecoming. The Denver police were called in, but since the theft of a single animal didn't rank high on their priority list, school security had to take the lead. Of course, all eyes were on our rivals for the big game, Henry Teller High, but that was a little too on the nose for me. I asked around, followed a few leads, and eventually fingered the true culprits, a couple of bad kids who had gotten expelled the year before. By the time kickoff came around, Ramsey was back on the sidelines in his blue and gold blanket, chomping away at his fresh hay. The return of the sacred mascot didn't help, though, the football team still lost the game by thirty-five points.

What started as a mission to impress my father turned out to be a bane of my existence. For the rest of the school year, my classmates wanted me to track down missing items and pets like I was the cowgirl version of Nancy Drew. I didn't get involved in another case until much later, and that's another story, too.

I looked Sam in the eyes. "Sam, I'll say it again. I'm not a cop, I'm a musician, I don't see what I can do to help. Even if I did, I wouldn't know how to investigate a death. I've never even seen a dead person outside of a funeral home."

"But you're good with people. They open up to you. Please, ask around and see if anyone else noticed anything."

I was about to respond when the chief approached. He looked

way too young to be the chief of police, but based on the nameplate on his shirt, that's who he was. The chief looked sixteen, but I assumed he had to be in his late thirties. He had reddish-brown hair clipped short, freckles on his nose, and a scowl on his face he must have developed over a lifetime of bullying people younger than him. I admonished myself for judging a book by its cover, so I smiled, put my hand out and stepped forward to introduce myself.

He stepped past me like I wasn't there and got right into Sam's face.

"Ma'am, please, I asked you not to talk to anyone. Find a spot to sit down and stay quiet. I don't want to put you in handcuffs."

Sam took a step backward; I took a step forward. "Can she at least change out of that shirt?" I asked.

The chief finally noticed me and looked at Sam, considered it for a moment, and nodded. "I would prefer to collect the evidence at the station, but I don't want you spreading it all over the room, either. You got something to change into?"

Sam shook her head. "Of course not."

"Here, I have a fresh shirt for you." I stepped off the stage and found the plastic tote we stored our merchandise in. I rooted around in there until I found a shirt for her. "You look like a medium, but I only have large. Will that do? And I've got a bag here that you can put the dirty one in."

Sam took the shirt and moved to step off the stage.

"Where are you going?" the chief asked.

"To the ladies' room to change."

The look in the chief's eye said everything, and Sam stopped in her tracks. "You need to change here, or not at all. Can't have you destroying evidence," he said.

Did I detect a slight smile curl up on his lips like a cartoon villain? Must have been a trick of the light, or the perception of the man I was building in my head.

"Fine." Sam stepped back onto the stage, turned so her back was facing us, and started taking off her shirt. To Bozeman's credit, he stepped in front of her and shielded her as best he could with his enormous frame. I was only a couple feet away, and I caught no glimpse of flesh during her quick change. A couple of seconds later, Sam turned back around, displaying my face on her chest. It was by far my favorite photo. Head back, wide smile, hand holding my hat on my head. She stuffed the soiled shirt into the plastic bag I handed her and passed the bag to the chief.

"Don't go anywhere, Sam. I mean it." The chief took the bag from her outstretched hand, knotted the top, then returned to his business.

"What's his deal? He doesn't seem to like you much," I said as I closed up the merchandise bin.

Sam took in a breath of air, then released it with a sigh. "I expect that's because he's asked me out a few times and I've always turned him down."

"Wait, you know him?" I asked.

"Of course. It's a small town. Everyone knows everyone. He comes into the bakery two or three times a week."

"And he's asked you out?"

"Yes. Like out for dinner, or to the movies, like a date," Sam said. The shirt I'd given her was too big, so she tucked it into her jeans.

"You've always said no?"

"Of course. I'm not really interested in seeing anyone right now. I'm still getting over my last breakup, so I've been throwing myself into my baking. Besides, he's not my type. I've heard rumors he can be... really mean. So please. Will you help me?"

I didn't know what to think. On the one hand, I had no business getting myself involved. On the other hand, I also had no business getting involved, but I had a desire to jump in anyway. The police were here, and they'd figure it out. All I had to do was pack up my gear, wait for my turn to be interviewed, and then ride off into the sunset like a good little cowgirl. I glanced at Bozeman, even though I already guessed where he stood. He shook his head, turned, and started coiling a microphone cable.

"Look, I can't make any promises. You can understand that, right?"

Sam smiled for the first time since she approached me. "Yes, of course."

"You expect people will talk to me? I am an outsider, after all. Not everyone will be an open book for me."

"Yeah, but they realize you're my friend, so you have that connection. Besides, you're a star. People always want to hang out with a star."

The term star was a little generous, considering I never played the Grand Ole Opry, but I understood what she meant. Most people enjoyed getting attention from the performers, which could be a benefit or a curse, depending on the situation. I admit, I've gotten better service at restaurants occasionally. And I once got upgraded from coach class to business class on a flight just because the gate agent liked my second album. A lot of times I let people down, regardless of how many autographs I give out or selfies I take with people. Most fans are great and only want to shake my hand and say hello, but sometimes people get a little too fanatical. On more than one occasion, Bozeman, or the venue security has had to rescue me from an eager fan who wanted to monopolize my time.

"I can't offer any promises," I said sternly.

"You said that already."

"I just wanted to make it clear. I'm way out of my element here." Out of my element was an understatement.

I couldn't stand the sad, hound dog eyes Sam was giving to me. "Okay, fine. But first, tell me how it was you came to have a shirt covered in blood? Tell me what happened. Leave nothing out."

"Like I said, I called Sherman a name, and he pushed me. After that, I went out the back door into the kitchen to cool off because I didn't want to make a scene."

"Stop. Back up. Why did you call him out in the first place? What precipitated that?"

"He must have had too much wine tonight because every time he was near, he'd give me a crack about losing my bakery. Or how he was going to own me, or how I'd be begging him for a job. Then, to top it off, he pinched me on the rear."

"He didn't," I said.

"He did," Sam confirmed.

"Anyone observe that?"

"I can't be sure. There was already a crowd of people around, and it happened so fast. That's when I turned around and called him a jerk. Then he pushed me, and rather than take it any further, I left the room," Sam said.

"Anyone see you?"

"Of course. Reba was right on my tail, and Shanna and some other folks were in the kitchen. They all saw me."

"Then what happened?"

"Well, Reba suggested I go to the restroom to wash my face, so I did. I stayed in there for perhaps five or six minutes, then came out."

"And then?" I asked.

"Well, then I ran into Dean."

"What do you mean by ran into him?" I asked.

"Just as I stepped out of the restroom, Dean was right there, as if he were waiting for me. He was angry that Sherman had pushed me."

"Did he say anything?"

"He was mostly just doing what I call his rattle. He gets all worked up to the point where he can't verbalize a single thought. The only clear thing I got from him was he said he couldn't believe Sherman had done that. Then he stomped off. I think he left the church to get some air. Walking around is his way of calming down. I swear, the man must put in thirty miles a day."

I hated to ask the next question, because I didn't quite get how to put it, so I said it as simply as I could. "Are you two... involved?"

She looked at me as if the words I said were in Arabic instead of English. I was thinking of a less subtle way to ask if they were spending quality time between the sheets together when things clicked for her, and she laughed at me.

"Oh, no. I dated him briefly, but we broke it off. We weren't compatible as a couple. I don't like him that way."

"Does he understand you're not a couple? Based on his body language alone, I'd say you two are the hottest item in town."

Sam blushed. "No. We're just... good friends. Dean is overprotective of me, and gets jealous sometimes, even though we're not together. That's one of the many reasons I couldn't get into a relationship with him. He has this old-fashioned way of thinking about what a woman is supposed to be, and I'm the opposite of that. He sees me as a stay at home, raise the children, and bake cakes type of woman who wears dresses and brings him a martini when he comes home at night. I'm the complete opposite of that. I enjoy being my independent self, and I don't feel like I need to be in any relationship where I can't be the person who I want to be."

Unfortunately, I wasn't sure she was telling me the whole truth, but for the time being, her relationships didn't enter the equation. "Go on. What went on after Dean left?"

"I headed back to the kitchen. I had stepped part way down the hall when I noticed the pantry door was ajar."

In my mind, I pictured the pantry on my bus, which spans from roof to floor, but is only a whopping twelve inches wide. "What type of pantry?"

"The church calls it the pantry, but it's only your average storeroom. It's used to hold the food donations they get for the giving box out front. It's also where they store the equipment that won't fit in the kitchen. Anyway, the door was open, so I wondered if anyone was in there. I tried to open the door wider, but something was blocking it from the other side. I pushed against it really hard, and finally it gave way, threw me off balance, and I fell in. When I did, I landed… by Sherman. And when I tried to get up, I slipped and ended up with my shirt a mess."

I nodded. Seemed plausible. Barely. "Anything else?"

"I had just regained my footing and was going to get help when Shanna popped in and started screaming. Within the next couple of minutes, people surrounded me, and they held me until the police got here."

I didn't really want to learn the in-depth forensic details, but there was one thing I needed to get. "How was he killed?"

Sam glanced at me, then stared at her feet. Never a good sign. "He… he got stabbed in the stomach."

I learned from experience, more my father's than my own, that getting stabbed in the abdomen wasn't always a death sentence. Unless the stabber nicked a vital organ or major artery. "Are you sure he was dead?"

"I don't know. After I fell and saw him, I freaked out. All I wanted to do was get out of there, so I didn't check."

"Could you tell if he was breathing?" I asked.

"I'm telling you, I don't know. Heavens, I'm a baker, not a doctor."

Sam's tone dropped, and the way she punctuated her words made her sound defensive. I stayed silent for a good two minutes, waiting to see if she'd offer any additional information, but she didn't.

"Did you hear if anyone called for an ambulance?" I thought by moving away from asking about her, she'd warm back up to me.

She stopped for a moment, as if trying to recall the memory. "I don't know. I noticed Ty was there pretty quick, but I only saw him briefly entering the room as I was being held outside."

After thinking for a moment, I didn't recall being introduced to a Ty. "Who's he?"

"He's the paramedic that runs with the volunteer fire department. Must have been his shift off, because he was here at the event, although he spent most of his time in the kitchen with his girlfriend, Bethany."

I made a mental note to reach out to Ty later. If he hadn't already taken off with the victim.

"So other than Dean and Shanna, you didn't see anyone else around when you found Sherman?"

Sam stayed silent for a moment. I could see her wheels turning. She shook her head. "No. I didn't see anyone. Although I could hear other people, which wasn't a surprise since the kitchen was just another few steps down the hall."

Sam stopped speaking, and I waited for her to fill in any other blanks voluntarily, but she didn't. At last, she looked me directly in the eyes.

"I'm in deep trouble, aren't I?"

I didn't quite know how to respond. It sure seemed like it to me. "I hope not, Sam."

I glanced up and saw the chief was charging to the stage like a man on a mission. He must've been watching us, because without a word, he took Sam by the arm and led her across the room and out the back door. I hoped he was taking her to the kitchen and not the police station, but I didn't desire to run after them and check.

Bozeman carried a microphone stand past me, folded it up, and set it on the floor.

"Bozeman, how long will it take us to get to Los Angeles?"

"Oh, ten or eleven hours, depending on stops and traffic."

"We have nothing planned on route, do we?" I asked. Sometimes we stopped off for touristy things, like a visit to the Grand Canyon. At other times we liked to visit friends or industry people while we were on the road.

"Nothing in concrete. We could drive it straight through if we had to. Are you thinking about staying around for another day or two?"

"Perhaps."

"You believe her entire story?" Bozeman asked.

I wanted to ask how much he heard, but I guessed it had to be the whole thing. Although he wasn't much of a talker, he was an excellent listener, even when he didn't mean to be. How much was believable? That's what it came down to. The stories people told could be one hundred percent solid truth. Or one hundred percent solid bat guano, and I suspect that Sam's tale lay somewhere in the middle, but hopefully more toward the truth end.

"There were a few parts in there I wondered about," I said.

"Yeah. Me too," Bozeman said.

"Although I guess I'll never find the full truth unless I seek it out."

CHAPTER SIX

In my head, I laid out a plan of attack, and then I scanned the room ahead of me. Since the committee had been involved in the circle of confrontation earlier, they composed the people I wanted to speak to first. Hopefully, they'd succumb to my charms and be open to discussion. Otherwise, it would be a night of quick conversations. It was just a matter of whom to approach first. It didn't take long to make my decision.

Reba had worked her way through almost an entire bottle of Sauvignon Blanc by the time I took a seat across from her. She let out a little yelp, as if it surprised her that anyone in a room filled with people would join her. She pulled the bottle closer to her, subconsciously telling me it was all hers and I'd have to get my own.

Reba gestured at me with the glass in her hand. "Do you always have blue hair?" I watched the wine climb three quarters of the way up the glass, then descend again.

"Not always, but for now. I like to switch it up. Blue, green, orange, white, black. All depends on my mood when I decide it needs a change," I said.

"Why? Why not keep your own color?" I'm glad I talked to Reba first. Her cheeks looked a tinge redder than when I met her earlier, and she was already slurring her words. I felt lucky to catch her before she nodded off into a grape-induced slumber for the evening.

"Want to hear a secret?" I asked.

Reba and I leaned in toward each other like we were girls gossiping in math class.

"I started going gray in my early twenties, so I started dying it blonde, but then I branched out to other colors when I got bored with the blonde."

Reba sat back, took a drink, then scoffed at me. "You think that's a secret? That's not a secret. You want to tell a secret, it has to be a juicy one. I got lots of secrets. I've been in this town for eighty years, and I know where they buried all those bodies."

Reba hadn't struck me as the town busybody when I met her, but I realized she could be helpful to me. If she stayed awake and coherent, that was.

I leaned across the table even further. "Oh my. Tell me a secret then. A juicy one."

Reba looked from side to side, then took a quick glance behind her to see if anyone was listening in. "Kayla's pregnant, and although Lionel thinks he's the father, he's not. And get this, Stevie, down at the farm store? He's cheating on his wife *and* on his taxes." Reba produced a wide grin, then sat back and outstretched her arms with her palms up. All she was missing was the hat and wand to make it a true magic trick.

It wasn't quite what I was looking for, but it was a start. I returned her grin in kind. "Wow. That's some dirt!"

Reba took another swig, then turned serious. "Oh, trust me, I have enough dirt to bury this entire town."

"I'll bet you do. You must have lots of secrets about the committee." It was a little pointed, but I felt I needed to direct the conversation, since I didn't really care who was having whose baby.

"Sure. Have you met Hanson, the florist?"

I nodded. "Yes, we've met."

"He likes to pretend he's gay, but he's not. He's dating a schoolteacher in the next town over."

Not what I was looking for, but I played along. "Why would he pretend to be gay?"

"Because the idiot assumes he'll sell more flowers that way. He's the only flower shop in the county. His brother owns the Quincey Inn. His brother, Harold, tells me Hanson's an idiot too. Hanson thinks his affair with that math teacher is such a big secret, but everyone knows." Reba thought that was hilarious and cackled like a witch over a cauldron.

I struggled to smile in response. "Affair? You said dating."

"I used dating as a loose term, dear. He met that teacher on one of those affair websites. She's as married as the day is long. Rumor has it she's related to Sherman Stier. A niece or cousin, or something. Can you believe that?"

That was a juicy tidbit. I tucked that one away for later.

"You know the diner's going to go under." Reba blurted it out so fast on the heels of the Hanson rumors, I barely had a moment to adjust to the topic change.

"No way. I ate there last night, and not a seat was open. The food was delicious, too."

"True enough. The word is that the resort is locking in exclusive contracts with all the local meat and produce vendors. Can you imagine what that would do to the diner? I guess they wouldn't last for more than a month if that happened."

I didn't have to imagine. Either the diner would need to ship in supplies from far away, find new vendors, or close the doors. Since Quincey was in such a remote part of the state, it wasn't a tough guess to determine the outcome.

"Wouldn't that be the same for Sam's bakery? If the resort got exclusive vendor contracts, wouldn't she lose out too?" I asked.

Reba considered the point. "I guess so, but I don't know for sure. Want some wine?"

I shook my head. I wasn't much of a drinker anymore. "No thanks, but you go ahead."

Reba refilled her glass with the bottle's dregs. Her eyes looked red. I suspected it would be game over for her soon.

"You hear of anyone here with a grudge against Sherman?"

She shot me a sly glance. "You mean, like a killing grudge?"

I nodded.

"Sweetie, take a peek around. Sherman Stier has either stabbed or threatened to stab everyone here in the back. I swear, he lives to screw people over. He wants to buy up the entire downtown area. Wants to turn the museum into a bowling alley, I'm told. He wants my B&B out of business. He even wants to close the local golf course because it would compete with his new one. Can you imagine that? The local course is only nine holes, and it's full of cactus and sagebrush. Also, there's some hold he has on the mayor, but that's one secret I haven't been able to crack. I'd say the only one who wouldn't want him dead is good Pastor Tom, and that's only because he's a decent man of God."

Reba drained her glass. "I wonder how long they're going to keep us here." She closed her eyes and slipped off to sleep without another word.

"She's nutty, you know."

I looked over at the next table. Shanna was there, scrolling through whatever on her smart phone.

I let Reba sleep and switched tables. "You caught all that?"

Shanna shrugged. "Didn't mean to. She's just… too loud. She gets that way when she's had too much to drink. Exactly like you saw her. She drinks, gets talkative and loud, then passes out."

"What will happen to her?" I asked.

Shanna shrugged again. I took it as a personal tic. "Tom or Hanson, or perhaps Dean will get her back to the B and B and she'll wake up on her couch tomorrow morning and do it all over again."

"It's terrible what happened here, isn't it?"

"No. Not really."

Shanna's blunt response surprised me. I'll admit it. "Why not?"

Shanna stopped scrolling and set her phone on the table. "Because. Sometimes, and by sometimes, I mean rarely, bad people get what they deserve."

I was speechless. Was this the same Shanna from earlier who gave me my muffin and, I guessed, could be the sweetest woman in the world? "Why do you say that?"

"He's been pushing people in this town around since he got here. Throwing around money, making threats to close businesses down. Reba was right about one thing. He's got something on the mayor for sure. I've overheard the committee and others around town have been to her with complaints either about the man or that resort, and she has done nothing about it. A rumor that Reba didn't tell you is that the mayor will be in the political fight of her life when the next election cycle starts."

"Why?" I asked.

"Because she won't be running unopposed for once. I have to

use the restroom."

Shanna picked up her phone as she stood and started for the door.

"Wait, who's running against her?"

She hesitated after a step, turned, and grinned. "Sam's boyfriend. Dean Williams."

I wanted to talk to Dean next, especially since Sam told me they weren't dating. When I finally spotted him, he was deep in conversation with Rob and Lisa, and I had no desire to intrude on the conversation. I really wanted to get him alone. Instead, I scanned the room. Besides the committee, there appeared to be around seventy-five people waiting to get interviewed by the police. By body language alone, I deduced most of them were itching to leave. My window of opportunity was closing. Fast.

I spotted Hanson near the stage. He was keeping busy by collecting the centerpieces he provided and placing them on a single table near the front door. I grabbed the one in the center of my table and grabbed the one from the table where Reba was currently napping, and carried them to Hanson.

I set them down on the table with the others. "These are really lovely. Can I help you collect the others?"

Hanson took a step back and almost tripped over a chair, but he quickly regained his balance.

I grabbed his arm to help him. "Hey, I'm so sorry. I didn't mean to startle you."

Hanson smiled. "That's okay. I got lost in my thoughts. What were you saying?"

"I said I like these centerpieces. They're pretty."

Hanson looked at the growing number of them on the table. "Oh. Thank you. They're nothing special. Carnations and daisies and whatnot. We didn't have a large budget for flowers."

"What are you going to do with them?"

Hanson blinked twice. I wasn't sure if he was all there or not.

"Usually people will take them, but I suppose with the... distraction, most of them are being left behind. I'll probably recycle the materials and the flowers will end up in the mulch pile."

"That's so sad something so beautiful will end up as mulch."

Hanson shrugged. "That's the nature of this business. Some flowers get dried and saved, or pressed into scrapbooks, but I'd say ninety-eight percent of them go into the trash."

"That's terrible. You'd assume they would donate them to a church, or a cemetery, or something."

"That occurs more often than not. Especially around the bigger holidays like Christmas, Easter, and Valentine's Day. But then what does the church and cemetery do with them when they've wilted away?"

I got the picture. "They end up on the mulch pile."

"Or in the town dump. Not a very romantic end, is it? It's the tragic irony of my business. People want to give flowers as a symbol of love and beauty, but the moment the flowers are picked is the second they start to wither and die."

"I never considered that." It was true, I hadn't. Although, to be honest, I've given flowers to no one, and I haven't received one since my corsage for senior prom.

"I saw you over there talking to Reba. Did she spin any wonderful tales for you?"

"You mean about your affair?" I said to myself. But I had the sense not to verbalize that. "She mentioned your brother owns the Quincey Inn. That's pretty cool. I read that historical plaque on the building when I passed by it yesterday. It seems like an interesting place. I'd like to go in and see it before I leave town."

Hanson gave me a look that told me he picked up what I laid down and was avoiding the topic.

"He's only a part-owner. I'm sure he owns fifty or sixty percent of the hotel, but you'd have to ask him."

"I don't recall meeting him. Is he here tonight? I thought he's on the committee."

Hanson wiped his brow on his sleeve and sat. "He's not in town. He's back in Taos with our parents. My dad broke a leg when he fell off a ladder, so Harold's up there helping mom take care of him."

"That's nice of him. You didn't go too?"

Hanson shook his head no. "No need for both of us. It's easier for him to get away. He's got an entire staff to run the hotel in his absence, so it's not uncommon for him to be away. Me, I've only got one assistant, and she's in junior college full time, so I have to run the flower shop mostly on my own. I would've loved to run home for a month or two, but that would have meant shutting the doors until I returned."

Made sense. I didn't detect any animosity between him and his brother. Well, maybe a small twinge of jealousy, and I could understand that.

"How did you get into the floral industry?" I asked.

Hanson rolled his eyes. "Actually, I wanted to be a mechanic, but I hated coming home every night dirty and smelling like grease. It was my mom's flower shop, so when she started talking about retiring, I became her apprentice and took over the place. So, Kelly, what is it you really need from me?"

I guessed the gig was up. "Codi. Not Kelly. I've learned from a couple of people that Sherman Stier had a lot of enemies in this town."

"Thanks for your honesty, Codi. That can be a hard thing to find around here." Hanson used a foot to shove a chair toward me, and I sat. "I try to keep my nose on my face and not in other people's business, you understand, so I won't tell you much. I'll tell you what I'm going to tell the cops if I ever get my turn. Yes, there was a lot of bad blood between him and a lot of folks here. No, I can't guess who he pushed to the breaking point."

"What about the argument you all were having earlier? What was that about?"

Hanson became interested in a fingernail and started picking at a cuticle. "Dean wanted us to approach the mayor tonight as a group, so maybe she'd finally do something about Stier."

"What resulted from that?" I asked.

Hanson forgot about his finger and paid more attention to me. "Beats me. I didn't want to get involved, so I slipped out of the back door and headed to the kitchen."

"What for?"

"To see if I could scrounge up another slice of pie and talk to some ladies."

"What happened?"

"Like I said, I had some pie, and talked to one lovely volunteer washing the dishes."

I went for the jugular. "Your girlfriend wouldn't object to that?"

Hanson looked a bit taken, then stood. "Nice talking to you, Kelly. Make sure you take a centerpiece with you when you leave."

Hanson walked away without looking back. Information-wise, he was a bust.

I grunted, hopefully loud enough for him to hear. "It's Codi."

I glanced up and saw Dean was sitting alone, nursing a bottle of soda. He saw me coming, looked for a place to escape to, and finding no safe passage, stayed where he was.

"Howdy," I said as I approached him.

He stared at me as if he didn't speak Texan. Dean took a swig of his soda and went to work peeling the label from the plastic bottle.

"You don't seem to like me much. Why not?" I asked.

His brow furrowed. "Mama said never to trust outsiders, and never to trust girls with guitars, and especially never to trust outsider girls with guitars."

I threw him my best smile. "That's sound advice. Your mama is a smart woman."

Dean scowled. "What are you here for?"

"I came to town to sing my songs and entertain y'all." I assumed that was self-explanatory, considering I'd spent most of the evening on the stage doing just that.

"No. I meant, what are you here for right now? I saw you sniffing around the others. What do you want from me?"

"Let me shoot it straight, slugger. Sam's a friend. We go way, way back, and she's about to find herself in a whole heap of trouble. I want to help her avoid that if I can. Can you tell me what went on earlier tonight?"

"I don't get what you mean." Dean set his soda on the table and crossed his arms. This wasn't going the way I expected or wanted it to.

"I saw the pow-wow y'all were having in the back, and I saw Sherman shove Sam."

Dean threw his left leg over his right. He was going into full shutdown mode. If there was a box or closet handy, I felt certain he'd go right for it.

"Well?" I asked.

Dean just pursed his lips tight and blew. I bet if I put a trumpet before him, he could perform *The Flight of the Bumblebee* with little effort. Perhaps I needed to change my line of questioning.

"I understand you and Sam are seeing each other. If you're sweet on each other, then for sure you'd want to help her, right? That's what I'm trying to do. Help her. Can't you help me? Do what's best for Sam?"

Had his eyes been lasers, he would have drilled a hole right through my forehead.

"Do you know why Sherman shoved Sam, and what happened afterward?"

Dean dropped his foot to the floor, put his elbow on his knee, and rested his chin on his elbow. He could have modeled for Rodan's *Thinker* if the statue was based on rage instead of logic.

"Can you tell me anything at all? Please? For Sam's sake?"

Dean's ears turned from pink to red, and I suspected there was an internal volcano churning inside him. I'd seen enough confrontations throughout my career to recognize when one was on the way. It was time to take my leave while the time was at hand.

"Okay. I'll go. But if you want to talk, I'll be around for a while longer. Think about Sam. Think about what she'd want you to do."

I left Dean stewing in his juices and looked across the room to see who else might have any helpful information.

I also needed to talk to Sam again and find out why she lied to me.

Looking around, I figured the pool of people I wanted to interview had reduced to about half, although I'd love another shot at Dean. I suspected he was hiding something behind that brick wall he threw up. Was it something to do with Sam? Was it something to do with a murder? I didn't know. One thing I knew for sure was I had to use the facilities, and since those were in the same hallway as the pantry, I hoped to get a look at that, too. I'm not a trained criminologist, but I figured I might spot something that the police overlooked. Like perhaps a signed confession, or the crime captured on video.

I walked through the room to the back door and turned right, which led me into the kitchen. The kitchen was empty, and I assumed that everyone who worked in there during the event had gone into the gymnasium. I turned around and walked down the hall. It only took a few strides to get to the pantry. The door was closed, and there was a giant X marked off in yellow crime scene tape. I wanted to open the door and look anyway, but when I reached for the doorknob, I noticed they covered it with fingerprint dust. I didn't want to add to that mess, nor did I want to be covered with dust, so I gave up that quest for the moment.

The restroom was just down the hall from the pantry, just like Sam had said. There wasn't much to the ladies' room. It was small. Three stalls and two sinks, and I was lucky enough to have the entire thing to myself. I selected the far stall and took care of business. It was good to be alone for a few minutes, and I soaked up the quiet like a sunflower basking in the sunlight. I closed my eyes for a moment and took a few cleansing breaths.

"I don't think Sam did it, even though everyone is saying she did." In the small room, the voice echoed over every fixture and shattered my moment of serenity.

"Are you talking to me?" I asked.

"Of course. We're the only two in here. C'mon out of there."

I got myself together, slid the lock open, and left the stall. Lisa stood at a sink. She was busy staring into the mirror and fixing her hair. I approached the remaining sink and washed my hands.

"Why does everyone assume she's guilty?" I took my time rinsing my hands. The water felt warm and relaxing, but I couldn't stay under there forever, so I shut off the tap and reached for the paper towels.

Satisfied with her look, Lisa turned from the mirror and looked at me. "Lots of reasons. They've been at each other's throats since they met. Sherman wanted to buy her out and close the bakery."

"I have firsthand knowledge of that. I was at the bakery earlier when he came in with a group of other men."

Lisa interrupted. "Investors from the city. Sherman doesn't… didn't have enough of his own money for everything he wanted, so he started bringing in investors about a year ago."

"He offered her a job at the new resort." I threw the used towels into the trash can.

Lisa laughed at that. "Oh, my. You think that he'd really give her a job there, and if he did, do you think she'd accept it? No way. Sam's too stubborn and way too proud to do that. Besides, she took that bakery from a place that was marginal to one of the top spots in town. You think she'd give all that up willingly?"

I pondered that for a moment. "No, I guess not. She was always headstrong and a fighter, even when I knew her back in school."

"Anyway, Sherman was always trying to push her buttons. In response, I've overheard her call him some things that I can't repeat in a church, or on the street, either. Sherman tried to get her arrested once, but Chief Jennings wouldn't do it."

That was an interesting tidbit I hadn't found out before. "Oh? What for?"

"Something about trespassing at the resort construction site. They've had problems with theft and vandalism up there. Sherman claimed he had video evidence of Sam and Dean snooping around. From what I got from the grapevine, the video wasn't clear enough to fully make them out, so Jennings did nothing but give them a stern warning."

A trip to the resort was another thing I added to my mental list of things to discuss further with Sam.

"Why do you think she didn't do it?"

"She cried over a bird once. I was at the bakery picking up a birthday cake and a robin flew into her front window and knocked itself out. Sam ran out there to see what she could do about it, and she picked that little bird up and held it until it revived and flew away. I can't imagine someone who would be so protective of a bird would take the life of anything, including a rude human."

I wasn't so sure about that. It made me daydream about the menagerie back on the bus. I've met plenty of horrible people that I'd trade in for a friendly skunk. "If Sam didn't do it, who do you suspect did? Someone stabbed Sherman. He didn't stab himself."

"I really shouldn't say." Lisa looked at the door to see if anyone might come in at that moment. I knew from experience that any time anyone said they shouldn't say, that meant they couldn't wait to spill the proverbial beans. "Dean has a terrible temper, and he's protective of Sam. They're dating. Everyone in town talks about that."

"Sam told me they weren't."

Lisa looked confused. "I don't know why she'd say that. Dean is at the diner almost every day and talks about her all the time."

Someone was lying, but I couldn't determine who. "Anyone else besides Dean? I heard Sherman wasn't much liked by many people in town."

Lisa's nose twitched. "Well, that's true. But I don't think there's anyone here who'd actually kill him. I say you don't have to look any further than Dean Williams, and that's exactly what I'm going to tell the chief first chance I get."

Lisa turned, yanked the door open, and stomped off. I washed my hands again and left the room.

CHAPTER SEVEN

I headed back to the gymnasium and stepped only a yard beyond the door when I literally bumped into Rob.

"Excuse me," he said. Rob pivoted around to determine who had run into his back, and his face displayed both delight and anguish to realize it was me. "I'm so sorry. I didn't see you."

"No, no. That's all my fault. I didn't watch where I was going. You got a second for me?" I asked.

I can't imagine where Rob's mind skipped to, but I pictured it went straight to me, inviting him back to my bus. That assumption I'd based solely on how intently he was looking to determine if his better half was watching us at the moment.

"Of course, I do," he said.

"Come with me then." I hooked my elbow into his and led him toward the stage. As we approached, I noticed Bozeman had finished packing the gear, which stood in a neat pile nearby. We couldn't leave until the cops cleared us, so Bozeman had settled into a chair with his feet up on another. He had his hat drawn low over his eyes, and a Louis L'Amour paperback in his lap. A quick glance would make you assume the book held his interest, but I guessed he was napping. He had been reading that same book for about four years, and he kept it stuffed in the pocket of his guitar case to be used more like a prop than a read. He figured people would be less likely to bother someone who was reading, and more often than not, he was right.

I led Rob onto the stage and over to the piano, where I grabbed my photo and handed it to him.

He looked at it, then looked back at me. "I like the blue hair better."

I glanced at the photo. Although I wore a hat, you still saw my long, raven black hair. I agreed. It wasn't a suitable color for me, and I never returned to it.

"Me too. I'm sorry we never got to play *Loving You, Leaving You*. I gather you were looking forward to it."

"Indeed. I'm sorry I didn't get to hear it in person."

"Hey, I got an idea. Wait here." I walked to the gear pile and returned with my guitar case. I extracted my acoustic from the case, sat on the piano bench, and played it for Rob. Even without Bozeman's accompaniment, it sounded good. The music end of it was pretty easy, just a simple, three chord progression that a billion other country songs had. But the magic of this tune I wrapped around the story it told, the story of loving someone so much you had to leave them. When I finished the song, I put the guitar away, closed up the case, and turned back to Rob. He had a tear in his eye.

"That was beautiful. That'll always be my favorite song, and I thank you for playing it for me."

I gave him an embarrassed smile and thanked him.

"Now tell me, what did you think of tonight's excitement?" I asked.

"I don't know. It all happened so fast. Sam and Sherman got into it. Then the next thing I know, Sherman took a swing at her."

"I caught that. You stepped in and saved her." I said.

"I had to. Wasn't right trying to hit a woman, no matter what she said to him."

"What did she say?"

"They argued about the bakery, and he said he had what he needed to take it from her. She called him a…"

Rob trailed off, searching for a word that he would substitute for what Sam actually said because he didn't want to repeat to me verbatim what he overheard. "… slimy weasel. Then Sam left the room while I held Sherman. After a minute or two, he pushed me off, then followed her."

Slimy weasel, not a jerk. Another inconsistency I'd need to ask Sam about.

"Did he catch her?"

"I don't know. I barely made it through the door when Lisa grabbed my arm and told me to stay out of it. She took me into the kitchen, so I can't tell you what happened after that. I didn't see Sherman again until I caught the scream and ran to the pantry."

"Who was there?" I asked.

"Shanna was the one who yelled. And I found Sam there, standing over the body. It was awful. I never want to go through anything like that again."

"Do you think Sam did it?"

"Well, she was the one closest to him, and she had his blood on her shirt, so I expect so."

"You don't consider anyone else might have done it? I understand no one around town really liked Sherman."

Rob scoffed. "Not well liked is an understatement. Everyone I know hated him. He's a cancer in this town. He even tried to start some trouble with me and Lisa down at the diner."

"Oh really? Like what?" For good measure, I batted my eyelashes at him. He didn't fall for it.

"I'm not usually for violence, but if Sam killed him, Mayor Mary should give her the key to the city." Rob held up the photo. "Thanks again for this. I'm going to frame it and hang it in the diner. I'm going to go show it to Lisa."

Rob rushed away from me like he needed to catch a train and left me sitting there wondering what to do next. I sat for a while and watched the crowd. Besides the committee, only two dozen people waited to be cleared to leave. The clock was ticking. I had perhaps twenty minutes to finish my inquiries before the long arm of the law reached in. I sighed, stood, and planned to introduce myself to the mayor.

Mayor Mary was sitting alone. Like Shanna, she seemed busy reading something on her phone. I hoped rather than social media; the mayor was using the downtime to get through some important town business. She spotted me coming and put her phone face down on the table.

"The famous Codi Cassidy. Thanks for coming to our small town and blessing us with your music. Mary Sweets. Nice to meet you."

The mayor stuck out her hand, and I shook it.

"It was my pleasure, ma'am. I'm just sorry I didn't get to give y'all the full concert I intended."

"Well, perhaps you can come back and play during our town harvest festival in October." She seemed all business, and although she presented a warm exterior, I detected a chill just beneath her surface.

"Sure thing. Have Sam pass me along the details, and I'll check if the dates work out."

"Sam? Sam Henry?"

"Yes, she's the one who booked me for this gig. We're friends. We go way back."

"Oh, well then." She said only three simple words, but the way the mayor said them caused the temperature in the immediate area to drop by twenty degrees.

"What do you think happened here tonight? It's horrible, isn't it?" I asked.

The mayor slipped into an unannounced staring contest with me. Although it tempted me to compete, I purposely blinked several times in succession.

"Why do you care?" The mayor slid back in her seat, checked her phone, and returned it to the table.

"Like I said, Sam's a friend, and I don't think she could have done what she's being accused of."

"I don't believe Chief Jennings has accused anyone yet. So far as I can tell, his team is still taking the initial statements of the people in attendance. Tell me, Ms. Cassidy, are you a detective?"

Her tone hardened, and I sensed a dressing down coming on. "No, ma'am."

"Perhaps you're an undercover agent with the F.B.I.? Or maybe a captain with the state police?"

I shook my head no.

"Is your napping partner over there secretly Columbo in a cowboy hat?"

I glanced over at Bozeman. He still had his feet up on a chair, but the book had fallen to the floor.

"No," I said.

"Maybe you should let the police do the police business, and if we need someone to write a ballad about it, we'll call you. Sound good?"

I recognized a dismissal when I got one, so I nodded and stepped away. Around the room I looked for Sam, saw she hadn't returned, so I wanted to share with Bozeman everything I learned and ask if he had any input. My plan traveled sideways, though, when someone wrapped a hand around my shoulder. I turned. It was Pastor Tom.

"You'll have to forgive Mayor Mary. She's under a bit of stress right now. It's not every day a benefactor of this town gets murdered in cold blood."

I wasn't sure I caught that right. "Benefactor? I found out he was trying to buy up every property he could to expand his business empire."

"Oh, no, no. It wasn't like that at all. Everything Sherman Stier did was to improve the community. Why, he had plans to update the library and city hall. Last year, the fire department moved into a larger station because of his generosity. Did you know he had plans to build an art museum dedicated to New Mexico artists? And he planned on hosting an artist's retreat yearly at the resort."

"He did, huh? Are you saying all the rumors I've been hearing about him are all wrong?"

The pastor looked in my eyes briefly, then picked a spot on my shoulder to stare at. I wondered if that was my angel's side or my devil's side.

He swallowed. "Well, you understand the human condition. No one is all good or all bad. People are by nature complicated, you understand."

Sure, I understood he didn't want to answer the question. "Yes, I get it. We're all flawed. But are you saying that everyone he threatened to ruin just misunderstood his philanthropy?"

"Did I mention the art museum? And the new fire department?"

"Yes, you did, Pastor Tom, but interestingly enough, everything you mentioned would come back and benefit him more than the town itself."

"No, you still don't understand. It's not like that at all."

"Why would someone want to stab him?" It was time to go for the blunt question. I didn't want a roundabout discussion. I never much cared for them.

"I have no clue. And I'm confident the chief will find the person responsible, and that person will go to jail, and may God have mercy on their soul after that. This is a place of God, not a place for violence. I'm sorry it had to happen here in this house of worship. What will happen to the congregation? How can people worship here without whispering about what occurred in that room? Who will clean up this mess?"

"One more question, Pastor Tom. How much money did he pledge to the church?"

Pastor Tom looked me in the eye without answering, so I supplied some options. "Ten thousand? Fifty thousand? A hundred thousand? More?"

At the word more, the good pastor's facial expressions told me all I needed.

"Strange that such an ungodly man would donate so much money to this church. What was it for? To clear his conscience? To tithe his way into heaven? Or perhaps there was something else going on. Was there, Pastor?"

His countenance changed, and I guessed there was, although I didn't know what. Yet another question I could add to my ever-expanding list of questions without answers.

"Have a good evening, Miss Cassidy. I will pray for you tonight."

Pastor Tom hastily moved away to the far side of the room. I couldn't tell what was going on with him, but I always hated to be called 'miss'. Did I look like a 'miss'? Come to think of it, with my small stature and my blue hair, I probably did, but that was well beside the point.

I was still stewing when I felt a tap on my shoulder. Once I spun around, I recognized the man in the uniform. I guess it was my turn with Chief Jennings.

"Chief Jennings, I presume?"

"Codi Cassidy, right? I apologize for being gruff before, but I couldn't have a suspect speaking to anyone. You mind answering a few questions?"

"Of course."

"Is Codi Cassidy your real name or a stage name?"

"Real name. Codi Lynn Cassidy. That's Codi ending with an I, not a Y."

"And your address and phone number."

I gave him a business card with the address of my post office box in Utah, along with my cell phone number and email address. He copied everything from the card down into a notebook, then put the business card in his shirt pocket.

"You don't have a physical address?"

I smiled. "My physical address is anywhere we park that bus out back. The post office box is a mail forwarding service. I have it to get the important stuff, like bills and my magazines. If you need to contact me, the best way is through text or email."

"Get a ton of fan mail, do you?" The question seemed innocent enough, but there was an underlying snarky tone to it.

I threw him a sweet smile. "I get a fair amount."

The glance he threw at me told me he didn't believe it. But it was true. I usually received ten or twelve fan letters a month, and that number typically tripled around my birthday.

"In your own words, can you tell me what happened here tonight? Anything you may have seen or heard?"

I sunk into the nearest chair to get comfortable. Chief Jennings stayed standing in his power position. I wondered if he meant what I saw and heard as an eyewitness, or saw and heard with all the snooping around I'd been doing over the past hour. I went with the former.

"There's not much I can tell you, chief. I spent most of my night on or near the stage. The only exception was when we had our meal break."

"Who's we?"

I pointed in Bozeman's direction. "Me and my partner, Bozeman James."

The chief raised an eyebrow. "Is that his real name?"

"I think his birth name is Jesse, but I've only ever known him as Bozeman."

"What can you tell me about the altercation?"

"I didn't witness any of that. I didn't know there was one until you stopped the show."

The chief looked up at me. "I don't mean the murder. I mean, the fight that happened right before."

"Like I said, Chief Jennings, I caught little of it since I was on stage performing my set. I witnessed Sherman push Sam, and when Sherman took a swing at her, a couple of guys stepped in and stopped him. Then, so far as I guessed, it was over. That's all I can really tell you."

The chief continued his notes, then closed his book. "How well do you know Samantha Henry? Rumor has it you're the best of friends."

That information didn't take long to get back to him.

"I wouldn't say that we're the best of friends. We were classmates back in high school, but I hadn't seen or heard from her after graduation until a couple of months ago."

"Why did she contact you?"

For the head of the police department, the guy seemed to be a dim bulb, and it shouldn't take remedial math to put this two and two together. "Well, she was in charge of the entertainment, and I'm an entertainer, so..." I held my arms out, hoping he'd make the connection all on his own.

"And you don't find it suspicious that she'd hire you out of the blue?"

"No. Not really. I get lots of contacts from people I've known in my past. Especially when they learn I'm coming back through town and they're looking for free tickets to the rodeo or something. Occasionally old friends like Sam will hire us to play gigs. Usually private parties or events like this one."

"People have seen you with her frequently over the last couple of days."

I didn't understand what he wanted to imply, but I didn't plan to fall for it. I usually had a long rope, but I was getting to the end. "Yes. We, meaning Bozeman and I, got to town around four-thirty yesterday afternoon. I ran into her when I was walking around town, and we talked for a bit. Then we ate dinner at the diner, and this morning I spent some time with her at the bakery. I'm not sure what it is you're digging for, but you will not find it. We're old friends, and if you think it's suspicious that old friends would want to reconnect after a long time, then I feel sorry for you."

"Did Sam ever say she wanted to kill Sherman Stier or anything like that?"

"No. Of course not. Why are you so focused on Sam? There were a couple hundred people here tonight, and any of them could have done it."

"And every single person here tonight is getting questioned, but the way it looks to us is that the evidence points right at your friend. She had the motive. She had the opportunity. She had his blood on her, she found the body, she had a vendetta, and most importantly, the knife recovered at the scene belonged to her."

"How could you possibly figure that out that already?" I sounded way too defensive, and I suspected I had to tone down my emotion. I had to remain calm and rational, so I took a cleansing breath. "Surely you couldn't have figured that out this quick, even if you were a top-notch detective."

Chief Jennings grinned. It didn't suit him. "It didn't take a detective. She engraved her name on the handle. So, if it walks like a duck..."

He had me there. It didn't look good for Sam. "Yeah, yeah. I got it. It's a duck."

"Of course, like I said, we're questioning everyone here. Everyone is a suspect as far as the law is concerned until we have definitive evidence that points to someone. Sam will get a fair shake from me."

I didn't know if I believed him, but I thanked him anyway, and he left me and headed over to Bozeman. Bozeman had woken from his nap, and their exchange didn't take long. Once Bozeman was alone again, I approached him.

"What did he say?" I asked.

Bozeman put his hat on the table and ran his fingers through his hair. "Probably the same things he said to you. We're free to go tonight, but we need to stick around town for a couple of days."

"He didn't mention that part to me."

"He probably assumed you would stick around, anyway. Let's get the bus loaded."

I hoped to talk to Sam again, but I didn't see her. A deputy had taped off an area around the back door, and cleanup had begun in the rest of the room. Lisa and Rob were supervising the removal of the remaining dinner service. Hanson was still collecting centerpieces, and Dean was helping Reba to her feet. I hadn't seen Shanna since I talked to her, so I assumed she was back in the kitchen. The mayor had disappeared, as had Pastor Tom.

Bozeman was in a hurry to get the bus loaded, so he rushed me along to get the job done. Once we loaded up, I got out of my gig clothes and slipped into my comfy jeans and tennis shoes. I added a jean jacket and a baseball cap to my ensemble and found Bozeman, who was already behind the wheel.

"Hey, I'm going to walk back to the lot, okay? I really need the fresh air."

Bozeman gave me the look. "Are you sure it's safe?"

"No. But I'm going to do it, anyway."

Bozeman sighed. "At least take Betty with you."

I reached around to my back and felt for Betty, already tucked into the holster, and hidden by my jacket. Betty was only a .22, and I always loaded her with nonlethal rounds. I made sure the probability was as low as possible that I'd actually kill someone, but it was all about having a deterrent available. "Already done."

Bozeman nodded. "Good. Don't dawdle. If you're not back at the bus in thirty minutes, I'm coming out looking for you."

"Deal." I stepped off the bus, helped guide Bozeman out of the parking lot, then headed out on foot.

Truth be told, I enjoyed wandering around at night, even if it was a little more dangerous. There was something about being out in the evening air that revived my spirit, and I often got song or poetry ideas while meandering around. Bozeman thought it was silly and dangerous for me to venture out like I do, but I disagree with him about it every time. Bozeman's the type who sees danger around every corner, and I'm nowhere near that paranoid, even if they are really out to get me.

I came to a corner, turned it, and took a few steps. As I walked past the church's main door, I realized I had ventured off in the wrong direction, so I did a one-hundred-eighty-degree turn and headed the other way. If it was one thing I hated, it was being directionally challenged. It was okay, though, because I always got to where I wanted to go, even if it took me a little extra mileage to get there.

I walked up the quiet road toward Main Street and noticed how dead it was. I had been to towns before where everything seemed to shut down at sunset, and this seemed to be one of those towns. Up ahead, a car passed by occasionally, but it was a rare sight. I passed a few houses with the curtains drawn, and behind them I could see flickering lights, so I knew it was television time in western America.

Past the houses, I came across a business. Was it one block of businesses before I got to Main Street, or two? I couldn't remember. I really needed to pay closer attention to my environment, which should be easy since I never have to drive, so I made a mental note to do just that. Another few steps and I passed an alley and then found myself in front of an electronics sales and repair shop. In the front window stood a variety of the old-time radios that people used to sit in front of before the TV came along. There was a single lamp burning inside the shop. By that light, I saw there were console televisions, giant old stereos, and even a couple of computers that must have dated back to the eighties. I wasn't sure how much of the shop was for sales and repairs versus how much of the shop was a museum of lost technologies.

Down toward Main Street I continued, my heels clicking on the concrete. I stopped again, glanced down at the soft-soled shoes I was wearing. No clicks. The hair on the back of my neck rose as I realized I was being followed. I continued walking down to the next storefront, then stopped and quickly pivoted. I didn't see anyone behind me.

Come on, Codi, get it together. No reason to get the jitters.

I started walking again and increased my pace until I was almost jogging. The clicking started again. Finally, I saw the traffic lights of Main Street half a block down. I hurried along, then as soon as I turned the corner, I dipped into the first inset entryway and extracted Betty from the holster and tucked her in my jacket pocket.

I waited and I counted to ten, then inched my head out to see if anyone was on the sidewalk. The coast was clear, so I stepped from the doorway, and crept back to the corner and glanced around the building. Nothing. I didn't realize I'd been holding my breath until I exhaled. I looked down Main Street and saw a group of teenagers milling around in front of a sandwich shop, so I jaywalked across the street and headed in their direction. As I got closer to them, I slowed down my stride and took a couple of furtive glances behind me. I still didn't see anyone.

Rather than continue on alone, I slipped into the shop.

"I'm sorry, we're closing up," the man behind the counter said.

"Look. I think there's someone following me. Can I wait in here for just a few minutes? I won't get in your way."

The man stepped around the counter, walked out the door, and came back in a minute later. "There's no one out there. Street's empty."

I didn't move. "Please. Just give me a couple of minutes."

The man stepped back to the counter and picked up where he left off with his cleaning. "I haven't seen you around here before."

"No. I'm from out of town. I was out for a walk and wasn't paying attention to where I was going, so I ended up on some side street."

"Where are you staying?"

Sometimes I believe that little white lies are much better options than telling the truth, so I lied. "The Quincey Inn. On Main Street. Where is that from here?"

The man pointed to the right. "Down that way, about six or seven blocks. You need me to walk you over there?"

I went to the door and looked outside. Not a soul in sight. "No. I think I'm okay now. It was probably nothing but my active imagination. It's always getting me into trouble. Thank you, though."

Before the man could respond, I left the shop and trotted up Main Street. I slowed four blocks later when the bakery came into view. Bozeman was at the corner waiting for me. He must have seen me coming up the street because he wore a look of concern on his face.

"Pleasant walk?"

I bent over, put my hands on my knees, and breathed deep a few times. "Could have been better."

CHAPTER EIGHT

At six the next morning, I was up, out of bed, and ready to go. I fed Gibson and filled a food bowl full of vegetables for Merle and Dolly. Since Sunday was treat day, I pulled some worms from the fridge for Merle, and opened a can of salmon for Dolly. There was no way to forget about Willie and Waylon, so I cut up half an apple for Willie, and half a banana for Waylon. I ate the other half of each fruit for my breakfast. Quiet not to wake Bozeman, I slipped out of the bus with the various food bowls and distributed them where they needed to go. Since daybreak was fast approaching, Merle and Dolly were still wide awake when I dropped off their dishes. Waylon and Willie were still in their little nest, dreaming about whatever chipmunks dream about, so I left the food outside.

In the breaking dawn, I stepped over to the bakery's back door. The door wouldn't budge, so I went around to the front. I saw the sign and realized I made a mistake. It was Sunday, and the bakery was closed for the day.

"Hey, you." The voice descended from above, and it startled me and made me jump back from the door. I took another step closer to the street and looked up. Sam was sitting on a small balcony drinking a cup of coffee. "Directly to your left is a door. It's unlocked. Come on up."

I found the door and took the stairs to the second floor, and Sam had the door to her home open before I hit the top step.

"Nice place." I looked around at the small, tidy space.

"It came with the bakery. It makes for a short commute in the morning. Would you like some coffee?"

"I'm more of a tea person."

"This is your lucky day. Follow me."

I tailed Sam into the kitchen. It was small, but functional. Sam filled a kettle with water and placed it on the stove to boil, then reached into a cabinet and found a mug. "Hey, I hope a tea bag is okay. I don't have any loose tea."

I laughed. "Steeping a bag is the only way I know how to make it."

Sam handed me a box of assorted fruit-based teas, and I selected a cherry one, opened the package, and dropped the bag in the mug. We waited in silence for the kettle to whistle, and when it did, Sam filled the mug. "Honey? Sugar?"

"Honey, please. That would be great."

Sam handed me a plastic bear of honey and I stirred in a dollop while Sam topped off her coffee. We took our beverages into the living room. Sam sat on the couch and threw a blanket over her bare legs. I sat in the only other chair in the room. I noticed she was still wearing my T-shirt.

"Rough night." I tried to take a sip, but the tea was too hot yet, so I held the mug between my hands to warm them.

"One of the roughest I've ever had," Sam said.

"What happened to you? I wanted to talk to you more, but you disappeared."

"Not by choice. When the chief saw me talking to you, he blew a gasket and had a deputy take me into the station. I had to wait there until the chief got back from questioning everyone else. I've only been home for a few hours. It seems I'm his prime suspect, and he's going to arrest me the second they process the evidence. Lucky for him, it all points back to me."

I stirred my tea and took a sip. "How do you know that?" I asked.

"Because that's a direct quote. So much for justice being blind, right?"

"Sam, look at me." Sam raised her eyes and looked directly into mine. "Did you do it? Did you kill Sherman Stier?"

Her gaze never wavered. "No, I didn't."

I could detect nothing in her voice or her body language to tell me she was lying.

"I talked to quite a few people last night. About half seem convinced you did," I said. I had a few sips of tea.

Sam took a drink of coffee, but then didn't respond.

"Sam, how did your knife get there?"

She drained the mug and set it on the table beside her. "I don't know. I took a few items to the church. Like a couple of pie cutters and three or four knives, but that knife was my favorite, so I wouldn't have taken it for fear of it getting stolen or misplaced."

"Why take anything? You told me the church had all the equipment you needed in the pantry."

"Yeah, but people donated most of the things they have and nothing is in the best of condition. It's not unusual for us to bring our own things in for the evening. Ask the McMurtrys. They do the same thing."

"What about Dean? Lots of people I talked to seemed to imply you two are dating, but you said otherwise."

"Because we're not. Like I said, we went out two or three times, and he was the sweetest guy ever. Then I made the mistake of sleeping with him, and he became downright possessive after that. That's when I broke things off. I can't be in that kind of relationship again."

I believed her. As far as I was concerned, she was three for three on the truth meter. Time for the big one. "Okay. What really went down with Sherman?"

Sam hesitated while she folded her blanket over to cover her bare calf. "He pinched me on the butt. Without even thinking, I spun around and grabbed him by his jangly parts and told him to never do that again or I'd castrate him. That's when he pushed me. So, then I made a wisecrack about his lack of manhood, and that's when he tried to take a swing at me. I guess I got him where it hurt him the most, huh?"

Sam chuckled at the memory. I smiled along with her. "Well, if you didn't kill him, we need to find out who did. Is the diner open on Sundays?"

Sam looked at a clock on the wall. It was one of those hanging cat ones where the tail and eyes moved. I thought those only existed in the movies. "It opens in fifteen minutes."

I got up and collected the mugs. "Then let's go get some pancakes. You go get dressed and I'll clean this stuff up."

By seven-thirty, we walked into the diner and grabbed the last table. It took me about three seconds of glancing at the menu to decide on the blueberry pancakes with a side of bacon. Sam, who said she didn't have an appetite, ordered raisin toast and coffee.

"The way I've worked it out, it's got to be someone on the committee," I said as I unfolded and refolded my napkin. "Although I talked to them last night, I'd like to talk to everyone again today to see if anyone saw or heard anything, or if anyone seems like a viable suspect."

"Do you really believe anyone on the committee can kill someone?"

"Would you prefer you remain the prime person of focus?" I asked.

"Um, no. After a second thought, perhaps someone on the committee did do it."

I unfolded and refolded my napkin again. One glance at Sam told me I was getting on Sam's nerves, so I put my napkin on my lap and started sorting the packets of sugar substitute by color instead. I hated waiting for meals to be served. I never knew what to do with my hands.

The server brought the food at last. Sam's raisin toast looked homemade, and my pancakes were larger than my head. After I covered them with butter, I added a portion of maple syrup. I forked off a corner and took a bite. I moaned in pleasure.

"My goodness gracious, that's delicious. Those blueberries just pop with flavor. Are they the same ones you use in your muffins?"

Sam brushed a toast crumb from her shirt. "Yes. We have the same supplier. Normally you can't grow blueberries in New Mexico, but there's a farmer in the next county over who specializes in them. He has whole greenhouses dedicated to fruits and vegetables that don't come from this area."

"How's the toast?" I asked.

Sam smiled. "It's perfect. I made the bread yesterday. What's the matter?"

"Nothing, it's just..." I took another bite and ran through the mental notes in my head while I chewed. "Yesterday, someone mentioned something about Stier destroying the diner's supply chain. I can't remember who I talked to, though."

"Is that relevant?"

I smiled. "It is if it gives someone else a motive."

I ate about half of the pancakes, and two out of three slices of bacon. Sam ate the remaining slice for me. Off in the distance, I saw Lisa, so I got her attention and waved her over.

"Good morning. Everything okay with your meal?" Lisa asked when she got to us.

"It was perfect," I answered. "Probably the best pancakes I've ever had. Listen, can I ask you a couple of questions? About last night?"

Lisa looked around the diner. "I really shouldn't. We're really busy this morning."

I gave her the puppy dog eyes. "Please? I'll only take a few minutes of your time, then I won't bother you again until I stalk you later for the pancake recipe."

Lisa scanned the area again. Everything looked to be running smoothly. "Okay, but I can only spare a couple of minutes." Lisa took the seat between Sam and me, and I asked her about what she saw or heard the previous evening. She added no further information from the night before, and her story didn't change.

I redirected the questions. "Is the diner going to be okay?"

A look of confusion crossed Lisa's face like a passing cloud. "Why wouldn't it be?"

"A little birdie told me that when they build the new resort, you're going to lose all your food suppliers and you'll need to close your doors. Now that Stier is gone, I imagine the diner is safe."

Lisa gave me the sternest look I've ever seen and seemed poised to give me the largest denial in history. The storm passed at once. Her face softened, and she threw me a smile as sweet as the pancake syrup at our table.

"You've been talking to Reba, haven't you? You got that nugget from her? She often mishears things, and then likes to repeat, incorrectly, I might add, the things she misheard. Yes, we have a lot of local suppliers, and we'd have to compete with any new restaurant for their business. Including Sam here. You know we get those blueberries from the same place?"

"Yes, she told me."

"Well then. However, even if a supplier can't fill an order, we have contingencies plans in place. Come with me."

Lisa took off from her chair, and I followed as close behind her as I could. We moved from the dining room through the swinging door in the kitchen. Behind the flattop was Rob, and around him were two other cooks, trying to keep up with the flurry of incoming orders. Lisa stopped in front of a large door, pulled it open, and gestured for me to join her in the walk-in freezer. The door slammed shut behind us, and the immediate chill hit me like a whack in the head from a tennis racket.

Lisa scraped the frost off a cardboard box. "Here, take a gander at that."

I read the box. Frozen beef. The box next to it held chicken breasts, the next contained pork. Lisa turned around and pushed the door open, and I followed, happy to leave the cold. She led me into another room where I saw large cans of fruits and vegetables. Along with them sat bags of various grains and even a couple of industrial sized boxes of instant potatoes.

From the pantry, Lisa led me to the small office and took a seat behind the desk. There was no other chair, so she pointed to the two-drawer file cabinet, and I sat on that.

"We try to be as farm-to-table as we can be, but the fact is that there are always supply chain issues and we have contingencies to deal with them. All that frozen meat you saw, all the canned goods? They all come from a distributor in Arizona. Here, look."

Lisa spun in her seat and grabbed a clipboard that was hanging on the wall. She flipped over a couple of pages and passed it to me. It was an invoice, one for ground beef, from a place in Tucson.

"If you opened that bottom drawer below you, you'd find lots of other paperwork showing the same." I had no reason to believe otherwise, so I didn't budge.

"We even have a backup plan if Sam doesn't come through with the baked goods we use. None of the frozen or canned food comes out as well as we'd normally serve, but we always tell our customers when there's a change. Believe me, in this part of the world, everyone is more than familiar with food, fuel, weather, or water disruptions."

I handed the clipboard back, and she returned it to its hook on the wall. "So, then the resort wouldn't have affected your business at all."

Lisa shook her head. "If it did anything, it may have made things crazier around here. I would imagine that there are some folks who would come into town for more of a home cooked meal rather than eat whatever option they had at the new resort."

I nodded. "You're probably right. I'm sorry I took up your time. No hard feelings?"

Lisa approached and took me into a hug. "Of course not. I know what you're doing and are looking out for Sam, and I appreciate that. Rob and I both love her to death, and to be honest, we need her here. She's just as much a part of this restaurant's success as we are."

She let me go and escorted me back to the dining room where I retook my seat.

"Well?" Sam asked.

"So far as I can tell, it checks out. I don't think they had the motive to kill Stier. They have a distributor they use if they can't source food from around here."

Sam shrugged.

"But you knew that already," I continued.

Sam nodded.

"Because you do the same thing."

Sam smiled. "Yes, I do. We use some of the same people, actually. I source mostly dry ingredients from their people. Flour, sugar, baking soda, that kind of stuff. Oh, and fruit when I can't get it fresh. My primary concern is typically eggs, but I also use a fair amount of dairy, like butter, milk, and cream. All depends on what I'm making."

"Wouldn't the resort cut into your dairy and egg sources?"

"Not really. I work with mostly smaller farmers, ones that wouldn't be able to handle that large a contract, anyway. And even if the resort somehow cut into the business, I'm not worried. It wouldn't be the first time I'd have to drive over to Tucson or El Paso for supplies. Oh, and honey. I have a local supplier for honey, but I could easily get by with store-bought stuff."

"What about chocolate?"

"Again, I wouldn't be affected. I'm a little particular about the chocolate I use, but I've teamed up with a bakery in Las Cruces that uses the same stuff I do. They're bigger than I am, so we go in on an order together and it gets shipped to them, then about once a month I head over there and pick up what I ordered."

"So, what you're saying is?"

"I agree with you, Codi. Rob and Lisa didn't do it. They didn't need to. They'll be fine with or without the resort. So now what?"

"Let's go over and see Reba. I'd be interested in seeing what she had to say."

Sam checked her watch. "It's after eight. We could wander that way and see if she's up."

"Why wouldn't she be? She owns a bed-and-breakfast, and she told me she's fully booked, so wouldn't she have to give her patrons breakfast?"

Sam stood, and I followed her out of the restaurant. "Breakfast is a loose term over there. She mostly offers cereals, packaged oatmeal, pastries wrapped in plastic wrap, that kind of thing."

I never noticed how fast Sam walked. I almost had to do double time to keep up with her. "That must thrill the vacationers."

"She makes up for it in the afternoon with a wine and cheese experience. Come on, we can walk over. It's only about eight blocks from here. You good with that?"

"Sure. Just slow down, okay?"

Sam dropped her speed in half, and I could resume a normal stride. I didn't mind the walk, and it was a beautiful morning. If I had to guess, the temperature was in the lower sixties, and there was a light breeze coming in from the south. We continued on in silence, and I wondered what must be going through Sam's mind. The last few hours must have been nothing but stress for her.

I was walking along, looking at a marvelous flower garden across the street when I slammed directly into Sam's back when she halted. I took a step backward, caught my heel on the sidewalk, and plopped to my rear.

"Are you okay? Anything hurt?" Sam asked as she offered me a hand up.

"Only my pride. Sorry about that. I wasn't paying attention."

Sam shrugged and pointed at a lovely, well kept Victorian home in front of us. "We're here, and I don't think we'll have to roust Reba from bed."

I looked to the house and noticed the old woman sitting in a rocking chair on the large front porch. She appeared to be napping. I approached her, trying to make as much noise as possible along the way.

"Ms. Reba? Hello?" I reached out for the chair's arm and gave it a gentle rock.

Reba's eyes sprung open like she got hit with a dose of adrenaline. She looked up at me. "I served the breakfast in the dining room off the kitchen."

"I'm not here for breakfast. Remember me from last night?" I took off my baseball cap and let my hair fall free. "You asked about my blue hair. Remember?"

She didn't seem to at first, but then she snapped to. "Of course, I remember. I'm not senile, you know!"

"Oh, I'm sorry. I meant no disrespect." I put my hat back on and crouched in front of her. "Can I ask you a few more questions about last night?"

Reba didn't seem sure, but she nodded anyway. I asked her the same things I had the night before, and she responded with more or less the same answers, although this time she left out Stevie's tax trouble. She was hazy on anything too detailed, and I chalked that up to the wine. This conversation led down to another dead end.

"You have a lovely home. Have you always lived here?"

She motioned for me to sit in the rocking chair next to hers, and for the benefit of my aching knees, I did.

"I was born in this house, as was my mother. This was one of the first houses ever built in this city. It was the mayor's house back in the day."

"Tell me more about it."

"Well, I used to live on the top floor, but once I got a little older, I moved to the ground floor. I converted a small office and sitting room into a little two room living quarters for myself. There are four bedrooms on the second floor, and a suite and another bedroom on the third. Has all the original woodwork, and the fireplaces are original as well. It's the best place to stay in town."

Sam tittered.

"What's so funny?" I asked.

"Since the motel closed last summer, it's the only place to stay besides the Quincey Inn."

Reba took offense and shook her frail fist in Sam's direction. "You build a hundred hotels, and this place would still be the best."

"I'd love to check it out. I love old houses," I said.

Reba shifted in her chair and pointed to the door. "Go on in. I have guests in every room at the moment, so don't go past the first floor, but you're welcome to look around."

I smiled, told them I'd be right back, and stepped into the house. The room I entered appeared to be the new sitting room, and it was marvelous. There were four large chairs at different spots around the room, and a table in the center. On the table was a chess game already in progress. From what I could tell, black was going to win in about four moves. On one wall was a fireplace, and where there weren't doorways or windows, there were floor to ceiling bookcases, each of them stuffed full of books. I walked through the room and scanned the shelves at random. There appeared to be a variety of things to read, from a leather-bound edition of Shakespeare's works to old western paperbacks. There were a few romance novels mixed in, along with a few contemporary thriller writers that I recognized. It was a nice home library where anyone could come in and find something to read.

There was a door to the left of the entryway, and I turned the knob and pushed it open. It appeared to be Reba's bedroom. She hadn't made the bed, and there were clothes piled on a chair. I closed the door behind me and continued down the hallway. The next room I encountered was a dining room with an enormous table that sat twelve easily. The furniture looked to be period pieces in great shape. There was a couple at the table eating breakfast, so I said hello and continued on to the kitchen.

Unlike the dining room, the kitchen was more contemporary in style. The stove, dishwasher, and refrigerator looked fairly new. I confirmed my suspicions when I saw the energy efficiency sticker on the fridge's side where one would hang magnets. Above and below, the cabinets were beautiful and looked recently repainted, and I looked at the floor. The hardwood gleamed compared to what I'd seen in the other rooms. Complete with the tour, I returned to the porch.

"It really is lovely. I like the kitchen. Was it redone recently?" I asked.

Reba nodded. "There was a sewer problem that damaged the lines underneath the kitchen. Had to tear the whole thing apart to fix it."

"That must have been horrible for you."

"You bet it was. The topper was the city wanted me to pay for it all, even though it was their problem. Can you imagine that?"

"How did that work out?"

"Well, deary, I contacted my insurance company who sent an insurance adjuster lady over, and she looked over the whole mess, and do you know what she said?"

How could I? "No. What did she say?"

"She said the city was liable and there was no way the insurance was going to pay. Then she got on the phone to some bigwig city lawyer, and a week later, some contractors were over here giving me options for new stuff. Can you dig it?"

I nodded. I dug it.

"You're sold out until fall?" I asked.

Reba nodded. "Yep. Things don't die down for me until after the fall festival. Then after that, I give the house a top to bottom deep cleaning, and I leave town for a couple of months."

"Where do you go?"

"My sister lives over in San Diego. I go there for

Thanksgiving, and I'm back here after New Year's. Got to be back for Valentine's Day. That's a big seller for me too. I can really raise the rates then, and people pay 'em if you get my meaning."

I got it, so I smiled and nodded. "How would it affect you if they built the resort? Would you still do all that business?"

Reba leaned over and let out a puff of air. "I don't care."

The answer surprised me. "Why not?"

"Blue hair lady, I'm eighty-four years old. The only reason I run this here business is to make enough to pay the property taxes and supplement my social security. And I enjoy having the people around for company. I'd be just as happy to move closer to my sister. Weather's nicer there, anyway."

"But what about this house? Your family legacy?"

Reba cackled at me. "You're a funny one. Someday, probably soon, I'm going to die, and it won't be more than a hundred years later, and this town will be dead right along with me. Eventually this house will rot away, and we'll both be worm food. Nothing lasts forever, even though people will tell you otherwise. Now if you don't mind, I need to see to my boarders."

Reba struggled to rise, yet stood without help, then shuffled into the house and closed the large front door behind her. I guessed we were no longer welcome.

Sam started down the walkway. "Well, did she do it?"

"No, Sam, I don't think she did."

"Because she didn't care about the resort?"

"Did you see her get in the house? She could barely grip the doorknob. I think she's got a severe case of arthritis going on there. Not only did she not have a motive to kill Sherman Stier, she wouldn't have had the strength to do it."

"So now what?"

"Now, my dear Watson, we move on to the next person."

CHAPTER NINE

Wwe took the short walk over to the flower shop and found the door locked and the closed sign in the window. It didn't surprise me as it looked like most of Main Street seemed deserted. It appeared the few businesses that opened on a Sunday wouldn't open until late morning.

I knocked on the door a few times and peered through the window. All I saw were plants, no humans. "I guess it's a strikeout. Do you know where Hanson lives?"

"On the west side of town, on the other side of the tracks," Sam said.

"Every time someone says that phrase, I wonder which side of the tracks is the good side," I said.

Sam smiled. "This is Quincey. Both sides of the tracks are fine. We consider the west side of the tracks the newer part of town because the homes over there are less than fifty years old. He moved out there when his parents moved out of town."

"Do you have a number for him? I'd really like to talk to him again, and I'd like you to be there. He wasn't exactly warm to me last night."

"Yeah, he can run hot or cold based on his mood, and if he gets into his defensive posture, he tucks his head into his shell like a turtle. It's just the way he is. I'm sure he'll come around."

"So, you have his number?"

Sam patted me on the shoulder. "Of course. I've got it in my address book at home. Speaking of home, do you mind if we call him a little later? I didn't sleep last night, and I'd really love to take a nap."

I would've preferred not to wait, but it was Sam under the spotlight, not me. If she needed a nap, I'd let her have one since I'd rather have a sharp Sam than a sleep deprived one. I looked at her and recognized she had bags under her eyes, and she looked exhausted. "Sure thing. Take all the time you need."

"I only need an hour or two. Will you be on your bus?"

"Yes. I don't plan on heading anywhere without you, so I'll wait for you there. I'm sure after a nap and a long shower, you'll feel a lot more alive."

Sam and I parted company, and I watched her disappear behind the door. I stepped around the side of the building and headed toward the bus. The lawn chairs were set up, so I assumed Bozeman had to be awake and about. As I got closer to the bus, I noticed that Waylon and Willie were out, and one or both of them had tipped over their bowl and were busy eating their snacks from the ground. They detected my approach, and both stopped, sat up, and looked in my direction. When they saw it was me, they returned to their feast. When I got to them, I bent over to pick up the bowl and Willie skittered over to me. I scratched his head and accepted the chunk of apple he held up to me.

"Aw, thanks, buddy. I had a big breakfast though, so I'm full. Why don't you take this back so it doesn't go to waste?"

Willie chirped at me, grabbed the apple from my fingers, stuffed it into his little cheeks, and ran back to Waylon.

I stepped onto the bus. Bozeman was in the kitchen making his breakfast. "Want some eggs?" he asked.

"No, thanks. I've eaten already." I didn't have the heart to tell him about the superb pancakes I had, especially since his eggs were always just on the edge of inedible. He tried, though.

I moved into my room, grabbed a book from the table, and I noticed I had left my phone there as well. I was one of those people who constantly misplaced their phone, so I often made a habit of leaving it in my room. Bozeman lectured me several times over the years about having it on me. He insisted it was for my own benefit. I could call him if I needed to, or hail a cab, or use it to get directions when I got lost, but I still hadn't gotten into the habit. I stuffed the phone into my pocket and headed back to the kitchen.

"Early morning?" Bozeman slid the eggs out of the pan and onto a plate. He grabbed a fork and sat at the table. I noticed he didn't have his coffee with him, so I poured him a mug and handed it to him. Like all cowboys, he took it black, with no sugar. I reached into a cabinet and pulled out a diet cola, my choice for my daily caffeine intake.

"Yeah. I was with Sam. We went to see the McMurtrys at the diner, and Reba."

"Find out anything useful?" Bozeman asked between bites.

I exhaled. "Yeah, none of them did it. Sam wanted a nap. We're going back out later. Want to come?"

"No thanks. I'll leave the detective work to you if you don't mind."

I smiled and left him with his eggs. I carried my book and cola outside and set them beside my lawn chair. Before I sat down, I put my head into Dolly and Merle's compartment. They were both present, accounted for, and napping. The bowls I gave them earlier were empty, so I pulled them out. Merle opened his eyes when I removed the bowl, then turned over and nodded back to sleep. Dolly never moved. They each had their own blanket, and I moved Dolly over a bit to check under hers. Dolly liked to collect stuff. I always checked her treasure haul to make sure she didn't get her paws on something that might be hazardous to either her or her roommate. She must have been scavenging during the night, because she had hidden under the blanket a penny, a bottle cap from a beer, three shiny rocks, and a stem with leaves. I confiscated everything except the rocks. Dolly liked rocks.

The penny and bottle cap I put into my pocket. I'd put the penny in the mug on my desk, and the bottle cap in the trash. The stem I was about to toss away, when I noticed there was a sticky substance on the end. I stepped into the sun and brought it closer and stared at it. It looked like a piece of thin green tape, and the edges of the leaves had a white dust on them.

"Dolly, what did you find here? And where did you get it?" There were times it tempted me to put a mini helmet on Dolly with a camera attached. I'd love to see where she traveled on her adventures, but since she didn't have one, this was just a mystery. I didn't know if the plant was poisonous or not, so I set it on the bus step as a reminder to throw it away when I tossed the bottle cap.

I took a seat, had a drink of cola, and opened the book. According to the bookmark, I was on page twenty, but when I glanced at the cover, I couldn't remember what the book was about. Was it something I started reading, or had I shoved the bookmark at a random spot to make sure I had one? I couldn't tell for sure, so I flipped back to page one and started the book from the beginning.

I shifted in my seat. Impatience was eating at me, and I couldn't concentrate. I read the same page repeatedly, and although I understood what the words on the page were, I couldn't get them to assemble in my brain to form the story they told.

I was reading through page one for the fourth time when a black SUV with dark, tinted windows pulled into the lot and came to a stop less than a foot from my seat. The engine revved for a second, and then the car shut off. I stayed where I was, and as I wondered who might be up for a Sunday morning visit, Mayor Mary stepped out of the vehicle. She wore blue jeans, a plaid western shirt, and the same scowl on her face I remembered from the night before.

"Good morning, Mayor." I put a little lilt in my voice to sound extra-friendly. "It's got the making of a beautiful day today."

The mayor stepped in front of me and removed her sunglasses. "I would've thought you'd left town by now."

I put my book on my lap. I didn't bother with the bookmark. "No, ma'am. Chief Jennings asked us to stay around for a couple of days in case he had any further questions for us."

"I'm sure that would be an inconvenience for you, since I imagine you have another performance to get to. I can square it with the chief so you can leave today. Don't worry. I'll call him just as soon as church lets out."

She was being pushy. I can be that way too, sometimes. "Thank you, but that's unnecessary. Our next gig isn't for a few days yet, and it's only a day's drive away, so we're in no hurry to leave. Besides, I like this town. Have you had the blueberry pancakes down at the diner? Delicious."

Mayor Mary smiled through clenched teeth. "I'm sure there are more… interesting places to visit on your way."

I doubted that. "Let's cut to it, Mayor, all the way down to the proverbial brass tacks. Why the bum's rush to get us out of town?"

Mayor Mary stared at me for what felt like an hour. I could tell there was something she wanted to say. I guessed since she was a bureaucrat; she was trying to find a delicate way to say it that wouldn't reflect poorly on her. That approach always rubbed me the wrong way, and I wanted to cut her off, but I waited.

"It's not like that at all. Look, even though you're just a musician, you're also a businessperson, correct? I'm sure you can understand what kind of pressure I'm under trying to do what's best for this town, and sometimes that involves making hard decisions. Look, I get it that people around here are talking about me, and how I invited Sherman Stier and his associates into the area, but it really was for the good of the community."

Did I catch that right? That she invited them in? That was a nugget I hadn't heard from anyone. "Like a new fire station or an art museum?"

The mayor smiled. "Exactly. Everyone will benefit from those. Just like everyone will benefit from increased tourism that the resort will bring. Business will be up, the tax base will increase, and I won't have to beg the state constantly for infrastructure improvement dollars. In the end, everyone wins."

Her words made sense, but I assumed that as a politician, she filled them with only half-truths. I took them with more than a grain of salt.

"Are you from Quincey, Mayor?"

"Why yes, I am. My family has been here for generations. My great-great-grandfather worked on the railroad, and my grandfather worked in a mine near here. I left town to attend college, but I came back home to be closer to family."

"That's nice. I'm sure your folks are really proud of you becoming mayor."

Mayor Mary grinned, the most authentic smile I'd seen her produce in the short time I've known her. "Yes, very. I'm the first female mayor in Quincey history."

"Congratulations. That's quite the accomplishment." I was genuine. I was all for girl-power. "Look, I don't mean to ruffle your feathers. Sam is still upset about what happened yesterday, and I want to stay around for just a couple of days to make sure she's okay. I'm sure you'd do the same for your friends, right?"

The mayor nodded, turned, and walked back to the car. "Fine. Stay if you like, but try to stay out of people's affairs, okay? We don't like that around here."

I nodded once. The mayor pulled out of the lot. I took a drink of my cola.

"She seems nice." Bozeman said. I'm surprised the mayor didn't notice him standing just inside the bus door, but then again, I was so used to his presence, I always sensed when he was around.

"Yeah, she's a peach," I said.

"You mind if I come out there and do some writing?" Bozeman asked.

"Of course not. There's plenty of room for you."

Bozeman stepped from the bus carrying a guitar in one hand and a notebook in the other. He sat in the other chair and opened the notebook to the tune he was working on. He started experimenting with different melodies and runs, trying to find the perfect sound for his new song. I picked the book back up and started again on page one.

I must have fallen asleep at some point, because I heard Bozeman calling my name.

"What?"

He pointed at me. "Your pocket's buzzing."

I had forgotten about the phone. I fished it from my pocket and accepted the call without looking to see who it was.

"Hello?"

"Codi Cassidy?" The voice sounded familiar, but I didn't know for sure who it was.

"I know who killed Sherman Stier, and I have evidence. I saw who did it. Are you interested?"

I sat up straight and came to attention. "Of course. Who is this?"

"This is someone who has the information you want."

"Why don't you go to the police? Take your evidence to the

chief?" That seemed logical to me.

There was a pause on the other end of the line. "I can't trust the chief. You shouldn't either. There are many people in this town you shouldn't trust for a lot of reasons, especially Sam Henry."

Now it was my turn for the pause. "Are you saying there's a conspiracy going on? That this is about more than a grudge against Sherman Stier?"

"Maybe," the voice said.

"Why come to me? If you don't trust the chief, why not call in the state police, or go to the mayor?"

"Can't trust the mayor either. And you're already here. Sometimes you have to bring in an outside exterminator to remove the rats. I won't say anymore over the phone. Meet me at the flower shop at two."

The line dropped dead.

Bozeman looked over at me. "What was all that about?"

"Beats me. It's someone claiming to have information about the murder. The mayor was right about one thing. We should have left town last night. I'll be right back."

I got up and walked around the building to Sam's apartment entrance. She locked the street level door, so I rang the bell and waited. Sam didn't answer, so I hit the bell several times in quick succession and stood on the street, waiting for Sam to appear. She didn't. I took a step back and yelled up at the window for her, but got no response.

I stepped over to the bakery and tried the door, but she had locked that too. I looked through the window, and everything looked buttoned up. The chairs were on top of the table like someone had recently washed the floor, and the empty display case gleamed. I moved to the rear of the bakery and tried the back door. Locked. I knocked on the door but got no response. I thought I heard something inside, so I put my ear to the door and listened. All was quiet again.

I fished out my phone and found Sam's number. She didn't answer, so I waited for the voice greeting to finish and left a message. "Hey Sam, it's Codi. I got a strange call, I suspect, from Hanson. He says he has information about the murder, and we're supposed to meet him at the flower shop at two. Call me back or come out to the bus when you get this message."

I hung up and headed back to my chair. Bozeman stopped strumming and gave me a look.

"She's not there. Although she told me earlier she hadn't slept all night, so she's probably napping," I said.

"Through all that racket? I heard you banging on the door and shouting for her from here. She must be a deep sleeper."

I checked the time on the phone. I still had a few hours to wait until two, and I guessed those hours would creep along.

At two o'clock, I tried rousing Sam, but again, I got no answer to my in-person visit or my phone calls. Since I was already late, I rushed over to the flower shop and stood outside on the sidewalk, only to find the door locked and the shop dark. Was I too late? I stood outside for fifteen minutes and tried to decide if I should write the phone call off as a prank, or if there was something else I should do. I ran with something else. The bakery had a back door, so I imagined the flower shop did as well.

I walked down Main Street to the end of the block, turned the corner, and ducked into the alley. I followed the alley until I came to the back door of the flower shop. Hanson's delivery van stood outside, and as I walked closer to the building, I noticed the door was ajar.

I pushed the door open wide and stepped across the threshold. "Hanson? Are you here? It's Codi. You called me this morning. I'm here."

The room was dark, so I checked the wall, discovered a light switch, and flipped it up. "Hanson?"

The back room of the flower shop was a mess. There was a large table with old plant clippings on it. An overflowing trash can was stuffed with greenery and wilted flowers stood to my left. There were flower boxes, vases, containers, and floral supplies everywhere. I took another step and discovered an open box filled with the centerpieces from the previous night. There was a doorway ahead, and I walked through that and found myself in the shop's front. The front was a complete opposite from the back. While the back was a mess of disorganization mixed with trash, the front was neat and organized. There was enough sunlight streaming through the large front window to see, so I walked quickly around the space to see if I could see anyone. Nothing.

I returned to the back room and to my right I noticed a walk-in refrigerator, much like I had seen at the diner. This unit had a small window in the door, so I got on my tiptoes and looked inside. From what I could tell, Hanson filled it with shelving units and flowers. I tugged open the heavy door for a better look. The first thing that caught my attention was the overwhelming smell of roses. The second thing was the body on the floor.

I closed the door, made an extremely hasty exit, and called the police.

Twenty minutes later, I was sitting on an overturned crate in the alley when Chief Jennings came out of the building.

The chief removed his hat, wiped his brow, and returned the hat to his head. "Yep, that's Hanson Johns in there. You want to tell me why you were here?"

The words 'you can't trust the chief' echoed through my head as I got the story together in my head. I didn't know where that fine line was between telling him everything I had to holding things back and having them potentially used against me later.

"He called me and asked me to meet him out front at two. When the time passed, I came around here, found the door ajar, and found him where you did."

"Did you touch the body?"

"No. I came right outside and called you guys."

Chief Jennings got out his ever-present notepad and wrote something down.

"Why did he want to meet with you?"

"He said he had information about Sherman Stier's death."

"So why call you, and not me, then?"

That was the question, wasn't it? Why indeed? "He knew I'm Sam's friend. I think he had information to clear her. He said he witnessed the murder."

Chief Jennings stared at me. I couldn't tell if he believed me or not.

"Did he leave you a message, or did you speak to him

directly?"

"I talked to him."

"Can I have your phone, please?"

I dug it out of my pocket and held it out to him.

"You got a lock code on there?"

I shook my head no.

The chief took the phone from me and called a deputy over and handed him my cell. "Samuels, get the numbers of any calls incoming or outgoing for today only, and get this right back to me. I'll be right back."

I watched as an ambulance pulled into the alley and the two paramedics exited the ambulance and talked to the chief. The door opened, and they wheeled a gurney into the flower shop. A few minutes later, they returned, loaded the sheet-covered body into the back, and left without lights or sirens.

A few minutes later, I saw Samuels give something to Jennings, and then the chief came back to me.

"You can have your phone back. The one incoming call was probably a burner number. Care to tell me about the fifteen calls you made to Sam Henry?"

That was the question I feared would come up. I told him how we got together for breakfast, and how she went to bed afterward, and I explained about how I tried to contact her multiple times after Hanson called me. I couldn't tell if I convinced him it was the truth or not.

"Am I a suspect here?" I wanted to be as blunt as possible, and I wanted to know if I needed to bring in a lawyer.

"Did you touch anything inside the building?"

I hated it when people answered questions with questions. I thought for a moment. "Let's see. I pushed the back door open. Then I turned on the light by the door, and I opened the refrigerator. I think that was it."

"Nothing else? You didn't handle the cash register? Or pick anything up, or lean on any surfaces?"

Did I? I was certain I didn't go near the register or handle anything. "No. I don't think so."

"Do you mind if we take your fingerprints? We'll get them

eventually, so you can provide them now, or we can take you to the station for a more formal questioning."

I wasn't one for formalities, and I knew they'd get them sooner rather than later. "You can have them now."

Chief Jennings called Samuels back over. "Get her fingerprints, will you?"

I held out my hand, expecting my fingertips to be dipped in ink.

Samuels shook his head. "We don't do it that way anymore, ma'am. Can you touch the screen?"

I looked down and saw Samuels had a device just a little larger than my cell phone. "What's that thing?"

Samuels smiled. "Portable ID unit. Scans all ten of your fingerprints right into the database."

"You have any outstanding warrants you want to tell me about?" Chief Jennings asked. "As soon as the prints hit the database, a search will start and will find out if you do."

"No. Not even an outstanding speeding ticket." At last, a simple question I could answer.

A few seconds later, Samuels got a beep from his phone and checked the message. "She's clean."

"Thanks." Jennings dismissed Samuels again, and Samuels returned to the flower shop.

Jennings turned his attention back to me. "You know, this is usually a nice, quiet town. Occasionally we'll get some knuckleheads drag racing through downtown, or we'll have to break up an underage drinking party. We get a fair amount of speeding tickets from the tourists who think the state highway has the same speed limit as the interstate. And of course, there's a bit of petty theft that happens at the market, but usually, it's pretty tranquil around here. And then you showed up and we've had two murders in as many days. What would you call that?"

I looked up at him. "An unlucky coincidence?"

"Don't leave town until I say you can go. No matter what the mayor says. I'm done with you for now. You can go on back to your bus."

I didn't hesitate for a moment. As I got to the alley's end, I noticed a small crowd had accumulated just outside the crime scene tape barrier the police had erected. I didn't recognize anyone. I ducked under the tape and made a beeline for the bus.

Where was Sam? Why hadn't she returned my calls? I didn't know if I was madder at her for ignoring me, or more concerned that something had happened to her, too. I needed to talk to Sam, so rather than return to the bus like I initially intended, I switched direction and stepped to her door instead. Still locked. I rang the bell.

A few seconds later, Sam appeared above me. "Hey, you."

I glared up at her. "Hey yourself. Get down here and let me in. We need to talk."

CHAPTER TEN

I waited a minute for Sam to come down and unlock the door, and then I followed her back up to her apartment. She sat on the couch while I paced back and forth in her living room.

"Where have you been? I called you like a thousand times."

"I took a nap. Look, I'm sorry, I said it would be a couple hours, but I was afraid I wouldn't be able to sleep, so I took a pill. Afterward, I dropped off like the dead."

"Poor choice of words. The florist is dead. I found him."

Sam looked stunned. "Hanson? Dead? What do you mean? I don't understand."

"I found him in the flower shop, in the fridge with the flowers."

"That's horrible!" Sam stood and came over to hug me. I didn't want to accept it at first, but I eventually let her put her arms around me. I admit, it felt comforting.

"Are you okay?" Sam took me by the hand and led me to the couch. We both sat.

"Yes. No. I don't know," I said.

"What were you doing at the flower shop in the first place?" Sam asked.

"That's why I've been trying to get a hold of you. Hanson called me and told me he had an idea who killed Sherman, and I was supposed to meet him at the shop at two. I was going to get you to meet him with me, but you didn't answer the doorbell or the phone, so I headed over there by myself. The back door was open, so I entered the shop, and when I opened the fridge, there he was on the floor."

"Oh, my. What happened?"

"Well, I called the police, and they came over and questioned me and took the body away."

"I don't believe it. Do you know how he died?" Sam asked.

I shook my head. "No. I only saw his legs, and that was enough for me."

"What about the evidence of who killed Sherman? Did you find anything there about that? Anything that would clear me?"

I shook my head again. Evidence? Had I said anything about Hanson having evidence? I couldn't think straight. The experience had scrambled my brain.

Sam leaned back in her seat and rubbed her eyes. "So now what do we do?"

I didn't really know. I felt like I was past the point of getting in over my head, and what I wanted to do most was get on the bus and head off to California for our next gig. But unfortunately, I had given Sam my word to help her out, and I hardly ever went back on my word.

"Your guess is as good as mine. I was certain someone from the committee did Sherman in, and I have to admit, when Hanson called and said he had the answer, my heart flipped with excitement. I'm so ready to put all this behind us. We've cleared the McMurtrys and Reba. Obviously, Hanson didn't do it unless there was a second killer out there somewhere. You didn't do it, did you? If you did, I've solved the mystery," I said.

I looked over at Sam, and finally, a smile appeared on her face. "No. I didn't do it. Did you?"

"I did not. So we can cross our names off the list. Bozeman didn't do it. I can vouch for him. Who does that leave? Dean Williams? Pastor Tom? Mayor Mary? Someone I never even considered? There were, what, a couple hundred people there last night? Any of them might have stabbed Sherman. And there wouldn't have to be a real motive. Maybe Sherman skipped someone in line, or stole a parking space. We live in nutty times, and people kill for nutty reasons."

"Yeah, but we don't have that kind of oddness around these parts. This is a pretty quiet little city," Sam said.

"I've been told that by the chief and the mayor."

We stayed silent for a few moments, each of us gathering our own thoughts.

"What about Harold Johns?" Sam asked.

"Hanson's brother?" I asked.

"Yes. I heard he was upset when the resort was first proposed. Said it would affect business at the hotel. And rumor has it he's already upside down on the property, so any change in business would end him."

I mulled it over for a moment. "Sure, that's a plausible motive, but Hanson told me last night that Harold is out of town, helping his folks. Is that true? When's the last time anyone talked to him?"

Sam let loose a long exhale. "That's right. He used to come into the bakery at least twice a week, but I haven't seen him in at least a couple of months. And I imagine they will confirm his story the second the police call Hanson's next of kin to report his death."

"True," I said.

"What about a hitman? Did someone hire some muscle to take care of Sherman, and then Hanson, to tie up loose ends?" Sam asked.

"If this were a large city, I'd say it was at least possible, but here, in Quincey, New Mexico? I doubt it. I'm sure people would notice a stranger in town. Heck, just yesterday I was a stranger in town, and you can't imagine all the looks I got from people when I was walking around before you found me. I got stares at the restaurant last night, and this morning. Small town folks seem to have a radar that alerts on people who aren't from here. Besides, did you see anyone at the event last night that you didn't recognize?"

Sam responded almost right away. "Well, no."

"Exactly. If a hired gun had come in and stabbed Sherman, I'm one hundred percent sure that someone would have remembered the person and reported it."

Sam nodded. "You're right. They would've stood out like a purple duck. Do you really think Pastor Tom might be in on it?"

I looked at her, then at my shoes. "You got me. I get he's a man of the cloth and all, but when I was talking to him last night, he seemed evasive about his relationship with Sherman. He gave me the impression that Sherman had donated a lot of money to the church. I can't figure out why he would, though."

"Maybe he was just doing a good deed? Like with improving the fire station?"

I shook my head and frowned. "No, I don't think so. If you build a new fire station, that benefits you if there's a fire. How does giving a chunk of cash to the church help Sherman? From what I've gathered, he's not the type of guy to offer something just because of the goodness in his heart."

"True. You want to go back to the church and talk to the pastor?"

"Why don't we wait until tomorrow for that visit? I would imagine Sunday is his busy day."

Sam laughed. "Yes. Of course, it is. I'd forgotten it's only Sunday. What makes you think the mayor's involved?"

I glanced over at Sam. "She came over for a visit this morning."

"No! What did she want?"

"The long and short of it was she invited me to hit the road at my earliest convenience," I said.

"But doesn't Chief Jennings want you to stick around?" Sam asked.

"He does. She gave me her advice before I found poor Hanson. Anyway, I don't think she stabbed Sherman herself, but I have a suspicion she's indirectly involved somehow."

"Why?"

"Oh, just a feeling, mostly. I also found it odd that business owners around town have brought their resort concerns to her attention, and what has she done about them all?"

"Well, nothing that I'm aware of. In short, she told us all about a month ago to bugger off about the resort completely."

"And that didn't strike you as odd?" I asked.

"Now that you bring it up, it does. Why would she so willingly side with an outsider to the detriment of the townies?"

"Exactly. So, either she's involved in something shady, and she had to get rid of Sherman. Or she's involved in something shady and was in league with Sherman. Either way."

"Or she might be completely innocent."

"Sure, Sam, perhaps she is. But I'd bet my favorite pair of boots that there's something going on there. And that leads me right back to Dean."

I looked over at Sam, who caught my gaze, then jumped up from the couch and headed for the kitchen. "You want anything to drink? I'm getting a root beer."

"Sounds good to me." I listened to the fridge open and close, followed by the sounds of Sam retrieving glasses from the cabinet. I picked up the sound of the pop top snap, and the familiar glug-glug sound of root beer falling into a glass. A few seconds later, she was back.

"Sorry, I don't have any ice." She held out a glass, and I took it. We touched glasses in a mock toast and drank. It was good. I couldn't remember the last time I had a root beer.

I hesitated, but I had to broach the subject again, and I assumed to Sam it was like a scab being picked at until it bled.

"So, Dean Williams."

Sam drained half her glass, then set it on the table beside her and looked at me. "I know, I know. You think he's the most likely suspect, right?"

I nodded.

"Why?"

I set my glass down and counted the points on my fingers. "First, he seems overprotective of you. Second, looking in from the outside, he appears to have anger issues. Third, he had an opportunity. You told me yourself he was right there just after you came out of the bathroom and just before you found the body, right? Fourth, I overheard him on more than one occasion talking about 'dealing with Sherman', and who knows what he meant there?" I dropped my hands and picked my glass back up. "Sorry to be blunt. I understand he's a friend."

"No. It's okay. That's one reason I asked for your help. I'm too close to this. I appreciate your fresh set of eyes on everything around here. Still friends?"

I smiled. "Of course. What's a little murder between buddies?"

We both laughed, and the tension washed away. I felt better, more relaxed. I didn't realize that I had built up enough internal pressure to run a V8 engine.

"Hey, what do you say—"

The doorbell interrupted Sam. She crossed over to the window and looked outside. "It's Shanna. Shanna, come on up, the door's unlocked."

Sam moved over to the apartment door, opened it, and soon Shanna stepped through.

I noticed Shanna had been crying. Her eyes were red and puffy and there was a faint black line on the side of her face where she'd tried to wipe away a streak of mascara. Sam noticed it, too.

"What's wrong? What happened?" Sam asked.

Shanna sniffed and gulped some air. "When I got home, I found this."

Shanna lifted her arm, and I saw in her right hand a plastic sandwich bag, and within that bag was an index card. She turned it around so we could read it. We both saw the words 'you're next' in big block letters in red ink.

I saw the note, then sat back down. Things were getting unreal. "Tell me everything about finding that," I said.

Shanna sniffed again. Sam motioned for her to sit on the easy chair and then passed her a box of tissues. Shanna grabbed a tissue, blew her nose, and took a breath. "I was at the gym. I go every Sunday to an afternoon yoga class. When I got home, I noticed this lying on the living room floor. I figured it was a coupon or something because people were always sliding things under my door, but when I turned it over, I saw that. I remembered what happened to Sherman Stier, and I got scared."

Sam and I looked at each other.

"Did you call the police?" I asked.

"Do you think I should?"

"Without a doubt. There's more going on here than you know. Here's what you should do. Go home, call Chief Jennings, and tell them exactly what you found and how you found it."

"I can't call from here?"

"You may, but the police would want to see where it

happened, so you'd have to go home, anyway."

"Okay. If you say that's best."

Sam gave Shanna a hug. "It probably is best that way. If you need us, we'll be here."

Shanna sniffed again. "Should I tell the chief I came here?"

Sam and I looked at each other again, but it was me who spoke first. "If it were me, I wouldn't bring it up. But, if you're asked if you went anywhere between the time you found it and the time you called them, tell them. It's important that you don't lie. Okay?"

Shanna slowly nodded. "Okay. Thank you."

Shanna got to her feet and took another tissue from the box.

"I'll call you later, okay?" Shanna said.

Sam ushered Shanna from the room and walked her down the stairs. I heard voices from the open window, but I didn't hear what they were saying. A few minutes later, Sam returned.

"Well?" she asked.

I drank some root beer and set down the glass. "Can this day get any more complicated?"

Sam exhaled. "I sure hope not. What do we do now? Do you want to find someone else to talk to, or should we wait and see what happens with Shanna?"

"Well, we said we'd be here, so I guess we should settle in for a bit."

We didn't know how long it would take for Shanna to call, so we found things to occupy our time. The first hour we spent talking about old times and gossiping about people we remembered from high school. Of course, I had to provide most of the information since I had a few dozen of them as followers of my social media.

After we ran out of people to talk about, we dove into a few magazines that Sam had lying around the house. Shortly after seven, Sam dug out a deck of cards and we played a rousing round of Go Fish, followed by a couple of games of War. Just as Sam's cat clock slipped into the eight o'clock hour, we finally heard heavy footsteps ascending the stairs.

A hard knock fell upon the door. "Quincey Police

Department. Open up. We have a warrant."

Sam and I passed confused glances, and she moved to the door and opened it. As she did, two deputies rushed into the room with guns drawn. One deputy motioned for Sam to join me on the couch, while the other did a sweep of the tiny apartment.

"All clear," the second deputy said as he joined the other one.

Sam didn't look well, and she started shaking. I put an arm around her and tried to steady her. "What's this about a warrant?" Sam asked.

Chief Jennings entered the room and stepped forward, offering Sam a sheet of paper. "Samantha Henry, I have a warrant for your arrest for the murders of Sherman Stier and Hanson Johns, and for making terroristic threats to Shanna Prescott. Please stand and put your arms behind your back."

Sam shook her head back and forth with such force I expected it to pop off and roll across the floor like a bowling ball.

"No. I didn't do it. I didn't do any of those things. You need to listen to me!" she screamed.

A deputy reached forward and grabbed Sam's upper arm. Sam responded by trying to become one with the couch. "No! Stop! I'm innocent!"

The other deputy stepped in, and between the two of them, they got Sam to her feet, spun her around, and slapped handcuffs on her. After that, Chief Jennings stepped over and patted her down for weapons.

"I'll bet you loved that, you pig!" Sam snarled. "You've always wanted to get your hands on me! Let me go! I didn't do any of those things!" Sam broke and the tears flowed. She looked in my direction and muttered something. I couldn't tell what it was, and before I asked for clarification, the deputies escorted her from the room.

The chief started looking around the room. I stood and followed him into the kitchen.

"What are you doing?"

"I'm executing a warrant, looking for evidence."

"I don't think —"

Chief Jennings spun around. "Look, I've had about enough

of you. You should leave before I charge you as an accessory to her crimes."

"There's no way. You can't. You don't have any evidence."

The chief threw me a sly smile. "Not to worry. I'm sure I could come up with something. Go back to your bus. Relax, have a nice evening, and then tomorrow, leave Quincey. Do us a favor and don't come back."

"No. You can't run me off, and you have nothing on Sam. You should let her go."

Before the chief could say anything, Deputy Samuels appeared in the kitchen carrying two small evidence bags and handed them to Jennings. "Got them. They look like they match to me."

"Thanks. Search the other rooms up here." Chief Jennings turned back to me and held the evidence bags directly in front of my face. "No evidence? See these?"

I tried to focus on what he had, but they were so close to my face I couldn't make out either item. After I moved my head back, and they came into view. I saw what they were, but I didn't know the relevancy. "Yeah? So what?"

"So what? She stabbed Sherman Stier with one of her own knives. Has her name on the handle, along with her fingerprints. She killed Hanson Johns with a pie cutter, one that looks just like this." Chief Jennings showed the bag with the pie cutter in it. "And she wrote the threat against Shanna on a card, exactly like the card like this that Sam writes recipes on. We've also found her fingerprints at the scene of each crime."

It all was hard for me to process. I was about to argue with him about being her alibi, but I realized I couldn't. Sure, I was with her at breakfast, and several people saw us then. And I was with her later in the afternoon, but that left a sizeable gap of time when I couldn't get in touch with her. Since the police already had my outgoing phone call log, they knew that. We'd been apart for about six hours. It was certainly enough time to off the flower man and leave a note under a door. Despite that, I believed my friend wasn't capable of such things.

The chief looked indignant and appeared to be waiting for me to say something. "Well?"

I coughed, then shook my head. "Look, I'm sorry, Chief Jennings, I didn't mean to come across as so aggressive. I'm just in shock, is all."

The chief must have taken my word for once because his shoulders slumped, and he slid into a more relaxed posture.

"Do you think I can see her? Please? I just want to make sure she's okay and that she at least has a lawyer. Would that be okay?"

The chief stared at me long enough for me to wonder if I had not said the words out loud.

"Yeah. Okay. But not tonight. It's already late, and she needs to go through processing. Tomorrow morning, come down to the jail and I'll make sure you can talk to her. Come early though, because we don't have a long-term facility, so we'll send her to the county jail in the afternoon."

I nodded. "I understand. Thank you, Chief Jennings."

It was time to leave.

"Cassidy?"

"Yes, Chief?"

"Don't do or say anything stupid. You've worn out your welcome here."

Without a word, I left the apartment, walked around the building, and entered the bus. Bozeman was in the kitchen making a snack. "Want a sandwich? Ham and cheese?"

My stomach rumbled. It was a busy day, and I hadn't eaten since breakfast. "I'd love one, thanks."

"Hot or cold?"

I smiled. I loved grilled ham and cheese. "Hot. Please."

Bozeman took a couple of extra slices from the bread, buttered a side of each, and slid them into the pan next to his. Bozeman was a chef of contradiction. He couldn't make a decent fried egg, but he could make a delicious sandwich. Give him a steak and every time it would turn out like jerky. Hand him a fish, and it would turn out flaky and delicate. I didn't understand it, but I had learned to work around it. If he was making a food he'd mastered, I'd always accept his offer for the meal. If it was something he couldn't cook right to save his life, I'd cook either just for myself or for both of us. Between the two of us, we got by fine at mealtimes.

"Where have you been all day? I thought you'd be right back."

I removed my baseball cap, tossed it on the chair, and ran my fingers through my hair. "You would not believe everything that happened today."

"Did you clear your friend of the murder?"

"Actually, I got her indicted in a second one. Oh, and accused of making a terroristic threat, whatever that is."

Bozeman turned around to face me, spatula in hand. "You're kidding."

I shook my head and frowned. I wanted to run to my room and cry or hide. But I also wanted the sandwich, so I sat tight. Gibson must have sensed my discomfort as he jumped up into my lap and nuzzled my chin. I giggled. "Hey, little man, your nose is cold and wet."

A few minutes later, Bozeman slid a plate in front of me and sat down across from me. Gibson moved to the seat next to me and laid his head on my leg while Bozeman and I ate in silence, which I was grateful for. After we finished the meal, I dumped the paper plates into the trash, washed Bozeman's pan, and rejoined him at the table.

"So, tell me about your day," he said.

CHAPTER ELEVEN

I didn't imagine I'd sleep that night, but I did, and I was glad about it. I woke up refreshed and ready to take on the day. Bozeman was still asleep, so I fed the animals and made myself a cup of tea. Every day I make a mental list of the things I wanted to accomplish during the day, and today's list comprised only two items. Find out who really committed two murders and get Sam out of jail. Easy peasy, squeezy lemon.

Around nine, I was ready to go, so I used my phone to find the directions to the local jail. To my dismay, it was over a mile away. I didn't have the heart to wake Bozeman to drive me over, and there didn't appear to be any ride share options in the area. So, I put on my most comfortable pair of sneakers and headed out for a walk.

I'm not a fast walker, partially because I'm so short, but mostly because I like to look at stuff as I go. Since I knew this morning I was on a mission, it took everything I had not to stop at a park I passed and sit on a bench and watch the birds. I had more important things to do, and I knew I needed to stay on task. That part wasn't easy, either, since I lived a non-structured lifestyle. Every day wasn't like the normal every day of the people who had to work nine-to-five jobs. I appreciated that, although I often let my thoughts wander, and sometimes didn't get the tasks done I wanted to do for the day. Today was different, though. Sam was depending on me, and I had to come through for her.

Around nine-thirty, I strode into the local jail. It was a small building that looked fairly new, and I wondered if Sherman Stier had put up the money for this one as well. I approached the desk and was about to explain what I needed when Deputy Samuels opened an inner door and motioned for me to follow him through.

"You have any weapons on you? Gun, knife?" he asked as he

ushered me into an interview room.

I was glad for once I had left Betty behind. "No."

"Sam will be right in. Usually, we don't let friends or family talk to the prisoners, so we're breaking the rules for you here."

"I appreciate that, Deputy. Thank you."

Samuels dropped his voice to a whisper. "Thank you for helping her. I like Sam, I really do, and I can't imagine she did these horrible things. But I can't let my personal feelings impede following the law. You can understand that, right?"

I smiled and nodded.

Another deputy led Sam into the room and cuffed her hands to a metal ring on the table I hadn't noticed when I sat down.

"Knock on the door when you're ready to leave," Samuels said. "There's also a camera in the upper corner of this room, so we will record you since you're not an attorney. There's nothing I can do about that. Got it?"

I nodded again. "Crystal clear. Thank you again."

Deputy Samuels closed the door, and the second it shut, I stood and gave Sam a hug.

"You look horrible in orange," I said.

Sam gave me a weak smile. "Everyone does. At least I don't have to wear the black-and-white striped outfit. That would be really embarrassing."

"How are they treating you in here? What's happened?"

Sam leaned over and ran her fingers through her unkempt hair. "It's not as bad as I pictured. I'm the only woman in here, so they gave me a cell of my own. I got fingerprinted, and my pictures taken, and they tried to ask me questions, but I said I wouldn't say anything until my lawyer got here."

"Do you have a lawyer? Do I need to get you one?"

Sam shook her head. "No, I'm good. I have a business lawyer on retainer for the bakery, and she's tracking down one who can handle the criminal charges. Should be here later this morning. Hey, Chief Jennings told me he told you about the evidence they have against me. I know it looks bad, but believe me, Codi, I didn't do any of it. I couldn't have."

Without being obvious, I glanced up at the camera. I half-expected it to be discreet so that you'd not notice it was there, or perhaps hidden behind one-way glass like in the movies. But no, it looked like a relic from the 1990s, and was out there in full view of anyone in the room. I couldn't decide if I should risk asking her further questions, or if I should keep my plan to myself.

"Sam, I believe you. I assumed you didn't do any of those things," I said.

"Can you do me a favor?" Sam asked.

"Sure. What?"

"Can you contact Dean for me and tell him where I am? He'll be worried about me, and I really don't want him to go off and do anything stupid. Sometimes he specializes in stupid."

"Sure thing." I didn't say it, but Dean was my next stop after this visit was over. He was still number one on my suspect list, and now that they had Sam behind bars, I hoped to use that pressure against him. If he really cared about her, perhaps he'd finally crack.

"Where can I find him?" I asked.

"After ten, he should be at the museum. Do you remember where that is? On Main Street, between the diner and the bakery?"

"I remember seeing it, so I should be able to find it. If not, I can look it up on my phone."

"Thank you."

I smiled. "Anything else?"

Sam was silent for a moment.

"What are you daydreaming about?" I asked.

She looked up at me. "My bakery. It's already past opening time. I can picture the people coming by for their daily bread and not being able to get it. And the McMurtrys. What are they going to do at the diner?"

Sam tried to remain strong, but cried. "This will ruin me here. I'll lose the diner contract with the McMurtrys, and this will shoot my reputation right between the eyes. People talk around here. I'll have to close the doors. I can't afford to start over. Not anymore. I can't do this."

I reached for her, held her close, and let her sob into my second favorite shirt. "It'll be okay. I'll stop by the diner on the way to visit Dean and explain things to Rob and Lisa, okay?"

"Okay."

"Could Shanna run the bakery while you're gone? Only to keep things going?"

Sam shook her head. "No, she's not ready. There's just so much to do."

"Can she at least let me in? We could put a sign on the window that says you're on vacation or something."

Sam's sobs turned to sniffles, so I let her loose and retook my seat.

"No. I locked the bakery, and the key is on my key chain. The police have that."

"Okay. Look, Sam, I haven't given up on you. We'll figure this out. Just give me a little time."

Sam nodded.

"Need anything else?"

"Yeah, could you break into the bakery and bake me a cake with a file in it?"

The statement gave me pause, then Sam gave a hesitant laugh, and I followed suit. The police had restricted her freedom, but hadn't constrained her odd sense of humor. I guess that was a good thing.

"It would taste like crap, but I could do it." I gave Sam a last hug, then knocked on the door. After a few seconds, a deputy let me out, and I walked through the police station and stepped out into the sunshine. Weather-wise, it looked to be a beautiful day. I hoped Sam would be out in time to watch the sunset. I exhaled and started walking toward downtown.

Twenty minutes later, I stepped into the busy diner. I must have missed the Monday morning breakfast rush because there were only two tables taken when I got there. I spotted Lisa when I entered the door, begged her for a glass of water, and explained as much of Sam's situation as I could without going into too many details. She seemed to understand. To my delight, she gave me her assurances that she and Rob would both stick by Sam through thick or thin, and I left the diner, relieved the conversation had gone so well.

It was the next talk I wasn't looking forward to.

It wasn't a far walk from the diner to the museum, but it seemed to take me twice as long to make that journey as it had from the bus to the jail.

The opening hour was ten, and I checked my phone and it was half past, so I tugged on the door, which opened freely, and I stepped into the building.

I had no expectations when I walked into the Quincey Museum of Local History. But I got a pleasant surprise when I passed through the door and stepped back into the 1800s.

The front admission desk looked like it came right from an old bank. The desk itself was about six feet wide, and below the waist, an artisan had carved an ornate pattern into it. Above the waist, there were three windows with ornate vertical brass bars and a small area below to pass items. Above the window was a sign with the word Teller spelled out in brass letters.

"Can I help you?" I noticed the person behind the window was a woman who looked to be in her early twenties. She dressed like I'd expect a male bank teller to be dressed, right down to the shiny vest and black tie. She even sported the visor I'd associate with the times.

"Yes. I'm here to talk to Dean Williams. Is he available?"

The teller picked up the phone and dialed a number. "There's a woman here to see you. Yes, she's short. Blue hair?"

I lifted my ball cap so she could check out the color underneath.

"Yes. She has blue hair. Okay." The teller hung up the phone and pointed down the hallway. "He was expecting you. Go through the exhibit. At the end of the first section, you'll notice a hallway with a sign that says genealogy. He's in that room doing research."

I put my hat back on. "Thanks."

I strolled through the room, impressed by what I saw. The museum had recreated a street scene of what the town looked like a few years after its founding. It featured a dentist's office, a general store, a hotel that looked exactly like the Quincey Inn, and a lawyer's office. Each building had windows to see artifacts, and there were several information signs I wanted to stop and read, but

I stayed on my mission.

Eventually, the street turned a corner to the right, and I spotted the hallway and found the genealogical library. That took my breath away, too. There was a wall lined with bookshelves that were stacked with all kinds of volumes. I spotted an old card catalog and several drawers that held tapes and microfiche. Against a wall stood a cabinet with drawers to accommodate large maps and two computer stations. In the center of the room, seated at a large table with three open books stacked around him, was Dean Williams.

He looked up from a tome and spotted me. "Come in. Sit down. Please."

I took a chair across from him.

His eyes dropped to the page, and without looking at me, he spoke. "I'd like to apologize for yesterday. I wasn't in my right mind, and I saw you as a threat, and now I realize you're just trying to help Sam."

"Apology accepted." I could be gracious. Sometimes.

He looked up and met my eyes. "I'd offer you a coffee or something, but there's no food or beverages allowed in this room. To protect the documents."

"I get it." And I did. At one time, I searched for leaves on my family tree and spent many hours in old libraries and the stacks of musty courthouses. I understood the rules. No food, no drink, no ink. "You have an impressive collection here."

"Yes. I've got the largest genealogical collection in this part of the state. I'm passionate about history, especially family history. A lot of the materials I've collected here are from closed libraries or from estate sales. I get donations from families as well who want to see their histories preserved. I've got records in here dating back to when this territory was still a part of Mexico."

"Impressive."

"So why are you here, Codi?"

"Did you know Hanson Johns is dead?"

Dean seemed interested in the book again and looked at the pages. He took a moment and wrote a note on a yellow legal pad beside him. "I heard that through the grapevine."

"Did you know they arrested Sam last night for both murders?"

That got his attention. He had been calm, but the fire I'd seen the night before passed behind his eyes. It quickly faded as he struggled to contain his anger.

"That I hadn't heard," he said.

I felt the need to press buttons since I was running short on time. "Do you believe she did it? Do you think she murdered two people in cold blood?"

"No, of course not," he said.

"Then who's your number one suspect? I can understand Hanson's murder if he saw who actually stabbed Sherman, but who, besides Sam, could hold the grudge enough to kill Sherman?"

Dean didn't say a word.

"You know, I really dislike the whole silent treatment thing. It's rude, and I'm confused by it. I thought you cared about Sam. Half the people I've talked to tell me you two are the hottest item in town, even though she denies it. Is she lying to me, Dean? Are you two a couple and for some strange reason, she doesn't want to tell me? Or is it the other way around? She's got the truth, and you're the one spreading lies around town about the two of you being together. Which is it? Tell me."

Dean exhaled and stared at me. He slammed the book closed, sprang from his seat, and carried the tome into the stacks. When he returned, his hands were empty. "Maybe it's time for you to leave."

I didn't move from the chair. "Maybe it's time you told me the truth."

He shook his head from side to side like a bull on the verge of rampaging. If he had anger issues like Sam said, perhaps I erred by not stopping back at the bus to pick up Bozeman, or better yet, Betty.

"You got something to say?" I asked. I guessed I was pressing my luck.

His chest puffed in and out as he breathed deep, but he remained where he was.

"Want to know what I think?" I asked.

"Not really," he said.

"I reckon you did it. You murdered two people and threatened Shanna, and you were the one who framed Sam to take the fall."

Dean took a step toward me. I stuck firm.

"Here's what I think happened, Dean-o. I think you did date Sam at one point, and I think she didn't care for the over-aggressive alpha male that you're displaying right now, so she dumped you. I bet you didn't handle that well and stalked her to possess her, if only in your own sick mind. Then Sherman came into the picture and pressed Sam to sell her bakery. You probably thought if you did the white knight routine and came to her rescue, then she'd change her mind. And you two would ride off into the sunset on your favorite horse. When Sherman threatened her with bodily harm last night, it was the final straw for you. So, you grabbed a knife from the kitchen, bull-rushed him into the pantry, and did the dirty deed. Unfortunately for poor Hanson, he soon came to the same conclusion I did, so you killed him too with the pie cutter you took from the church yesterday. How the note to Shanna figures in, I don't know, but the police can solve that piece. That sum everything up nicely for you, Dean?"

Dean took another step toward me, bent over, and screamed in my face. "I love her!"

I had enough, so I pushed the chair back and leaned toward him so close our eyebrows almost touched and screamed right back at him. "You love her so much she's going to get the death penalty for something you did?"

Dean made a move, and I thought he was going to hit me. Instead, he grabbed a book from the table and threw it across the room. It landed with a bang on top of a cabinet, then it slid across the surface and dropped to the floor. I wondered if he was going to toss me across the room next.

He clenched his teeth. "I wouldn't do that. You've got me all wrong. You don't understand."

"Everything okay in here?" Dean and I both looked at the door. The teller was standing there, her phone in hand, and she looked like she was ready to call for help.

Dean stepped back from me and smoothed out his shirt. "Yes, Amy. Everything is fine, just fine. We're just having a friendly discussion. You can go back to the front." Amy raised an eyebrow, paused for a moment, then left the room.

"Dean. Sit down. Please. Help me help Sam. If you love her, do it."

Dean took a step for the door, then stopped. After a couple of seconds, he returned to his chair, and I took mine as well.

"Help me understand you. Come on. For Sam," I said.

He stared at the table surface, which was fine by me. "I know I'm out of control. There are… I've had some issues in the past, and I'm seeing a therapist about them. We're trying different medications, but we don't have the correct… balance yet. I love Sam, and I don't blame her for not wanting to be with me and my… dark side. But I didn't kill those people."

"Tell me what happened Saturday night when the fight started."

"Sherman was going to hit Sam, so I grabbed his arm. He tried to wrestle away from me, but I contained him for a moment. Then he let an elbow fly, and I caught it right in the face. See?"

Dean lifted his head and pointed. Right at the hairline was a bruise I hadn't noticed before. So much for my great powers of observation.

"After he whacked me, I relaxed my grip, and he slipped free, and followed Sam out the door. Of course, I was hot on his tail, but Rob intercepted me and dragged me into the kitchen and pushed me up against a counter and held me there."

"Did you try to get away from him?" I asked.

"Of course. But you've met the man. He's a giant. And he knows I go through these… spells, so he just held me there for like five minutes until I calmed down somewhat. Then he let me go."

"What did you do?"

"I needed some air, so I headed for the nearest door, almost knocked Sam over when she came out of the women's room. She looked okay, so I rushed outside, walked down the street like three or four blocks to clear my head, then slowly wandered back to the church. By then, they discovered Sherman's body."

"He was in the pantry. Did you see him in there? You walked right past it on your way out."

Dean thought for a moment. "No. I think the door was closed, and if it wasn't, I didn't notice. Sometimes I'm like a horse with blinders on, and I can only see what's directly in front of me."

"Where were you yesterday afternoon?"

"What? What are you talking about?"

"When someone killed Hanson."

Dean rose, stepped over to another desk, shuffled through some items, and returned carrying a sheet of paper. He handed it to me, and I glanced at it. "What's this for?"

"It's a receipt for some books I purchased at an estate sale yesterday around two. It was in Deming, which is a little over an hour from here. After the sale, I went out with a couple of guys for a bite to eat. I'm sure I can scrape up the receipt for that, too."

I dropped the paper on the table. He deflated my theory in an instant, like an old balloon. Now what?

"I can see why you thought it was me." Dean looked at the floor. "I'm sorry to disappoint you."

"Actually, I'm more disappointed, for Sam's sake. I'm almost out of ideas," I said.

Dean looked back at me. "If I were a betting man, I would've put my money on the mayor."

That got my attention. "What? Why the mayor?"

"Hold on."

Dean went to the map drawer and returned a few minutes later with a roll of paper and a couple of books. He found the end of the paper and placed a book on it, then unrolled the rest and set a book on the other end. I saw it was a map.

"This is a plat map of the Quincey and the surrounding areas. It's a little outdated by sixty or seventy years, but it'll work for this demonstration."

He looked around the area, found another book, and set it near the top of the map, then placed a second book right next to it. Then he extracted a dollar bill from his pocket and placed it along the bottom of the two books.

"Okay, look here. The books represent where the new resort will go. There are two proposed routes to get to that resort. The first is to the top, which is the main road that will run right through town on the county road and eventually feed into the interstate. The second route would cross right through that dollar bill, which would get to the interstate quicker and without going through town."

"So what?" I asked.

"The mayor currently owns that land and wants to sell it to the resort for a sizable amount of money, but Sherman's been blocking that sale."

"Let me guess. He's been stringing along the mayor until he got all the other improvements around the area he wanted."

"You got it. She's been having the planning commission rubber stamp practically everything he wants. Besides that, she's been tamping down all the complaints from the local businesses."

"I would imagine a direct feeder to the interstate would damage the local economy?"

"Some folks would be fine. I imagine there'd be a fast-food place or two and a gas station built at the brand-new exit. But if they did not force people through town, then they wouldn't know about the inn, or the diner, or this museum."

"You think the mayor killed Sherman so she can get his fellow investors to buy her land?"

Dean shrugged. "It's plausible."

"And that's the reason you're going to run against her?" I asked.

"Yes. I do genuinely care about this town and would prefer to see it thrive, rather than just the investors from other parts of the state."

"Now I understand why she was pushing me to leave town. Where would she be now?"

Dean rolled up the map and stacked the books in a neat pile. "At city hall. It's a couple of miles from here."

I exhaled. "Sounds like I should get walking, then. Thanks for your time and all the clarifications."

I picked up my hat and left the room. I was outside the

museum when someone tugged me on the arm. It was Dean.

"Come on, I'll drive you."

CHAPTER TWELVE

Dean's little green Honda stood right by the front door of the museum, so we got in, and he started the engine. Since I was used to riding high on the bus, as Dean sped up, it was like being in a go-cart for me. Dean made three consecutive right turns and a left, and we were back on Main Street, heading west. He seemed in a hurry. When we got to a stop sign and had to wait for a woman with a stroller to complete her long journey through the crosswalk, Dean showed his impatience by drumming his fingers on the steering wheel and shifting in his seat. Once she cleared the curb, Dean hit the accelerator, and I settled back into my seat like I was on an Apollo mission leaving Earth.

"Do you always drive like this?" I asked.

Dean glanced at me, and I snuck a peek at the speedometer. He was already going ten miles over the limit and getting faster.

"You told me you were in a hurry," he said.

"Not that much. Let me ask you, do you ever do nothing?" I asked.

"Nothing? What do you mean, nothing?"

"Like sitting outside and looking at the moon and stars? Without thinking about anything and letting your mind clear out?"

"No, why?"

"Perhaps it would help you gain some focus. Maybe help you slow down a bit."

Dean slammed on the brakes, and as the momentum threw me forward in the seat, he turned a corner and stopped in a parking space with a final squeal of the tires. "We're here."

I considered walking back as I undid my seatbelt and left the car. Dean seemed to know the way, so I followed him into the building. It was a fairly new structure, two stories, rectangular, with the only splash of color being the United States and New Mexico flags waving in the wind out front. I assumed he'd been there before since Dean bypassed the information desk in front. He took an immediate left and started ascending the stairs to the second floor. Once at the top, he turned left again and followed the hallway to the end. At last, we stopped at the door to the mayor's office.

Dean held the door open for me and we stepped into the outer office. There was a receptionist's desk there, and although there was a steaming cup of coffee on it, there wasn't a person in sight. Dean took that as an invitation to go farther in. He stepped around the desk, rapped a knuckle on the inner door, peeked his head in, and opened the door wide.

If it surprised Mayor Mary to see us, she didn't show it. We walked into the room and stopped right in front of her desk. The mayor, who was reading a document, looked up at us over her glasses, exhaled, turned the document upside-down, and sat back in her large leather chair.

The mayor took off her reading glasses and dropped them on the desk. "What do you people want?"

I wanted to speak, but it was Dean who took the lead. Without asking or an invitation, he settled into the visitor's chair in front of her desk. "The sheriff arrested Sam Henry."

The mayor looked at him, at me, then back at him. "I already know that. He told me last night."

"She didn't do it," Dean said.

Mayor Mary shrugged her shoulders. "That's up for the court to decide, not you."

Dean stood suddenly and pointed his finger at the mayor's face and started screaming at her. "Look, Mary, we're all tired of you and your crap. I know you were involved, not Sam. You were the one who brought that weasel Stier to town, and you were the one who was looking to get rich while the rest of us suffered. I don't imagine things were going your way, so you got rid of him, didn't you? And you set Sam up to take the fall at the same time. Clever, Mary. Brilliant. Now that Stier's out of the way, I'm sure you've already started getting buddy-buddy with his investor friends, haven't you?"

Dean picked up the mayor's phone, held the receiver out to her, and lowered his voice to almost a whisper. "You need to get on this phone, call Chief Jennings, and get Sam out of jail. She doesn't belong there. You do."

The mayor didn't make a move, so Dean dropped the receiver. It landed on the desk with a thunk, then bounced and slipped off the side of the desk.

"Listen to me, you ass. I had nothing to do with the deaths of anyone. I didn't do it myself. I didn't have it done. You have no evidence to the contrary. Likewise, you have no evidence that I'm doing anything inappropriate regarding the new resort. You have nothing on me." The mayor leaned over, grabbed the phone's handset, and put it back on the base.

"We're done now. You can leave, either on your own, or I can get security to remove you. I'm happy either way."

Dean glared at her, and she glared right back. It was a contest of iron wills, and Dean broke first. Without a word, he got up, brushed past me, and left the office.

Mayor Mary looked at me. "Well?"

I gathered all the information I needed to. "I'll be leaving, I suppose. Have a nice day."

I left the office and retraced my steps back to the stairs and took them to the first floor. I assumed Dean would wait for me in the lobby, but he didn't. When I stepped outside, he wasn't there, either. I made my way to the parking lot, scanned all the spaces, and noticed his little green Honda was gone. Damn. There went my ride. I thought that was for the best.

I checked the map on my phone to make sure I had the directions right and started walking down Main Street. After fifteen minutes, I found myself in front of the police station, and I was happy to discover I was at least headed the right way. I continued down the street, not so much in a hurry anymore since I had run out of people to talk to. My suspect list had neat checkmarks next to every name, cleared completely, and I didn't know what to do. I'd run out of ideas.

As I walked, I overheard a church bell ring in the distance.

Without thinking, I counted the peals in my head. It was noon, and since I had nothing for breakfast, I was hungry.

When I got to the diner, the lunch rush was on. Lisa spotted me, escorted me to the last table in the room, and handed me a menu.

"Want anything to drink, sweetie?" she asked.

I asked for water, and she scurried away to retrieve it while I glanced at the menu.

"I'd go with the meatloaf sandwich. They serve it open-faced with a side of mashed potatoes and gravy."

I looked over my menu and discovered it was Pastor Tom, offering his advice. "Do you mind if I join you? There's no other place to sit."

I used my foot to push a chair out for him. "Go ahead." As he sat, I returned to the menu. "The meatloaf wouldn't be too much food? I don't like being overstuffed."

"No. They serve it as a half-portion for lunch."

Lisa returned and dropped off glasses of water for me and the pastor. "Have you decided?"

I looked at the pastor. "I understand the meatloaf sandwich is good. Let's try that."

"Same for me," Pastor Tom said.

Lisa scratched the order on her pad and left us.

I unwrapped a straw, sunk it into the water, and took a drink. The ice water tasted refreshing after the long walk I just took. "What's on your mind today, Pastor Tom?"

"My conscience, mostly. I saw Sam Henry at the jail today," the pastor said.

"Why were you there?"

"I go over there three times a week, talk to any inmate who wants to talk. Try to provide some comfort to them."

"Did you talk to Sam?" I asked. I took another drink. I'd almost drained my glass. Pastor Tom noticed and pushed his untouched one my way.

"Oh, yes."

"What did she say?"

"That she was innocent, but she feels like she's going to

prison. She'll be one of those wrongfully convicted people you read about on the Internet. Her words, not mine," Pastor Tom said.

"Do you believe her? About being innocent?"

"Of murder? Yes, of course. She has fine Christian values."

That took me aback. "She didn't mention she attended your church."

Pastor Tom smiled at me. "No, I didn't say she was a good Christian. I said she had good Christian values. She doesn't attend my church, or any other church around town so far as I understand, but I see her at events, bake sales, Christmas programs, that sort of thing. What I meant to say was, she doesn't need to attend church to prove she's a good person, because she just is. She's generous with her time, and her humor. She bakes extra bread for the shelter, gives free cookies to the children, even makes a batch of dog treats once a week for any customers that have pooches. I've never seen her say an unkind word to anyone."

That sounded exactly like the Sam I remembered. "Except Sherman Stier?"

Pastor Tom got up and returned shortly with another glass of ice and a pitcher of water. He refilled my glasses, then poured himself one. Pastor Tom took a sip of water. "Well, that's a unique situation, isn't it? She was only fighting to protect what is hers, and we can't fault her for that, can we?"

I shook my head. After I took another drink, I dabbed my lips with a napkin.

"I can't wrap my head around this whole thing, Tom. I get Sam didn't do it, but I was so sure it was someone else from the committee who did. Lisa and Rob don't have a motive, and Dean Williams has an airtight alibi. Hanson is dead, and although I strongly suspect the mayor is up to some shenanigans, I don't think it's murder."

I looked up at him. "You didn't kill those men, did you?"

I thought I'd offended him. Instead, he broke into a hearty laugh. "Oh, my, no. It wasn't me."

"Sorry, Pastor, I had to ask. But you took some money from him, didn't you? I was right about that one?"

Pastor Tom frowned, then nodded. "Yes. One hundred and

twenty-five thousand dollars. In cash. He handed it to me in a brown paper bag, like he was passing me a turkey sandwich."

"Why did he give you the money?" I asked.

The pastor swirled the straw in his glass as he thought for a moment. "One Saturday night I was working late, preparing the church for Sunday services, when he came in and plopped himself down in the back pew. As I got closer to him, I could tell he was drunk. His eyes were bloodshot, and he smelled like a distillery."

"What did he want?"

"He wanted to make a confession," the pastor said.

"A confession? You hear confessions?" I asked.

"Oh yes, all the time. I'm not Catholic, so I don't have the fancy confessional, or have people do Hail Marys or penance afterward, but I get confessions all the time. Sometimes people can't hold a secret, and the person they seek to tell is someone in the church. It comes with the position."

"And then you have to keep their secrets?"

"Oh yes. And I keep secrets much better than Reba Chestnut does, bless her."

We both laughed.

"And you keep everything in confidence? No matter what horrible thing they tell you?"

Pastor Tom took another drink. "No, not everything. If someone confesses to me about a crime against a person, I'll report that to the authorities."

"I thought that was against the rules."

"If I were a Roman-Catholic, it would be, because I would violate the seal of confession. But I have to look at it from the other perspective too. I can't stand by knowing that someone could have committed a rape, or assault, or even murder and not be accountable for it. In those cases, I would persuade the confessor to go to the authorities themselves, and if they didn't, I would."

"So, if I told you I stole a Snickers bar from the grocery store, you'd keep that secret, but if I shot the store clerk during the act, you would tell the cops?"

"Yes. That's right."

"I've never heard of that before."

"I believe I'm the exception, not the rule. Ah, here's lunch finally."

Lisa dropped off the food and left without another word. Pastor Tom bent his head and said a prayer, and although I wasn't really religious, I stayed silent as he did so to respect his beliefs. When he finished, we dug into our meals.

Pastor Tom had indeed made an excellent suggestion. The meatloaf was moist, seasoned properly and, in a word, excellent. It was so good; I ate three quarters of it, instead of my usual half. Then again, I had skipped breakfast, except for the tea. When I finished eating, I pushed my plate to the side.

"So Sherman Stier came in to confess about something. Since they didn't arrest him for anything, I assume that means he didn't confess to physically hurting anyone."

I looked over at Pastor Tom. He stayed silent, but he gave me a nearly imperceptible nod.

"Can you tell me what happened?" I asked.

Pastor Tom finished his meal, wiped his mouth with his napkin, then wiped up the crumbs on the table in front of him.

"He gave me his confession, begged me to keep his secret, and left in a hurry. A week later, he handed me a sack full of cash and told me to consider it a gift to the church for my help."

"He wanted to buy your silence."

"Yes. Although I would have kept his secret, anyway. I've heard much worse things during my time in the church."

"What are you going to do with the money?"

"I considered returning it to him, even recently, but now that he's gone, I suppose I'll keep it. That kind of money will go a long way to feeding the hungry and clothing the needy."

I couldn't find fault with that logic.

Pastor Tom rose suddenly. "Thank you for letting me join you for lunch. I have to run over to the retirement home. Don't worry about the check. I'll pick it up on the way out."

I smiled. "Thank you, that's quite kind."

Pastor Tom turned to leave, but came back, leaned close, and whispered in my ear. "You know, love is a strange thing. When people fall into it, they're so happy. When they fall out, sometimes they're sad, other times they're angry. Furious, even."

Pastor Tom stood, gave me a wink, and left me sitting by myself. I finished my water, left a tip for Lisa, and exited the diner.

I didn't have any place else I needed to go, so I jaywalked across the street, and did some window shopping as I ventured to the bus.

Our lawn chairs weren't outside, the area looked cleaned up, and the door was locked tight, so I used my key to enter.

"Hello?" I said as I entered. "Anyone home?"

Silence greeted me, so I stepped over to the table and saw the note. Bozeman had gone for a run. Bozeman liked to keep active, and with our constant time spent on the road, he liked to use any downtime to exercise when he could. If we were in a town large enough to have the gym he had a nationwide membership for, he'd go there. If he didn't have that opportunity, he'd trade in his six-gallon hat and cowboy boots for a pair of shorts, a T-shirt, and running shoes. I had the place to myself.

There was a pile of black and white fur on the bench seat, curled up beneath the window, and although it could be mistaken for Gibson, I knew it was Merle. Merle lifted his head to watch me as I moved to the fridge and pulled a handful of raspberries from a pint.

"What are you doing up here? Fighting with your sister again?" Merle perked up when I sat next to him and waited for the treat he knew I would give him. First, though, I had to make sure the raspberries were nice and sweet, so I ate a couple myself. The little red morsels exploded in my mouth, and I moaned in delight.

"Want one?" I held one out for Merle, and like a gentleman, he took it in his front left foot and shoveled it into his mouth. He seemed to enjoy it as much as I did. I gave him my last raspberry, and he then crawled onto my lap and rolled over to get his belly scratched. My skunk was such a ham.

"Tell me, what's going on?" I knew he had gotten into a scuffle with Dolly. Although they loved each other most of the time, now and then they got into a minor argument, much like two dogs, or two cats, or two human siblings would do. When that happened, we usually brought either Merle or Dolly onto the bus, whoever was less grumpy at the moment, just to separate the two for a brief period. Obviously, a scuffle had ensued while I was gone, and Bozeman had to step in and be the mean parent.

"Where's your twin?" If I had to guess, Gibson was in his usual spot on the pillow tower atop my bed. "You'll never believe the last couple of days I've been having. Every time I seem to have a handle on this thing, it just slips away from me again. So frustrating, you know?"

Merle raised his head. One would think he was paying attention. In reality, I knew he just wanted me to scratch the little white stripe that ran down his forehead between his cute black eyes. Merle has always been a diva.

"I'd better go see what your sister is up to. Do you want to go back downstairs?"

Merle answered that question by rolling off my lap and curling back into a ball on the cushion beside me. I took that as a no, so I rubbed his cute little ears and got up to go see what Dolly was up to.

I opened the door to Dolly's cage and glanced inside. As usual, Dolly had snuggled up in her blanket. Bozeman had given her a bowl of vegetables, but they didn't look touched.

"Hey Dolly. How's my girl?"

Dolly raised her head and looked at me. I rubbed her head and scratched her back. Usually she loved it, but on this occasion, she turned around and ignored me. Dolly could hold a grudge when she wanted to. Since she didn't want to be sociable, I looked under her blanket for her most recently collected treasures. I found two more rocks that I added to her growing pile. She had found the bowl end of a plastic spoon broken in half. She also had a bent Eisenhower dime, and a silver button, and all those items I took with me onto the bus and tossed them into the kitchen trash.

I thought for a moment about what I wanted to do to pass the time, then elected to write some music. There was a song I'd been working on for the better part of a week that was giving me some trouble. I had the lyrics where I wanted them, but there was something about the melody that I didn't like and wanted to change. The hard part was figuring out what that change was.

Having the desire to figure it out, I went to my room, grabbed my notebook and my Martin, and took them back to the parlor. I got comfortable and strummed the guitar. I woke Merle up with the noise, but since he and the other animals were used to music on the bus, he put his head down again.

For several minutes, I worked through some chord progressions before changing the tune to a different key altogether. It turned out I hated that even worse, so I changed it back again, and worked through different iterations until I had something I was almost happy with. I picked up my pencil, made a few notations, and then, as was my habit, rather than put the pencil back on the table, I moved to place it between my lips. I lost fewer pencils when I chewed on them while I wrote. Just before the pencil touched my lips, I looked down and noticed a white substance against the yellow-painted wood. I brought the pencil closer to look at what it was, and then I saw the index finger and thumb of my right hand contained particles as well.

I moved over to the sink, turned on the water, rinsed my fingers, and watched as the substance combined with the water and disappeared down the sink.

Where had I seen that before?

I watched the water swirl in the bowl for a moment, then shut it off.

"Wait. Wait, a moment…"

I grabbed the kitchen trash bin, tipped it over, and then watched as the contents spread over the counter. Among the banana peels, a few crumpled sheets of paper, and a small amount of other random kitchen trash, I found what I was looking for. The button I had just thrown away. I picked it up and saw right away the white substance I had transferred to my fingers. I realized I had seen it before, and it took a simple swipe through the remaining refuse to find the flower stem I had thrown away the day before.

Certainly, I wasn't a chemist, but they looked the same to me, and at last the synapses in my brain connected enough to realize I'd seen it before. Literally right on the tip of my nose.

Flour.

From the bakery.

Somehow, Dolly had been exploring the area and brought back two items covered in flour. I studied the button and realized I had seen that before, too. I closed my eyes and mentally replayed conversations I'd had with anyone over the last few days. There was only one person I could remember who was wearing a jacket with buttons like this.

I smiled.

I had a new suspect.

CHAPTER THIRTEEN

My tunnel vision was in full effect when I stepped off the bus.

I didn't notice Bozeman performing his post-run stretch, and tripped over his outstretched leg. My arms flailed before me, and I performed a graceful face plant in the dirt. To his credit, Bozeman didn't laugh, but he took a moment to help me up.

"Where are you going in such a hurry?" he asked.

I pointed across the lot. "To the bakery."

I left Bozeman behind and raced to the back door. Of course, I expected it to be locked, and it was. I pushed and pulled on the door but didn't get it to budge. I examined the area, and on the ground, a foot to the door's side, was a small pile of flour. Directly in the center of that pile looked to be a handprint, except it was too tiny to be a human hand, unless there was an infant loose in the parking lot. It was Dolly's. I tried the door again, and of course, it didn't move a single inch.

I looked up at the building and discovered a small window I hadn't noticed before. It was only about fourteen inches square, and even I wouldn't fit through it, but it would still give me an idea if anything was amiss inside. The problem was, I was about two feet too short to peer into it.

"Hey Bozeman, come over here. I need a boost."

To his credit, Bozeman didn't ask a single question. He simply came over and did what I needed him to do. I had him bend over. I put a foot in his cupped hands, and he lifted me easily over the ledge so I could gawk into the bakery. A fine dusting of flour covered the window. I tapped on the window, hoping some of the flour would drop away, and to my surprise, the window swung inward.

"Lift me a little higher, Boze."

Bozeman complied, and I grabbed the ledge and stuck my

head through the open window. My shoulders were too wide for the opening, so I got no farther, but I was in enough to see the bakery's inside. For sure, someone had been there. There were a few pans and several other items on the floor. The usually clean stainless-steel counters and appliances all had a layer of white on them, like it had snowed inside the building. To me, it didn't seem like someone had vandalized it. More like someone had a tantrum and took it out on items within reach, like when people toss vases or lamps during outbursts in movies.

"Okay, you can let me down." I pulled the window closed as well as I could, and in a couple seconds my feet were back on the ground.

"What's going on?" Bozeman asked.

"Someone's been in there. It's a mess. The door's locked, and I suspect the front door is too. Sam says the only key is with the cops, so that means that either someone took it from them, or there's another key out there."

"So what?"

"Next to the sink on the bus are two items I took away from Dolly's stash. I guess one is the bottom part of a broken boutonniere, and the other is a button which I'm pretty sure came from a denim jacket."

"Where did Dolly get them?"

"Right around here. She left a footprint." I pointed to it, and Bozeman squatted to inspect the area.

"Yeah, that's hers," he conceded.

"I encountered a denim jacket yesterday. Shanna was wearing it when she came to Sam's apartment with the note she found."

"You guess she's in on this?"

"Oh, yes, big time. Now I only need to find her."

"You realize that the phone you carry is good for more than phone calls and giving you directions. Where is it?"

"I left it on the bus."

A few moments later, Bozeman was looking through my phone while I gave Merle belly scratches. It took him only ten or fifteen minutes, but he soon picked up my pencil and jotted an address down in my notepad.

"She's over on Madison Street, about five blocks from here."

"How did you figure that out?"

Bozeman smiled and set my phone on the table. "I used the bakery's social media pages to find pictures of Shanna, which I used to do a similar image search until I found her personal pages. She doesn't have them set to private, and in one photo she had a photo of a birthday card she received, but she didn't block out or hide the address. Not very smart. Anyone can find her."

I leaned over and gave him a hug. "Thanks, Boze. I'm so glad you're smarter than you appear."

Bozeman grinned. "I know. That isn't too hard. Are you going out again? Do you need me to go with you?"

"No. I'll take Betty, and I'll be okay."

"Alright then. I'm jumping in the shower. Take your phone with you and call me if you get into any trouble, which, knowing you, is a distinct possibility."

I tore the sheet from the pad, left the table, strapped Betty in for the journey, and jumped from the bus. I knew where Jefferson Street was, so I assumed they were in presidential order and figured Madison had to be the next block over. To my surprise, I was right. I was getting better at this navigation stuff.

Shanna's house was in the middle of the block, a quaint-looking Craftsman style home with a few potted flowers on the front porch. I was undecided whether I wanted to go in aggressive with guns blazing, or passive like I was just passing through. Shanna decided for me when the door opened before I'd even reached for the doorbell.

"What are you doing here?" she asked.

"Just figured I'd stop by and check on how you're doing and if you've talked to Sam."

Shanna let go of the door and moved into the living room. Although she hadn't invited me in, I followed her anyway and took a seat on her couch. She paced across the room and back before she settled into a wooden rocking chair near the front window.

"No. She's in jail. How would I have talked to her?"

I looked around for the jacket she wore yesterday, but it wasn't in the room. I doubted she'd let me search the rest of the house for it.

"Do you wonder what you're going to do next? Like if Sam goes to prison and can't run the bakery?"

Shanna smiled. "I'm going to run it. Keep the bakery going."

That was a surprise to me. Sam had mentioned Shanna wasn't ready for the big time yet.

"You've talked about that with her?" I asked.

Shanna hesitated. "Oh, sure. We've talked about it. Like, not in the context of her going to jail, but like what if she got really sick, or wanted to take an extended vacation? Scenarios like that."

Somehow, I doubted that's how the conversation actually happened. Besides, she looked up and to the left, so I suspected she was lying. Or was it up and to the right? I never remembered which way it was. Didn't matter. I still had her dead to rights.

"The bakery wasn't open today, was it? I could really go for one of those muffins. You haven't been over there, have you?"

"No. Like I said, I haven't talked to Sam yet, but I'm sure she'll want me to get it back in business as soon as I can."

"You haven't been over there?" I asked again.

"I said no. Not since…Saturday. Yeah, it was Saturday morning."

"Oh yes, I remember now. When that awful man came in."

Anger flushed through Shanna's face so quickly I almost mistook it for a lapse in my vision. She looked at her feet, then at the ceiling, then at the wall behind me.

"What did you think of Sherman?" I asked.

Her eyes continued to flit around the room, and finally they settled on me.

"He was… I never had… I don't know," Shanna sputtered.

"Why not? No one else I talked to liked him. He seemed to be a mean, spiteful man, only in search of his next dollar."

Shanna smiled. "Oh, no. He had his sweet side too, he…"

Somewhere in another room, I heard a phone ring. Shanna excused herself and left to answer the call.

While she was gone, I sat still and looked around. It was a

modest living room. Besides the couch and the rocking chair, there was a small side table next to the couch, holding a lamp. There was a basket overflowing with magazines next to the rocking chair, and a wooden teacart on which a small television sat. On the wall behind the television, I saw framed family photos, so I got up and studied the pictures. The one that caught my attention was a photo where a lawman was standing with two small kids on either side. A boy and a girl.

"That's my dad with me and my brother."

I hadn't heard Shanna approach, so she startled me, not that I wanted to give her that satisfaction. "Your dad was a cop?"

"Yep. Spent thirty years with the New Mexico State Patrol. Retired a few years ago and moved to Florida."

"Why Florida?"

Shanna shrugged. "No clue. He never really gave us a good reason for that, just said all retired people should move to Florida."

I leaned a little closer to the photo, and I could just make out his name tag. J. Jennings. Holy moly. Jennings. "Um, your brother wouldn't be Chief Jennings, would he?"

"Yes. Daddy was so proud that one of us followed in his footsteps. He practically burst his buttons when Jack made chief."

I figured right then I had a problem with her brother being the chief. It was a struggle, but I smiled anyway. "I'll bet he did. Speaking of buttons, did you lose one lately?" I played it cool and returned to the couch.

"I'm not sure what you mean."

"On that jacket you came to Sam's in. The denim jacket. It has those distinctive buttons. I found one today, covered in flour, and I'll bet if we looked at that jacket, we'd find you're missing a button."

"So what? Lots of people lose buttons."

"Yeah, but you told me you haven't been to the bakery in a couple days. Obviously, that was a lie."

I expected her to confess to her crimes a la every dramatic courtroom scene I've ever seen on television, but Shanna just stared at me, not speaking, not moving.

I stepped in with both barrels. "Shanna, I think you did it.

You killed Sherman Stier, and you killed Hanson when he saw you do it. Then you let Sam take the blame. I just don't understand why you'd do it."

A flashing light caught my eye. I looked out the window and saw the chief getting out of his car. I smiled. "The calvary has arrived."

Shanna grinned even wider as she reached to open the door. "It's not what you expect."

Chief Jennings entered the room and nodded at Shanna, then approached me. "Get up and turn around."

I didn't understand. "What? Wait!"

The chief didn't wait. Instead, he grabbed me by the upper arm and lifted me with ease to my feet. He spun me around, and before I realized what happened, He handcuffed me and marched me right out of the house.

"What is this?" I yelled as he forced me down the sidewalk. "She's the one. She did it."

"You're under arrest for trespassing." He bent me over the hood of the car. I saw neighbors coming out of their houses to watch the show. That was going to be great for my public image. I considered for the briefest of moments making my booking photo the cover art for my next album.

"What's this?" The chief found Betty, removed her from my holster, removed the clip, checked the chamber, and set the gun on the hood. "I guess I need to add carrying a concealed weapon to the charges."

"I've got a permit for that. It's in my wallet."

Jennings ignored me as he checked my other pockets for weapons. He didn't find guns or knives, but he found my phone and wallet. After he was done, he placed me in the backseat of his squad and got in the front.

He turned in his seat so he could face me. "You want to explain what you're doing here?"

I didn't know if I wanted to. He was her brother. How could I accuse her of a double murder to her brother? I wouldn't think that would have the impact I wanted. I needed to see how far I could stretch the truth without throwing out any accusations.

"Sheriff, I only came over to talk to her. About if she's seen Sam, and about the bakery."

"Why?"

"I told you before, Sam's my friend."

"Sure, fine. But why would you care about the bakery? You don't live here. You don't have a vested interest in it."

Okay, he had me there. I shrugged my shoulders. "I like the blueberry muffins she makes. Come on, chief, let me go. I just came over here to talk. Nothing more."

"Shanna said you forced your way in uninvited and wouldn't leave. Are you saying that's not true?"

"No. Look, I don't expect you to trust me. I have proof back at my bus."

"What proof?"

"Dolly found a button from Shanna's jacket, and one of Hanson's flowers."

"So, you want me to get a statement from Dolly?"

"No. You can't talk to her. Dolly's a raccoon." I knew I made a mistake the second the rushed words passed my lips.

"Raccoon? You collected evidence from a raccoon? Did the raccoon give you a statement? Does it talk? Can it give a description to my department sketch artist?"

At that moment, I wished I could put my hands over my face and hide.

"Have you had any drugs or alcohol today?"

I shook my head. "No, I don't do those. I'm sober."

He didn't take that as gospel either. Based on the Dolly talk, I couldn't blame him.

"Perhaps I should talk to another officer. Do you have someone else I could talk to? Like maybe Deputy Samuels?"

He rolled his eyes. "You obviously don't know how that works. Complaints go up the chain of command, not down, and I'm at the top of the chain. Why would you need someone else? Are you going to lodge a protest?"

I was getting frustrated. "No. That's your sister in there. Surely, you're going to take her side about anything I have to say."

"You assume I can't be impartial?"

I shrugged and noticed the insulted look on his face. I struggled a bit, but I managed to sit up straighter. "No."

"You're wrong. If it's one thing my daddy instilled in me was a love for the law, and he also taught me that the law was equal for all people."

I swallowed. Maybe I had more in common with him than I thought. "My dad told me the same thing. Nothing made him angrier than when rich people got to skirt around the law while some lawmen harassed the poor."

That got his attention. "Your father was a cop?"

I nodded. "Detective with the Denver police."

His voice softened. "You see it all the time. Lots of criminals think they can get away with stealing the moon because they have relatives who wear a badge. Makes me sick. I'm not like that. If I caught Shanna driving drunk through town, or high on drugs, or running naked down Main Street, or holding up the pharmacy at gunpoint, you can bet your bottom dollar that I'd have no second thoughts about arresting her."

"Why all the aggression with me? I did nothing wrong. I came here to talk, not shoot her to death."

"Then why are you carrying a gun?"

"After the event Saturday night, I walked alone back to the lot behind the bakery where we parked the bus. I thought someone was following me," I said.

I wasn't sure if he believed me or not.

"Who was it?" Sheriff Jennings asked.

"I don't know. All I heard were the footsteps, and when I looked behind me, I didn't spot anyone. It freaked me out."

"Can anyone confirm that?"

I thought for a second. "Yeah. I ran into the ice cream place on Main Street. I told the guy there."

"Bigger guy? Gray hair and mustache?"

"That's him."

"Paul Patterson. What did Paul do? Call the police?"

"No. He looked around outside, but there was no one there by that point. He offered to walk me back to the bus, but I declined. After that, I started carrying the gun for my protection. Like I said, it's registered and I have a permit."

Chief Jennings opened my wallet and found the paper. He scrutinized it for a few moments, then put it back where he found it.

"This is all a big misunderstanding," I said. "Why don't we go back in there and talk to Shanna and straighten everything out? Or we could go back to my bus and I'll show you what I found."

"Okay. You wait here. Don't move."

Chief Jennings left the car and returned to the house. From where I sat, I saw him knock on the door, then enter.

"Don't move. Funny," I said aloud to no one. I couldn't if I wanted to since I wore the handcuffs. Even if I got out of those, I'm sure he locked the back doors. And there was a plastic partition preventing me from going into the front seat, and I surely could not dig my way through the backseat into the trunk. I waited patiently for the chief to return.

I expected him to return right away, but he didn't. After five or six minutes, I wondered what kind of fairy tales Shanna was telling about me.

At last, the door opened, and Chief Jennings came out. He was moving fast, but not quite running. He seemed to know that the neighbors were still watching. Rather than get back in the car, he came to my side and opened the door.

"Get out."

I did as I was told, and he turned me around and gently removed the cuffs. He opened the passenger door. "Get in."

I got in the front seat and waited for him to slide into the driver's seat. "Are we going to talk to Shanna?"

He picked up the radio handset. "No. She's gone. He pressed the button. Unit one to base."

The radio crackled for a second, then the response came through. "Go ahead, Chief."

"Base, I need you to put a BOLO out on Shanna Prescott. She's probably driving a silver Ford pickup. If anyone spots her, don't approach. Just let me know where she is."

"Copy that, Chief."

"Unit one out." Jennings replaced the handset and started the engine.

"Now what?" I asked.

"Now we're going to your bus. I want to see what you have."

The chief did a U-turn in the street and headed for the bakery. It didn't take over three minutes to drive the short distance, and he parked the patrol car and followed me into the bus.

Bozeman was watching TV when he saw the chief appear. He got to his feet immediately, let me pass, then stepped into the space to separate me from the chief. "What's going on here, Codi? Everything okay?"

"Everything's fine, Bozeman. He just wants to see what Dolly found." I glanced around for a moment. The items were still on the counter. "Where's Merle?"

"Downstairs with Dolly."

"Who's Merle?" the chief asked.

"He's… my cat." I almost lost him trying to explain Dolly. I didn't want to have to explain why I also hung out with a skunk. "Over here."

I pointed to the items on the counter and stepped aside to give him room to look. Rather than touch them, he bent over to get a closer look.

"What do you think?"

He stood straight again. "Yeah, that looks like a button from her jacket. It's her favorite, so I've seen her in it probably a thousand times. I don't get the significance of the twig, though."

"I didn't either until I went to the florist's shop to see Hanson. That green tape at the bottom is a florist's tape that they used to hold flowers and such together. I'm pretty sure that's the remains of the boutonniere Hanson wore on Saturday night. I'm also certain the white substance on both items is flour."

"You have a couple of plastic bags?"

Bozeman was closest to the pantry, so he opened the door and handed a couple of baggies to the chief. Chief Jennings took a steak knife from the butcher block and used the knife to push the items over the counter's edge and into their respective baggies. He put the knife back, sealed the bags, and stuffed them both into his shirt pocket.

"What makes you think it's flour?"

"Come on, I'll show you."

I led Jennings out into the parking lot, and over to the bakery. There, I pointed out Dolly's tiny footprint. He took a few pictures with his phone, then collected a sample of the white powder into another baggie. Since he was taller than me, he had no trouble boosting himself up to the window like I had done and taking a peek inside. After he took a couple more pictures, he led me back to the cruiser and gave back my belongings, including my gun, which I returned directly to its holster.

"Well, chief, what do you think?" Bozeman asked.

The chief looked at Bozeman and pointed a thumb in my direction. "I think that Codi's on to something here, as baffling as it sounds."

"It was the raccoon that convinced you, wasn't it?" I asked.

The Chief was about to answer when the radio unit he carried squawked. "Base to unit one."

"Go ahead."

"Chief, someone spotted Prescott's car speeding west out of town. As requested, the deputy held back, but followed at a distance. Prescott went up to the construction site. Do you have further orders?"

"Have the deputy stay there, but don't pursue. I'm on the way. I'm out."

He looked at me as he opened the door. "Well? Are you coming?"

CHAPTER FOURTEEN

I didn't need to be asked twice, so I jumped in the car and by the time I reached for my seatbelt, we were already speeding out of the lot. As Chief Jenning drove, I kept my mouth shut and watched the outside world pass by faster than I had ever before. Jennings slowed at intersections to ensure we'd get through safely, but only slightly. I sat in awe as we ran through red lights and as cars pulled over to let us pass. I took the ride as a proxy power trip.

Once we got outside of town, Jennings stomped the accelerator like he was executing a cockroach, and we shot through the scrubland like a rocket ship. I glimpsed another patrol car ahead and thought for sure Jennings wouldn't be able to stop in time. But I admit, it impressed me when we came to a halt within a foot of the other car without so much as a squeal from the brakes.

The deputy came alongside, and Jennings rolled down his window. "She still up there?"

The deputy turned and looked up at the road and back at the chief. I noticed the deputy was a woman, tall, skinny. Her uniform shirt looked too large for her, and it billowed in the breeze like a ship's sail.

"Yes, sir. Unless she drove off the road on the far side of the property, but I think there are still old cattle fences out that way, aren't there?"

"I think so. Stay here in case she doubles back. I'm going up to find her. If you don't hear from me in fifteen minutes, call dispatch for some backup."

"Okay, Chief."

The deputy backed away and watched us pass, and the chief turned onto a gravel road. Unlike before, when he drove fast enough to peel the paint from the car, this time he barely crept along.

"Does this road lead to the new resort?" I asked.

"Yeah."

"I thought it wasn't under construction yet."

"Most of it isn't. The first phase is laying sewer and prepping the land for the building foundations," the sheriff said as he steered around a pothole. "That's where they are now."

"Why would Shanna come up here?"

He didn't answer. The only sounds came from the crunch of the gravel beneath the tires and the occasional chirp from the radio. We got to the top of a rise, and below I discovered where they laid out the bare bones of the resort. I saw stacks of unlaid sewer line, several trenches dug, and large machines lined up along the road. There were lots of stakes sticking out of the ground with pink ribbons waving in the breeze. Throughout the property, roads of gravel resembling tendrils spread out in several directions.

At the far end of the area, I spotted a construction trailer with the contractor's name on the side, and two other sheds. As we drove closer and rounded a bend, I caught sight of Shanna's truck parked behind a shed. I didn't spot her, only the open door of her Ford. Jennings slowed the vehicle and pressed on until he parked on the opposite side of the shed from the truck.

"Stay here," he ordered. The stare he gave me matched his stern words.

He opened the door, stepped outside, and I watched as he used the shed's corner for cover, determined it was clear and slipped around to its side. Not wanting to miss anything, I disobeyed orders and followed his trail. I met up with him soon after, and when he discovered me coming, he put a hand up for me to stop and shook his head. He put a finger to his lips, so I tried to be quiet.

Jennings crouched behind Shanna's truck. With his gun drawn and with a quick motion, he popped up, looked into the truck's bed and got down when he realized it stood empty. Slowly, he made his way to the open door, peered in, and came back to me.

"She's armed," he whispered.

"How do you know?"

"The rifle rack is empty, so she must have it on her. You should get back in the car and drive back to the deputy. I made a mistake bringing you down here."

"Well, I'm not going back. You should either arrest me, or let's press on." It was a tossup to which one he'd choose, but in the end, he nodded.

"At least stay behind me or something else. Stay out of the line of fire. I'm going into the construction trailer next. You stay outside. I mean it this time."

We edged to the end of the shed, and I got a good view of the trailer. It looked like a manufactured home, but it stood on wheels and had cinderblocks beneath it to keep it level and steady. We were on the end of the trailer, which contained an air conditioner unit and no windows, so we made quick time hustling up against the building.

Jennings took a snap look around the corner. "There's only one door in, and three small windows. I didn't see any rifle barrels sticking out, so that's a good sign. You stay here. I'm going in. Okay?"

I nodded, and Jennings crept around the corner. True to my word, I stayed put. Well, I kind of stayed put. I tiptoed to the corner and looked around it. Jennings stood still by the door with his hand on the knob. He opened the door an inch while I held my breath.

"Shanna? It's me, it's Jack. I want to come in there and talk to you, okay?"

"No." Shanna screamed loud enough that I easily understood her.

Jennings opened the door wider so he could peek in. I worried he was making another mistake, especially if she really had a rifle.

"Shanna come on, put the gun down, and I'll come in and we can talk about it, okay? Everything's going to be fine. Look, I'm going to put my gun away, and you can put yours away, okay?"

If Shanna answered, I didn't pick it up. She must have relented, though, because Chief Jennings holstered his sidearm and moved inside, leaving the door open.

I moved around the corner, so I had a better chance of eavesdropping.

"Shanna, put the rifle down. Daddy told you never to point a gun at a person, remember? Remember, he taught us both that? Do you remember how important that was to him? To never point a gun at someone? Put it down, Shanna."

Shanna murmured something in response.

"Tell me, why did you run from the house? Why did you tell me Codi broke in on you? What's going on? Talk to me Shanna."

Again, I got no response.

"Shanna, NO!"

Chief Jennings screamed the last word, and I caught the rifle's report. It hadn't even finished ringing in my ears, and I was already trying to figure out what to do. Go back for the deputy? Run in like the savior? I seemed trapped between opposite reactions, but I decided quickly when I realized the chief might need immediate help, and I couldn't leave him.

I reached around and pulled Betty from my holster and held her down by my side. When I moved, I positioned myself right in front of the door. Once there, I glanced inside where one of Chief Jennings' legs stretched out in front of me, unmoving.

"Shanna? This is Codi Cassidy. I'm coming in now. I don't mean you harm. Let me check on the chief, okay?"

I got no words, but a loud wail that transformed into a heavy sob. I stuck in my head far enough to peek and looked toward Shanna. She sat on top of a desk, her hands in front of her face, crying. The rifle stood on the floor in front of her. I kicked it into gear, rushed into the room, grabbed it by the still-warm barrel, and chucked it out of the trailer.

"I, I, I k-k-killed my only brother." Shanna sobbed and bawled even harder.

I didn't want to look, but I did. Chief Jennings laid face down in front of a filing cabinet. I thought he was dead, but I noticed his body shake, and he stirred slightly.

"Help me," he sputtered.

I honored his soft plea and helped him roll onto his back. Shanna hadn't killed him after all. The shot got him in the shoulder, and the impact spun him around and he fell, hitting his head against the file cabinet on his way down.

"Shanna. You didn't kill him. He's not dead. He's moving."

Shanna was still crying, but she dropped her hands and looked over at us. Chief Jennings threw her a half-hearted wave.

Without prompting, Shanna rambled. "I didn't mean to do it. I just got so angry with him. He said he loved me. He said he'd take me away from here once the resort was done. But when he came to the bakery that morning, and didn't even acknowledge me, I knew it was all a lie. I was just another toy to him."

I helped the chief sit up, and he leaned his back against the cabinet. "Shanna, what did you do?"

"It was an accident. I had a knife from the bakery, and I was… practicing with it at home. I didn't think Sam would even miss it, but then I felt guilty, and I was going to return it to her that night. There I was in the kitchen when Sam came bursting through the door and then Sherman came in after her. I took him into the pantry and I told him I loved him and that he should forget about the stupid bakery. But he said he didn't love me. He wanted the bakery. He wanted her. Don't you understand?"

Jennings and I looked at each other, then back at her.

Shanna sniffed, then wiped her nose on the sleeve of her denim jacket, and I noticed right then, that yes, the bottom button was gone.

No one said a word, but it was Shanna who lost the game of silence first. "When he tried to push his way past me, I got him. He fell, and I left the pantry and ran back to the kitchen. I was going nutty in there and didn't know what to do, so I went back to the pantry, and that's when I saw HER on the floor next to HIM, and I lost it. I refused to take it. She didn't deserve him, only I did. I screamed, and when the others came, I went back to the kitchen."

"Why did you stick around?" Jennings asked.

Shanna shrugged. "I wanted to see if he was still alive, and when I found out he wasn't, the police were already there and wouldn't let me leave. And then what did I see? I saw her talking to you!"

Shanna punctuated her sentence by pointing at me. I was glad

I had the foresight to toss the rifle outside.

"The next thing I knew, you were waltzing around the room like the queen, asking stupid questions, and I knew you had to be dealt with, too. After you finished talking with me, I returned to the kitchen to find myself another knife, but I didn't. The best I got was one of Sam's pie cutters. I was so furious I couldn't wait to get you outside."

Shanna laughed to herself. "Do you get how happy it made me when you walked back to the bakery instead of riding in that big bus of yours? I was ecstatic."

"It was you who followed me."

Shanna nodded. "I almost got you, too, but then you turned that corner, and those kids were across the street. I knew I lost my chance when you ran into the ice cream parlor."

For once, my intuition was on point.

"After that, every time I tried to find you, you weren't alone. Lucky for you."

I looked at Jennings. He didn't look good. Nearby was a work shirt draped over a chair. It looked clean enough. I balled it up and applied pressure to his shoulder. His head was bleeding too, but I didn't have another compress, and his shoulder was much worse. He gritted his teeth but otherwise took the pain without complaint.

"What about Hanson Johns? How did he fit in?" Jennings asked.

"Sunday morning, out of the blue, he called me and said he saw me there. He wanted me to give him five thousand dollars, or he was going to turn me over to you. Yeah. Like I have five thousand dollars just lying around. If I did, I wouldn't have come back to Quincey, that's for sure. We agreed to meet at the flower shop at one, and when we met, I lured him into that cooler and gave him the present I had meant for her."

Again, she pointed at me. I got the feeling we wouldn't be best friends.

"Then I thought, why don't I get rid of her first, so I could get to you next, even though I had planned it the other way around? That was the easiest thing ever. I just made that fake note and got you to believe I was being threatened, and when I turned it over to

Jacky here, he couldn't arrest Sam fast enough. Good riddance. She deserved it for taking my man away, although I'd rather see her go to the cemetery than to prison."

I was so concerned about Jennings' shoulder that I had paid little attention to Shanna, other than passing glances. I looked over at her and saw she'd transformed. When I first entered the trailer, she was upset, almost hysterical about shooting the chief. Now she was sitting there calmly, relaying this story to us like we were chatting while having tea. Her tears had dried up, and although her eyes were red and puffy, they now had an appearance that leaned toward evil rather than sadness. She looked psychotic.

I leaned over and whispered into the chief's ear. "Where are your handcuffs?"

"Left side." His voice was weak. His shoulder wound didn't appear fatal, so I guessed he'd suffered a concussion when he hit his head. I reached over his body and got his cuffs.

"Chief? Stay awake. Don't go to sleep." I yelled his name and shook him gently. His left eye opened and tried to focus on me but he couldn't. "Shanna, your brother needs an ambulance. Can you call for help? There's a deputy just up the road."

"No. In fact, I've come up with a brand-new and improved plan. A much better one. I've decided you're going to prison with Sam."

"For what? I did nothing wrong."

"For killing the chief of police. You'll probably get the chair for that."

I looked up and noticed that Shanna had Betty pointed in my direction. How in the world did I lose my gun? Then I remembered. I set Betty on the table when I grabbed the shirt. Dumb. I wouldn't make that mistake again. Even if I lived through this.

"Although I have a better idea. I'll explain you shot Chief Jennings when he confronted you about killing the others, then I shot you. It's a winner-winner chicken dinner scenario for me. I'll probably be a hero. I'll have my picture in the paper and everything. Maybe Mayor Idiot will even give me a key to this stupid city."

That story made no sense to me. Why would I shoot anyone? I have no motive since I've only known these people for three days.

I detected a faint siren in the distance. Finally, the posse was on the way.

"Hey, Shanna? The police are almost here. Drop my gun and step back. You're finished."

Shanna moved back and glanced out the window. "You're right, time is running out. Say goodbye to the chief." Shanna pulled the trigger.

In the tiny trailer, the sound was deafening, even though Betty was only a .22. As expected, the muzzle flashed when the gun erupted, but no bullet came whizzing by. Only the shell casing that did a lazy loop in the air and bounced off the wall and onto the floor.

It was my turn to grin. "You can't kill him with blanks." I got up and took a step toward her. "Give it up. You can't hurt us anymore. Give me my gun back."

It was a bluff. Only the first bullet in the clip was a blank, but she didn't know that. I hoped she would drop the gun and give up. She didn't. Instead, she pulled the trigger again, and this time I felt the bullet rush past my head and the chief yelped like a kicked dog behind me. There was a pair of scissors and a large stapler on the table next to me, so I grabbed the stapler and threw it with all my might in her direction. My plan involved causing enough distraction so I could run out of the open door to safety.

Shanna fired again when I made my move. She was the best shot in the world, or I was the luckiest person on the planet because the bullet clipped the stapler enough to change its direction slightly. Rather than take a round to the chest, I got hit in the shoulder. I didn't have another chance to do anything else. Behind Shanna, a window broke, and then the world lit up.

I was only vaguely aware of the flurry of activity around me. I felt the trailer rock as several people entered, and I heard people screaming, although I couldn't understand the words. As my vision came back, I saw Deputy Samuels had Shanna in custody and was escorting her from the building. I sensed someone nearby, and the deputy I had met only a few minutes earlier was at my side, helping me to my feet. With her help, I staggered outside and collapsed on the ground when I got a few feet from the door.

An ambulance arrived, and the paramedics rushed into the building to tend to Jennings, and I tried to get up, but I couldn't.

"Whoa, there, tough girl." The deputy held me down, and I blinked a few times and hoped my mind would clear enough to read her tag. She noticed my struggle. "Can you hear me?"

I nodded.

"You can call me Daisy. We threw in a flash-bang grenade when we heard the gunshots. You'll be okay. You have some ringing in your ears?"

Ringing was an understatement. I nodded again.

"Don't worry. That will go away in a few minutes. Your normal vision will return too. Are you injured?"

"I got a bullet to the shoulder," I said.

"You don't have to yell. Just use your normal speaking voice." Daisy gave me a bottle of water, and I struggled to swallow the first mouthful. The fresh liquid helped clear my mind and my throat from the smoke created by the grenade. As I drank, Daisy tore my shirt and looked at my shoulder.

"You're not bleeding, but you'll probably have a hell of a bruise. Are you sure she shot you?"

I nodded for the third time. "Yes. It was a rubber bullet, though, and it hit something before it hit me, so I was doubly lucky. Is the chief going to be okay?"

"I don't know. They're working on him now."

Daisy stayed with me, and together we watched the trailer's door. After an eternity passed, two men carried the chief out through the narrow door, then put him on a gurney, and put the gurney on the ambulance. A few seconds later, the ambulance left, sirens blaring, leaving only a cloud of dust behind.

Deputy Samuels appeared and crouched down before me. "Chief Jennings will be fine, I think. He has a shoulder wound and a concussion for sure, and a possible broken rib or two. We'll have to wait for the x-rays to see for sure. Are you okay?"

"I think so," I said.

"Good. Deputy Daisy will take you to the hospital to get that shoulder checked out."

I was going to argue that it was fine, but it started to throb and stiffen. "Okay."

Daisy and Samuels helped me to my feet and into Daisy's car. As Daisy got in the driver's seat, Samuels buckled me in.

He gave me a smile. "It'll all be okay. Oh, and don't leave town. I'll have some questions for you."

I looked him in the eyes. As I focused, I noticed he had pretty green eyes, with a speck of gold in the bottom of one iris. "I should have left town three days ago."

Samuels nodded and closed the door. I rested my head against the window and closed my eyes. A few moments later, we were on the move.

CHAPTER FIFTEEN

The next day I slept in. Normally I was an early riser, but I was dead tired, which, in retrospect, was better than being just dead. I opened my eyes around eleven in the morning and I woke to a pair of pretty kitty eyes staring at me.

"Hey Gibson. Are you trying to steal my soul?" I got an arm above the covers and scratched his ears. Gibson purred in response, then jumped off the bed and ran from the room.

I got up, did my morning business, then returned to my room. Rather than the full cowgirl regalia, I slipped into a pair of teal sweatpants. Before I pulled on my T-shirt, I studied my shoulder in the mirror. The x-rays confirmed I had no broken bones the day before. The rubber bullet didn't break the skin, but a large, deep red bruise the size of a half dollar had already developed. It hurt to look at it, so I didn't bother trying to touch it.

I ran a brush through my hair, and brushed my teeth, and, feeling somewhat normal, I ventured out into the world.

The bus was empty, so I assumed Bozeman was outside, and when I stepped down the stairs, I found him waiting for me.

"Sleep well?" Bozeman asked as he put the magazine he was holding down in his lap.

"I did. It must have been the painkillers they gave me at the hospital."

"Hungry? I could make you some eggs," he said.

Bozeman reminded me of my mother that way. They both carried the superstition that food would cure any ailment, hurt feelings, unpleasant experiences, or any general malaise.

"Not really. I could go for one of those, though." I pointed to the bucket of small orange juice bottles Bozeman had near his chair. He passed me a bottle. I opened it and drank. It tasted delicious.

"How's your shoulder? Is it going to be okay?"

I knew Bozeman was concerned, but I also guessed he was hinting around to see if I could play our next gig on Saturday night, which, by my count, was only three days away.

"It should be. I've got a nasty bruise, and it's a little stiff, but I should be ready to go."

"If you're not up to it, we could get a session player to stand in for you. I have a few guitarists in mind who could fill in."

That was the beauty of being me. Although I considered myself a talented songwriter, and of course, a great singer, Bozeman was the lead guitarist, and I mostly only played the rhythm. We could hire just about anyone to do that. Especially for the more traditional country songs we typically had on our set list. Those were usually simple three or four chord progression numbers with not much complication. And many of them were well-known country standards that any guitarist worth their weight already knew.

"Let's see how I feel tomorrow. I should be able to know for sure if I can play," I said.

Bozeman picked up his magazine and found the page he was on. "Fair enough."

I took another drink of orange juice, then looked at the sky. It had the makings of another beautiful day. The sun was bright; the sky was a light blue, and I tracked but a single cloud as it raced across the troposphere. I closed my eyes and felt the sun's warmth on my face.

"You have a visitor coming," Bozeman announced.

I opened my eyes and turned my head, and saw Sam walking across the parking lot carrying something covered by a towel. When she got to us, she handed the item to Bozeman.

"Hey there," she said to me.

"Hey yourself." I got to my feet, and we hugged. My shoulder was tender and throbbed during the embrace, but I still didn't want to let go, and apparently Sam didn't want to let go either. Finally, we separated.

"I was over earlier, but Bozeman told me you were still sleeping."

I turned to Bozeman. "You didn't tell me she was here."

He shrugged. "I forgot."

"I assumed you might be hungry." Sam lifted the towel and exposed the four blueberry muffins on a plate.

My mouth watered like one of Pavlov's dogs, and I reached for one.

"You told me you weren't hungry," Bozeman said as he pulled the plate away.

"That was before. This is now."

Bozeman brought the plate forward, and I took the muffin. I held it beneath my nose and inhaled. Oh, that smell!

"Here, Sam, take my seat." Bozeman set the plate on a bus step and selected a muffin for himself. "I'll go see what the kids are up to."

Sam grabbed a muffin from the plate and handed it to Bozeman. "Here, they can have one too. There are plenty more where these came from."

Bozeman took the muffin and sauntered off to give the animals a treat.

Sam and I hugged again, and then we both sat.

"When did you get out of the pokey?" I asked.

"Last night around ten. I was just in there reading a book, and the next thing I knew the cell door opened, and in walked Shanna in an orange jumpsuit. They brought her in and took me out."

"I would've loved to see the look on your face."

"Me too. Come on. Shanna? I never would have guessed it was her."

With great anticipation, I peeled the paper from the muffin's bottom and broke off a chunk. I liked to eat the bottom first and save the crown for last. I was weird that way.

"Me either."

"Is it true she tried to kill you?" Sam asked.

I nodded as I popped a piece into my mouth and chewed. My eyes rolled as I savored the bite and then swallowed. "Yes. She probably would have too if I used real ammunition. She hurt Chief Jennings really badly though. Have you heard how he's doing?"

"No."

"Did you know they are siblings?" I asked.

"No. Neither one ever mentioned it to me. I can't imagine why."

I shrugged, ate another part of the muffin, and drank some juice.

"Listen, I had to come over and thank you for everything you've done for me. I wouldn't be free if it wasn't for you," Sam said. She didn't have to say a word. Her expression told me all I needed.

I smiled. "Anytime."

We sat for a moment in silence, staring at each other.

Sam leaned forward. "You didn't mean that, did you?"

I laughed. "Actually, no. I don't enjoy getting shot."

Sam smiled. "I don't blame you." Sam stood. "Listen, I need to go. The bakery's still a mess, and I need to get that cleaned up. And I have a million orders to fill."

"You need any help?" I asked.

"From you, no. One other thing, Lisa's having a small get together later at the diner. Starts at seven. Make sure you and that hunk are there, okay?"

"We'll be there."

I sat back in the chair and finished my muffin and looked forward to a lazy day.

At seven on the dot, Bozeman and I walked through the diner's door. They had rearranged the room a bit, and pushed several tables together in the center of the room to form one big seating area. Around the table were most of the people I'd interacted with over the previous days. Sam, Dean, Reba, and Pastor Tom were all in attendance. As we approached and said our hellos, Rob and Lisa appeared from the kitchen carrying dishes of food they placed on the table to serve family style. Bozeman and I found our seats, and Pastor Tom started the meal off with a quick prayer.

When the blessing was over, I looked around the table at the food. There was a platter holding a mountain of fried chicken. There were big bowls filled with mashed potatoes, buttered corn, and green beans with slivered almonds. Of course, there was not one, but two baskets of fresh-baked dinner rolls.

A server appeared and took our drink orders. Bozeman asked for a beer. I asked for lemonade. Soon, plates we passed around the table and filled them, and the sound of small talk and clinking silverware filled the air.

Everyone stopped eating and looked up when the door opened, and Deputy Samuels entered.

Rob stood and held out his hand for Samuels to shake. "Deputy, please, join us. There's plenty of food."

Samuels shook his head. "Unfortunately, I can't. I'm on duty. I'm in charge while Chief Jennings takes some time to mend."

"How's he doing?" I asked,

"He's good. The worst he got was the concussion, so they're keeping him under observation for another day or two for that. Otherwise, they patched up the shoulder pretty good."

"What about his ribs? Broken?"

Samuels shook his head. "No. Only bruised. Good thing you had non-lethal rounds in that gun. Oh, that reminds me, the chief wanted me to give this to you." Samuels reached into his coat and handed me an evidence bag. Betty was inside.

"I didn't expect I'd ever see this again. I assumed you'd need it for the trial."

"It's unnecessary. We've already got Shanna on two counts of murder. The chief's not bothering with the added assault charge. He also asked me to give you a message. Asked me to write it down even so I wouldn't get it wrong."

We all waited while Samuels extracted a piece of paper from his shirt pocket. He unfolded it, cleared his throat, and read directly from the paper. "Codi, please accept my gratitude. I'm in your debt. If I could ask you for one more favor, please leave my town as soon as you can."

I protested. "That's not what it says!"

Samuels handed me the paper, and I read it. He had read it word for word from the sheet.

"Son of a gun," I said.

Everyone at the table laughed at the joke at my expense, including Bozeman.

"By the way, the chief also wanted me to tell you that he turned all the evidence you had against Shanna to me, since I'll be doing the investigation. He didn't want anyone to expect he couldn't be impartial since his sister is the accused."

I smiled. "Thank him for me. That means a lot."

A squawk came from Samuels' radio. He answered the call, excused himself, and rushed from the room.

The meal continued on, and as the servers cleared the table from dinner, Dean stood and clinked a fork against his glass to get our attention.

"Hey, everyone. I just wanted to make a toast to Sam and welcome her back." He waited as the rest of us applauded but didn't take his seat. He looked uncomfortable, but he spoke again. "I'd also like to apologize to everyone here. I've been going through some… things, and it's been a personal struggle for me. Because of that, I haven't been on my best behavior, and I've been a rotten friend to all of you. I'm sorry. Sam, I've been especially hard on you, and I would accept being your friend, even if you never want nothing more than that."

Sam smiled, then stood and gave Dean a hug. "We'll always be friends, Dean. All of us here will always be friends."

Rob interrupted. "Not friends, family."

Everyone applauded again as Dean and Sam sat.

I leaned over to Bozeman. "I wonder what's for dessert."

Lisa overheard my question. "We'll serve dessert shortly. Give it a little time. Let your dinner settle."

I looked across the table at Reba. She winked at me, then produced a bottle of white wine, filled her water glass, and an instant later, the bottle disappeared again. She was quite the magician, and amazingly, I don't think anyone else at the table noticed, and if they did, they ignored it.

Reba took a swig of wine and looked me in the eye. "I knew all about them."

"Who?" I asked.

"That Sherman Stier and Shanna. I had a suspicion they were involved with each other. I have a lot of secrets that I know about a lot of people."

Pastor Tom put a finger to his lips to shush Reba. "Reba, dear, we've talked about this. The Lord doesn't like idle gossip."

Reba dismissed him with a wave of her hand. "Pfft. This isn't idle gossip, Pastor, this is active gossip. There's a big difference."

The pastor looked taken aback, and I could tell Bozeman was on the verge of laughter, so I elbowed him in the ribs to squelch it.

Reba took a drink, then continued. "They thought they were being sly, but I always have my ear to the ground, always. I learned they met up in Taos, where Sherman is from. Shanna met him at some bar up there, and he got smitten with her pretty looks and whatnot. Next thing you please, they were living together. I guessed right away that wouldn't work out. Shanna's too possessive, and Sherman is… was too much in love with money to be fully in love with her. That's why she moved back here."

Dean turned to Sam. "Did you know any of this?"

Sam shook her head no and was about to answer when Reba spoke up.

"Don't interrupt. I'm telling the story. Anyway, when he showed up in Quincey, Shanna assumed, incorrectly, that Sherman was interested in her. What he was really interested in was growing his fortune. Sure, they casually saw each other a few times, but he wanted nothing more from her."

"Bah, that's probably just a rumor," Rob said.

Reba pointed a finger at him. "Rumor my butt. Why, they came and stayed at my place one night. Shanna booked it with all the fancy sides I have. Wine, cheese, flowers, bubble bath, the works. I think that was her attempt to woo him back."

I leaned over and whispered to Bozeman. "Do people really woo? I thought that was just in the movies."

He shrugged.

Reba continued. "And although he had carnal relations with her that night, he didn't want her for forever, so she got furious at him." Reba took another drink and settled back in her seat, the story over.

"Love and money, the two biggest motives for murder," I said. "Pastor Tom, was that the big secret that Sherman came to you with? That he had that lurid affair with Shanna?"

I put the pastor on the spot. He tugged at his shirt collar and glanced around the table, only to notice that every pair of eyes focused on him. "I can't say, of course, I can't break the rules of confession. That would go against doctrine. I'm surprised you would even ask me that."

"My apologies, Pastor Tom."

Pastor Tom noticed he wasn't the center of attention anymore and threw me a quick wink. I smiled back at him.

"Anyone hear why Mayor Mary didn't show up tonight? Was she not invited?" Sam asked.

Lisa brushed away some crumbs on the tablecloth before her. "I invited her. I called her myself. She asked who else would be here, and the second I got to Dean's name, she politely declined the invitation, then rudely hung up on me without another word said."

It was Dean's turn to be the center of attention. "Well, what a few of you may not have heard is that our good mayor did some… inappropriate things on behalf of the town when dealing with the resort. Since those things have come to the surface, I think she's having second thoughts about being mayor."

I was curious, so I asked. "Are you still going to run for the job, Dean?"

Dean looked at me. "Yes. I still believe I can make a difference in Quincey."

"What about the future of the resort?" I asked.

"Well, from what I understand, Sherman was only the point person on that project, so whoever steps in to fill his position will probably carry it through. Although Stier, and to some extent, the mayor, went about things the wrong way, I think we all agree here that the resort would be a boon to this community. If, I mean when, I'm elected, I'll work with whoever's on that board to make sure that we meet the town's interests before those of the resort."

Rob raised his glass. "Here, here."

I glanced across the table at Sam. "Speaking of filling positions, I imagine you'll need someone new at the bakery."

"Why, Codi Cassidy, are you saying you'd like to give up that life as a country star to settle down and become a baker?"

I shook my head immediately. "No way. I wouldn't do it even if you paid me with blueberry muffins. That's a hard pass."

Lisa dropped her napkin on the table and stood up. "Actually, I might help you out there." She went through the swinging door into the kitchen and returned a few minutes later, dragging a young woman by the arm.

"This is Heather. She's my niece and she's come to stay with us for a few months. She's a hard worker, no, an excellent worker, and I think she'd be a great fit for your bakery."

Rob put a hand to his face so fast, he inadvertently slapped himself.

Sam noticed, along with the rest of us. "Do you have something to add, Rob?"

Rob shook his head, but Heather stepped forward. "Well, Rob's a nice man, and what he won't tell you is that I'm a walking disaster. I take orders wrong, I'm clumsy, and I spilled an entire bowl of soup on someone's lap yesterday."

Reba perked up at that news. "Who was it?"

Rob's face turned a shade of red. "Paul Peterson."

Reba laughed so hard her laughs turned to coughs, and when she took a swig of wine, it must have gone down the wrong pipe because she coughed even harder. I thought she might have a coronary, but she took a few sips of actual water and calmed down. "I can just see it, that pompous Paul Peterson with a lap full of... what type of soup was it?"

Heather glanced at the ceiling. "Tomato bisque."

Reba chuckled. "That's perfect."

Lisa broke in. "Oh, come on, dear, give yourself more credit. You're polite, and you're a quick learner. Maybe you're just not made to work in a diner. Not everyone is. Sam, what do you think?"

Sam looked Heather up and down. "Do you have any cooking experience?"

Heather shook her head.

"Have you taken any classes? Ever baked anything outside of a batch of brownies at home?" Sam asked.

Again, Heather motioned to the negative.

Sam paused, and we were all silent, waiting for the response. In the end, Sam smiled. "You know, I'm a sucker for hard-luck cases. Be at the bakery at six tomorrow morning, and we'll get started, okay?"

***

The next morning, I stepped off the bus at just after seven with bowls of food for the kids when I saw Sam walking across the lot, wearing her white apron and a wide grin. She was carrying a large box, and I hoped it was full of blueberry muffins.

"Here's a treat for the road. Thanks again for everything."

I called for Bozeman, and when he stuck his head out, I handed him the box. I nodded toward the bakery. "Did Heather show up at six?"

"No. She showed up fifteen minutes early. From what I've seen so far, it'll take her a bit to get going, but I think I can turn her into a baker."

We hugged.

"I'm going to miss you. The town will be quiet and boring without you here," Sam said.

"And I'm sure that's the way y'all will prefer it. Nice and quiet."

A tear formed in Sam's eye. "I owe you so much, you know."

I waved it off. "No, you don't. You carry no debt with me."

"When are you leaving?"

"Another hour. I need to feed Merle and Dolly, and Bozeman likes to give the bus a once over before we travel."

"Where are you headed next?"

"California."

"I hear there's gold there."

I shrugged. "We'll see."

I thought Sam was going to hug me again, but she didn't. She kissed my cheek, turned, and walked back to the bakery. I felt happy for her, and I was proud of her for showing such strength over the last few days. Someday, I hope to be strong like her.

I got back to work. I fed Merle, Dolly, Waylon, and Willie, then I cleaned out Dolly's stash for the day. It must have been rough scavenging because all she had under her blanket was a single shiny paper clip. I gave everyone some scratches, and ensured everyone was ready to travel, and then I double checked the area around the bus to make sure we would leave no trace.

Bozeman was ready to go when I buckled myself into the passenger seat.

"Ready?" he asked as he turned the key in the ignition.

I nodded. "Let's go. Time for our next adventure."

Ballads
and
Bloodshed

CHAPTER ONE

I caught my reflection in the side mirror of the bus as we rolled down the highway, and my small, elfin face looked back at me. The window was partially open, so the passing wind threw my hair in various directions, making me look like a modern-day Medusa. I undid the hair band I hadn't taken the time to put on correctly in the first place, closed the window, corralled my unruly locks, and slipped the band over my head.

I looked over at the driver, who appeared, to my delight, to be keeping his eyes on the road. "Do you think I need a color change?"

Bozeman James glanced over long enough to make it appear he was looking at me. He shrugged his shoulders, which signified his typical response since he didn't talk much. Occasionally, when he had too much to drink, he would ramble on for an hour or more, but those moments were few and far between.

"What do you think?" he asked, returning his attention to the highway.

Another Bozeman trait, passing the question right back to me, and he should have, since I was going to do what I wanted to do, anyway. I checked my locks in the mirror again and paid close attention to where my hair reached the scalp. The first little bits of gray and white peeked through. I could go another week or two, and afterwards I'd have to change, but until that time, I remained happy with the current color, which was a light, almost ice blue. Thanks to poor genetics, I started going gray in my mid-twenties. Since no one wants to see a young country singer with gray hair, I keep it dyed, and usually I go for different colors when I do so, simply to mix it up. Other than the dyed hair, I'm your sweet, run-of-the-mill traveling musician and cowgirl poet.

"I think I'll give it a couple weeks and I'll switch it out to something else. Perhaps a shade of green next time or pink. Perhaps orange."

Bozeman grunted. "You hated orange the last time you tried it."

"Did I?" I wasn't being coy. I honestly didn't remember. I'd have to check the book. Each time I did my hair, I made a brief note in a notebook to describe the specific color and whether I liked the result. Ah, well, that remained a debate for another day.

"Have we ever been to Sunny Station before?" I couldn't remember. Since Bozeman drove the bus, he had a better idea of where we'd been in the past, since he had to pay attention to the road. I, the owner of the shotgun seat, spent my time napping, reading, or looking out the window as we traveled the country's highways and byways from gig to gig.

"No, we haven't," he said.

Sunny Station was a small town nestled south of the San Bernardino National Forest, east of Los Angeles, west of Palm Springs.

"Why is your friend having the release party there instead of L.A.?" I asked.

"He's from there. He titled his new album *Going Home Again*, or something like that, so he thought it would be a good gimmick to have the first release party there. I think the studio's giving him another one in the city in a few days, but he put this one together for his family and friends to get a preview of the album."

"Nice of him to invite us to play," I said.

Bozeman nodded. "Yeah, it's gracious of him. We're only the opening act though, so we'll only get to play for a half hour or forty-five minutes."

I smiled. "That's long enough." I knew it took little effort to get new fans if you had a great sound and presented yourself in an open and fun manner. Even a couple of songs generated enough interest for some people to buy CDs or other merchandise or sign up for our social media sites. It always made me happy to expand our fan base, and even as something as simple as being an opening act would accomplish that.

I knew we weren't getting paid a fortune for this gig. In fact, we'd barely make enough to break even considering the cost of gas and how much it took to feed the bus, but that was okay, because I loved to play.

I got that love of music from my mom, who worked as a traveling musician herself until she met my dad and settled down in Denver with him. She taught me how to play piano, and later, guitar. Mom taught me all about music theory and all the technical stuff that goes into it that no casual listener ever thinks about. She taught me about songwriting, and how a country song, especially, was really about telling a story that condensed down to three minutes. It was tough work, but I loved it, even as a kid, and when I was little, I used to dream about being a country star someday.

I remembered my first songs I played for a room full of other kids in my middle school talent show. I dressed up like Dale Evans, in a white cowgirl outfit. Complete with the strips of leather fringe dangling from the arms and legs, white boots, and a white cowgirl hat to match. Mom bejeweled the outfit with rhinestones, of course. We even decked out my guitar, with my name, Codi Lynn Cassidy, written on the body. I had a little stage fright at first, but when I saw my mom and dad out there in the audience, I got even more nervous.

Then I played my first chord.

My mom had told me that once you strum the guitar, the muscle memory takes over and the nerves go away. But of course, I didn't believe her. She was right, though, and all my stress melted away with the first chord I struck. My set comprised two Dolly Parton numbers, and I won third place. You would think they'd just inducted me into the Country Music Hall of Fame with the praise I got from both my parents.

As time passed, I adopted more of a traditional cowgirl look. I dropped the rhinestones and sequins for blue jeans and non-frilly shirts. The cowgirl boots and hat stayed a part of my stage persona, but when I'm not performing, I like to go with a pair of comfortable sneakers and a baseball cap. Oh, and I dropped the 'Lynn' from my stage name, and now I only go by Codi Cassidy because I'm a sucker for alliteration.

"You know if he wants covers, or can we do original

material?" I asked.

Although Bozeman offered some input, I usually came up with the set list, and I normally liked to have it figured out at least a day or two before the show.

"Usual set is fine," he said.

The usual set meant we would go on the heavy side with our original materials, with a couple of covers thrown in. Typically, I did a Willie Nelson tune, but we stayed versatile enough to do about anything, including a couple of pop-rock numbers if we needed to. When I added the covers to the plan, I usually put two or three numbers in the slot, so we decided on stage what to sing. It all depended on the audience, really. If it skewed older, I'd break out some Reba McEntire, or Tanya Tucker. If it tended to be a younger crowd, Carrie Underwood or Taylor Swift. Sometimes, if Bozeman was in the mood, he'd pick a number for himself and would sing anything from Elvis to Garth Brooks. In the end, it was all about having fun, and if Bozeman and I had a good time, that usually caught on like wildfire with the audience, and they would have a great time, too. The usual set worked great for me, since it took little work for me to pull it together.

"When are we going to be there?" I asked.

Bozeman grunted his usual response when I asked that question. Okay, I asked it more to annoy him than anything. From where I sat, I could easily see the GPS, and according to that, we were almost where we needed to be, which was a county park about a mile or so outside of town.

"Are you going be able to play tomorrow night?" he asked as he checked all the side mirrors for cars in his blind spot.

In response, I rotated my shoulder and stretched out both my arms. I still had a sore arm where I had taken a bullet less than a week before, but I wasn't stiff anymore, and I felt good. "Sure thing. Don't you worry about me."

Bozeman grunted again. That one translated into 'he didn't believe me'.

"After we're parked, I'll play a few songs for you. If you're not satisfied with my performance, we can call in a session guitarist, okay? Deal?"

Bozeman nodded. "Deal. Hold on."

We had arrived at the park, so Bozeman turned the wheel and the bus followed. The park had a gravel road with a myriad of potholes that Bozeman navigated around like a downhill slalom skier at the Olympics. The front wheel on my side dipped into and out of a hole, and I bounced in my seat. I caught the sly smile on Bozeman's face once I settled back into my spot.

Bozeman followed the road past a baseball diamond to the parking area. There were two sizeable areas marked off, and each had a sign next to it. Bozeman did a wide arc, so we'd be facing out and parked the bus next to the sign that had his name stenciled on it. He turned off the ignition and exhaled. The ride from New Mexico had taken only ten hours, including a couple of stops along the way, but I could tell Bozeman seemed tired. He often reminded me that being behind the wheel of a thirty-foot tour bus wasn't quite the same as driving the family sedan. I had to take his word for it, since he didn't allow me to drive the bus. At four-foot-ten and with a skinny physique, I couldn't easily handle the beast. Although I was good for a quick jaunt, I certainly couldn't handle it across the interstates of America. Besides, I never judged the turns around corners quite right, and often drove over curbs, which, for some odd reason, made Bozeman really nervous.

It was mid-afternoon, and a warm, blue-skied day when I stepped off the bus. I walked in circles for a bit, then did some stretches to get the kinks out of my lower back.

Bozeman stepped off the bus and walked past me.

"Where are you going?" I asked.

Bozeman didn't answer, just pointed ahead of him and kept walking. Ah, the park had bathroom facilities, which were nice. Although we had such amenities on the bus, Bozeman hated emptying the black water tanks with a passion, so we used alternate options whenever we could.

When I heard the gig was at a park, I didn't quite know what to expect. Some parks we've played were really nice, complete with permanent structures and food vendors. Other parks were nothing more than a mowed patch of grass with not so much as a shade tree to camp under. This park was on the nicer side. Beyond the restrooms Bozeman was making a beeline for was what looked to be an Olympic-sized swimming pool. That made me hope the restroom included a shower of some sort. About a hundred yards south of the pool, there was a small amphitheater, complete with a covered stage, and I assumed that was where the concert would take place. Overall, the venue pleased me.

I got back on the bus and walked to my room, which was at the rear of the bus. It was past the small kitchen/living area combo, Bozeman's bedroom, the phone booth-sized bathroom, and the room we used to store our gear. On my bed was a small pile of pillows. I usually stacked them with care, but they must have succumbed to the jostle of the potholes because two out of four of them were on the floor. My tuxedo cat, Gibson, seemed unfazed and was in the middle of the bed giving himself a bath when I entered. He spotted me, gave out a half-meow, and returned to work on his tail. I saw he was fine, so I gave him a couple of pets, then let him be.

Outside the bus, I opened the under-bus storage compartment where Merle and Dolly lived. They were both asleep, and it didn't surprise me since, as a skunk and a raccoon, respectively, they were both more active during the nighttime hours. They both slept on old blankets, and I ran a hand beneath Dolly's blanket to see what treasures she had.

Dolly was a three-legged raccoon and loved to bring shiny or interesting things home when she was out gallivanting at night. Every day, I checked her stash and removed anything that could be a danger to either her or her roommate. When I opened my hand, I found a penny and a half-dozen colorful rocks. The penny I kept for the change jar, the rocks I put back where I found them. I don't understand why Dolly has an attraction to rocks, but she always picks up a few every day. When she had too many beneath her blanket, I picked through them and kept the most colorful ones, and the rest I tossed back into the parking lot.

Merle didn't collect stuff except lots of hugs and kisses because he loved being the center of attention. Usually he'd appear around dinner time, would spend the night doing whatever he did, hang out with us during breakfast, then head to bed for the day.

Both of their food dishes were empty, so I removed those, unhooked their mostly empty water bottle, then left them to their dreams.

They were good, so I moved to the rear of the bus to check on my other two friends. Waylon and Willie were a pair of chipmunks who had made a nest in a smaller compartment where a hole had rusted through the compartment door. As I got closer, I could hear them chittering, and they were excited to see me. I pushed aside a bit of chicken wire we used to close the hole when we were in motion and said hello. Usually, chipmunks lived in nests made of leaves, twigs, bark, grass, and sometimes garbage. But Waylon and Willie had top-tier accommodations and lived in nests composed of a holey T-shirt and a pair of socks that Bozeman donated to them.

I held my hand flat, and Willie jumped into my palm and sat still. Once I gave him a scratch between the ears, he jumped to the ground and ran off. Waylon followed, and while they skittered away, I collected their little food and water dishes. I then removed and shook out their bedding and put everything back as I found it.

I took all the bowls to the kitchen and washed and dried them. The water bottle I rinsed out and refilled with a jug of water from the fridge. I was just about ready to give them some food when Bozeman returned.

"Please tell me there's a shower available over there," I said.

"A nice big one. I'm headed back for one right now." Bozeman disappeared into his room. A few minutes later, he came out with a small canvas bag filled with a fresh change of clothes and the sundry items he'd need for a shower.

"I'll head that way too once I'm done feeding the kids. You got your keys?"

"Yeah," Bozeman said as he stepped back off the bus.

I opened the fridge and found some leafy greens for Merle and Dolly to share. For Merle, I picked out a few cherry tomatoes, which were his favorite, and for Dolly, I unpeeled a banana and sliced it into small pieces. The chipmunks got a treat of a handful of trail mix. Before I put it in the bowl, I painstakingly removed the chocolate pieces from it because I was greedy and liked to save those for myself. I was feeling extra-generous and added a small cracker with a dab of peanut butter on it to the mix. They'd be living high on the hog when they got back to the nest.

Merle had half an eye open and watched me as I set out the food and replaced their water bottle. He was still groggy, so he barely moved when I scratched him on the nose between his eyes. Usually, he enjoyed having his belly scratched, but he didn't seem to have enough energy to roll over. I knew how that was. I didn't like to get up sometimes either.

Once my chores were complete, I did just as Bozeman had done and collected everything I needed for the shower. For ease, I slipped out of my jeans and into a pair of sweatpants, and I traded in my socks and sneakers for a pair of flip-flops, then trundled off to the bathhouse. The shower facilities were even nicer than I'd expected. There were a dozen lockers to keep things in, and four individual shower stalls. The one I picked seemed to be almost new. The stainless-steel fixtures gleamed, the tile was immaculate, and although I'd leave on my flip-flops, the floor looked clean. I turned on the water, then stepped out into the main locker area to undress, then grabbed my soap, shampoo, conditioner, and towel, and returned to the shower.

To me, there was nothing better than stepping into a nice, steamy shower. Since we spent so much time on the road, we used our on-bus shower sparingly and didn't dawdle when we did. In here, I could take my sweet time, and could even rinse and repeat, just like the instructions on the shampoo bottle suggested.

I didn't time myself, but I stayed in there long enough to wash the road grunge from my body and sing an entire album's worth of tunes. Although my fingers looked like prunes, I wanted to stay in there even longer. I knew I couldn't, so with a frown and a pout I shut off the water, dried myself off, wrapped the towel tightly around me, and went into the locker room. I was the only one in there, so I took my time getting dressed and then brushing out my hair. As I did so, I looked at myself in the mirror.

"Purple next time. A nice deep purple," I said to my reflection.

My transformation was complete, and I felt relaxed, clean, and ready to take on the world. I looked around to make sure I had everything with me, then walked back to the bus.

Bozeman was already there and had been so for a while. He had set out our favorite lawn chairs next to the bus, and between them was a small cooler. He had a beer in his hand and was reading through a tattered copy of an old Louis L'Amour western. I noticed my guitar was laying across my chair, which was a giant hint that Bozeman expected me to keep my word about playing for him. He watched as I set my shower bag on the bus steps and took up the guitar. I slung the strap over my head, checked the tuning, and broke into a small set of about half the songs I'd already sung in the shower just a few minutes earlier. I thought I sounded pretty good, considering I hadn't played for almost a week.

When I finished, Bozeman nodded at me, then went back to his book. I took my guitar, picked up my shower bag, and headed to my room to stow everything where it belonged. I would've loved to leave things out and deal with them later, but I found that living in such a small space really didn't lend itself to being too much of a slob.

Once I finished, I rejoined Bozeman outside, and he handed me a bottle of lemonade from the cooler. Which I gratefully accepted. I opened the lemonade and had a drink. It wasn't as good as homemade, but it was good enough to be refreshing.

"Are you worried about tomorrow?" I asked.

Bozeman glanced at me over his book, then set it in his lap. "Why would I be?"

"It's got to be a little nerve-wracking for you. Having your friend get picked up by a big label with his career seemingly on the upswing. Yet you and I drive around in this old bus playing in venues just large enough to hold a large bingo tournament."

Bozeman rocked back in his chair and took a swig of his beer. "Not really. I lived that lifestyle for a long time, back before we even met, and I actually prefer what we have. We don't have to worry about promoters or agents or managers. We have control over our lives that he won't have. We play the gigs we want to play, cut albums when we want to, write music when we want to, take a break when we need to. The problem with being a star is you don't have control over anything, from what you eat to how you dress. No, I'm not jealous at all. If anything, I'm sure in a couple of years, Toby will be jealous of me."

"Yeah, but he'll probably be rolling in dough."

Bozeman shrugged. "Maybe. Maybe not. All depends on how ethical the people around him are. You've heard plenty of stories of musicians and actors bilked out of their hard-earned money because of terrible managers or dirty deals, right? There's no way to tell. So, I'm good here. Besides, we seem to be doing just fine."

I nodded in agreement and let it drop. "Any idea on when your friend will be here?"

Bozeman finished his beer, then pulled another from the cooler. "I'd say in about ninety seconds."

I turned and glanced at the road, and headed in our direction was a tour bus that made the same arc Bozeman did and pulled into the spot right next to ours. It was my turn to feel embarrassed. I had bought our old bus from an old musician friend of my mom's. It was a good thirty years old and showed its age sitting next to the shiny new model that pulled up beside us.

It was time for the event to begin.

CHAPTER TWO

The bus rocked a bit after the engine shut down, so I guessed there were more people on it than just two. Five minutes later, the door opened and a tall man with pale skin and shoulder-length dark hair rushed out. He glanced at us and turned and jogged to the restroom.

"Is that your friend? He's kind of rude," I said.

"No, that's not Toby. I have no clue who that is. Here he comes now."

Bozeman stood and watched as the next man from the bus approached. Bozeman offered his hand to shake, but the man took Bozeman into a bear hug and laughed. "Jesse James, it's so good to see you. Man, it's been forever."

The man let Bozeman go and turned his attention to me. "You must be Codi Cassidy." He smiled after he spoke and held out his hand. I offered mine, but rather than a real handshake, he lightly grabbed my fingertips for a second, then released his grip in a hurry. "I'm Toby Madden. It's so nice to meet you. I've heard great things about you."

I smiled back at him. He wasn't a bad-looking man. He was roughly six feet tall, only a couple inches shorter than Bozeman, and he had light brown hair that had a slight curl, and deep blue eyes. Beneath his shirt, I noticed he had a bit of a beer belly starting, but I imagined he'd work that off pretty fast once he got on tour. "Thank you. And thanks for inviting us to open up for you. It's a real honor."

"Jesse tells me —"

Bozeman interrupted. "Bozeman."

Toby turned around and faced his friend. "Huh?"

"Bozeman. I've told you that like a hundred times. I haven't gone by 'Jesse' in twenty years."

"Why not? Jesse James is a cool name."

"It got old when every person I met either made a stupid crack about me robbing a train, or put their hands in the air, expecting me to take their wallet. Honestly, I don't know what my parents were thinking when they named me that. Since I'm from Montana, most people started calling me Bozeman anyway, so the name stuck."

Toby looked at me. "So, Codi, my guess is that you're from Wyoming?"

I shook my head. "Close. I'm originally from Denver. My parents named me after my mom's favorite aunt."

Toby didn't know what to do with that information, so he smiled for a moment. I saw a bit of relief pass over his face when he noticed a couple of women get off the bus.

"Hey, meet some of the band," he said to us and turned and yelled for the women. "Girls, come over here and meet these folks."

As they approached, I could tell they certainly weren't girls, which was a term that pricked at my brain like an ice cube on an exposed tooth cavity.

"Meet Frannie Love, she plays bass."

The first woman stepped forward and extended her hand. She was, in a word, gorgeous. She was as tall as Toby, had beautiful, tanned skin, mid-length wavy blond hair, and emerald green eyes. I suspected Bozeman was already in love and was currently visualizing his happily ever after with her.

"It's Fran. I'm pleased to know you."

The second woman took my hand without waiting for an introduction. "I'm Laurel Preston. I play the fiddle and sing background vocals."

Laurel was a little more my size. She looked to be about five foot two, had a head of curly red hair, and small gray eyes. Her hand was warm, although somewhat sweaty in mine, and she lingered for a moment longer than was the norm.

I let go of her hand, and as I stood, I discreetly wiped my hand on my jeans. "It's good to meet both of you. I'd love to have a bassist and a fiddler in my band. Why don't you come over and join me? I'll trade the two of you for Bozeman, and we could be the next great all-female trio."

The group laughed, then out of the blue, Laurel winked at me. "I'd be all for that," she whispered, which generated another round of laughter.

The man who ran for the restrooms strolled back and joined the group. Of all of them, he looked the most out of place. He stood about five-ten, had pale skin, long hair that I could tell was dyed black, and dark brown eyes. I pegged him at being in his mid-twenties, a good ten years behind everyone else. He dressed head to toe in black but looked nothing like a Johnny Cash lover.

Toby motioned toward the man. "Here's the newest edition to our group. Gabe Galvin. He's my new drummer."

"Nice to meet you." I stuck out my hand, but Gabe simply looked at it like he'd never seen one before. I let my arm fall back to my side. Without a word, Gabe left and got back on the bus.

"Sorry about that. Gabe's having trouble transitioning into our band. He used to play with a death metal group out of L.A., but he was looking for a change, and my agent asked me to bring him on as a favor. My previous drummer called it quits on me, so I needed one in a hurry and said yes."

I doubted that was the case, but since it wasn't my band, it wasn't my business, either.

Toby looked around the area. "That's all my people. Where are yours?"

I sat back down in the chair. I never liked to just stand around and talk. It always felt awkward to me. "Don't have anyone else. It's just the two of us."

Fran looked confused, so I explained. "I have backing tracks for everything else on the computer. Drums, piano, bass, whatever we need."

Laurel frowned. "It's not the same."

"I know, but we're a small-time operation, and it works for us, and to some extent, gives us more flexibility. Although, I'm thinking of adding a fiddle player." I threw Laurel an exaggerated wink.

Laurel giggled and grabbed Fran's arm. "Come on, I need to

go use the facilities. See y'all later." Laurel and Fran turned and headed toward the restrooms.

I watched as the women literally skipped away, and the image changed when a short, rotund man stepped into view. Unlike the rest of us, he dressed in tan slacks rather than blue jeans, and a button-down dress shirt rather than the casual T-shirts everyone else wore. He came forward and presented Bozeman with his business card. Bozeman glanced at it without really reading it, then shoved it between the pages of his book. I knew it was bad business card etiquette, and I hoped it wouldn't offend the man, even though he offended me by ignoring me completely.

"Cody Cassidy, I presume," the man said to Bozeman.

"No. Over here. I'm Codi Cassidy. With an I, not a Y, like what's written on the bus you're standing next to."

The man glanced at me, swiveled his head to read the side of the bus, then settled his eyes back on me. His cheeks were reddening, which meant I had embarrassed him, which I didn't mind since he was the one with the bad assumptions to begin with.

"My apologies, Ms. Cassidy." He started over and handed me a business card, which I shoved right into my back pocket without reading.

"Please. Call me Codi."

"Codi. Fine. Thank you. My name is Russell Davidson. I'm Toby's manager and promoter."

I glanced at Toby. He caught my gaze and rolled his eyes in return. "I'll bet you are."

Russell did his best to recover, stood straighter, and donned the smile of a businessperson looking to make a deal. "May I ask who your representation is, and if you're happy with their services?"

Behind Russell, I saw Toby's chin drop to his chest. He shook his head and took several steps backward to exclude himself from the conversation.

I grinned at Russell. I could play the game too. "Tell me, Russell, how much do you charge?"

"Twenty-three percent."

I exhaled. "You must be good. I thought the typical ceiling

was only twenty percent."

Russell subconsciously fiddled with one of his shirt's buttons. "Yes, I believe in going well above and beyond in my service."

"What's your contract length?" I asked.

"Three years," he said without pause.

At that, I sent up an eyebrow. "Twenty-three percent for three years? What if I don't make any money over that time?"

"Well, I take my percentage off the top, of course."

I looked over and saw Bozeman glaring at me so hard it would give me a headache if I kept up the eye contact, so I broke away.

"And what would I get for your services?"

"I'd line up performances, take care of advertising, social media, accounting, taxes, all that sort of thing. Of course, I handle all the business operations, so you're free to concentrate on your performances."

"I see. To answer your original question, we're represented by CB Management, dis-incorporated."

Russell shook his head. "I've never heard of them."

I grinned. "You just met them. I'm the C of CB, and Bozeman over there is the other half of the outfit, and yes, I'm happy with our services."

Russell glanced over at Bozeman, who returned his acknowledgment with a tip of his beer bottle.

Russell looked back at me. "Surely you can't do all that work yourself. You're only a… musician."

I stood, wondering what the word was he originally wanted to use, and felt pretty confident that it was *woman*. I took a step toward him, and although I was a good four inches shorter and a hundred-plus pounds lighter than he was, he yielded the ground to me and stepped back.

"Only a musician? Do you mean I can write songs and learn melodies, but somehow, I'm too stupid to run a business? For your information, I do the bookings, and we have gigs for forty-eight weeks a year. I do the promotion, I run the social media." I threw a thumb in Bozeman's direction. "This hunk over here does the accounting and makes sure we pay the bills, and we hire out a person to do the taxes. We can do everything you can do, and do it better, because we know how to run the business the way it best suits us. So, no. We don't need or want your three-year contract, and certainly not for twenty-three percent." I paused for a moment, let the moment pass, and gave the sweetest smile I could before I put a bit of country twang in my words. "But thank you kindly, sir, for the offer."

I retook my seat.

Russell turned to Toby and was about to say something when Toby stopped him and clapped him on the back. "I'll tell you what, Russell, why don't you quit while you're behind, and run onto the bus and check e-mails or something?"

Russell looked at Toby for a moment, then stomped off in a huff.

Toby sat on the bus steps. "Sorry about that. He can be a bit of a pill to swallow."

Bozeman extracted a beer from the cooler, twisted off the cap, and passed it to Toby. "How did you find that guy?"

Toby drank, emitted a soft burp, and shrugged. "Excuse me. Yeah, the record company saddled him with us. I didn't really have a say in the matter. Once you get past the snark and bluster, he's not that bad."

"Does he really save all that work for you?" I asked.

Toby's facial expression told me everything. "Like I said, he came included in our contract. To be honest, though, we were getting by fine without him. Laurel and Fran handled most of the promotion stuff, and to an extent, still do. The studio hooked us up with an accountant, so Russell primarily sets up the gigs, then acts as the manager once we get on site and need the stage set up."

I chuckled. "Sounds like a great deal to benefit him. Really doesn't add up to twenty-three percent in my mind."

"Codi, don't move." Toby whispered.

"What? Why?"

"There's a mouse right by your foot."

I leaned over and looked, despite the warning. It was Willie. I bent over and held out my hand. Willie climbed into my palm, then sat down, and I sat back in my chair. "This isn't a mouse. It's

Willie. He's a chipmunk. Haven't you ever seen a chipmunk before?"

Toby leaned in closer. "Sorry, I'm not wearing my glasses. Looked like a mouse to me. Why are you holding a chipmunk?"

At that moment, Willie twitched, expelled a nut from his cheek, and dropped it into my hand next to him.

"Apparently, he thought I needed a snack."

Bozeman and Toby both laughed.

"We have two chipmunks. Waylon is probably running around here somewhere, or he returned to his nest. It's getting pretty late in the day. Thanks for the nut, Willie, but you can have it."

I picked up the nut and held it out for Willie. He grabbed it with his cute little chipmunk paws and shoved it back into his cheek. He started turning in circles, which was chipmunk talk for putting him down, so I lowered my hand to the ground, and he ran off to the bus.

"That's the strangest thing I think I've ever seen," Toby said.

I smiled as I thought of Merle and Dolly. "Trust me, I can show you stranger."

"No, that's okay. I'll pass."

Bozeman got up and shifted his chair so he could more easily see his friend. "Tell me about the new album."

Toby took a swig, and I took that as he meant to think about it for a moment. "Well, I think you'll like it. It's not really the old-time country, but not like the pop-inspired country of today either. There's plenty of guitars and fiddle, but it doesn't sound like a rock album, if you know what I mean."

Bozeman nodded. I got the gist as well. Lots of country stars out there played music that would transcend past the traditional country fan to more of a broad base.

"What about the release party tomorrow night? What are you expecting?" I asked.

"Guest list is invitation only, mostly to friends and family, a couple hundred people. I'm originally from here, so I wanted to do something special for the home folk. Of course, it's a public park, so I suspect the crowd may get to twice as large with people who just show up, and I'm good with that. Gates, as they are, open at six, party starts at seven."

"What about amenities?"

"There'll be a couple of food trucks here. The record company's sending them over. They're also sending out a crew in the morning to take care of the sound system and lighting, so y'all won't need to worry about that. If you have any special equipment you want, make sure you take it over when they get here. Russell will be on hand to supervise everything, so go to him for anything you need."

I wanted to get down to the brass tacks, primarily, what they expected from Bozeman and I. "What about us? How long should our set be?"

"County law says we need to be shut down by eleven, so you can play for an hour or an hour and a half if you want to. Do you got enough material to cover that?"

I nodded. "Of course. What do you think, Boze?"

Bozeman ciphered it in his head. "Probably an hour at most will be good. We should do a fifty-minute set and come out for an encore."

It sounded like a good plan to me.

"Do you have merch to sell?" Toby asked.

"Yeah, but nothing too wild. CDs, signed photos, T-shirts, stuff like that. Can we set up a table?"

"For sure. If you're good with it, Fran and Laurel can run it for you while you're onstage, and a bit after until you can take over. You can trust them, and they're pretty good salespeople. They could sell anything to anyone, and like I said, they're both trustworthy, so you don't have to worry about the till."

"Sounds good. Appreciate the favor," Bozeman said.

"Good, then maybe you two could do one for me in return. Come on up and join me and the band for our encore."

I looked at Bozeman, who seemed fine with it. Usually when we were on a bill with other acts, we'd usually catch anyone playing before us, then stay for most of the act following us, then head back to the bus. Neither one of us was big on traditional after parties.

"We can do that. What's the song?"

"It's an original. Real easy standard three chord progression, you'll pick it up pretty fast. We'll practice it at sound check tomorrow at four. Does that work?"

"Sure thing." It didn't bother me. We had nowhere else to be, and all day to travel the couple hundred yards to the stage.

Fran walked up, put her hands on her hips, and leaned in toward Toby. "Are you going to fire up the grill, or are you going to sit here chatting all night? Come on, your crew is hungry." She grabbed Toby's arm and forced him to his feet.

"Okay, okay, I'm coming. Would you two like to join us? Dinner is nothing fancy, just burgers, beans, potato salad, and the like, but you're welcome. We've got plenty of food."

I turned to Bozeman. "What do we have on the menu for tonight's feast?"

He thought for a moment. "Well, you can have your choice of canned beef stew or a peanut butter and jelly sandwich."

I looked back at Toby and Fran, who still had a tight hold on his arm. "We'll be right over."

After Toby and Fran left, Bozeman and I cleaned up our little area and while Bozeman carried the cooler onto the bus, I checked on Dolly and Merle. Although it wouldn't be dark for another hour, they were both stirring from their naps. I noticed the banana and tomato treats were already gone, and I took the time to give them both head and belly scratches. I left the door open so they could roam when they wanted to, and I got on the bus to wash my hands and grab a light jacket since I usually get a chill once the sun sets.

A few minutes later, Bozeman and I strode over to Toby's bus. The way Fran talked about the grill, I expected one of those small charcoal things that only fit a couple of burgers at a time. It amazed me to see that the bus came with a full outdoor kitchen.

Toby had on a chef's hat and an apron that said 'kiss the cook', and he was working a flat top grill that easily held eight hamburgers. Next to that was a pan filled with onions and mushrooms, and another burner held a pot of baked beans. A portable picnic table large enough for ten people was set up, and

Fran and Gabe were setting the table. Laurel stepped off the bus carrying a tray of hamburger buns and a basket filled with a bottle of ketchup, at least four types of mustard, salt and pepper, relish, and other condiments.

Toby impressed me with his prowess in the kitchen. "You got that going quickly. You just left us like ten minutes ago."

Toby looked up and smiled at me. "Yeah, well, we all work as a unit. Gabe got everything started out here while the girls prepped all the food. Russell's still in there making some coleslaw."

"He can cook too? Besides all the other duties he performs?"

Laurel laughed at me. "I wouldn't call it cooking. It's mostly pre-made. He just has to dump everything into a bowl and stir. The rule is for everyone to eat, everyone has to contribute to the meal."

"That sounds great, but who do you decide who does the dishes?"

"That's easy," Toby said. "If no one volunteers, we play one round of Texas hold'em, and the two weakest hands share the cleanup duties."

Laurel elbowed me in the ribs. "That usually means it's Gabe and Russell. Neither one is lucky at cards."

I shrugged. "Well, that only means they must be lucky at love."

Laurel wrinkled her nose at the prospect. "Eww. So gross, Codi. Why don't y'all grab a drink over at the fridge there and take a seat?"

Bozeman needed no further invitation, so he went and came back with a beer for himself and a bottle of water for me. We both found seats and Laurel, Fran, and Gabe joined us. Toby came over and dropped off a bowl holding the onion and mushroom mixture, and another containing the baked beans, then went back to the grill. Russell appeared with his coleslaw and found a seat, and then Toby returned with a platter of hamburgers.

I waited, wondering if someone was going to say grace or something. Instead, Toby cleared his throat and picked up his glass. "A toast to our friends, Codi and Bozeman." We all clinked glasses together and dug into our evening meal.

glasses together and dug into our evening meal.

CHAPTER THREE

The next morning at eight on the dot, I was about to step off the bus when I received a knock on the door. When I opened it, I looked out and noticed Laurel standing there with a box in her hands.

"Good morning. Would you like a donut?" She smiled at me as she lifted the small box as if paying tribute.

It was a gracious gesture, offering someone you just met a donut, and I was more than happy to take her up on the offer. "Only if you'll have one with me. Come on in."

I stepped back into the common area, and Laurel followed me. I pointed to the small bench table. "Have a seat. Would you like some coffee or something?"

Laurel placed the box on the table and slid into the seat. "You won't believe this, but I can't stand coffee. Tea or juice or even a can of cola would be fine."

I moved to the refrigerator to determine what we had in stock. There was a pitcher of what I remembered to be orange juice, but when I picked it up, I realized one of us had put it back in the fridge empty. In our world, that wasn't considered a spiteful act. It usually meant that either Dolly or Merle was aboard, and we didn't want them getting into something they shouldn't. Sometimes our fridge contained more empty, dirty containers than actual food. Until, at last, one of us broke down and did the dishes, or needed room after a grocery run. No luck, so I stepped over to the pantry.

"I've got Diet Dr. Pepper or water I can offer you. Got a preference?"

"I'll take the Dr. Pepper," Laurel said.

"It's in a can. Would you like a glass, or ice?" I should have checked if we had ice before I offered her some.

"Nah. I can take it right out of the can."

I grabbed a couple of cans and some napkins and sat at the table.

Laurel took a can, wiped the top off with a napkin, popped it open, and took a sip. "Thanks. This is great. Have a donut."

She pushed the box toward me, and I flipped the lid open. There were four donuts inside, and I immediately gravitated to the Boston Creme, like a shark going after an injured fish. As graceful as a giraffe wearing oven mitts, I picked it from the box and took a bite. I loved the taste of chocolate on my lips and the explosion of pastry creme onto my tongue.

"Those are my favorite, too." Laurel reached into the box and extracted what looked to be a blueberry cake donut.

As we ate in silence, I looked Laurel over. When I met her, she was standing next to Fran, who, because she resembled a Greek goddess, took all the attention. But as I looked at Laurel as she sat by herself, I discovered she could more than hold her own. Today she had her fiery red hair pulled back in a bun, and her complexion was flawless, except for a small mole on her neck just below her right ear. She wore no makeup that I could tell, and she was what my mom would refer to as a classic beauty. Even though she dressed in dark blue sweatpants and a gray T-shirt with an alien on the front.

I finished my donut, wiped my mouth and fingers with a napkin, and pointed at her shirt. "You believe in aliens?"

Laurel gave me a crooked smile, brushed her donut crumbs into her hand, and placed them atop her napkin. "You'll probably think I'm a kook, but yes."

"Why?" I hoped the question didn't sound as rude out loud as it did in my head. "Sorry, I'm just curious."

Laurel smiled at me. "No problem. For me, it's just math. Even within the Milky Way, there are probably forty or fifty billion planets that may support life as we recognize it. Even if there was a one percent chance of life on those planets, that would still be forty million populated worlds out there."

I nodded. The numbers made sense to me. "Then why didn't the little green people contact us yet?"

"Good question, and my answer is, think about it. Let's say there is life on other planets. You can't assume that those life forms are in the same advanced stage we are, right? I mean, it took humans, what? Six or seven million years to evolve to where we are now? There might be millions of life forms out there that haven't reached our stage of maturity yet, still discovering fire and such. Or lifeforms that aren't as advanced technologically to cross the stars."

Made sense to me. "Do you think we'll ever get visited by aliens?"

She winked at me. "Who's saying we haven't been? Who's saying the whole human race isn't an offshoot of some civilization from some faraway planet?"

We sat in silence for a moment, eyes locked. I broke it first. "It's way too early to be having this conversation."

"So, where's Bozeman this morning?" Laurel asked.

"If he's not on the bus, and he wasn't outside, he is in the shower or out for a run."

A sly smile crossed Laurel's face. "If I may be so bold to ask, what's the deal with you two?"

I knew what she meant by that. It was the same question in one form or another that I got asked almost every time I met a new group of people.

"There's nothing going on there. We're just business partners."

"Oh. I see."

I wondered if she did. It seemed the concept of two people living on a bus and traveling around the country playing music together, yet not being romantically involved, was over many people's heads. Most people didn't believe me. After all, Bozeman's a good-looking guy. Tall, dark, and handsome with the six-pack abs and flashy smile, like he just stepped out of a cheesy romance novel, but there were zero sparks for either of us. We were friends and colleagues, and that was the extent of it.

"Honest. Ask him out if you want to," I said.

Laurel tilted her head and tugged at the neck of her T-shirt. "No, he's not really my type. He'd probably find Fran more attractive, anyway. Everyone always does."

A second later, Laurel shrieked and pulled her legs up onto the bench seat. She tried to speak, but couldn't, and instead pointed at the floor behind me.

"What?" I turned around and saw Dolly sitting on the floor, her whiskers twitching in our direction. I bent over, Dolly came forward, and I swooped her up in my arms. "I must have left the door open. This is Dolly."

Laurel determined she wasn't in danger, and returned her feet to the floor. To my surprise, she leaned toward Dolly and held out a hand. "She's a raccoon! Can I pet her?"

"Sure," I said and held Dolly out so Laurel could reach her better.

Laurel moved her fingers closer and Dolly reciprocated by wrapping her tiny human-like hand around Laurel's finger. It looked like they were shaking hands.

"Give her a scratch on her nose there between the eyes, and she'll be your friend forever."

Laurel did as I suggested, and Dolly squirmed in my grip until I let her go. She walked across the table and plopped down in front of Laurel.

"She's so cute. Can I give her a donut?"

"Maybe. What do you have left in the box?"

"Another blueberry cake, and a jelly filled."

"Go with the blueberry. And only half, okay?"

Laurel nodded, opened the box, pulled the donut in half, and closed the box. She broke the donut into smaller chunks and offered one to Dolly. Dolly, who was never shy when being offered food, took it in her paws and nibbled away at it.

"She's adorable. Where did you get her?"

"I got her from a veterinarian as a kit. Someone had found her and brought her in because of her leg. She was born without a back leg."

Laurel held the donut up in the air, so Dolly had to reach for it. When Dolly extended her body, her birth defect became apparent. "That's amazing. Okay, girl, last chunk." Laurel fed the remains of the donut to Dolly.

After she ate the last bite, Dolly jumped from the table to the seat next to me, and then to the floor. She took a couple of steps, then groomed herself, much like a cat would.

"If you think that's amazing, grab that other half of that donut and follow me," I said.

Laurel grabbed the donut and trailed me outside. We stopped by the door, and I bent over and saw that Merle was home and still awake, which was a good thing. He had a tendency to be grumpy if anyone woke him, a trait we shared. I reached into the cubbyhole and brought him out.

"This is Merle," I said.

Laurel's jaw dropped in surprise. I couldn't judge what was going through her mind, and she didn't speak for a good twenty seconds. "Can I hold him?"

"Sure. Sit down."

Laurel sat in Bozeman's lawn chair, and I put Merle on her lap. "He like belly rubs, tomatoes, and blueberry donuts."

Merle did a quick circle in Laurel's lap, determined she wasn't a threat, and laid down on his side. Laurel broke off a chunk of donut and offered it to him. "Where did you get a skunk?"

"Picked him up the same place I got Dolly."

"You're too much, Codi. Any other surprises around here?"

I shook my head. "No. Just a cat and a couple of chipmunks. How is it you're so good with animals?"

Laurel broke off more donut. Merle was enjoying his morning snack, or rather, since he was mostly nocturnal, his bedtime snack. "I grew up on a farm. I've been an animal lover since I was a little girl. When I was young, I wanted to be a vet or work in a zoo."

"And you ended up playing fiddle in a country band?"

Laurel gave me a smile with a hint of sadness behind it. "Yeah. You know, life impedes your plans sometimes, right?"

I nodded in agreement. I knew how that went.

"What are you three up to?"

I turned and saw Bozeman. I hadn't even detected his approach, and usually I was well aware of my surroundings. He dressed in sweatpants and a T-shirt and was carrying his shower bag, and his hair was wet.

"I'm just introducing Laurel to the kids."

Bozeman nodded at Laurel. She nodded back, and he got back on the bus. As she fed the last of the donut to Merle, I saw Dolly stepping off the bus. Merle noticed her as well, shifted in Laurel's lap, and jumped to the ground. From there, they went into their compartment.

"It's bedtime for them," I explained.

Laurel frowned. "Is it safe for them to live in a storage compartment under the bus like that?"

"Sure. They prefer it over living on the bus since it's more like they're used to in the wild. Bozeman even fixed it up, so it's well-ventilated, heated in the winter, and cooled in the summer. In short, whatever the temperature is on the bus, it's the same temperature in their little apartment."

"And you let them run free?" Laurel asked.

"Sure. They always know where home is. We only lock them up when we're on the road, so no one falls off the bus. We wouldn't want that to happen."

"This is too much. Hey, I've got to get going. See you later, right?"

"Of course, we'll be here all day."

At quarter to four, Bozeman and I walked over to the amphitheater, ready for the sound check. I lugged my favorite Martin guitar with me while Bozeman pulled a folding wagon holding his pedal board and his Gibson. As we got closer, I could see a crew had been hard at work setting up for the event. There was a soundboard set up, a professional lighting rig over the stage, and a literal tower of large black speakers and amps. From the looks of it, people wouldn't need to come to the park to hear the concert. They'd be able to enjoy it from their house if they lived anywhere within a three-mile radius.

Russell appeared from out of nowhere and stopped us from going any farther. "Hold up here. Toby's going to do a short sound check, then I'll get you settled."

Although the amphitheater had paved aisles running from the top of the hill to the stage, it didn't have traditional seats. Instead, the seating area looked like an agricultural terrace and had eighteen-inch-high steps set into the hill. At the end of each step was a brick wall, about twelve inches wide, topped with a capstone for seating. Bozeman angled his wagon into the step so it wouldn't roll to the stage and sat. I followed suit, setting my guitar case at my feet.

I looked at Russell. "What's the plan?"

"Toby's band will play though four or five songs until the sound engineer is happy. If we're lucky. Then you two can set up and do a quick check, and then y'all will run through Toby's encore."

"Why if we're lucky?"

Russell shrugged. "Sometimes Toby gets into a snit with the sound guys and plays the same song repeatedly until he's happy. It drives everyone nuts. The engineers, the band, me, but he insists on doing it."

At that moment, Gabe appeared on stage, followed by Fran and Laurel. He ran through his drum kit to make sure he liked the positioning of the equipment while the women checked the tuning on their respective instruments. Gabe looked into the audience at Russell. Russell checked the venue to make sure everyone was in place, then gave Gabe the thumbs up. Gabe clacked his sticks together, then began a beat. A few seconds later, Toby strolled out on stage, and the sound check began.

At first, it was a bumpy beginning to get the sound levels correct for the venue. Once the technicians had the sound figured out, the band settled into a short set to get warmed up. I was enjoying the music when I heard a gruff voice behind Bozeman.

"Excuse me, sir. Could you remove that ugly hat?"

Bozeman and I both turned, and Bozeman jumped to his feet. "Well, I'll be. Tommy Skye! How are you, man?" Bozeman held out his hand and Tommy shook it.

"Been better. Codi, I assume. Nice to meet you."

I offered my hand.

"Tommy Skye is one of the best guitar players in the business. What are you doing down here? I thought you were with the band."

Tommy looked at the stage, then back at Bozeman. "Nah,

we've had a falling out. I'm not with them anymore."

"Got a new gig?" Bozeman asked.

Tommy sniffed, produced a ragged tissue from his pocket like a magician, and rubbed his nose. "No. I haven't played in a while."

Bozeman nodded. "Well, it's good to see you. You're looking good."

Bozeman and I must have a different opinion of what good looks like, because the man didn't look good to me at all. He was five-eight, and I could tell he'd lost a lot of weight recently based on how much tongue hung from his belt loop. He wore a buttoned denim jacket that looked to be three sizes too big for him, and his gaunt appearance made him look like a living skeleton. I wondered if the falling out he mentioned had anything to do with illegal narcotics.

Russell whistled at us from the stage and waved us over. I hadn't noticed Toby's band was done with their check. We said our goodbyes to Tommy and climbed to the stage where Bozeman set up his pedal board, and I removed my guitar from the case and gave it a quick tuning. We took our positions with me out front and center and Bozeman just a step behind and a pace to my left. Together, we worked through two songs until I got the signal from the sound engineer that we were ready.

When we finished, Toby's band joined us on stage, and Toby explained his idea for the encore. The first song was an old Willie Nelson standard I could play in my sleep, and probably had at one time or another. The last song we'd sing was the first released single of the new album.

"Just watch the monitor there for the lyrics and chord changes," Toby instructed. "We'll run through it two or three times, so you get the feel."

I looked down near the front of the stage and noticed the black box I thought was an amplifier was actually a video monitor that looked like an amp. From the audience side, it would look like a piece of audio equipment, and they wouldn't be able to tell it fed the musicians the lyrics and chord progressions. The band started, and I watched the monitor as they played through it once so we could hear it. Overall, it was a nice, albeit old-fashioned country ballad about a cowboy alone on the plains, reminiscing about a lost love. The tune was catchy, and the lyrics told such a poignant story. I knew it had the makings of a gold, if not platinum, record.

Russell appeared from the wings and gave us each a copy of the sheet music to *Dancing Teardrops*, the song we'd just played.

I glanced over at Bozeman, and he looked unhappy. He wore a snarl on his face, and his cheeks were turning red. The paper he clenched in his fist. My first thought was he was suffering a seizure. "Boze? Are you okay?"

Bozeman shook his head, jumped from the stage, and ran up the hill. Everyone had gone silent behind me, and I turned to see all the inquisitive faces staring at me. "Um. He had a thing. I'd better go check on him. Excuse me."

I stepped onto the bus and noticed two things. Bozeman had crumpled the sheet music into a ball, and the door to our equipment storage room was open. Since the door opened toward me, I couldn't look in, but I heard Bozeman rummaging around for something.

"Bozeman? You okay in there?"

Bozeman grunted, like he had just lifted something heavy. "Yeah, I found what I'm looking for. Be out in a second."

I made my way back to the table and sat. A few seconds later, the door closed, and Bozeman approached with a cardboard banker's box I'd never seen before.

"It has to be in here." Bozeman opened the box, and I saw it stuffed with notebooks and random sheets of loose-leaf paper. He grabbed a handful of notebooks, set them on the table, and pushed them my way. "Here. Check the inside cover for dates and pull out anything from ten or eleven years ago."

While Bozeman checked the loose papers, I did as he asked. In the end, I had set aside two notebooks from that timeframe. Bozeman placed the box on the floor and threw all but the two notebooks into the box. He grabbed one notebook and slid the other over to me. "Okay, now go through and see if you recognize anything familiar."

I was confused. "Familiar how?"

Bozeman grabbed the paper ball, smoothed it out, and handed it to me. "Familiar like this."

I opened the notebook and scanned through the pages. I knew Bozeman was a songwriter, but I didn't know he was so prolific. Every page I turned offered a new page of handwritten lyrics with chords or notes penciled in the margins. I checked the notebook's cover, and it said it held eighty pages. Assuming all the pages were there, and each song covered two pages, Bozeman had at least forty songs in this notebook alone. I continued to turn pages until something finally caught my eye. I compared the notebook to the sheet music and turned it around.

"Is this what you're looking for?"

Bozeman nodded. "That's it exactly."

Bozeman took a minute to compare the notebook to the sheet music. "He changed the title, but the music and lyrics match. I thought that song sounded familiar, and now I know why. He stole it from me, that son of a—"

Without continuing his sentence, Bozeman grabbed the notebook and music and raced from the bus. I got up immediately, but by the time I left the bus, Bozeman was already out of sight. Since there was such a height difference between us, and he was a runner and I wasn't, there was no way to keep up with him. By the time I reached the stage, Bozeman was already there and on top of Toby.

"You stole my song!" Bozeman screamed as he threw wild punches at Toby. Although Bozeman had Toby trapped under his gigantic frame, Toby wrapped his arms around his head. Most of Bozeman's manic punches landed with no actual harm.

I stepped forward and grabbed Bozeman's arm. "Help me," I implored the others standing around me. They looked like statues, but finally Gabe came and helped me pull Bozeman off of Toby.

"That's enough," I ordered. "Back off, Bozeman."

Gabe helped Toby to his feet. Toby looked ruffled and had a tiny cut on his chin that was barely bleeding, but he didn't look bad at all. I'd seen worse injuries at a post-Thanksgiving sale at a local big box store.

Bozeman's chest heaved as he breathed, and he stuck his

finger out at Toby. "I ought to hang you, you thief."

A tense cloud passed over the stage. I didn't know how this stalemate would end. Of course, being the smallest-stature person around, I grabbed Bozeman's arm and pulled him toward the stage stairs. "Come on, cowboy, let's go take a break."

CHAPTER FOUR

 I held on to Bozeman and led him all the way back to the bus. To his credit, he never once tried to pull away, even though he could have done so without expending a single calorie's worth of energy. Instead, he trudged along like a zombie.

When we got to the bus, I sat him down in his chair and stood over him like a scolding mother. "I can't believe you did that! He could cancel our gig tonight and sue you for assault, or get you arrested! Are you out of your mind?"

Bozeman threw the puppy-dog-eyes look my way, and I knew I couldn't stay mad at him for long, especially since I wasn't good at anger to begin with. To show him I remained upset, I crossed my arms and sat down with a huff.

"He's not going to call the cops, and he's certainly not going to sue me," Bozeman said.

"How can you be so sure?"

"Because. It will cause him a lot more trouble when it gets out that Toby poached someone else's song, and I sue him for copyright infringement. The record company will drop him like a hot rock."

I picked up the sheet music from the ground where Bozeman dropped it and checked the citation. It claimed the music and lyrics came directly from the head of Toby Madden. "Maybe it was a mistake. If you talked to him, perhaps he'd change it to give you the writing credit. Then everybody wins, right?"

"That's not going to happen in a billion years. Once it gets around that he stole my song, I'm sure any writer who has ever known him is going to scour Toby's back catalog to check if he stole anyone else's work. And for sure, he won't want to part with any of the royalties he'd have to give up."

"You're not even going to talk to him?" I asked, hoping he'd at least apologize.

Bozeman stood. "What I'm going to do is go for a nice, long walk. I'll be back by six-thirty at the latest."

I watched as Bozeman skulked off in the opposite direction of the stage, so I hoped he wouldn't circle back and cause any more trouble. Conflicted, I felt trapped between going after him and letting him blow off the steam. I opted for the latter.

Instead, I wanted to find Toby and ask if we were still the opening act or if we should get our gear and leave. As I passed his bus, I noticed him headed in my direction, so I stopped and waited for him. The cut on his face had already stopped bleeding, and although his clothes looked wrinkled from the tussle, he didn't look like he'd been in a fight. He saw me, slowed his gait for a few seconds, reconsidered and sped up again and stopped a foot from me.

Toby crossed his arms and tipped his chin up. "Did you come to apologize for him?"

I shook my head. "No. Bozeman's a big boy. That's up to him to do. What I need to find out is if we're still good to open tonight."

Toby glared at me for a moment, then dropped his posture. "Nice and candid. I appreciate that. If I had anyone else on the bill, I'd call the cops and have you removed from the park, but since it's just the two of us, I'm going to let it go. My fans are expecting you, and I still want you to perform. However, the minute your set is done, I'd like you to be gone. No merch, no shared encore. Get on this..." Toby glanced at my old bus and pointed to it. "...machine and go."

I didn't like the deal, but since I had no other options, I nodded. "Yeah, okay. Can I ask you one question, though? Did you steal his song?"

Toby glared into my eyes. I expected him to scream a denial at me, but he turned for his bus without uttering so much as a syllable.

"I'll take that as a yes," I whispered to myself.

He stopped in mid-stride, as if to return, then kept walking.

"Did he fire you?"

It was my turn to be startled. I jumped when I heard the voice, then looked behind me. It was Laurel. I hadn't seen or detected her approach, so I assumed she learned how to teleport, or at the very least, was a ninja.

She smiled at me. "Sorry. I didn't mean to scare you. Are you still playing tonight?"

"Yes. But we need to leave right after our set, and we can't sell merch."

"Good. I have all your albums," she said. Laurel smiled. "I'm a big fan."

I blushed. During meet-and-greets I heard those words often, but when a fellow musician said them, it just hit differently. "Thanks. I appreciate that."

"And don't worry about the merch. Toby told me and Fran yesterday about the table, and we'll still run it for you."

My brow creased. "Oh, no, I can't have you getting into any trouble for me."

Laurel waved her hand at me like she shooed away a fly. "What trouble? Toby returned to the bus, and he'll be there until like five minutes before we go on stage. Sometimes he's even late for the set, and once we start to play, he'll spot some blond in the crowd and focus on her all night. I'm sure by the time our gig is half-over, he'll have forgotten about everything."

"Are you sure?"

"I'm positive. So, what do you say?"

I thought about it for a quick minute, then made my decision. "Come on, I'll show you what I have."

I led Laurel to the bus, opened a storage compartment, and brought out the three totes I had filled with various merchandise. We sold signed photos of myself, copies of my CDs, Bozeman's CDs, and, of course, a variety of T-shirts with my pretty face on them. I put the totes on a portable hand truck, and together we wheeled the load to the top of the amphitheater where Russell was busy stocking Toby's merchandise. Although we offered the same stuff, Toby's presentation blew mine away. He had a small, covered portable gazebo for his merch. I had a plastic table. It would do, though. One benefit of having only a couple samples out and working from totes was it only took a few seconds to clean everything up in case of bad weather or a quick getaway.

With Laurel's help, I got things going, and once I showed her the price sheet and how to take credit cards, I excused myself to get dressed for the show. Back on the bus, although I was alone, I could tell Bozeman had been there. The banker's box had disappeared, so I assumed he put it away, and I sensed a hint of his cologne in the air.

I moved to my room and picked out my outfit for the night, which wasn't hard because I had a set wardrobe to choose from. I had three pairs of jeans to choose from. All three were the same brand and style and the only choice I had was color: either black, blue, or dark green. I also had three western shirts, again, same shirt but in different colors. I had a practical system, and everything went together, so I could literally get dressed in the dark and everything in my ensemble would match. Tonight, I went with the black jeans and navy blue checkered shirt. I brushed my teeth, put on my boots, found my hat, and was ready to rock out, or rather, country out.

Ready to go, I was about to leave my bus when I felt a paw on my calf. I looked down, and there was Gibson, working hard to get my attention. I took a step away from him, and he plopped to the ground, expecting belly rubs, which I happily provided while I cooed at him.

"You be a good boy and watch the bus. I'll be back in a couple of hours."

There was still no sight of Bozeman when I got to the stage, but Gabe was there making last-minute adjustments to his kit.

"We really haven't talked. I'm Codi."

Gabe didn't speak.

"Toby told me you're new to the band. Came over from metal, right?"

He looked at me, but again, didn't utter a syllable.

"What's your favorite band? Black Sabbath? Megadeth? Led Zeppelin? Although I think they consider Led Zeppelin classic rock by now. Mine is Metallica."

His eyes widened, so I assumed I had him. "You're familiar with Metallica?"

"Of course, darlin'. My favorite song of theirs is *Enter*

Sandman. I love the guitar sound of that song. When I first heard it, I played it repeatedly until my parents begged me to stop. Or rather, the neighbor next door got my parents to make me quit."

To show I learned the tune, I sang a few bars for him.

"Of course, I love *Nothing Else Matters*, too." I sang a bit of that as well to him, and Gabe stood there grinning. I couldn't blame him. Certainly, the boots and hat weren't a typical look to match the music.

"Wow, I'm impressed. I'm surprised you've heard of them. It seems like metal would be outside of your wheelhouse."

"Why? Music's an art and I appreciate it all. Rock, blues, jazz, folk. There's nothing I don't enjoy occasionally. Well, except opera, but I'm sure I'd like that better if I understood Italian. And all those genres borrow from each other. So how you like being in a country band?"

Gabe twirled a drumstick in his hand. "It's so different from what I'm used to. There's not as much energy."

"You mean you miss the younger crowd, more bass guitar and the intensity?"

He tilted his head. "Yeah, kind of."

"I can understand that. What I first started out; my manager would book me into these country bars. You ever been in one?"

Gabe shook his head no.

"Some of them were okay. Nice stage, agreeable sound, respectful crowd, and those weren't so bad at all. Other times, he'd get me a gig at these real rowdy places where they surrounded the stage with chicken wire and the crowd got meaner as the night got longer."

"Why the chicken wire?"

"That was to prevent the band from getting hurt when the locals started throwing beer bottles."

Gabe laughed. "They must have hated you to throw bottles."

"Sometimes. Other times, the locals considered it a sign of respect. Where I came from, respect wasn't throwing glass at people, but different strokes for different folks. And in those places, you could bet that at least one fight would break out during the evening, and we'd just keep on playing like there wasn't a riot happening three feet in front of us. Although one night, a drunkard jumped on my stage, threw a punch at my drummer, and knocked him clean out."

Gabe's eyes widened. "Oh, wow."

"Exactly."

"What did you do?" he asked.

"Well, we took a break long enough for the bouncer to throw out the guy and to wake up the drummer, then we finished the set."

"That's incredible," Gabe said. His ear-to-ear grin told me he liked that story.

"It is. Anyway, I remember there was one night just after we finished a gig in Texas at the roughest place they had ever booked us to play. I was sitting on a barstool, picking bottle glass out of my hair, and my favorite shirt smelled like a brewery. I looked around and wondered how I had gotten there, and how long I'd have to spend playing places like that. It was right then I decided I had enough, so I fired my manager and broke up that band, and vowed to never play in another dive like that again."

I had the eyes from him again, so I could tell I'd lost him. "Long story short, Gabe. Although it was scary, I made a change that, although hard, was better for me in the long run. I'm in a much better place today, mentally and professionally, than had I not gotten out of that comfortable groove I was in. Get it?"

"I think so."

"Take advantage of the opportunity you have now. You can never tell where it will lead, right?"

"That's true."

"What are you talking about?"

I hadn't even noticed Bozeman had joined us. There he was, standing with his guitar slung over his shoulder and pick in hand, ready to play, and when he spoke, it startled me.

I smiled. "Nothing much, just Metallica."

Bozeman rolled his eyes at me. Although I enjoyed a wide range of genres in music, Bozeman was more of a purist. He enjoyed only two types of music: country music produced before 1960, and country music produced after 1960. It was only through my insistence that songs from other genres popped into our set list occasionally.

"It's almost show time," Bozeman said.

I looked out at the sound engineer's booth and spotted the digital clock perched on the table front. A red number ten was visible, so I realized it was only ten minutes before we were on. I did a last-second spot check of my equipment and walked offstage with Bozeman and Gabe into the wings and waited for our introduction.

A few seconds later, Russell appeared at my side. "You ready?"

I looked at Bozeman, and he gave me a nod.

"Yes. We're ready to go," I said.

Russell stepped to center stage and positioned him in front of my microphone. "Ladies and gentlemen, thank you for coming to the show tonight. I know you're all excited about seeing Toby Madden, but before we bring him out, we've got a fantastic act for you. Please help give a warm welcome to Codi Cassidy."

I plastered on a smile, and Bozeman and I took our places on stage. I wouldn't call what we received a warm welcome, more like a smattering of polite golf clapping. That was okay, though, because I knew we weren't the ones the crowd had been hand-selected to see. Tonight, we were only the appetizer for the main entrée.

I ran off a three count, and we hit the opening chord together. In a normal set, Bozeman and I started off with songs that worked well with just us and our two guitars. Once the audience knew it was us behind the magic, I fired up a computer that provided accompanying tracks of different instruments for other songs. I relied on the magic of technology for my pianist, drummer, bassist, fiddler, and any other music we'd need during a set. I also had the program set to where the lights would synchronize with the music. But tonight, I didn't need to worry about running the machine. The engineer was running my computer, and the studio had provided a lighting crew.

We started the set with two of my original songs, and then I slowed it down with a rendition of Dolly Parton's *I Will Always*

Love You. I loved that song, not only because it is one of the best songs ever written, but it fits nicely into my vocal range. That was a good one to play for a crowd that didn't know my music. We played a couple more of my songs, then I turned the stage over to Bozeman.

Bozeman stepped forward and played one of his originals, but as he did, I could see that something wasn't quite right with him. He seemed… off, like he wasn't really there. Sure, that was him picking and singing, but I noticed he was really just going through the motions, which was something he never did. Bozeman loved to play live shows, and that joy always translated into an animated performance.

Had this been a rehearsal, I would've stopped the session right there and asked him what the deal was. Since there were a couple hundred people watching us, all I could do was keep up appearances and go on with the show.

Instead of displaying his normal on-stage self, he powered through his song by rote, gave the crowd a thank you, and passed the floor back my way.

I gave a brief introduction of the next song to the crowd. It was more for the benefit of the engineer to let him know he needed to activate the backing tracks on my computer. As I spoke, I looked into the crowd. I spotted Tommy Skye still sitting where we had left him. He saw me looking at him and raised a can of beer and tilted it in my direction. At least he was enjoying the show.

With the music backing tracks, we picked things up a bit, and we intermixed a few popular upbeat country songs into the set that fit in well with my original tunes. That always worked well with a crowd that didn't know my music and kept them up on their feet and cheering and dancing.

I checked the clock on the engineer table and saw it displayed a green three, which means we had time for one more song. I did a quick introduction of my most famous song, *Loving You, Leaving You,* which broke into the top forty of the country chart, and we played that. It was the song that usually got the most applause and cheers, not only because it was an excellent song but also because most people didn't know it had come from me.

Just like that, our part of the show was over. Instead of the polite, golf clap cheers we'd opened to, we received a hearty ovation upon our exit. We'd whipped the crowd up for more music, so I stood satisfied that as the opening act, we had done our job.

Bozeman and I each said thank you to the crowd and took a couple of bows, then headed for the wings.

Russell was there, holding a grin and bottles of water for each of us. "That was great, fabulous! When Toby suggested you as an opening act, I was skeptical, but, boy, you won me over."

"Thank you." I opened the bottle and drank down half the contents.

Bozeman had already emptied his bottle and set it on top of an amp box. "Is there a restroom here, or do I have to use the one by the pool?"

Russell pointed toward a short hallway behind Bozeman. "Follow that hall. Can't miss it."

Bozeman turned and headed in that direction. I wanted to remind him about the merchandise booth, but he was out of sight by the time I thought of it. "When does Toby start?"

Russell stepped around me and looked at the clock. "Just over sixteen minutes. You don't have too much gear. You want the roadies to take it to your bus, or do you want to haul it yourself?"

"Just have them make a small pile and we'll go through it first and make sure we have everything." It was a simple answer. I, along with probably most performing musicians, had found ourselves burned before. It wasn't often intentional, but in the rush to clear the stage, it wasn't uncommon for gear to be misplaced. Not that we had much. I had one guitar and my computer, and Bozeman had two guitars and his pedals, along with our mics and stands, and a handful of assorted cords.

"Hey, I'll be right back." I left Russell and made my way to the merch area at the top of the hill. Laurel was selling a CD to a customer, so I stood aside and waited for the transaction to finish.

When the middle-aged man turned around, he gasped when he noticed me. "Ms. Cassidy, that was such a good show. Would you mind signing this for me?"

I smiled my sweetest smile. "Of course." I stepped around the table and found a small tote that contained all the miscellaneous things I usually needed. From the tote, I grabbed a marker and held out my hand for the CD. The man gave it to me, and I slipped the insert out.

"What's your name, sugar?"

He told me, and I wrote the obligatory "To Tom, Love, Codi Cassidy", and slid the inset back into the case. I passed the CD to him and shook his hand. "Thank you for your support."

I turned back to Laurel. "Thanks for running the booth for me. I really appreciate it. I'll help you pack everything up."

Laurel grinned at me. "No need. There's nothing to pack. You're sold out."

Her words confused me. "Everything?" I pulled the bins from beneath the table and looked inside. They were empty. "Laurel, this is amazing. I've never done so much in sales in one night. You've done a fantastic job."

Laurel blushed. "It wasn't me. You sold yourself with that super performance. People really enjoyed your act. Hey, I've got to go. Can you handle things from here?"

I nodded. "Most definitely. I'll take the bins back to the bus, and should be back in plenty of time to see you play."

Laurel left, and I cleaned the table off and stacked the empty bins onto the hand truck and wheeled it to the bus. We had everything locked up, so I used my keys to unlock the storage bin and stowed all the gear, relocked everything, and headed back to the stage. When I got to the wings, Toby's band looked ready to go. Gabe was twirling a drumstick, Fran had her bass strapped to her body, and Laurel was checking a couple of strings to make last-second adjustments.

I looked around, but didn't see the man himself. "Where's Toby?"

Fran rolled her eyes. "He's such a diva. Sometimes he waits until the last moment to join us, and sometimes he waits until we're already playing before he steps onto the stage. The man's a big drama queen."

Outside, the crowd was getting restless and was clapping in

rhythm, as if the act would draw the band out.

"We can't wait anymore," Russell said as he turned his frown into a smile and headed on stage. The cheering intensified as he took to the microphone. "And now, here's what you came here tonight to see! Ladies and gentlemen, The Toby Madden Band!"

Russell rushed offstage and Gabe, Fran, and Laurel took his place. Gabe knocked out a beat on the drums, and Fran added a bass line a few seconds later. Laurel stood poised and ready to go. There was only one thing missing. I looked around behind me, but there was still no sign of Toby.

Russell growled. "Damn him." I saw him signal to Laurel, and Laurel started on her fiddle. Unlike most shows, the opening number was going to be an instrumental song without the headliner.

Russell turned to me and put his hand on my shoulder. "Could you do me a favor and go check the bus while I see if he's passed out in the men's room?"

"Sure thing." I left the building and half-walked, half-trotted to Toby's tour bus. I knocked on the door and called for him, but no one answered. Hurriedly, I knocked louder, and tried the handle. The door opened.

I climbed the stairs onto the bus. It had a similar layout to mine, but since it was a top-of-the-line model, and a good thirty years younger, it put my old bus to shame. I opened doors and checked rooms as I made my way from the front to the rear, and eventually I came to the last door. I rapped on it, then gently pushed it open. The moment I saw him, I knew he was going to miss his dramatic appearance onstage.

Toby Madden was dead.

CHAPTER FIVE

When I first saw Toby, he was lying on the bed, face down, one arm sprawled over the side, like he had thrown himself there after a hard day in the mines. My initial, more optimistic thought was that he had a few too many beers and had passed out as a result, but he remained too still, too quiet. I walked around the side of the bed, and when I spotted his eyes, they stared straight off into the great beyond. I rushed from the bus and ran back to the stage.

Russell was already back where I had left him, and I gulped for air, and bent at the waist with my hands on my hips as I reached his side. I wasn't a runner. "Call the police. Toby's gone."

"Gone? What do you mean, gone?"

I took a gulp of air and straightened my stance. "I mean he's…" I looked around to determine if anyone was in earshot. "Dead."

Russell opened his mouth, closed it, and repeated the process. He looked like a guppy tracking down food. "I don't understand."

I pointed in the general direction of the bus. "He's in his bed. Dead. I saw him. You need to call the police."

Russell stood, unmoving. He picked a great time to play the statue game.

"Give me your phone," I ordered.

Russell complied, and I took it and called 9-1-1. After a few seconds, the operator answered the call, and I explained what had happened and where we were. I hung up and offered the phone to Russell, who was still doing his best fish impression.

"What are we going to do? People are expecting him to play," Russell said, as if that happened to be the most pressing thing on his mind at the moment.

I shook my head. "He's sung his last song."

I looked out at the stage. The band was on their third

instrumental song, perhaps their fourth, and I could tell the crowd was growing restless at the lack of Toby's appearance.

"You've got to stop the show," I said.

Russell nodded and finally came back into his own head. "Yes. Of course, you're right. Thank you."

Russell stepped onto the stage and said a couple words to the band that I didn't catch and approached the microphone. "I'm sorry folks, but because of unforeseen circumstances, Toby Madden won't be able to play for you tonight. I appreciate you coming out, and please stay safe on your way home."

As expected, a chorus of boos erupted from the crowd, but when they watched Fran, Gabe, and Laurel leave the stage behind Russell, they disbursed.

We clustered in a small circle. Fran took off her bass guitar and handed it to a roadie. "What's going on?"

I waited for Russell to say something, but when I looked at him, he was already looking at me, expecting me to break the bad news.

I exhaled, followed by a deep breath. There was only one way to rip off this bandage. "Toby's dead. I found him on the bus."

Fran's eyes jumped immediately to mine. "You're kidding."

I stayed silent, but I held her gaze.

"You're not kidding," Fran realized.

Laurel started crying. Russell moved closer to her and put his arm around her shoulder, and she surprised me by taking a step farther away from him. "What happened?" Laurel asked.

"I have no clue. I found him and came back here and called the police."

If on cue, sirens whined nearby, got louder momentarily, then stopped.

"I'd better go. Since I found him, the police will want to talk to me," I said.

I left the stage and headed for the bus. I noticed there was already one squad parked beside it, and off in the distance, I spotted another two cars and an ambulance coming up the road. Much of the crowd that had left the amphitheater clustered around the immediate area.

I waited by the patrol car's hood for the trooper to appear. A couple of minutes later, he stepped off the bus and approached me.

"You the one who called this in?" I looked at the officer. I read the name Marvin printed on the name tag of his county-issued brown deputy's shirt.

"Yes. I'm Codi Cassidy. I found him. He was supposed to play tonight, and didn't appear for the show, so his manager asked me to search for him. No, Codi with an I, not a Y." It was a common mistake, and I thought I'd help him out as he took notes.

Another man was making a beeline for us. I could tell by the way he moved he was the person in charge.

"What do we have here?"

"Well, Sheriff, I just arrived. There's a DB on the bus. This is the person who called it in."

"Sheriff Cross, ma'am. Can you explain what happened here?"

I sighed. I hated repeating a story, but I did. When I finished, the sheriff nodded in understanding and addressed the deputy. "Lee, why don't you work with the others and clear the crowd, okay? Close the park if you need to."

Deputy Marvin took the order and left us. A paramedic stepped into the place the deputy had recently vacated.

"Well?" the sheriff asked.

The paramedic did a head-bob toward the bus. "He's gone, Sheriff. I can't tell for sure how long, but probably more than an hour. You'll need to get your investigative team on there before we can move him. It's too tight inside, and we'll have to carry him out without a gurney."

"Okay. I'll tell you when you can take him," Sheriff Cross said.

The paramedic returned to the ambulance to wait, and the sheriff moved to his car, opened the trunk, and returned with a duffel bag. He caught the questioning look in my eyes and took a moment to explain.

"It's a little joke around here. I am the investigative team."

While I waited, I walked back to my bus and retrieved my lawn chair from its storage cubby. After I set it up, I wanted to check on the kids. Fortunately, Merle, Dolly, Waylon, and Willie were all present and accounted for. Although I typically left their doors open so they could come and go as they pleased, I thought it best to keep them locked up for the time being. It was not the time and place for either a skunk or a three-legged raccoon, regardless of how cute and friendly they were.

I sat and waited. After ten minutes, Gabe appeared over the horizon, pulling my wagon behind him, and Laurel and Fran followed him, each with a guitar in hand. They stopped when they got to me.

"We brought your gear," Gabe said as he stopped right before me.

"Thanks. I appreciate that. Everything except the wagon goes on the bus."

Gabe reached for the door. "The door's locked."

I stood and fished the keys from my pocket. "Sorry about that. I must have locked it when I came out last time." I unlocked and opened the door, grabbed my guitar case, and hauled it inside. The interior was dark, so I flipped on a few lights. I carried my guitar to my room and set it down next to the bed.

Gibson wasn't in his normal place, so I looked around for a moment until I finally spotted him curled in a ball underneath my table.

"Stay in here, okay? Only for a little while."

Gibson threw me a half-hearted meow in protest as I closed the door behind me. When I got to the common area, Gabe was there holding Bozeman's pedal assembly and Bozeman's two guitars were at his feet. Laurel was cradling my laptop, and Fran was looking in my fridge.

"Follow me with that," I said.

Gabe did as he was told, and I opened the gear storage door and directed him where to place the pedals. He headed back for the guitars and stored them in the room and returned to the parlor and slid into the booth next to Fran.

I pointed at the laptop that Laurel still held, cradled like a baby to her breast. "I'll take that."

Laurel looked down. "Oh, yeah. Okay."

She passed me the computer, and I set it on the kitchen counter next to the microwave.

"Might as well have a seat." I pointed at one of the two remaining chairs in the room. Laurel sat in one. I took the other.

Gabe looked from person to person until his eyes settled on me. "So now what?"

I shrugged my shoulders. "Beats me. Have any of you seen Bozeman?"

Laurel and Gabe shook their heads.

Fran sat forward. "Nope. Not since you played. Wonderful set, by the way. I'd never heard any of your songs before. I really enjoyed it."

"Thanks." It wasn't the best of times for a compliment, but I took it anyway.

We waited in awkward silence for a good fifteen minutes for someone else to say something, but no one did. I felt relief washing over me when I caught a knock at the door.

"Come on in," I called.

A second later, Sheriff Cross appeared and stood tall before us. "I need to ask you all some questions. Would you mind coming with me? Let's start with you."

He pointed at Laurel, who sat closest to him. She got to her feet and followed him out of the bus.

"Interrogation time," Gabe said. He developed a sudden interest in his left thumbnail and started picking at it.

The wait continued. Perhaps an hour passed before Laurel returned, and Sheriff Cross removed Gabe from the room.

Laurel returned to her original chair and looked at the floor.

The silence was driving me nuts. "Well? What was that about?" I asked.

Laurel glanced at Fran, then looked at me. "I'm not supposed to talk about it until he's talked with everyone."

I nodded in understanding. It seemed logical to me. Once again, silence descended on us like a warm blanket as we waited.

The knock on the door returned, and the sheriff came for Fran. Laurel's brow furrowed as she noticed Gabe wasn't with him. "Where's Gabe?" Laurel asked.

She moved to get to her feet, and Sheriff Cross motioned for her to remain seated.

"Don't worry about him. He's outside. Sitting right outside the door here."

I stood and looked out the window. Sure enough, he was in my favorite lawn chair, the interest in his fingernail returned. I nodded at Laurel. "He's fine."

Laurel relaxed, and Fran followed the sheriff off the bus.

I wondered if I should turn on the television or make some tea or something when Laurel whispered in my direction. "Have you talked to them yet?"

"Just a little. Why?"

"Did he ask you about anyone you think could have done it?" Laurel asked.

"Done what?"

"Toby. The sheriff said someone murdered him."

That was news to me.

"He's been getting alibis from all of us and asking questions about everyone else. He wants to know if anyone saw anything," Laurel said, keeping her voice low.

"Go back. Someone murdered Toby? How?"

Laurel looked at the door, then back at me. She leaned so far forward in her chair I thought she'd fall over.

"They said they strangled him to death. How horrible."

I nodded in agreement and sat back. It was horrible.

"They also want to know —"

Laurel stopped the moment she detected the door open. A heartbeat later, Bozeman appeared.

I felt a sense of relief. "Hey, stranger. Where have you been?"

Laurel looked at Bozeman, then at me, then back at Bozeman. "I have to go. I'll talk to you later." Without another word, she scampered from the bus in a hurry.

An expression of confusion passed over Bozeman's face. "What was that about?"

I shrugged. "Don't know. So where were you?"

Bozeman took off his hat and placed it in the seat Laurel had just vacated. "After the gig, I talked to a few fans, then left for a walk around the park. What's going on? What's with the cops and the ambulance?"

"You don't know?"

Bozeman shook his head.

"Someone strangled Toby to death. I found him on his bus when he didn't show up for his set."

Bozeman's expression changed, and his face looked like he had just taken a big gulp of curdled milk. "Wait, what? Murdered? You're kidding."

"Come here." I got up and had Bozeman join me at the window. I opened the blinds and pointed outside to where the ambulance was still waiting. Several of the sheriff's department were milling about, trying to appear busy. "Does that look to you like I'm kidding?"

Bozeman slowly shook his head and took a seat at the table. "What's going on?"

"The sheriff's been taking statements from Toby's band mates, and I imagine he's going to want to speak to us too."

Bozeman was about to respond when the sheriff appeared. "Ms. Cassidy, could I have a few more words with you?" He passed an odd look in Bozeman's direction as I stood, then he escorted me from the bus.

When I stepped off the last stair, I noticed Gabe had moved the lawn chair to the end of the bus, and there were two deputies guarding my door.

"Right this way." I followed the sheriff away from the buses and over to a small picnic area. On a picnic table was an upside-down notepad covered by a rock. His duffel was on the ground next to the table. "Have a seat."

I sat down at the table and swung my legs in so I was facing forward. Since he was just under six feet and had a bit of a paunch, he put only one leg over the bench when he sat.

"How long have you known the deceased?" the sheriff asked.

"I just met him yesterday."

He picked up the rock and set it aside, turned the paper over, and jotted a note, then looked at me. "You just met? How did you become his opening act, having never met?"

"He's Bozeman's friend. They go way back," I explained.

"Where were you between the hours of six-thirty and eight?"

That was an easy enough question. "I was setting up our merch table, then we played our set."

"Do you have any witnesses?"

I smirked. "Of course. Everyone here did. We started promptly at seven and finished just a couple minutes past eight."

"No, I mean, can anyone verify you setting up your merch?"

"Yes. Laurel was with me the whole time. She and Fran ran it while I was playing."

"Where was Mr. James during that time? Didn't he help?"

"No. It only took the two of us. There wasn't a lot to do."

"Can you vouch for his whereabouts for the half hour before you took the stage?"

Could I? I thought hard about the question, and I realized there was really only one answer since I had interacted with only one person during that time frame.

Sheriff Cross didn't wait for an answer. He set the pen on top of the pad. "What about the fight Mr. James had with the deceased earlier today?"

My stomach did a somersault. I finally understood where this was going. I didn't lie, but I did try to soften things.

"It was just a disagreement."

"Over what?"

"One of Toby's songs. Bozeman recognized it as a song he'd written back when they were partners and wanted to ask Toby about it."

"Mr. James wasn't happy about it?"

I shook my head.

"Did he threaten any physical violence to the deceased?"

You mean other than to kill him?, I thought. "He was upset, sure, and I don't blame him. But Bozeman's a big teddy bear, and he wouldn't really hurt anyone."

"Would you be able to explain this?"

Sheriff Cross leaned over and took a plastic evidence bag from the duffel. He had a crumpled piece of paper in the bag, and when he turned it around, I recognized it right away.

"It's sheet music. To the song we were supposed to join Toby on during the encore."

The sheriff nodded. "Right. Can you guess how this piece of paper got jammed into Toby's throat?"

That one I had no answer for, although I wanted to provide a sarcastic one. In the end, I found it best to keep my opinion to myself.

"Thank you, Ms. Cassidy. That's it for now."

As the sheriff took a couple more notes, I excused myself and stepped back to the bus. The deputies near the door eyed me warily, but neither prevented me from entering. Bozeman was sitting right where I left him.

"Bozeman. Be honest with me. Where were you after the rehearsal?"

"You know where I was. I went for a walk."

"Yeah, but where?"

"Just here. Around the park. This place is massive. There are a couple of ball diamonds over that way, a soccer field, a disc golf course, a kid's playground, and a bunch of nature trails. Why do you ask?"

"Did you talk to anyone? Interact with anyone? Anyone recognize you?"

I stared at him as he searched through his memories.

"No. I didn't talk to anyone. It was pretty quiet over there. I saw a couple of guys playing disc golf, but they were way off in the distance and probably didn't see me. Come on, Codi. What's up?"

"Bozeman, listen to me." I walked over to him and placed my hand on his upper arm. "Remember earlier today when you got into that fight with Toby?"

"Yeah. Of course."

"Remember the part where you called him a thief and said you should hang him?"

Bozeman blinked. Twice. Then realization struck and struck hard. His chin dropped to his chest, and he rubbed his forehead.

"The cops think I did it, don't they?"

I nodded. "I'm pretty sure you're suspect number one."

"And they asked you about the threat I made? And where I've been? You told them?"

"Bozeman, look at me."

Bozeman looked back up at me. I could see a mix of fear and sadness in his dark brown eyes. "Have you ever known me to tell a lie?"

He shook his head.

"Would you want me to?"

"No. Of course not. You're the most moral person I've ever met, Codi. I know it's not in you to lie to anyone. Even if you did..."

I knew where he was going. "Yep. Even if I did, there were a half-dozen others who heard what I heard and saw what I saw."

"I'm so screwed."

"Did you do it?"

A flash of anger shot through his eyes, followed by a moment of hurt that I'd even asked the question.

"No. I didn't. You know I could never."

I believed him. I'd seen him angry, and I'd seen him drunk, and I'd seen him say or do stupid things. But none of the things I'd witnessed in the past led me to believe that Jesse James was a killer.

I heard the door open, and someone climbed the steps. I looked over and saw Sheriff Cross and Deputy Marvin standing there. The sheriff had a pair of handcuffs in his right hand.

"Bozeman James, I'm Sheriff John Cross. What can you tell me about the death of Toby Madden?"

Bozeman denied it right away. "No. Only that I didn't do it."

"Where you were this afternoon after the fight?"

Bozeman looked up at the sheriff, but didn't answer.

"Can you tell me anyone you interacted with, anyone to provide any kind of alibi?"

Bozeman stayed silent.

"Okay. We'll do this down at the station. Stand up and turn around."

Bozeman complied with the orders, and the sheriff placed Bozeman's right wrist in the cuffs.

"Bozeman James, you're under arrest. What was that?"

"I said my given name is Jesse. Bozeman's my stage name. That stays here."

Sheriff Cross chuckled. "No kidding? Jesse James? For real?"

Bozeman nodded. "Codi, give him my driver's license, okay?"

"It's in his room. Can I go get it?"

The sheriff nodded. "Marvin, go with her."

The deputy followed me into Bozeman's room, and I found Bozeman's wallet on his table right where he left it most of the time. I grabbed the wallet, removed his license from the plastic window, and returned the wallet to the table. The license I handed to the deputy, and we returned to the main room. The deputy passed the card to the sheriff, who examined it carefully. Cross put the license in his left shirt pocket, and from the right, he extracted what looked like a laminated business card.

"Son of a gun. Okay, then. Jesse James, you're under arrest for the murder of Toby Madden. You have the right to remain silent."

Bozeman struggled against his cuffs. "Wait, no. You've got the wrong guy! I didn't do it! I'm innocent!"

"Bozeman!" I got the attention of all three men in the room, and they each turned to look in my direction. "Shut up. Use that right."

Bozeman nodded, and the sheriff went back to the recital. "You have the right to remain silent. Anything you say can and will be used against you in a court of law. You have the right to an attorney. If you cannot afford an attorney, one will be provided for you. Deputy, escort him to my car, please."

Deputy Marvin took Bozeman's elbow and guided him to the bus door, and then they were both gone.

"What happens next?" I asked.

The sheriff looked at me. "Well, I'll hold him at the county jail until he can get a preliminary hearing in front of a judge. We're a little backed up, so it'll probably be Tuesday or Wednesday next week at the earliest."

"What do you think the judge will do?"

"It really depends on the judge, but since this is a murder charge,

I suspect the judge will hold him over for trial. I shouldn't say anything about anything, but I'd recommend you get him an excellent lawyer, and line up a bail bondsman. Otherwise, he'll stay with us until he goes to trial."

I followed the sheriff down the stairs and into the night. At some point, they must have removed the body because the ambulance was gone, and there were only three police cars left at the scene. In the car nearest me, I saw Bozeman in the back seat, head down, not moving. Sheriff Cross got into that car and drove off.

At Toby's bus, I saw Deputy Marvin bark orders to another deputy who was busy sealing the bus door off with police tape. Once the task was done, Marvin nodded and drove off in his own car. The final deputy, whose name I did not know, slipped behind the wheel of his own vehicle, but didn't go anywhere. I suspected his order was to stay on site and protect the crime scene from the public, even though they'd cleared the public from the park.

Up into the dark California sky I looked, just in time to see a shooting star pass overhead, and I took a moment to make a wish. I hoped had the strength to carry it through.

CHAPTER SIX

I was sitting in a captain's chair, cuddling with Gibson, when I heard a soft knock at the door. I wasn't expecting company, nor did I want any, so I ignored the sound. A few seconds later, the knock resurfaced, this time a little louder. I ignored it again, but the knock returned for a third time, and this time it sounded like whoever was pounding on the door was using a baseball bat to do so. I relented.

"Come in," I yelled.

The door opened with a squeaking noise I hadn't noticed before, and I made a mental note to write that down in the log I kept for Bozeman's bus maintenance tasks. The thought of Bozeman and the running list of chores I had for him around the bus made me sad and I wept again, which sucked because I hate to cry.

"Hey, hey there. Are you okay?" It was Laurel. She dropped the backpack she was holding, kneeled down, and wrapped her arms around me, which sucked, because I hate being held while I cry. If I have to cry, I like to do it alone. It seemed to make Laurel feel better, though, so I didn't pull away. So, I wept for a bit and threw in an intermittent sob for effect. I took a deep breath, and Laurel loosened her grip and pulled away.

She got back to her feet, headed into the kitchen, and returned with a paper towel, which I used to blot my eyes.

"I'm sorry," I said.

"Hey, there's no need to apologize to me. This has to be hard on you."

Laurel noticed Gibson. "Oh, I hope I didn't squeeze your skunk. I didn't notice him before."

I shook my head. "No. He's not a skunk. It's Gibson. He is my cat."

When he heard his name, Gibson picked his head up, which he had nuzzled into my torso, and looked around. He saw Laurel and reached out a paw.

"He likes you. Shake his hand."

Laurel did as she was told. "Nice to meet you, Gibson."

Gibson responded by struggling to his feet. He did a move I called the Halloween Kitty in which he stretched out, arched his back, and pointed his tail straight up in the air. He held the pose for a five second count, jumped to the floor and lazily walked to his food bowl.

I sniffled one last time, wiped my eyes, and blew my nose. I balled up the paper towel and tucked it under my leg.

"What are you doing here?"

"I've got a favor to ask. Would it be okay if I stayed with you? Only for tonight?" Laurel pleaded.

"Don't you want to sleep on your bus? It has to be far and away more comfortable than mine."

"We can't. The police taped it off and we can't return to it until they finish their investigation. They let us on under supervision long enough to grab enough personal items for a couple of days, but that's it. We can't get back on until they release it."

I got up and threw the used paper towel in the kitchen trash. "Just you?"

Laurel nodded. "Gabe's roughing it in the park. He's got a tent and a sleeping bag. Russell and Fran rode into town to find a hotel."

I thought about it for a moment. I didn't remember the last time I'd spent time alone on the bus. It had to have been months. I didn't mind being alone, and it's not like it scared me or anything, but it was always nice to have another person around if I wanted to talk. I could always talk to Gibson, Merle, and Dolly, but they never held up their end of the conversation. I was going to decline, but then my heart dropped when I saw Laurel standing there looking put out like Little Orphan Annie.

"Okay. You can stay for one night. You'll have to sleep out here, though."

She nodded. "Deal. That chair looks comfortable enough."

"No, not the chair, silly. The dinette there will convert to a bed. Here, I'll show you."

Laurel got out of the way, and I moved through the steps for her. First, I removed the tabletop, then the tables support pole from the middle. I removed a bench cushion and set the table into the built-in tracks, which bridged it across the space. Then I rearranged a couple of pillows to make the mattress, and with a little effort and sixty seconds worth of time, Laurel had a place to sleep.

Laurel looked at it like it was a magic trick. "That was easy. I guessed it converted, but I didn't know how."

"I'm sure you would have figured it out with some trial and error," I said.

Laurel picked up her backpack and put it on the bed and sat in the other captain's chair.

"Why didn't you go to town for a hotel?" I asked.

Laurel's cheeks reddened. Apparently, I'd touched on a sensitive subject. "I'm… a little short on funds. I haven't gotten paid in a while, and what little I make, I send home."

"How long is a while?" It wasn't my business, but my curiosity got the best of me.

Laurel thought about it. "I don't know. Two months, perhaps three."

That surprised me. "That long? I was expecting you to say a week or two at most. Why so long?"

Laurel shook her head. "You'd have to ask Russell that question. He and Toby never discussed the finances with us, and anytime Gabe, Fran, or I needed spending cash, we'd just ask Toby, and he'd reach into his pocket and hand us money."

"So, you're saying there was money? It wasn't a case of just being broke?"

"Oh, no. There was plenty of money. Toby always had a roll of bills in his pocket, like in those old gangster movies. He and Russell never lacked for anything, and there was always food and drink on the bus, and we never ran out of gas, so there must be cash coming from somewhere."

"Did Fran or Gabe get paid regularly?"

"I never asked. Since most of our needs are taken care of, it wasn't a big deal if we got paid sporadically."

I understood the logic to a point. I found when on the road, there wasn't a lot of time to go on shopping sprees, and as long as we didn't need food or other necessities, there wasn't much need for money. Most of it got deposited into the business account.

"You don't have a bank account to draw from?"

Laurel looked offended at the question, and I wanted to apologize for digging in too deep, but she answered before I said anything.

"Of course I do. I earmarked most of that for my grandmother. She's been ill, and I have a care provider for her."

"I'm sorry. Where is she?"

"Bakersfield," Laurel answered.

"You see her much?"

"When I can. I'm sure you recognize how it is with the schedules we keep."

I nodded. The life of a traveling musician wasn't all people romanticized it to be, especially when it came to staying in contact with family and friends.

"Although, I do video chat with her every day. Hey, Codi, if it means anything coming from me, I don't think Bozeman killed Toby. He doesn't seem like the type."

"Thanks. And he's not. Actually, it's a rare occurrence when he even loses his temper like he did today. The only other time I've seen that has been when he's protected me. All I need to do is clear his name. Sounds easy enough, right?"

Laurel nodded that she agreed, but the look on her face told me she didn't seem totally convinced.

"Do you mind if I ask you a few questions?" I asked.

Laurel brought her feet up below her and sat cross-legged in the chair. I had to give her points for that, since there was no way I could ever accomplish that acrobatic task. "Go ahead."

"How long did you work for Toby?"

Laurel gazed up at the ceiling for a while as she accessed her memory. "It's been more than a year. Fourteen, fifteen months maybe? They brought in me as a session player for his last album, and he asked me to stay as a regular in the band for this latest one."

"Did you ever have any trouble with him?"

"Like what? Like, did he come on to me, or did we fight, or whatever?"

I nodded. "Sure. Either, or both. Or more."

Laurel laughed. "A big no, and no. He and I had no animosity outside of the studio, and I wasn't really his type, so I never had to worry about him making a pass at me."

"What's his type?"

"Oh, the typical things that men go for. Tall, blond hair, blue eyes, thin, tan."

I smiled. "It sounds like you're describing Fran to a T."

"Almost. Frannie has hazel-green eyes, not blue, and she wears colored contact lenses, but still."

"Did they have a thing? Toby and Fran? Like, romantically?"

Laurel shrugged. "I don't know for sure. If they did, they kept it pretty well hidden. Ask Fran about that. I'm sure she'd be happy to tell you. She doesn't have much of a filter."

"How long has she been around?"

"Let's see," Laurel glanced back up at the ceiling. "Eight months? She wasn't around for the recording. She came in after Rusty left."

"Who's Rusty?"

"The old bass player. He'd been with Toby for years, then one day, he said he'd had enough, packed up his gear, and left us at the next city we came to."

"Sounds like they had a pretty big fight."

"They got into it something good all right, but I never figured out what they were fighting over."

I wondered if it had something to do with stolen lyrics. At least I had a lead on a suspect other than Bozeman. I got up, headed to the kitchen for a couple of cans of Diet Dr. Pepper and handed one to Laurel. She smiled, and we opened our cans and drank in unison.

"Have you seen Rusty around lately?" I asked, resuming my line of questioning.

"Sure did. I saw him last Saturday."

I raised an eyebrow.

Laurel reached into her pocket and extracted her phone. She clicked a few buttons, then passed the phone over to me. I looked at it and watched a video of a band playing at a theater. I watched half the song, then passed the phone back.

"Let me guess, the bass player is Rusty?"

Laurel took the phone and nodded.

"You know where and when that video was from?"

Laurel looked at her phone again. "A week ago Friday, Atkins Theater in Syracuse, New York."

Even I didn't think it was plausible that a guy would span the entire country to commit a murder.

"Rusty moved on and found a new band."

"He sure did. He's playing for someone now who's up and coming. The new guy has promise and will probably be bigger than Toby would ever hope to be."

I let out a heavy sigh. "Well, there goes my suspect pool."

Laurel smirked at me. "Don't give up so easily. You still got the rest of us. Me, Gabe, Fran, Russell…"

"Hey, that's true. Did you kill Toby?"

Laurel laughed. "No. I didn't kill Toby."

I wanted to take her at her word, but there were just a couple more things. "Did you ever leave the merch table during my set? Go to the bathroom? Get something to eat or drink?"

Laurel shook her head. "Nope. Stayed there from the time you left me until you returned."

"What about Fran?"

"Frannie's heart isn't really in sales. She showed up maybe ten minutes after you left, took a quick break in there to go do whatever she did, and left about five minutes before you came back."

"You know where she was?"

"Before and after, no. During, I'm pretty sure she wanted a snack because I saw her walk off toward the food trucks. Well? Did I do it?"

I looked at her in the eyes. "No. You didn't. No opportunity, no motive."

"I may be lying, you know. I might have shut down the merch table and did the deed and returned later. You wouldn't have noticed."

"No, you didn't. I checked the timestamps on the credit card transactions. At most, there was a four-minute gap between them. You didn't do it."

"I'm glad you believe me," Laurel said. She smiled at me, then took a drink.

"Me too. Hey, what about Gabe? What was their relationship like?"

Laurel stretched her arms in the air, then scratched her head. "Gabe's been with us for only a couple of months. He used to be in a metal band, then got shipped off here for some strange reason. To be honest, I don't understand it. He's a good drummer, but he's not a country music drummer, you know what I mean?"

I nodded. I understood. Different music, different rhythms, and methods.

"Gabe and Toby ever have any words?"

"No, but I imagined there would have been some, eventually. Toby was always on Gabe about his playing. Gabe was doing the best he could to learn the music, but occasionally, he'd make little slip-ups. Not enough to affect the song ever, but it was enough to throw us other musicians off."

"His playing presented a problem with the band?"

"Laurel paused again. "I'd say not really. Fran's not the best bassist in the band, but she always keeps the correct tempo, and I have to give her credit for that. I mean, she's got a head for timing. She could play something in a four-four-time signature and have a different person around her playing in three-four, and she'd still hold her own. Anyway, Gabe always leaned on that. Every time he messed up, he just followed Fran right back to where he should be."

"But Toby didn't like that, I'll bet."

"No. He sure didn't. I remember one time at rehearsal, the kid kept messing up and Toby kept getting angrier and angrier at him. I mean, it was frustrating. We had to restart the same song at least eight times by then, and I was sure Toby wanted to bust his guitar over Gabe's head by then."

"What happened?"

"In the end, Toby screamed a bunch of things at Gabe I don't want to repeat, then he left and returned to the bus."

"And what about Russell? Does he have any issues with Toby?"

Laurel frowned. "Ask Russell that one. To be perfectly honest, when we first met, Russell was a little too forward toward me, if you know what I mean. Since then, I've been trying my best to keep my distance and never be alone with him if I can help it."

I nodded. "Smart girl."

Laurel yawned, and I felt bad for her. It had been a long, emotionally taxing day, and I realized how tired I was, too.

"I'll get you some bedding."

"Great. You have a place I could change?"

"Sure. Use my bedroom. It's at the end of the hall."

Laurel picked up her backpack and hauled it into my bedroom and closed the door. While she was gone, I retrieved a set of sheets, a blanket, and a pillow from the equipment room and made up the bed for her. I heard the door open. When I looked over, Laurel stood before me wearing flannel pajama bottoms with penguins on them, and a T-shirt that featured an alien flashing the peace sign. I couldn't help but grin.

"I like the ensemble."

Laurel plodded to the bed while I checked that all the blinds were properly closed, then I locked the door. "If you need anything, I'm right down the hall. And if anyone comes to the door, don't answer it. Come and wake me up, okay?"

Laurel nodded and pulled the covers up to her chin. "Good night."

"Good night, Laurel."

I shut off the lights and walked through the dark to my bedroom. Within a few minutes, I got changed and dove into my bed. I felt Gibson jump on the bed, and within a couple minutes, he was lying on my chest and purring. I didn't know if I'd be able to sleep, but there's something calming about a cat's purr and within scant seconds I drifted off to dream land.

The next morning when I got up, Gibson was no longer with me, which was unusual for him. After I slid into some jeans and a shirt, and used the bathroom, I went to check on my guest. I found her back in the captain's chair, reading a book. Gibson was on her lap, licking his tail.

"Good morning," I said, trying to sound chipper.

Laurel looked up and smiled. "Good morning. Sleep well?"

"Surprisingly, yes. You didn't need to do that."

Laurel had folded up all the bedding and turned the bed back into a dinette.

"It was no trouble. I appreciate you letting me stay over. What do you plan on doing today?"

I opened the fridge and looked in. There was plenty of food for the kids, not so much for me unless I wanted a salad for breakfast. "Well, after I get cleaned up and feed the animals, I'll probably venture into town and see if I can visit Bozeman."

"Want some company?"

I thought that over, then agreed. "Sure. But you have to have breakfast with me, too. Does that work for you?"

Laurel nodded and put down her book. "Sure, if I can grab a shower first."

"Let me feed the beasties, and I'll come with you. I could use one myself."

Laurel slipped into more appropriate clothes while I dropped off a plate of vegetables for Merle and Dolly. Both were sleeping and didn't notice me. Willie and Waylon were both chittering away when I opened their cage. I could tell they were happy to get into the morning sun when they jumped to the ground and bounded away without so much as a hello. I cleaned out their abode and dropped a couple of shelled walnuts into their dish as a surprise treat upon their return. When I turned around, Laurel was there, backpack in hand.

I went back aboard the bus and grabbed my shower things, and met her back outside. We didn't talk as we walked to the shower house, but I thought it was still nice to have someone along with me. Like the previous day, the place was empty. We each selected a stall, showered, dressed, and headed back.

We were halfway to the bus when we saw Gabe headed in the opposite direction. Based on his look, he had gone through a rough night. His hair looked tussled, and I thought his face seemed paler than the day before. Something else I hadn't picked up on was that he wore eyeliner. I only noticed it then because it had smudged overnight, giving him a wicked raccoon appearance.

"Good morning, Gabe," Laurel said to him as I wondered if she was always so perky in the morning.

"Hey." Gabe's greeting came out more like a grunt than an actual word.

I thought this would be an excellent time to get his take on things. "While I have you here, you mind if I ask you a couple of questions?"

Gabe thought otherwise. Without stopping, he grunted again and kept walking.

Laurel turned her smile on me. "He's not really a morning person."

After we returned to the bus, I made sure I had my phone, wallet, and keys on me. I was never much of a purse-girl, especially since I usually had my guitar case with me that I could shove stuff in. Laurel was already outside waiting for me, and I locked up the bus and was ready to go.

"I wonder how far we need to walk to get to the jail."

"Oh, we have three options on that. We could either walk, which is about four miles from here, or, if we wanted to wait for Neil, he could give us a ride, or we can get a rideshare."

"Who is Neil?"

Laurel turned and pointed toward the police car stationed near Toby's bus. "Deputy Neil over there. His relief doesn't get here for another hour, but he said he'd give us a ride if we needed it."

Before I could answer, my stomach rumbled loud enough for Laurel to hear.

"I'll get us a rideshare," Laurel said before I could answer her question. "Can you share the cost? I scraped up about thirty bucks, but that'll have to last me until I can get to a bank."

I agreed. Laurel performed some magic on her phone, and within fifteen minutes we were in the back of a van headed toward town. The driver dropped us off at a diner. We entered, and I happily worked my way through a Denver omelet with toast while Laurel downed a plate of pancakes. As she ate, Laurel used her phone to find the county jail, which, to our mutual joy, was only four blocks away.

After breakfast, we walked to the jail. Out front there was a marble monument dedicated to law enforcement surrounded by benches. Laurel got comfortable on a bench and pulled a book from her backpack as I entered the building.

I didn't know quite how to frame my question as I approached the desk. What was Bozeman? Inmate? Suspect? I wasn't sure as I made my request. "I'd like to see someone in your custody, please."

The desk sergeant looked at me, then tapped the small sign next to the desk that read 'no visitors without prior approval'.

"I'm here about his lawyer."

The sergeant looked me up and down. I was wearing blue jeans, a T-shirt, a zippered sweatshirt, and a baseball cap to hide my blue hair.

"You don't look like no lawyer to me," he said.

"No. I'm not his lawyer, I'm his business partner. I'm here to see who he wanted to contact for his lawyer. We have several that we use." That was a little white lie, since we had only one. But in my defense, my person knew people.

I could tell the sergeant was about to deny my request when Sheriff Cross appeared. "Ms. Cassidy. Sign in there and come with me."

I looked down and jotted my name on the visitor log, along with who I was going to see. The desk sergeant collected my hat, phone, keys, and wallet, and handed me a visitor's pass to clip to my shirt. From there, I followed the sheriff into a small room, and he directed me to a chair. He left, and I waited. Ten minutes later, the door opened, and Bozeman entered, followed by a deputy, and then the sheriff.

Sheriff Cross nodded, and the deputy left the room. "You can take all the time you need, but since you're not legal counsel, we'll be watching and listening."

He pointed to the ceiling corner to show us the camera. He unlocked Bozeman's left handcuff, ran it beneath a metal bar attached to the table, and cuffed his wrist.

I waited to speak until he left the room, which was silly, considering we were being recorded. "Are you okay?"

"Yeah."

"You don't look so good. Didn't you sleep much?"

"Not really. The only benefit to being a murder suspect is I didn't have to share a cell with anyone. They think I'm a menace to society."

"Who should I call? You got a lawyer in mind?" I asked.

Bozeman shook his head. "Never needed one. I certainly don't want a public defender, though. Think Mac could find me one?"

Morris MacDonald was our entertainment lawyer. He stepped in when we had things that involved complicated contracts. Like when we hired musicians, producers, and booked studio time when we cut new records. Occasionally, we had him look over the paperwork when we got approached by a larger music festival or some other promotion company. He was a good guy, and always weeded out the bad deals for us.

"Criminal law is outside his area of expertise, but I can get a recommendation from him."

Bozeman nodded. "I've been trying to wrack my brain around who would do this, but I can't come up with anyone. And since they've got the witnesses saying I made the threats, they're pretty sure I'm the guy. I wish we'd never found that notebook."

"What do you mean?" I asked.

"Well, I wasn't one hundred percent sure he'd stolen my song until I confirmed it with the book. I mean, I thought it sounded familiar when we played it at rehearsal, but that happens all the time since so many songs like to sample from other songs."

"Wait, Bozeman. That notebook would prove you wrote the song."

"Yeah, so?"

"I mean, if you could prove you wrote the song, wouldn't it make more sense to sue the pants off him and the record company for copyright infringement?"

Bozeman exhaled. "Again. Yeah, so?"

I smiled at him. "So that takes away your motive. You'd be better off keeping him alive. You wouldn't see a penny with him dead. I need to find that notebook."

CHAPTER SEVEN

Laurel and I caught a rideshare back to the park, and she followed me into my bus. I had Laurel take a seat at the dinette while I headed to Bozeman's bedroom to search for the notebook. The room appeared just as I'd left it when I got his license, except his wallet wasn't in the same place I'd gotten it from. Bozeman was, in a word, a neat freak. Although he'd never been in the Army, you wouldn't guess that by looking at his room. He made his bed with military precision, and he stowed everything away where things should be. The only place that usually looked cluttered, and I'm using the word cluttered loosely here, is his table. The surface usually held his wallet, phone, and other things he used most often. Currently, there was a notebook, along with a mug filled with pens and pencils. The notebook was open to a page which was half-filled with lyrics and chords. No doubt a new song he was working on. I turned the notebook over, and sure enough, it had a blue cover, not a red one.

I did a quick spot check around the room, including under the bed and in the small closet, but saw no signs of the book I wanted.

"He must have put the thing away," I said to myself, and that made sense because he had an annoying habit of putting things back when he finished with them. Half the time I don't think he even realized he did it. It was automatic.

After I left his room, I trekked to the storage room and retrieved Bozeman's banker's boxes. I remembered him pulling out only two, but I found four, and I wrestled them all out into the hall and set them next to the dinette table. I opened the cover of one and set the box on the table.

"Here, help me sort through this. We're looking for a notebook with a red cover."

Laurel and I dug through the box and repeated the exercise Bozeman and I had gone through the previous day. Although this time, I didn't have his organized mind to ease the task.

When we finished, we had four books stacked on the table.

I took the top one and gave it to Laurel and grabbed the second for myself. "Let's go through these first."

"What are we looking for?" she asked.

"That song Toby wanted to put out as his first single. The one he planned for us to sing together at the encore before the big fight happened. Somewhere in one of these books are the handwritten lyrics that Bozeman wrote years ago, and they seemed to be a perfect match to the sheet music Russell gave us. Sheet music."

Where did I put the sheet music? I assumed what the sheriff had in the evidence bag was Bozeman's copy, but where did I put mine?

Unlike Bozeman, who will put things away when he's not using them, I will often leave items out a little longer before I deal with them, much to Bozeman's chagrin. Sometimes it gets to where he will stow them somewhere without telling me, and I'll spin in circles, sometimes literally, trying to find the item I wanted.

My go-to place was the dinette table, but since Laurel and I currently sat at it, I knew that was out. I checked the kitchen counters and the kitchen trash before I returned to my bedroom to search there. Unlike Bozeman's barracks, my room looked a little more lived in. Today, I pulled the bedcovers up and stacked the pillows on the bed. I did that more for Gibson's benefit than mine since he liked to sleep on the top of the pile. I checked my table, which currently held my computer, a bunch of random, unrelated papers, a handful of guitar picks, and an inkless pen that I'd yet to throw away. No sheet music.

I exited my room and walked back to Laurel. "You wouldn't have a copy on you, would you?"

Laurel shook her head. "I left my copy on the other bus. Are you sure you had yours?"

"I'm pretty sure. I had it when I followed Bozeman back here. Then we rifled through the notebooks, and I'm pretty certain we compared them to his copy, because he crushed his into a ball, and

I had folded mine. Then he left, and I gave the kids a snack, and…"

I remembered where I put the thing, so I stepped to the fridge, opened the door, and right on the top shelf I discovered the piece of paper, neatly folded in half. I brought the paper back to the table, opened the sheet, and set it sideways so we could both use it for reference. Of course, I tried to act as if keeping things in the fridge was normal for everyone.

"Page through the book and find the sheet that matches the lyrics. I'm pretty sure Bozeman had a different title, but I don't remember what he called the original."

"I understand," Laurel said as she reached for the book.

Laurel and I started working through our respective books, and the bus stayed quiet. Until Laurel suppressed a laugh, then didn't hold it back.

"What's so funny?" I asked.

"I did the same thing once; except I lost my phone. Usually, I set my alarm for seven, but for some insane reason, I woke up early, and I was the only one up, and I must've put my phone in the fridge when I looked for something. Of course, at seven, the alarm rang, and wouldn't turn off, so it kept dinging. You couldn't hear it from outside the fridge. When Russell opened the door, he suspected someone planted a bomb in there, so he slammed the door shut and ran off the bus."

"That's not funny." Then I pictured Russell scampering away and I laughed. "Okay, that's a little funny."

I completed my notebook first, then grabbed another. I was about halfway through when Laurel closed hers and reached for the last book. When I finished, I waited for her. Nothing. I put all four notebooks back in the box and returned the box to the storage room while Laurel started on the next box. In the second box, we had five notebooks to search through. In the third box, there were zero red-covered ones, and in the fourth box we found six. After two hours, we'd been through all the boxes, and the notebook wasn't in any of them.

"Now what?" Laurel asked. She had a good question.

"Hold on a minute. Bozeman took the notebook with him back to the stage when he confronted Toby. Did you see that?" I asked.

Laurel nodded. "Didn't miss that. He almost shoved it up Toby's nose."

"Then the ruckus started. Maybe Bozeman dropped the book and didn't pick it back up before I dragged him away. Do you remember seeing it?"

Laurel thought for a moment. "No, since I focused on the fight. I suppose it might still be by the stage."

"I doubt it. There must have been, what, three or four dozen people backstage after that? Someone probably found it."

"Let's go check, anyway," Laurel said.

I imagined that would be a hopeless exercise, but Laurel was right. We should at least look and cover that base. Together, we walked to the amphitheater and stepped backstage. It was empty. Russell's road crew had packed up all the gear and equipment and hauled it away. From what I could tell, the crew was top-notch, and they impressed me with the pack out. Not even a remnant of gaffer tape remained on the floor where they'd affixed the cables.

"Someone might have picked it up and put it in a random road case," Laurel said.

I exhaled. "Yeah, you're probably right. Someone found it and shoved it in with a random piece of gear. Now all I'd have to do is find that gear. Is the sound and lighting company the same as what you guys normally use for a show?"

"I don't think so. This was supposed to be a big deal, so the record company brought it all in from Los Angeles."

I frowned. If that were true, there would be no way I would track that stuff down. It would either be in a warehouse or on its way to the next gig.

"Damn," I said.

Laurel took me by the arm. "Come on, there's nothing here. Let's go back."

I let Laurel lead me from the stage and we trudged back to the parking lot. As we got closer, I noticed two things. The first was more police activity on Toby's bus. The second was Gabe sitting nearby, still in my favorite chair. We walked over, and he grunted in acknowledgment.

Laurel pointed at the police. "What's going on?"

Gabe shrugged. "I'm not sure. Perhaps the cops are doing another pass-through for evidence or whatnot. The one guy yesterday said they were going to do that."

We watched for a while. I saw Sheriff Cross appear once again, front and center, with his duffel bag in tow.

"We didn't have time to talk this morning. Can we do it now?" I asked.

Gabe shrugged again. "I guess."

"I take it you're not much of a morning person?"

"No. Not really. You know how it is in this life, right? Sleep until mid-afternoon, get up, do a gig, party all night."

I didn't know what life he was talking about. It certainly didn't fit with my experience of show business, which rarely included after-parties or staying up all night. Unless it meant driving to the next show. Bozeman and I usually woke up early every day, or at least I did, since he did all the driving and sometimes slept in after a long road trip. There was too much on the business side of show business to do.

"How did you get along with Toby?"

Another shrug. At least his shoulders were getting a good workout. "Okay, I guess."

"I heard he would come down on you during rehearsal," I stated, more like a fact than a question.

He paused. "Where'd you hear that from?"

"It doesn't matter. Is it true?"

"Sometimes. But he was like that with everyone, not just me."

I didn't respond and waited for him to fill in the growing uncomfortable silence. It worked.

"Okay. I admit, it's taking me a bit to get in the groove. I'm used to different music. When I was with the other band, I could play anyway I wanted, and I got to do solos."

"And Toby?"

"Oh, he was always on me. Gave me music to listen to and expected me to learn how to drum from that. Anytime I missed a beat, it seemed he wanted to beat me. But look at it from my perspective. I'm new to this. I don't know about all this country stuff, and I made a mistake coming here."

"Anyone else have any trouble with Toby?"

Gabe erupted out of the chair so fast there could have been a spring beneath him. Laurel took an instinctive step back, but I stayed anchored in my spot.

"Why are you bothering me? Ask her. Ask any of them. I don't care. Just leave me alone!"

He huffed with a side of growl, and he puffed his chest out. A scowl crossed his face, and I knew at that moment that I misjudged the kid. I thought he was a shy wallflower type trying to find his way. But with the outburst, he seemed to be one of those internal-volcanic types who was prone to blow under the least provocation.

He stepped closer. The toe of his shoe contacted mine. I didn't back away, though.

"Before you say anything else, or do anything you'll regret later, I suggest you look to your right," I said.

He hesitated a moment, then looked. Deputy Marvin was leaning up against his car, watching the whole thing.

Gabe took a step to the side. "I have to use the bathroom. Don't talk to me again."

Gabe turned and stomped off toward the restrooms. I took advantage of his leaving and folded up my lawn chair, carried it back to my bus, and locked it in the storage space where it belonged.

"Is he always like that?" I asked.

Laurel looked back, probably to confirm he hadn't returned. "Not always, but he's been getting worse over the last couple of weeks. I wonder what his issue is."

"Well, if I had to guess, I'd say he has two issues. Anger and drugs."

"No. Do you think?"

"I think he's using something. What, I'm not sure. He probably ran out of whatever he was on a couple of weeks ago, and now he's going through withdrawal and can't handle it," I said.

"Are you sure?" Laurel asked.

"Not a hundred percent, but somewhere in the high nineties. I've seen it before. You think Toby or Russell are wise to his problem?"

It was Laurel's turn to shrug. "I have no idea. Obviously, it's a surprise to me."

I was about to comment on something else, but before I could, Sheriff Cross approached.

"Ms. Preston, do you know where Mr. Davidson is?"

Laurel answered right away. "Well, if he's not here, he's probably still in town. Why do you need him?"

"We're all done here. We've got a few things we're taking for evidence. Here's a list of the things we took." The sheriff handed her a sheet of paper that she didn't bother looking at. "Also, I'm releasing the bus, so you're all free to go back. You two have a nice day now."

We watched as the sheriff casually moved to his truck, got in, and drove off, leaving Laurel and me there alone.

Laurel glanced at the paper, seemed disinterested, then looked at the bus. "I hope they didn't lock up behind them. I don't have a key."

"You don't have a key to your own bus?"

"No. Russell was always paranoid about security. Only him, Toby, and the driver had a key. It usually wasn't an issue, since one or more of them were always around."

"Driver? I don't think I met a driver."

"Yeah. I'm not surprised. He and Toby didn't get along much. Steve's only around when we need to drive somewhere. When we're not on the road, I don't see him much."

"That seems odd to me. What was their riff?"

"No clue. You'd have to ask Steve. I imagine he'll be around today sometime since we're free to leave. Speaking of which, I'd better call Russell."

Laurel took her phone from her pocket, looked at it, and returned it. "My phone is dead. Like an idiot, I forgot to grab my charger yesterday. Come on, let's go get it."

I followed Laurel, and luckily for us, the sheriff had left the door wide open.

"Whoa. I hope I don't have to clean up this mess."

I looked around the common area, and I could tell the sheriff and his crew had done a thorough search. Although they destroyed nothing, they'd also returned nothing to the exact spot it had been. There were seat and couch cushions awry, items spread out, and I could see in the kitchen area where cabinets and drawers were half or fully open. It looked like a small tornado had come through since I'd been on the bus last.

"I'm going to check out Toby's room," I said.

Laurel nodded and took the lead, but turned left into her space while I headed to the rear. The door was open, and I stepped into the room and saw pretty much what I expected to. The bedding was gone, and there was black fingerprint dust everywhere. There was a bedside table with a drawer, so I reached over and slid it open. Inside the drawer was an open pack of AA batteries. I also found a crossword puzzle book, a broken pencil, and an adult magazine with the photo of a blond with very impressive breasts on the cover. I closed the drawer and turned my attention to the closets. It didn't take me long to determine there was nothing to see.

I left Toby's room and returned to Laurel's. She didn't have a room as much as she had a dedicated sleeping space. She didn't have a door, but a sliding privacy partition. Her space included a cot-sized bed with under-bed storage, and a small nightstand that also served as a table. She also had a small portable wardrobe that appeared to be made of cheap press board.

She saw me hovering and screeched at me. "Don't come in here!"

"Why not?" I asked.

"It's embarrassing," Laurel said.

"It's not so bad." I stepped over and sat down on her bed. I couldn't confirm, but I think her mattress had concrete instead of padding. "Before I bought my bus, Bozeman and I were touring the country in an old van from the seventies. We spent more time broken down on the side of the road than we did playing music."

Laurel relaxed and checked her phone. It was on the charger, but apparently didn't have enough juice just yet.

"Really? You and Bozeman slept in a van together?"

"Sure did. It had a bench seat that fit me perfectly, but poor Bozeman had to sleep either sitting in the passenger seat or curled around the gear in the back. Most nights, he slept in a pup tent outside, which wasn't so bad in the summer. Or so he claims. You'll have to ask him about it sometime."

"What do you suppose this is?" Laurel asked.

I looked at the finger Laurel was holding out to me.

"It's fingerprint powder. They probably wanted to get the prints of everyone who was on the bus. Did they take your prints when they questioned you yesterday?"

Laurel shook her head as she grabbed a tissue and wiped the powder away. She used the same tissue to clean up the mess on the nightstand.

"They might, just to exclude you as a suspect," I said.

"You sure know a lot about police work for a singer."

I smiled. "Well, my dad was a cop."

I let it go with that. I didn't mention that dad was actually a detective in the Denver Police Department, nor did I talk about my proclivity for getting in and out of mysteries.

"You mind if I look around the bus some more?"

Laurel wrinkled her nose. "I don't know about that. Toby had a pretty strict rule about not going into each other's spaces, you know?"

"I get it. Everyone needs their privacy, right? You think I could at least use the toilet?"

"That you can do. Go back toward Toby's room. It's on the right."

I left Laurel to her cleaning and stepped into the hallway. I waited for a moment to ensure we were alone, since I didn't want to get caught by anyone. Then I drifted in the general direction of the bathroom. After I looked back to see if Laurel was watching, I opened one door and saw a small bunk area. I assumed it was Gabe's, based on the messy appearance and drumsticks laying on the bed.

The next room over belonged to Fran, I assumed because of the bass guitar leaning in the corner, and the pictures of herself hanging on the far wall. She must have done modeling work at one point, because none of the shots appeared to be selfies or from a point-and-shoot camera. Her room was a little larger than Gabe's area, and although the bed was small, the area was extensive enough for a real closet and a dressing table. She'd cluttered up the dressing table with bars and bottles of makeup and other cosmetics that I never used.

Russell's room was next, and it was larger than Fran's, and smaller than Toby's. His amenities included a full-sized bed, a closet, a bookshelf stuffed with books and papers, and a small desk. Although I wanted to enter that space and rummage through all his papers, I didn't want to break my promise to Laurel. I just took in what I could see from the doorway.

I saw nothing of use to me, so I left his room and went to the bathroom. Their bathroom was larger than the one on my bus and included a full-sized toilet, vanity, and a shower stall that looked like an old phone booth. I did my business, washed my hands, and went back to Laurel.

"Everything good in here?" I asked.

I found her still scrubbing away at the nightstand. "No. I don't think this powder will ever come off. Can you look around to see if they messed anything else up like this?"

Someone had folded over the covers on her bed, as if they had gone through the three under-bed drawers, and one wasn't closed properly. I crouched down, opened the first drawer, and peered in. It was where Laurel kept her personal hygiene and beauty supplies. The second drawer she'd stuffed with socks and underwear. The third one, which wasn't on its track, was full of music books and correspondence. As I fixed the drawer, I thumbed through the contents.

"That's all music and old letters and cards from friends and family. I trained in classical music before I switched over to country, so I like to practice that stuff sometimes to keep sharp."

I pushed the drawer closed and sat back on the bed. "Hey, Laurel, I'm sorry. I didn't mean to pry."

Laurel looked into my eyes for a second. "Yes, you did."

I thought she was serious for a moment, but then she laughed.

"Got you. It's okay. I've got nothing to hide. Check the closet, will you?"

I opened the wardrobe and looked inside. It had three sections. The top half had a bar to hold hanging clothes. From what I could tell, Laurel's wardrobe consisted mostly of jeans and casual shirts. There was also a rain jacket, a heavy jacket, and two sweatshirts on hangers.

On the left side were three drawers. I opened and closed all the drawers quickly. Two held T-shirts, and the third held four pairs of shoes, three casual, and one pair of black high heels that matched the only dress she had hanging in the closet.

On the right side, below the hanging clothes, was an area to hold just about anything, and in that space, there were four violin cases. I touched one, and a violin bow tipped over and fell out of the closet.

Laurel heard the sound and glanced over. "What's that doing out? I keep all the bows in their cases when I'm not playing. It's too easy to damage them otherwise. Find out where that goes and put it away, will you?"

I took out the first case and looked in. Not being a violinist, I didn't really know what I was looking at, but it looked like the type of violin I'd seen in every orchestra I'd ever watched. The top had a place for bows, and this case held two of them. I closed the case and opened the next one. This violin looked like it was from outer space. It was missing most of its body, although it had the neck, fingerboard, and chin rest the previous one had. It looked to be missing the body.

"What is this?" I asked.

"Oh, that's my new baby. Full electric. I love it and want to transition over to it. Not as temperamental onstage as a classic violin."

"You weren't playing it yesterday, were you?"

"No. Toby won't let me play it in concerts. It didn't match the pure country image he wanted."

The violin had its bow, so I moved on to the last case. I put the case on the bed and opened it.

"Laurel? How did this get here?"

Laurel looked over and she and I stared at the red notebook stuffed into her violin case.

CHAPTER EIGHT

Laurel looked flustered and spoke up immediately. "I didn't put that there."

I reached into the case, removed the notebook, and opened the cover. Sure enough, Bozeman had written his name, along with the date range the contents spanned. I had a choice to make: whether to believe Laurel, or throw her back into my suspect pool. If I had the supplies, I would dust the thing for fingerprints myself. Regardless of the training my dad gave me, I never picked up that skill and always smudged them, thus making them unusable.

"You don't know how this got here?" I asked.

"No. Of course not!"

"This isn't the fiddle you played last night?"

"No. That's an old one I never use. Check this out. I damaged one of the tuning pegs, and I haven't gotten it fixed yet. About two months ago, I broke it."

I picked up the violin and glanced at the instrument. Even though I didn't play a violin, I knew enough about stringed instruments to tell one of the tuning pegs seemed askew. I placed the violin back in the case, added the bow, and closed it.

"Besides, how would I know the notebook would be so important? And if I took the thing, why would I hide it where someone would find it so easily? It's not like I have a lot of secret stashes here. I don't even have a locking door. Anyone who wants can come in here." Laurel waved her arms around the small space and then crossed them in defiance.

I thought Laurel made a lot of really excellent points, even though she sounded a little defensive. Although I imagine I'd be acting the same had our positions been reversed.

I looked at Laurel. Nothing about her body language suggested she tried to hide anything from me, and I did believe deep in my heart that she knew nothing about the book.

"What's going on here?" a voice said.

Laurel and I ended our staring contest, and both looked over to see Gabe standing in the hall.

Laurel picked up her phone and held it out. "I forgot my charger. I need to call Russell and tell him we got the bus back. Or do you want to?"

Gabe huffed. "Yeah, right. Like I'm going to call him. Have fun."

He left, and I guess based on his direction, he was going to his own room.

"You mind if we go back to your bus? I don't want to be with him here alone."

I thought she made a reasonable request, so I followed Laurel off her bus, and she followed me onto mine. Truth be told, it seemed empty without Bozeman around, so I was happy to have her there.

"Looks like someone's hungry." Laurel pointed at the floor.

I looked over and noticed Gibson's stainless-steel bowl was empty, and he was sitting before it, hitting it repeatedly with his paw. It made a slight ting sound every time one of his nails came into contact with it.

"He can be demanding when he's hungry. Here, take this and find the song."

I gave the book to Laurel, and she sat down at the dinette while I opened a cabinet and pulled out a plastic container filled with dry cat food. "Are you hungry, little man?"

I filled the bowl about a quarter full, then set it back on the floor. Gibson rubbed against my leg, then moved in for the snack while I put the container away.

"Laurel, would you like something to drink?" I asked.

"Yes. I'll take a bottle of water if you have one."

I nodded and opened the fridge. There was plenty of Bozeman's favorite beer in there, but no water. I walked back to the storage room, found the fresh case I remembered we had in there, pulled out a couple of bottles, and sat down opposite Laurel. I slid the bottle to her, and she opened it up and drank half before setting it down.

"Thanks. I was really thirsty," she explained.

I thought it was odd when Laurel got to the last page, then closed the book and handed it to me.

"It's not in there. Wrong notebook."

I made my signature confused scrunchy face. "It has to be. It was the only notebook that he removed from the bus. The rest are all in storage."

Laurel passed me the notebook, and I opened it and started from the beginning. I wanted to rush through, but I took my time so I wouldn't miss it. I remembered it was somewhere in the middle, but I didn't find it, and soon, I too got to the end without success.

"This makes no sense." I lifted the book and shook it in the air. "It has to be in here."

As I shook the book, a piece of paper about the size of a single snippet of confetti floated down and hit the table. Laurel and I both followed its fall, like we were watching a bald eagle descending on a field mouse.

"Oh, no," I said.

I started from the beginning and paged through the notebook again. This time I paid particular attention to the margins on the spiral end where the paper connected to the wire. I found the spot I was searching for and pulled out another snippet of paper.

"Someone ripped it out."

Laurel leaned in and examined the book. "How can you tell?"

I lined up the two pieces of paper on the table before her.

"When they ripped out the pages, they left behind a couple bits of evidence."

"How do you know Bozeman didn't rip those pages out himself? It might be he didn't like whatever he was working on and removed it. It could still be the wrong book."

I flipped back a few pages, didn't find what I wanted, then flipped forward a few, and pushed the notebook back to Laurel. "If he didn't like something, he put an X through it and moved on."

Laurel looked at the page and the ink marked that stretched

from corner to corner. She paged through the book and discovered another one shortly thereafter.

"I'd also be willing to bet that if I counted the pages in the other notebooks, they would match the count on the cover," I said. "And this one would be short, although I don't want to go through that experiment. Unless you'd like to."

"No. I'll take your word for it. What does it mean?"

"It means someone understood the importance of that notebook and that song, and I mean to figure out who it was. Got enough battery to call Russell yet?"

Laurel checked her phone, nodded, and made the call.

*

Two hours later, Laurel and I were sitting outside, me in my favorite chair, Laurel in Bozeman's, when a car pulled up and Russell and Fran emerged from the vehicle. Russell carried a backpack and a computer bag. Fran had a carry-on suitcase, and she looked like she was returning from the airport.

Fran waved her fingers at us before she climbed onto the bus, but Russell didn't acknowledge us at all.

Fifteen minutes later, Fran stepped off the bus carrying a large mesh beach bag. She had a pair of flip-flops wedged in the side, the top of a bottle of shampoo sticking up from a pocket, and there was a towel under her arm.

"Hey, keep your eye on things here for me, would you?" she said in our direction.

Without waiting for Laurel to answer, I jumped out of my seat and double-timed my gait until I almost caught up with Fran. Since she was taller than I was, I had to walk a little faster than I normally would just to keep up with her.

"Fran. Hey, Fran, slow down!"

Fran stopped, looked behind her, noticed it was me, and smiled.

"Hi, Codi."

"Do you mind if I talk to you?"

"Sure. Walk with me. I'm sorry about your friend getting arrested. He seemed like a nice guy. I was hoping to spend some time with him."

On instinct, I rolled my eyes. It seemed Bozeman had a knack for attracting attention in practically every place we played. Not that it surprised me since tall, dark, and handsome didn't go out of style, and he always kept his six-pack, regardless of how many twelve-packs he put away. To his credit, though, he rarely caught any of the passes that women threw his way. When he did, he never brought a date back to the bus, which is something I was eternally grateful for.

"Well, I hope you get your chance. I called a lawyer this morning, and she thinks we can bond him out by tomorrow."

Fran smiled. "How nice for him."

"I'm sorry about Toby. How long were you with him?" I asked.

Fran smiled again. "You mean with his band, or with him personally?"

I stopped in my tracks. "Are you saying you had a relationship with him?"

"It wasn't really a relationship. I had certain needs, he had certain needs, and we fulfilled them for each other."

"What did you need?"

"A job. When I was a young girl, I wanted to be a model or a guitar player. I modeled, but I assumed that wouldn't last forever. I mean, I'm going to turn thirty in a couple of years, can you imagine? And take a glance at this…"

Fran pointed to her forehead. I expected to view a pimple or mole or something, but her skin looked fine to me, even without makeup.

"At what?"

"Look. Closer. A wrinkle. Can you imagine?"

I couldn't. I probably had a few myself, but I never scrutinized myself in the mirror to seek them out.

"Lucky for me, my parents had me take up guitar when I was a little girl, and when I became a teenager, I switched over to bass guitar. Bass is sexy."

I nodded, wondering where this was going.

"I was lucky enough to be a part of a photo shoot for some of Toby's promotional material, and I told him I wanted to be a part of a band. He had me audition, and before I even finished, I was in the band. How fortunate for me."

I didn't want to know, but I had to ask. "Okay, so what did Toby get out of the deal?"

"Sex. What else?" Fran said it so matter of fact that the candor surprised me.

"Isn't he married?"

"Yes. Well, he was, I guess. Millie, or Maddie, or something from Texas or Virginia. I don't recall. I only met her a few times," Fran said.

"Did she learn you were having an affair with her husband?" I asked.

Fran shrugged. "It beats me. I don't really care. He got lonely on the road, and she refused to travel with him, so it was her own fault."

I didn't understand the logic behind that, and at the moment, it didn't matter. In my mind I added Millie, or Maddie, or something to my suspect list, but I doubted in this case the wife did it. I didn't think she would understand the significance of the stolen song. Still, I wanted to ask about her.

"Did you ever have any minor or major disagreements with Toby?"

"Oh, no. None. Not one."

"I heard he could be hard on people during rehearsals."

"Who told you that? Gabe?" Fran asked.

I didn't confirm or deny.

"If it was him, then yes, he was tough on that little pill-popper because he plays the drums like one of those wind-up monkey toys. But Toby said nothing negative to me. Ever. Well, that's not true. He did once, but I corrected him, and he fell into line, and I never had a problem with him again."

"How did you correct him?" I almost didn't want to get the answer.

"Why, Codi, I denied him access to these."

Fran dropped her bag and lifted her shirt, exposing her bare breasts to me. I have to say, based on that move, she was self-confident. And perky. She dropped her shirt while I looked around to check if anyone else had seen her, but we were alone.

"Did Russell ever have any issues with Toby?" I asked after a pregnant pause.

"Oh, sure. They argued all the time about everything. Anything else? I really need a shower."

"No. I guess not. Thanks for speaking to me."

Fran bent over to retrieve her bag, and I took a step toward the bus, then stopped. "One more question. Do you get paid regularly?"

"Sure. Every week like clockwork. Every other week direct deposit from the record company, and on the off weeks I get a cash bonus from Toby." Fran winked at me, then frowned. "I guess I'll need to find a new band."

Fran shrugged and walked away. I figured she didn't kill Toby. No motive, and without him, she'd lost her position and her perks. After I exhaled, I headed for the bus.

I was about halfway back when I felt someone's eyes on me. I looked to my left, saw no one, turned to my right, and spotted Tommy Skye leaning up against a tree. He waved, but when I took a step toward him, he turned around and ran across the field.

I was in no mood to chase him, so I didn't. Instead, I continued on and took my seat next to Laurel.

"Did you know Toby and Fran were sleeping together?" I asked.

"It wouldn't surprise me if Fran was sleeping with everyone on that bus. Well, except me, she's not really my type. Let me guess, did she show you her boobs?"

I nodded. "How did you know that?"

"For some nutty reason, she gets off on being topless. It drove Toby nuts, and I can't imagine what it did for Gabe."

"She mentioned in passing, Gabe is a pill-popper. You ever catch him taking anything? Notice any bottles lying around?"

Laurel shook her head. "Not that I can remember. Although pills are a little more discrete than say, something like cocaine, right? I mean, he could hide them in an aspirin or vitamin bottle, and no one would be the wiser."

I agreed. "Look, I hate to ask, but is there a way you could look around? See if he is hiding anything like that? Don't feel pressured, though. You can say no if you want to, and I won't think anything less of you, and won't say another word about it."

Laurel didn't answer right away, and I could tell she was mulling it over, which only added to the respect I had growing for her.

"If it'll help your friend, I'll do it," she said after a few minutes.

I nodded, and we sat together in silence for a few minutes. Then, without a word, Laurel rose and left me.

"I saw you talking to that nasty woman."

To my credit, I didn't flinch when I caught the voice, but I looked to see where it came from. It was Tommy, who had positioned himself behind my bus so I could only see his head.

"So what?" I asked.

"Did she tell you lies about me?"

"Why don't you come over here and we'll talk about it."

"No. I don't want them to see me. Come over here," he said.

"Okay, but I'm warning you, I'm armed."

"Fine. I'm not."

I picked up my chair and hauled it over to where Tommy was. Rather than set it down hidden from anyone else's view, I placed it at the end of the bus's bumper, just in case. "What's up, Tommy?"

"Did she tell you lies about me?"

I got up and adjusted my chair. I had placed one leg on top of a hole, so I was in danger of tipping over at any point. "No. She never mentioned you."

Tommy rolled his eyes, then spun in a full circle. "Sure. She didn't tell you she got me kicked out of the band?"

Before he spoke those words, I was ready to remove myself from the conversation, but now he had my rapt attention.

"How did she do that?" I asked.

"Let's just say it had something to do with those melons she showed you. I'd been with Toby since the beginning, before he even cut his first record. You look at the liner notes, and you'll see me in there. Tommy Skye on bass. Played with him through the dirty bars and county fairs. Then that album hit, and he started becoming a celebrity. When the second album dropped, that's when we started doing the bigger tours. Auditoriums. Arenas. Inside gigs, you get what I mean?"

I did. Some people didn't mind playing outside, and I've enjoyed a cool breeze running across the stage while under the fiery lights. But the benefit of the indoor concert was the show continued on as scheduled. Didn't have to worry about rain, snow, lightning, heavy winds, or excessive heat. Or insects, or birds. I even had a bat swoop over my head once.

"So, what happened?" I asked.

"We were doing a promotional piece for an upcoming tour, and someone thought it would be a good idea to bring a couple models in as arm candy for Toby. We'd done it before, but the only difference is, this model plays bass and never left when the shoot was over. Before you would say lickity split, I was off the tour and hitchhiking my way back home."

"Where is home?"

"I'm originally from Kansas, but I've been in L.A. for about twenty years now."

"Were you mad at Toby?"

"Of course. But oddly, I couldn't blame him. He's always been a sucker for a big-boobed blond."

"Is his wife a big-boobed blond?" I asked.

"Allison? No way. She's an average-looking brunette. She's the type where if you passed her on the street, you wouldn't even glance at her."

"So then, why did he marry her?"

"I think they were high school sweethearts."

"Any chance she lives around here?"

Tommy gave me a Cheshire Cat grin. "And found about her husband's indiscretions and did him in for revenge? Nope. Sorry. She lives somewhere in upstate New York with her parents."

"Oh. Did you ever do any songwriting with Toby?"

"No, sorry, ma'am. I'm strictly a player. Never had much of a talent for writing. Tried it once, but it didn't work out for me. I'm sure you get it."

"Sure. It's not for everybody. Do you know who he collaborated with?"

"Not really. I wasn't a part of that. I didn't get involved until there was a song to play. Sometimes I helped on the music end, suggesting riffs, or runs, or key, but that was about it."

"Hmm. Did you ever observe anyone accuse Toby of using their songs without permission?"

Tommy gave me the grin again. The first time, it was odd, this time, it was bordering on creepy. "You'll like this one. We were at a concert at some venue in Tennessee doing a soundcheck. Out of the blue, we got interrupted by a guy who came right up to the stage and started screaming at Tommy about stealing his song. Had a lawyer there with him and everything."

"What happened? Did the guy get physical?" I asked.

"No. Just a lot of shouting went on. The venue security came to throw the guy out, but the lawyer stepped in and stopped them. Next thing in an odd turn of events, Toby and Russell are talking to the pair all nice and civil like. The lawyer took a sheet of paper out of his pocket and handed it over to Toby. He read it, gave it to Russell. Russell read it, then must have said something to Toby, because he took the paper back, signed it, and gave it back to the lawyer."

As Tommy spoke, I visualized the events in my head. "Sounds to me like Toby got caught and got a choice to settle on the spot, or get dragged into court, and since I've heard nothing about it, he must have settled."

"Yeah. If he had any money. We weren't exactly living high on the hog back then, especially with Russell managing things," Tommy said.

I sat back and folded one leg over the other to get comfortable. "Tell me more."

Tommy leaned up against the bus. He was pretty close to the chipmunk nest. I hoped Willie and Waylon were out somewhere playing a nearby tree and not wanting to get into their house for the next few minutes.

"Well, Toby always thought that Russell was taking more of the pie than just his normal cut. He told me about a time he went to ask Russell about the budget, then Russell kicked him out of the room and made Toby come back an hour later. Russell showed him the books, but Toby figured what Russell showed him wasn't the complete picture."

"Skimming a bit off the top, you mean? Fudging receipts and numbers and whatnot?"

Tommy nodded. "Yep. You got the picture good."

"So why didn't Toby fire him? Or get the record company to replace him?"

Tommy shrugged. "Soon after that, Fran was in and I was out. By that point, I didn't care who managed the band."

"Did you overhear the name of the guy who accused Toby of pilfering his work? Ever seen him before?"

Tommy shook his head. "No. But like I said, we were in Tennessee. Could have been anyone. You get how Nashville is. There are so many songwriters there, you could use them to pave the way to Hawaii. Then have enough left over to create a different route back."

I had to laugh. I had heard that line before, although I didn't remember where. It reminded me of that old saying about every server in Los Angeles having a screenplay ready in their back pocket in case they served lunch to a big-name producer.

"Did you see the argument yesterday? Between Bozeman and Toby?" I asked.

"Yep. Saw the whole thing. It reminded me of the other time I just told you about. Except Bozeman didn't have a lawyer with him."

"Do you think Bozeman killed Toby?"

Tommy took off his baseball cap and scratched his head. A few strands of hair came away when he did, and he looked at them indifferently and let the breeze take them before putting his hat back on.

"No. I don't. I've known Bozeman a long, long time, and I don't expect he has the stomach for it. The cops have the wrong man. I'm certain of it."

"You seem to know all the players, so tell me, Tommy, who do you think did it?"

"Well, if I were a betting man, I'd put my money on —"

Tommy was ready to spill the proverbial beans, but then I heard a yell from behind us.

I turned in my chair and saw Russell rushing toward us. He was screaming something, but I couldn't make out the words. "What do you suppose he wants?"

I turned back to Tommy, but Tommy had disappeared like a shadow at midnight. "Tommy?"

I looked back, and Russell was still on his way. He was wearing a light green polo shirt with his jeans, which was a mistake since the sweat from his exertion was darkening the fabric. It wasn't a good look. I wanted to give Willie and Waylon some space, so I picked up my chair and moved it back to where I normally had it near the bus door. I sat down just as Russell arrived.

"Hey Russell. What's up?"

CHAPTER NINE

W hat was he doing here?" Russell demanded.

"Oh, not much. Just talking to me."

Russell eyed me with suspicion. I wondered if he was the paranoid type who always worried about what was being said about him. Since recent conversations didn't paint him in the greatest of lights, I didn't blame him for it.

"You wanted to talk to me, so talk," he said.

He got that right. I wanted to talk to him, and the more people I spoke to, the more questions I had for him. What should I accuse him of first? Fund theft? Copyright infringement? Murder? Toby's infidelity? So many choices, so little time. I threw him a softball.

"It's a shame about Toby. I really liked him. Were you two friends long?"

Russell looked at me with some apprehension. "We've known each other for a fairly long time, yeah."

"It's quite the rag-tag band he has, isn't it? I mean, if you put Toby, Fran, Laurel, and Gabe together in a room filled with musicians and told everyone to divide into a group, I wouldn't see it forming naturally."

"I don't get what you're saying."

"Well, take Bozeman and me, for example. When we met, I looked for someone to play the lead guitar. I had somewhat of a vision of what I wanted. So, I asked around, got a few names, did a few interviews, listened to people play. That's when I found Bozeman, and we had this natural chemistry that makes our partnership work. I don't feel the chemistry in Toby's band."

"Good thing you're not in the band, then. I've got things to do. Catch you later."

Russell pivoted to leave and got a step away before I threw out the next pitch. "Is it true Toby paid off a songwriter in

Tennessee?"

That got his attention. Russell returned to my side. "You have no clue about that."

I didn't, really, since I had information based on a secondhand account. "Are you saying you didn't have to compensate a Nashville songwriter over a song Toby claimed to write? He figured out the theft, like Bozeman did, brought in a lawyer, and signed over the rights in a fair exchange for a payout. And I'll bet there was a nice non-disclosure contract to go with that as well. Am I right?"

Russell didn't speak. He simply stared at my forehead.

"Am I in the ballpark?"

Still no response, so I changed my approach.

"Fran seems like an odd addition to the group. Tommy out, Fran in? Can you tell me about that?"

"Nothing to tell. Tommy got erratic. He's a druggie. Everyone on the team knows we don't allow drugs anywhere near Toby."

"How do you find out Tommy did drugs?"

Russell sneered. "How would I not? He started having erratic behavior, losing weight, missing rehearsals. He had to be replaced. For the good of the band."

"And the best you found in all of country music was a bass player who happened to be a model at the time?"

"It's not like that. Frannie can play. She's a natural, and she's serious about her craft. She's well-respected. Ask anyone."

"Okay. How do you explain Gabe as the drummer? I understand he can't hold a beat."

Russell leaned in and pointed a finger at my face. "Come on, lady, I've had enough of you and your questions. I get what you're trying to do, trying to find someone else to pin Toby's death on, but the simple truth is, they've already got the right guy in custody. Your man."

Russell turned and stomped off. I didn't know what to do next, but then I felt a light tapping on my shoe. I looked down and spotted Merle nuzzling my leg. "Hey, Merle. Come here, buddy." I leaned over, picked him up, and set him in my lap. "What are you doing up already? Couldn't sleep?" In response, Merle shoved his nose up under my arm. I laughed.

"Stop, that tickles." I adjusted Merle so that I had access to his underside and gave his belly a good scratching. You would think a skunk wouldn't like that, but it was one of Merle's favorite things in the world.

"Well, where do we go from here? I'm not any further along with getting Bozeman out of trouble than I was yesterday. Do you have any ideas?"

In response, Merle spread out his legs and started smacking his lips, a sure sign he enjoyed his time with me. Merle must have realized I needed some attention because after fifteen minutes, I felt better and had a bit more clarity in my mind. I had devised a new plan, and the first step involved talking to Bozeman's lawyer.

"Come on, Merle." I picked him up and carried him with me onto the bus. I placed him on the floor, retrieved my phone, and found the number I needed. It took a few moments to dial the number, and the person picked up after the second ring.

"Jennifer Collins."

"Hi Jennifer. Codi Cassidy here. Bozeman James' friend?"

"Hi Codi. What can I do for you?" I imagined Jennifer leaning back in an oversized leather chair and putting her feet up on her desk. I also thought that happened the same way when all white-collar professionals talked on the phone.

"Do you have any word on Bozeman's arraignment?" I asked.

The line fell silent, and I thought she hung up on me, but then I heard a door close and some papers shuffle. "No, sorry. It may take a couple more days. From what I'm told, the county judge is out sick and they're trying to find a replacement for him."

"Is there any hope at all of getting him out soon?"

"No, sorry. Not until he's been before the judge."

"Is there anything you can tell me about Toby's death?" I asked.

"Sorry, I'm not supposed to say anything that would jeopardize the case. I'm sure you can understand that."

I hated not getting straight answers, but that only added to my persistence. "Hey, Jennifer, I'm trying to poke around here to see if I can find any answers, and I'm pretty much running out of options, so if there's anything at all you can tell me, please do."

Again, there was a long pause, and once more I thought she'd disconnected the call, but a second later, she whispered to me. "Okay. I would get in trouble with the court by releasing this, but I have a colleague at the morgue. The official cause of death is asphyxiation."

"Thanks. Anything else?"

"Yes. They did a rapid drug screening, and it turns out Toby had drugs in his system, although I won't have the full workup until the lab tests come back. They sent those to an external lab, so it will be a few days before I get the report. Hopefully, that will help you."

"Thanks. I appreciate the information," I said.

"I have to go. There's another client I have to meet with."

This time, Jennifer disconnected, and I put down the phone. I heard some crunching, so I did a quick glance over at Gibson's food bowl.

"Hey, Merle. I've told you a billion times that you shouldn't be eating the cat food."

I picked up the bowl and placed it on the counter. "You want a snack?" I opened the fridge and found the container of cherry tomatoes, which was Merle's absolute favorite. I counted only three remaining in there. Based on the space in the rest of the fridge, I guessed I needed to make a grocery run soon.

Bending over, I gave Merle a tomato, and he chirped like a bird as he grabbed it and munched on it. I was about to feed him a second one when there came a knock at the door.

"Codi? It's me."

"Come on in, Laurel."

Laurel entered, and once she was inside, she pulled a plastic baggie from her pocket and placed it on the counter next to the tomatoes. The bag contained a variety of pills and capsules.

"Sorry it took so long. I had to wait until everyone else was off the bus. This is a sample of everything I found in Gabe's room."

I picked up the baggie and looked at the contents. There were perhaps eighteen pills and capsules in all. A few things I recognized right away, including an aspirin tablet and a vitamin C supplement, but there were a few I didn't recognize. A squeal interrupted my investigation. I looked down and saw Merle looking up at me with a displeased look on his face. If a skunk did such a thing.

"Do me a favor and give Merle those tomatoes. One at a time, though, or he'll make a big mess with them. I'll be right back."

I retreated to my room, retrieved my laptop, and returned to the dinette. Once I was there, I fired up my machine, and while I waited for that, I removed all the drugs from the baggie and lined them up on the table.

"What are you doing?" Laurel asked as she joined me. She still had one tomato in her hand, but I imagined that would be gone once Merle realized she had run away with his treat.

"Looking up these drugs." I handed her a white tablet. "See the imprint number on there?"

Laurel studied the pill. "Yeah."

"Each drug is supposed to have a marking like that. It helps to identify it. What is the number?"

Laurel told me, and I searched for it. "It's generic aspirin, just like I thought. What's another?"

Laurel picked up a capsule and read me the number from the side.

"That's an antihistamine."

We repeated the exercise until we identified all the over-the-counter drugs. There were three left. One was a capsule with a green body and a cap the same color as a robin's egg. The other two were pills. One was bright yellow with a sun stamped into it, and the other was a light purple adorned with what looked like the eye of Horus. Despite my best effort, I didn't identify those.

"What do you think these are?" I asked.

Laurel shook her head. "I have no clue."

"Where did you find them?"

"They were inside of a fake book. I wouldn't have found them; except I accidentally knocked the book over when I was reaching for something else. I have an idea. Take one, and I'll observe what happens to you."

At first, I thought she was serious, but then Laurel let loose the laugh she tried to suppress. "I'm sorry. I couldn't help myself."

The three unidentified drugs I put back in the baggie, and the rest I swept into my hand and tossed them into the trash.

"Oh, Merle." I grabbed a paper towel and wiped up the remains of a tomato from the floor, then wet another towel and washed over the area again to clean up the sticky mess. I tossed the paper towels into the trash and looked around for Merle. He wasn't anywhere in the area, so I assumed he was somewhere searching for trouble.

The storage room, Bozeman's room, and the bathroom doors were all closed, which left my room as the remaining place to check. I looked in. Gibson was in his normal spot on the pillow pile, and although he lifted his head to look at me, he didn't move at all. I checked the floor under the table and in the closet, but I didn't find the skunk. I glanced at Gibson again and was going to ask him where his brother was when I noticed his mass was twice the size it normally was. It took me a step closer and a second longer to register what I saw. Rather than go back to his normal spot, Merle had curled up with Gibson for his nap.

I was lucky that all of my animals, most of the time, got along with each other. Although Gibson looked moderately annoyed by the disturbance, he wasn't angry about it. As far as Gibson was concerned, Merle was just some strange breed of cat who wanted to share a nap space.

"Everything okay?" Laurel asked when I returned to the living area and plopped into a captain's chair.

"Yeah. I'm just getting frustrated. You and I are certain Bozeman didn't murder Toby. I also recognize all the evidence points in his direction. I don't know where to go from here."

"Who's your money on?" she asked.

"A better question is who it isn't. I'm ninety-eight percent sure that you didn't do it."

A mock-angry look crossed Laurel's face. "Only ninety-eight percent? There's still a two percent chance you think I did it?"

"Yeah, but that's only because I don't want to rule anyone out completely. Don't take offense. Deep down in my heart, you're innocent."

Laurel smiled. "That's good enough for me. I'll take it. So then, if not me, then who?"

"Fran? She had an affair with Toby."

Laurel considered it for a moment, then dismissed her. "No. I don't think so."

"Why not? Because she's a woman?" I asked.

"Of course not. Women commit murder all the time. I don't think she would do it because she doesn't really hide anything. She got her job because she slept with the boss. Everybody knows, and she doesn't care. She's sleeping with a married man. Again, she doesn't hide it, because she doesn't care."

"She'd care if Toby's wife suddenly showed up," I said.

Laurel chuckled. "That's a fact. Still, I don't see Fran caring about that, either. I doubt she'd get in one of those classic girl fights over Toby. She'd be more likely just to cut him loose and move on. She's like a shark in a tight skirt."

I nodded and agreed. It was a good analysis, and aligned with what my impression of her was too. Fran was the type to use her sex appeal to get whatever she needed. At least, until those wrinkles she worried so much about ended all that.

"What about Gabe?" Laurel asked.

"To tell you the truth, I had Gabe all but scratched off my list as well, but now that you found those drugs, I'm not sure. What you don't know is that Toby had drugs in his system when he died."

The look on Laurel's face told me it surprised her to hear that news. "Are you sure?"

"Pretty sure. I can't reveal my source, but I'll tell you that fact came right from the county coroner."

"Might there be a scenario where Gabe was supplying Toby those drugs, and something moved sideways and Gabe killed Toby?" Laurel asked. I liked the way her mind worked.

I shrugged. "Perhaps. Or it was the other way around. Toby was the dealer, and Gabe was the junkie? Then something moved sideways and Gabe killed Toby."

"That would explain why Toby always had a roll of money.

Either way, Gabe kills Toby."

"Yeah. I'd have to push that one around in my head for a bit. What you haven't learned is that Toby was also giving Fran a bi-weekly cash bonus," I said.

That fact Laurel never expected, and it hit her hard. "No, really? Are you saying that I've been going without a paycheck and begging for pocket cash while Fran's been getting double?"

"It looks that way, yes," I said.

"What about Gabe? Has he been getting extra, too?"

"That I need to figure out yet."

Laurel shifted in her seat. I could tell the whole money thing bothered her, and I couldn't blame her for that. It seemed everyone was getting a cut of the pie while she had to go without. In the back of my mind, I wondered if she really knew all about that and extracted her cash along with a pound of flesh. It seemed plausible, so my confidence she hadn't murdered Toby dipped down to ninety percent.

"That gets us to Russell. What do you think about him?" Laurel asked.

"To be honest, there's so much there, he's almost too obvious of a suspect. Every time I talk to someone new, I get more details about potential shady stuff he's involved in. It seems to me, though, that Toby and Russell were equally complicit in their partnership."

Laurel shifted in her seat, then rose from the dinette, stood, and stretched her arms toward the ceiling. "Yeah, but again, could something have gone on there? Toby was going to turn on Russell? Wanted to cut him out of a deal? Or maybe Toby wanted to come clean and confronted Russell about it."

"Again, maybe, but either way, with Toby's career taking off, why would Russell kill the golden goose if he was taking a percentage of the profits? That's the part that doesn't stick with me."

I was about to say something else, but as I opened my mouth, something hit the side of the bus. The impact wasn't strong enough to move the sturdy vehicle, so neither Laurel nor I were affected, but it surprised us both.

"What was that?" Laurel asked.

"Beats me," I said.

Since Laurel was already standing, she was almost out the door before I even got out of my chair. By the time I stepped into the afternoon sun, Laurel was on her knees in front of someone. I rushed over and saw Gabe lying on his back, foaming at the mouth.

"What's wrong with him?"

Laurel looked scared. "I don't know. What should we do?"

"Let's roll him over so he doesn't choke. We'd better call 9-1-1," I said.

"I'm already on it." I looked back and saw Fran behind us. In the excitement, I never noticed her.

I overheard Fran on the phone giving our location while Laurel and I rolled Gabe onto his side. As I steadied Gabe to make sure he wouldn't fall again, Laurel shoved her finger in his mouth, wiggled it around, and removed it quickly.

Her quick action amazed me. "That was gross," I said.

Laurel shrugged. "I wanted to make sure there are no obstructions. It wouldn't do much good to have him on his side if he is choking on his tongue."

"That's a good point."

Fran hung up and stood over us. "Ambulance is on the way." She looked around like she should do something, couldn't decide what that something was, then stepped backward to give us room.

I looked up at her. "What happened to him?"

"I'm not sure. We were both on the bus. I was in the front parlor reading a magazine, and he was in his room. Next thing that happened, he screamed and ran past me, right off the bus. I followed him out. He grabbed his head and ran around until he ran headfirst into your bus. Then he dropped to the ground there."

"Is there anything else we can do?" I asked.

Laurel grabbed Gabe's wrist and felt for a pulse. After thirty seconds of stillness, she let go. "Pulse is erratic. Fran, do you know if he took anything?"

Fran shook her head. "Like I said, he was in his room."

"Do you know where Russell is?"

"No. He's not here. I think he headed to town about an hour ago."

Off in the distance, I heard sirens, which was a good sign for Gabe. A couple of minutes later, an ambulance and a sheriff's car pulled up next to the bus. Fran and I both moved away to give the experts more room. Laurel provided a brief recap of what happened, then joined us while the paramedics worked on Gabe.

I saw one start an intravenous line while the other checked Gabe's heart. They took as short of time as possible before they loaded Gabe onto a gurney, loaded the gurney into the ambulance, and drove off, sirens blaring.

"We should go to the hospital," Fran said.

"Hold on. I have a few questions for you first."

All three of us turned around at once and saw Deputy Marvin standing by his truck, notepad in hand. "Starting with all your names and what happened here."

Fran stepped toward him. "You have our names. You were literally just here a couple of days ago."

"I know. Sorry. New incident, new report. If you could give me your IDs, that would be great."

We split off to retrieve the requested documentation, then met back at the truck, where the deputy patiently waited for us. Once there, he asked for the details of Gabe's adventure. Fran provided most of the story, and Laurel and I contributed what information we could. It didn't take long to write up what he had, then he gave us a ride to the local hospital.

When we got there, it surprised me when we turned the corner into the waiting room and saw Russell already there, seated in a chair, thumbing through a magazine.

Fran spoke up first. "What are you doing here?"

Russell set the magazine down on the seat next to him. "Sheriff called me when they brought Gabe in. I've only been here like five minutes."

We all sat and waited. Fran picked up the magazine Russell

had rejected while Russell fiddled with his phone. Laurel amused herself by watching the television news. The sound was off, but the closed captioning was on, so she read each of the stories as they ran by.

I spent that time watching the three of them. I expected that since they lived and worked together that there would be some interaction, but there was none. They could have been three strangers waiting for a report on three different people. They didn't speak to each other, and except for passing glances, they didn't look at each other.

After about an hour, a doctor appeared in the room. The doctor was a giant of a man, at least six feet tall, dark skin and eyes, black beard, bald head. At first look, he could have passed for a wrestler or a bouncer, but his white coat and the stethoscope hanging from one pocket said otherwise.

"Who's here for Gabe Galvin?"

Four hands shot up in the air at once.

The doctor stepped into the middle of the room and gave us the report.

"Your friend had an overdose. Also suffered a minor seizure and a heart attack. We had to pump his stomach, but he's stabilized now. He'll have to stay overnight, perhaps two nights until we can release him."

"Do you know what he took?" I asked.

"Based on the stomach contents, some designer opiates. One of which was laced with a rat poison."

The doctor's pager went off. He checked it, then ran from the room.

I understood little about the drug trade, but I guessed rat poison wasn't a common additive. To me, at least, it made little sense to get someone dependent on a drug, only to turn around and kill them. That sure didn't help with repeat business. Somehow, I needed to get myself out of the room and back to my bus and see what was in that capsule I couldn't identify.

I got out of my chair and tried to pretend I was invisible, but somehow, it didn't work.

"Where are you going?"

I turned around. It was Russell who asked, although Fran and Laurel were looking at me too.

"I'm just going to the restroom. I'll be right back."

CHAPTER TEN

I had to use the restroom, so I didn't tell a lie, because I headed straight there. What I didn't mention was that I had no intention of going back to the waiting room, so once I finished washing my hands, I walked directly to the main exit. Once I stepped through the automatic doors, I realized I made a mistake. Other than walking, I had no way to get back to the park. Normally I wouldn't mind the hike, but I felt the uncomfortable pressing of time against me, so I needed to return as soon as possible.

From my back pocket, I pulled out my phone and searched for rideshare services. I hadn't asked which one Laurel used when we traveled to town the previous day, and I had too many choices, so the multiple options stumped me. I have to admit that my biggest failing as a person was the inability to fully grasp the magic of cellular technology, which, I understand, makes no sense. Even I didn't understand how I can sit down at my laptop and program background music for the band. With accompanying fully synchronized light shows, yet I couldn't order myself a taxi.

Frustrated, I shoved my phone back into my pocket and stepped back inside and approached the desk receptionist.

"Hi. This is embarrassing, but I need a ride back to where I'm staying. Would you do me a favor and call one for me? I would do it myself, but my phone battery is dead," I said. Passing him a look, I tried to appear wiped out and pitiful, which wasn't far from the truth.

I expected some push back, or a question or two, or at the least a raised eyebrow, but I got none of those. The receptionist picked up his desk phone, dialed a number, had a ten second conversation, and hung up.

"Cab will be here in three minutes, right out front there."

I gave him my best smile. "Thank you. I appreciate it."

I returned to the front walk and waited. As I did, I kept looking behind me, expecting Laurel, Russell, or Fran to pop out of the building and ask where I planned on running off to, but luckily for me, no one did.

The seconds seemed to stretch on, but eventually I saw an old-fashioned yellow taxicab slow down and stop right next to me.

"Where to?" the driver asked as I slipped into the back seat.

I looked into the rear-view mirror and caught the guy's eyes. He was an older gentleman, in his early sixties at least, with salt-and-pepper hair. He wore a gray flat cap, and there was a pair of fuzzy dice hanging from the mirror. I wondered if I entered a time machine instead of a taxi.

"The county park. The one right outside of town."

He didn't pull off right away like I expected, instead he just stared at me. He probably thought I was taking him for a ride.

"My tour bus is there, so I'm headed back to pick it up."

My answer seemed acceptable, because he shifted the car into drive, and he sped away from the curb. Ten minutes later, the driver parked right next to the first bus he came to, which turned out to be Toby's. That seemed fine to me. I had it in me to handle the extra thirty feet.

"That'll be sixteen dollars even."

I thought it was a little expensive, but I handed him a twenty and didn't wait for the change. I climbed from the cab, walked to my bus, unlocked the door, and entered. My heart skipped a beat when I noticed the baggie of drugs sitting on the dinette, because I realized at that moment, I should have locked them away with Merle on board. Gibson, by definition, is a curious cat, but he has nowhere near the ability to get into as much stuff as Merle or Dolly. They were the reason we didn't leave food out and triple checked the cabinets. With the curious critters aboard, all of the hatches had to be battened.

I shoved the bag into my pocket, then I checked my room to make sure everything was okay. Gibson was sitting at the foot of my bed washing himself. When he spotted me, he passed me a glance that let me know he wasn't happy that Merle, who still slumbered on the pillow tower, had usurped his spot.

I stepped back outside and looked to check if anyone was around, but I was alone. I walked over to Toby's bus and wanted to climb aboard, but the door didn't open for me. Hoping to find something, anything, I checked the bus storage bays, but the only one unlocked was empty.

At the rear of the bus, my luck turned for the better. The wall panel that closed off the kitchen was open, so I had the entire area to explore. I had access to the fridge, a small sink, a pull-out grill, and several cabinets. Carefully, I snooped through everything. Sadly, I found nothing but cooking utensils, a drawer of spices, unbreakable dishes, and a few aprons and towels.

I slammed the last door closed, turned, and noticed the trash can had tipped over. Beside the can was a small mass of used paper plates and napkins, and trailing away from that on the far side of the bus was a trail of garbage leading into the woods. I followed the trail like a bloodhound, and just inside the tree line, I discovered the large, black garbage bag with a hole in it. Based on the hole's size, I suspected a larger critter had been in there, like a raccoon, possum, or coyote, and I hoped it wasn't Dolly.

Most of the foodstuff spread out on the ground away from the bag. I recognized remnants of the dinner we'd had the other night, including burger parts and plenty of coleslaw. I also recognized a banana peel, some coffee grounds, and a pancake with a single bite from it. What caught my eye was a small, bright yellow plastic package with a mouse on the front along with a giant red X and a skull. Although the top of the package looked zipper-sealed, there was a hole chewed through the bottom. I guessed some poor creature was going to have a bad day.

Not wanting to touch the pouch, I looked around me until I found a stick of suitable size. I shoved the stick into the chew hole, lifted it, and carried it back to Toby's bus, where I set it on the table. From the cabinet, I grabbed a dark blue melamine plate and placed it next to the pouch. I extracted some granules from the package and made a small pile of them on the plate. Then I took the capsule from my pocket, opened it, and dumped about half onto the plate next to the pile. I carefully closed the capsule and returned it to the bag and my pocket. Relying on the entirety of my high school chemistry experience, I compared the two small lumps of powder. I expected the capsule to be a mixture of drugs and poison, but it surprised me to see there was no difference between the pill pile and the package pile.

"Oh, boy," I said to myself.

I needed to keep the package, so I checked through all the cabinets and drawers to find something to store it in, but I found nothing. In a last-ditch effort, I opened the fridge and spotted a bunch of sliced carrot and celery sticks in a gallon-sized plastic bag. I assumed that would do nicely, so I dumped the vegetables onto the table, and replaced them with the rat poison package.

"Was your little science experiment successful?"

The voice startled me, so I let out a squeal as I jumped back. It was Tommy again.

"Why do you insist on always sneaking up on me?" I asked, harshly.

"I don't sneak. You're just inattentive."

I took some offense to that remark, but I didn't comment on it. One thing my detective dad taught me was to always be well aware of my environment.

Tommy took a step toward me. "What do you have there?"

I adjusted my grip on the bag so it was as obscure as I could make it with my tiny hand. "I have a big bag of none of your business. What do you want?"

"I want to know what you have there."

Tommy stepped in and reached for the bag. As he did, he pushed me against the table. I took the table's corner right in the hip, and the jab of pain brought stars to my eyes.

"Let me go!" I screamed as loud as a banshee, but I'd have to do better than that to attract any attention in the empty park.

I held the poison as far away from my body as I could, but Tommy clawed at my arm, desperately trying to reach it. Although he was physically larger than me, he wasn't as strong as he looked. When he made another thrust forward to get the bag, I sidestepped, put my left foot behind his leg, and pushed him.

Tommy pinwheeled his arms to regain his balance, but it was too late for that. He fell at an awkward angle and screamed when his left elbow took on the full weight of his body when he hit the concrete parking lot. I watched him for a moment to see what he'd do, but he didn't get up. He just rolled over onto his butt and rubbed his elbow. The tough guy started crying. Not an ugly cry, but the tears were flowing.

"You witch!" he screamed. "You don't understand, and you'll ruin everything!"

I took a few steps backward to keep him in sight as I retreated toward my bus.

"Yeah! You'd better leave. Get out of here before things get super bad for you! Leave and stay away for good!" he yelled after me like a playground bully.

I took a few more steps and determined he wouldn't follow me. I turned around and ran back to the bus, climbed aboard, and locked the door behind me. I shoved the rat poison into the cabinet beneath the sink, washed and dried my hands, and rushed to my bedroom.

Neither Merle nor Gibson were on the bed, which was good. I kneeled on the floor, threw the bed blankets onto the top, and opened one of the under-bed drawers. This was the drawer that held my safe, and all my secrets. Well, not secrets exactly, just rather important paperwork like my birth certificate and passport, a few thousand dollars in cash, and Betty. Normally, I don't carry Betty around with me. Since there was a murder, an attempted murder, and a physical assault all within a couple of days, I decided it was time for a little self-protection.

I punched my six-digit code into the keypad, then pulled on the handle, but it didn't open. I closed my eyes, took a deep breath, and counted to ten to calm myself. When I opened my eyes, I punched in the code again, slower, and pulled the handle, and this time the door opened. I grabbed Betty and a clip of ammunition, closed the safe and the drawer, and smoothed the bed blankets back into place.

Once I had Betty, I grabbed her holster from a hook in the closet, put everything together, and strapped her on. Dad trained me how to use a gun and I wasn't afraid to carry one. That came as another advantage of having a detective father. He taught me how to shoot handguns and long guns when I was still in my early teens. He taught me how to use them, clean them, and respect them. I'd have to say I'm a pretty excellent shot, although I practice as little as possible. Sometimes when we have a down day, Bozeman and I will find a range and take turns practicing with his rifle, but those days are few and often far between.

One thing my father and I disagreed on was whether to shoot to kill or shoot to stop. He always told me that once I got to where I had to draw my weapon, the time for niceties was over. At that point, I needed to shoot to kill because the aggressor might overtake and disarm me. I told him he had a valid point, but I disagreed with him. I didn't want to take a life if I could help it, and that's why Betty only held non-lethal rounds. Also, she was only a .22 caliber, so with that, she was the biggest weapon I dared to carry. Yet I still felt protected. I doubt I would ever kill anyone if I shot them, but for sure I would give them a reason to let me be, especially if I did the double-tap dad trained me to do.

Armed, I snuck back out to the living area and looked out the window. I saw Toby's bus, but not the back end where I'd encountered Tommy. I didn't see him near Toby's bus, and I checked several other windows and didn't see him near mine, so I thought the coast was clear.

Against my leg, I sensed a nudge. I looked down and saw Merle head-butting my shin just above my ankle. That was his signal to me he was ready to leave the bus. I picked him up, scratched his head, and opened the door. Before I walked out, I looked left, right, and left again, just like I was crossing a street. Then, seeing no one, I stepped into the parking lot. Tommy wouldn't realize I was now armed, but I hoped that if he saw me, a skunk would be enough of a deterrent to leave me be.

Merle twitched in my arms, so I set him down and watched him scamper away. I could tell it was time for him to do his business, and I was happy to let him. Although I trained Dolly to use Gibson's litter box, Merle couldn't pick up that skill.

Thinking of Dolly, I needed to check on her to make sure she was safe and sound. The last thing I wanted to learn was that she was the one who ate through the rat poison package in the woods.

Still on high alert, I checked the area as I walked to Dolly's compartment. The door was open, which was the standard when we parked, and I looked in and saw Dolly's pretty black eyes staring back at me.

"Hello, Dolly," I whispered.

Dolly stretched like a cat, then moved toward the door. When she was close enough, I picked her up and scratched her head. In response, she climbed higher up my chest, and put both paws over my left shoulder and set her chin down. In that position, she looked like a big hairy baby waiting to be burped, but it was actually a demand to give her back a good scratching, which I happily did.

As I gave Dolly her scratches, I walked around the bus, looking out for Tommy. There was no sign of him, so I walked over and looked around Toby's bus as well. Tommy wasn't anywhere around there, either.

I spotted the trash can and realized I needed to clean that mess up. If it was one thing I believed in, it was being a good steward of the environment. I carried Dolly back to my bus, set her on the ground, and opened the compartment where we kept our maintenance supplies. From there, I grabbed a pair of gardening gloves and a large black trash bag.

I put on the gloves and carried the bag into the woods, where I dumped the other trash bag into mine. Then I collected all the litter in the area and cleaned up the trash trail that led from the bus to the woods. Back at Toby's bus, I threw away the melamine plate holding the rat poison, and all the paper products. The celery and carrot sticks I gathered up and threw into the woods. The local animals could eat those. Once I gathered all the trash, I closed the bag, put a knot on the top and set it inside the trash can. The trash can had clamps on the side to hold the lid on, although I imagined any smart animal could get past that. But I was too tired to haul the bag over to the dumpster the park provided. Instead, I returned to my bus, put everything away, and set up my chair.

I thought about getting a book or something to drink when I saw a flash of gray fur run past my feet, followed closely behind by a flash of black and white. Instead of moving, I sat still and watched Merle and Dolly play. They had this weird game they played, which seemed to be a combination of tag and hide and go seek. One would chase the other, and tackle them once they caught them, then they'd switch, and the pursuer would become the pursued. It was fun to watch, but I never wanted to play. Too much running for my taste.

I heard a car approach, so I leaned over so I could see better. It was a green sedan, and it pulled up and Laurel got out of the back seat.

"There you are. I thought you were going to the restroom," Laurel said with more relief in her voice than disappointment.

"I did. Get yourself a chair and sit down."

Laurel found a chair, unfolded it, put it next to mine, and settled into it. We were sitting with our backs to the sun, and the rays felt warm and comforting on my shoulders.

"What are you doing here?" she asked.

"Babysitting."

As soon as I uttered the words, Merle popped out from behind a tire, did a full circle around Laurel's feet, and ran under the bus. On instinct, rather than out of fear, Laurel picked up her feet. A few seconds later, Dolly raced by, backtracked, and sat down right in front of us.

"He went that way." I cocked a thumb in the direction Merle went. Dolly looked at me, then headed in the general area to which I pointed. The encounter was priceless, and Laurel and I laughed. It felt good to laugh.

"How's Gabe doing?" I asked.

"The doctor says he's going to need to stay in the hospital for a couple of days. By the time I left, we still didn't have any details of the drugs he took, so I have no clue if they were uppers, or downers, or what."

"I'm more interested in the rat poison. I found a package in the trash near your bus. Then I compared it to the contents of that capsule you gave me, and it looked the same to me. Do you know anything about that?"

"What? No. Of course not. I didn't know we had anything like that on the bus. Why would we? I've never seen a single sign of rodents aboard."

I nodded. "It would have taken time to fill those capsules, and you saw no one doing anything like that?"

"No. I think I'd not only notice something like that, but I'd certainly question it."

I looked over at Laurel. "We need to get the rest of those drugs and turn them over to the police. Hopefully, they'll have a way to identify them."

"Perhaps they could get fingerprints off the pills."

I doubted that could be done, but I didn't want to say otherwise. "Maybe. Hey, you've got a visitor."

Laurel looked at the ground. Merle was sitting at her feet.

"He wants some attention. Pick him up if you want to."

Laurel grinned and didn't hesitate. Within seconds, she had Merle on her lap and was stroking his fur. "You're such a pretty boy, aren't you?"

"Do you know Tommy Skye?" I asked.

Laurel nodded. "Not formally, but I know of him. Why?"

"He's been lurking around here the last couple of days. I had an encounter with him earlier. He seems intent on running me off and out of the park."

Laurel's eyes widened. "Are you okay?"

"I'm fine. He got more banged up than I did. I just wanted you to know that he's out here somewhere. And based on the way he shows up at the most inopportune moments, he's probably camped out on the edge of the woods somewhere."

"Okay. But why?" she asked.

I shook my head. "You tell me. I don't know what he's doing here. He told me he lives in Los Angeles."

Laurel moved to place Merle back on the ground. "I'd better go get those drugs before Fran and Russell get here. They should be back soon."

"Do you have the bus key?" I asked.

Laurel thought for a second. "Actually, no, I don't."

"Then you can stay where you are and cuddle with the skunk. The door's locked."

Laurel exhaled in frustration. "It sure would be nice to be

treated like an adult and part of the team."

"Sorry, but the team's about to be over. Y'all were here for Toby. Toby's gone now, so then, so is the band."

Laurel frowned. "With all that's been going on, I haven't even thought about that. I guess I won't need a key after all."

"Have you thought at all about what you're going to do next?"

Laurel shook her head. "Not a single thought. I don't know. Maybe I'll go spend time with my grandmother, although I really do like being out on the road and playing for people."

"I agree. There's nothing like it in all the world, being up on that stage and having all those people listening to your music."

Laurel smiled. "Well, I'm not worried. There's always a band looking for a good fiddle player, right? And if that doesn't work out, I can always switch back to classical and join an orchestra somewhere."

"I'll bet you could. Before you go, I need your help with just one simple thing."

"Sure. What is it?"

"Help me get Bozeman out of jail and back home."

CHAPTER ELEVEN

Dolly noticed Merle was getting all the attention, and couldn't have that, so she climbed up the side of my chair and plopped right down in my lap. She nuzzled at my hand until I scratched her nose right between the eyes. Afterward, I worked on her ears, and she relaxed, and I felt her go limp. I knew from experience if I kept it up, I'd have a raccoon sleeping on my lap within five minutes.

"What's our next move?" Laurel asked.

I glanced over at Laurel, who was still playing with Merle. Normally, the kids were shy around strangers, but they both took to Laurel like bees to clover. "Well, I'd like to get Gabe's drugs and turn them over to the cops, and I'd love the chance to search his room. Too late, though. It looks like the rest are back."

When the Ford van pulled up, the brakes squealed in a pitch that assaulted my ears. It must have been twice as bad on Merle and Dolly because they both jumped from our laps and scurried toward their nest.

I watched as a man whom I had never seen before stepped out of the passenger seat. He looked to be as average as a man could be. Average height, light brown hair, and a runner's build with the beginning of a rounded stomach. Unlike Laurel and I, who dressed in jeans T-shirts, the man was wearing black dress slacks, a white button-down shirt, and a skinny black tie.

He must have recognized Laurel because he walked right over to us.

"Hey, Steve. This is my friend, Codi Cassidy. Codi, this is Steve Ridgeway. He's the bus driver. Are we leaving soon? We must be if you're back."

Steve shook my hand when I offered it. He had a firm, but not overpowering, grip. "Nice to meet you. Yeah, I got a call from the record company. We'll be shoving off today."

"Hey, Steve, can I have the key? I need a jacket, and they locked the bus, and I'm the only one here."

Without comment, Steve fished a key ring from his pocket, picked through until he found the right one, and held it out for Laurel.

"Here. Put them in the driver's seat when you get in."

Laurel took the keys and smiled. "Thanks, Steve. Keep Codi company until I get back, will you? She doesn't like to be alone."

Laurel got up and Steve replaced her in the chair. For a few moments, we looked at each other like we were on an awkward first date.

"So, you're a musician too?" he asked.

I smiled. "Yes. You've heard of me? Are you a fan?"

"No. I saw your name written on the side of your bus there."

Talk about deflating someone's ego. I took my turn at the unpleasant conversation. "So how long have you been Toby's driver?"

Steve stared at me for a second, and I guessed that he wouldn't answer, and at worst he would walk away, but he leaned back in the chair and crossed his legs. "Oh, I don't know for sure. Three, perhaps three and a half years."

"Driving is hard work. I always feel bad for Bozeman. He's my partner, and he has to drive this hunk of metal around."

Steve didn't comment.

"Laurel told me you don't stay on the bus when you get to a location. Why is that?"

"Why do you care?" he asked.

That question seemed to raise his dander. "I don't, really. Only thought it was unusual. I thought drivers always stayed on the bus."

Steve uncrossed his legs. He noticed a small rock near his right foot. He kicked at it, and it skittered under my bus.

"Toby and I have an arrangement. I take care of other areas of his business, so I stay off site so I can concentrate on it without all the distractions that go on around the bus."

"That's interesting. I thought Russell as the band manager handled all of Toby's business affairs."

Steve glared at me for a moment and rose. "Nice meeting you, Codi Cassidy. Have a nice day." He said the 'have a nice day part' so cold and sarcastic that the words still hung in midair as he turned and walked to Toby's bus. I hoped Laurel had finished whatever she was doing in there, because she'd been gone too long to have simply gone for a jacket.

Steve stepped onto the bus and disappeared from sight. I pledged to wait only five minutes for Laurel to come out, and if she didn't return by that time, I would go over and find her myself. I pulled my phone from my back pocket, found the timer feature, set it for five minutes, and pressed the little green button. For a couple of seconds, I watched the numbers flip to make sure it was running and turned my attention to the bus. I waited. Five minutes dropped to four. Four eventually became three. After what seemed to be an hour, three turned to two, then finally to one. My eyes darted from the phone to the bus as the last minute ticked away.

The alarm rang, and I fumbled for the button to shut it off. Once my phone was silent, I got to my feet and started walking toward the bus. I reached a little over halfway when Laurel bounded down the steps and skipped off in my direction.

She was wearing a bright yellow raincoat that looked to be at least one size too big for her. She looked, in a word, ridiculous, especially considering there wasn't a single rain cloud to be seen in the big blue sky.

"Come on." She interlocked her elbow into mine, spun me around, and escorted me back aboard my bus. There, she removed the raincoat. "Did he follow us?"

I looked out the door and the parlor window. "Nope. I don't think so."

"Why are you wearing that coat? It looks silly on you."

"It protects me from the rain," she answered matter-of-factly.

"But it's not raining out."

"Oh, I also love it because it has lots of internal pockets to protect other things from the rain and from spying eyes."

Laurel picked up the coat and rummaged around inside. "I've got some presents for you."

She handed me what looked to be a pill bottle. The bottle label said it was a generic multi-vitamin, but I could tell right away the label was fake because someone had misspelled the word vitamin. I twisted open the top, tipped over the bottle, and a few of the pills I hadn't been able to identify tumbled into my palm.

"Thanks. That's what I've always wanted."

"Wait. There's more," Laurel said.

Laurel reached back into her coat and removed a baggie. In it were over a dozen of the tainted capsules.

"Nice. Those were in that fake book you told me about?"

"Yep. And that fake book got me thinking. If he had one item like that to hide stuff in, maybe he would have more. So…"

Laurel dipped into her coat for a third time and extracted a yellow legal pad. She handed it to me and sat back in the captain's chair. "Last present. Good things come in threes."

I took the pad and looked at it. The first page had doodles. Nothing artistic, only random lines, boxes, triangles. I flipped the first page over, and the second page was the same, except the sketches seemed to be someone's initial attempt at artwork.

"What is this?" I asked.

"To me, it looked like he was trying to come up with a personal or band logo, and not doing a good job at it."

I looked at it again with that in mind, and some images kind of made sense in that respect. The lines I'd mistaken as scribble lines now resembled drumsticks, at least a little. I wasn't sure what Gabe was going for, but he convinced me if he really wanted his own logo, he should ask a graphic designer or someone at the record company about it. Drawing was not in his wheelhouse.

"Why am I looking at these?" I asked.

"Keep turning the pages," Laurel said.

I flipped to the next page and found a list of songs. I looked up at Laurel. "Toby's set list?"

"Not in order. Just some of the common songs we'd play during a show. Some we always play aren't on there, and there are a couple included we haven't played in forever."

"Where did you find this?"

"There was a false bottom in one of his drawers. In there was a dirty magazine, and this. Please, keep going."

I turned the page, and this got my attention. It was a block of text, written in block letters. After I cleared my throat, I read them aloud to get their full effect.

"I don't know why I'm here. I hate them all. Why can't I leave? I hate Fran, always flaunting her sex like a peacock in heat and flashing her boobs at every opportunity. I hate Laurel and her oh, shucks, look at me I'm a down-home country girl who's so innocent."

My eyes slid from the page, and I looked at Laurel.

She smiled and shrugged. "Well, I guess he doesn't like me."

I turned back to the note. "I hate Toby. He walks around like he's God's gift to country music with his stupid sequined jackets and his flashy boots. If people learned the things I did about him, he wouldn't be able to serve beer at a country bar, let alone be a country star. If it wasn't for Billy running his mic through the computer, he'd sound like an old goat chewing on a tin can. Who's Billy?"

"He's the lead sound engineer," Laurel said. She got up, crossed to the pantry, and helped herself to a bottle of water. She brought me one, too.

"Is this part true about Toby's singing?"

"Well, I am under an NDA, but I will tell you that Toby would never get confused with Frank Sinatra. And you know all those singers who have a unique voice? Willie Nelson? Kenny Rogers? Bob Dylan?"

"Yeah, of course. I named one of my chipmunks after Willie."

"Well, they would never consider Toby in that class, either."

"So, you're saying he's a fake? The computer Gabe mentions. Is it voice modulation or pitch correction?"

"Both." Laurel held her hands up in front of her. "You didn't hear me say anything of the sort, now did you?"

I let it drop and returned to the note. "The world needs to learn the truth, and I think I should be the one to tell them. I will destroy him for what he did to me. Well, that got cryptic quick, didn't it?"

Laurel nodded. "Yeah. It had a strong start, especially that part about Fran, but it lost its steam after a few sentences. Not bad for a manifesto start, though."

I flipped to the next one. It was blank, so I closed the book and offered it to Laurel.

Laurel refused to take it. "No. You missed the best part. Keep going."

I took it back and paged through it again. After a few blank pages, I found the real prize. "Holy moly. It's Bozeman's song."

I removed the two sheets of paper from the pad and put them on the dinette table like they were museum exhibits. I grabbed Toby's sheet music from the counter and handed it to Laurel.

"Here. You compare the two and tell me what you think."

Laurel took her time and compared Toby's song to Bozeman's. After five minutes, she set the paper down on the table. "Except for the title and a couple of word changes, it's exactly the same."

"Did you check the dates?" I asked.

Laurel picked the paper back up, found the music copyright date, and compared it to the hand-scrawled date on Bozeman's page. "It looks like Bozeman's is a good ten years earlier. What are you going to do now that you have this back?"

"I don't know for sure. I might get Bozeman's lawyer looped in and see what she says. Hypothetically, of course. Excuse me."

While I trusted Laurel, I didn't want to include her in my conversation with Bozeman's lawyer. So, she waited where she was while I went into my bedroom and made the call. It didn't take long for us to come up with a game plan.

I returned to the other room.

"Well?" Laurel asked.

"Hold on." With my phone, I took pictures of everything Laurel had brought me. I snapped photos of every page on the legal pad, as well as Bozeman's handwritten lyrics and the sheet music. "She recommends we turn everything over to Sheriff Cross."

"Is that really a good idea?"

"I asked that same question. Bozeman's lawyer said yes, though. The lawyer won't be able to use the evidence at the arraignment hearing. But she might use it to persuade the district attorney that Bozeman isn't the killer. I want to make one stop first."

Rather than put everything back in Laurel's raincoat, I instead found a brown paper grocery bag that fit everything nicely. We got off the bus just in time to see Fran and Russell exit a ride share car. I jogged over to the driver's window.

"Hey, can you take my friend and I to a couple places?"

The driver checked his phone to see if he had anyone already slated. "You're good. Get in."

I climbed into the seat behind the driver, but as Laurel reached for the handle of the other back door, Russell grabbed her arm.

"Where are you going?" He sneered.

Laurel looked over at me, then back at Russell. "I'm just going back to check on Gabe."

"You can't. We're leaving. Right now."

"You know as well as I do it will take at least an hour for Steve to get everything cleaned up and ready to go. Just give us an hour, okay? If I'm not back by then, you can leave without me."

Russell let go of her wrist and opened the door for her. "I'll be generous. Two hours. No more."

Laurel climbed in and Russell slammed the door behind her. "We don't have a lot of time."

I nodded, then instructed the driver to take us to the county hospital. I told the truth when I said I would turn it over to the sheriff. Forgetful me, I didn't mention I wanted to have one last conversation with Gabe about it first.

We arrived at the hospital and found our way to Gabe's room. When we approached, the door was closed, and Laurel took the lead and opened it a crack. I could see the lights were out, but the random flicker told us the television was on.

"Gabe? Are you awake?" Laurel said, just above a whisper.

"Who's there?"

"It's me, Laurel. Codi is here to see you, too. Can we come in?"

There was a delayed answer. "I suppose."

Laurel opened the door wide, and we entered the room.

There were two chairs nearby, one on either side of the bed, so we each took a seat.

I knew Laurel had little time, so I got right into it. "Gabe, can you tell me about the drugs?"

"What drugs?"

I fished the bottle out of the bag and held it out. The TV didn't cast enough light, so Gabe pressed a button, and an over-bed light came on. I shook that bottle in front of him. The pills rattled inside.

"Those aren't mine," he said.

Laurel leaned over to Gabe. "I found them in your room, Gabe. And the doctor said they pumped those same types of pills from your stomach. You want to stick with the 'you never saw them before' story?"

Gabe looked at Laurel, at me, then back at her.

"Okay. Look, you don't understand the pressure I'm under. They help keep me balanced, you know? Mellow. Attentive. I'm only doing them for the good of the band. For Toby and the rest of you."

I fished out the baggie and held it before his eyes. "What are these supposed to do?"

Gabe looked at the capsules briefly, then stared at the television. There was a baseball game on with the sound turned down. "He told me those would help me sleep."

"Who's he? Who gave these to you?"

Gabe shook his head. "I can't tell you that."

"Did you know what's in these? Rat poison. Your doctor confirmed it, and I found the package in the trash can on your bus. Whoever you're trying to protect gave you rat poison. Sure, those will help you sleep, especially if your intention is to sleep forever."

Gabe focused on me again. "You're trying to trick me. I'm never going to tell you."

"You want to tell us about this, then?" I put the drugs back in the paper bag and pulled out the legal pad.

"Where did you get that?"

Laurel spoke up. "I found it in your secret drawer with your copy of Boob Monthly. You saying this isn't yours, either?"

Laurel reached over, grabbed the pad from my hand, and

turned to the second page. "Are you saying you didn't do this? You're not trying to design a logo for your bass drum? Thinking about starting your own band?"

Gabe reached up and ran his fingers along the page. "No. This pad is mine. I just haven't seen it in a long time. A few weeks ago, I lost it. I'm just surprised you found it. Why would you even care? It's just a stupid logo."

"We don't give a toot about the logo. We care about your manifesto."

"What are you talking about?" he asked.

Laurel flipped to the correct spot and read it to him. As she read, I watched Gabe's face for any micro-expressions. The only one I noticed was a general look of confusion that anyone could see.

"Let me see that," Gabe said.

Laurel handed him the pad, and Gabe studied it. "I didn't write this. I wrote none of these things."

"Come on, Gabe. Fess up," Laurel said.

"No. Okay, I'll admit that those drugs were mine. I can't deny that. But this I didn't do."

"We don't believe you, Gabe," I said.

Laurel and I hadn't considered doing the good-musician, bad-musician routine on him, but it seemed to work.

"Look, watch, bring that tray closer."

I looked where Gabe was pointing and saw an adjustable bedside table. I wheeled it over and put it over the bed so Gabe had full access to it. On the table was a pen and a crossword puzzle book that someone had brought him to help ward off boredom. Crosswords must not have been his thing, though, because the puzzle the book was open to only had five words filled in. I could tell just with a glance that the answers to two questions were wrong.

"Give me a sheet of paper."

Laurel looked at me for approval, and when I nodded, she tore the last page from the legal pad and set it on the table.

Gabe picked up the pen. "Okay, now read me the note again."

Laurel read, and Gabe wrote what she said.

I noticed something was off right away. "Hold it. Gabe, you're writing in cursive. Do block letters, like in the note."

Gabe crossed out what he had written. "Sorry. Let's do it over. Anytime you're ready, Laurel."

Laurel read the note again, this time slower, because it took Gabe longer to write in the same style of the note. Laurel got through three sentences before I stopped her and asked for the pad.

I set the pad on the table and placed Gabe's version right next to it. At first, I only scanned it, then went back and read it with more intention and I compared them one letter at a time.

I looked at Gabe, then at Laurel. "He didn't write this note."

"How can you tell?"

"Get closer and look. Not even close to being the same," I said.

"Maybe he faked his handwriting when he wrote it just now," Laurel argued.

"He could have, but I don't think so. There are too many discrepancies in the way he wrote the letters."

"Good. Does that mean I'm off the hook, then?" Gabe asked.

"Not yet. I've got one more question. Have you ever seen this before?" I removed Bozeman's song from the pad and placed it on the table.

Gabe leaned forward and was about to grab it when I stopped him. "No. Don't touch it."

Gabe removed his hand from the area and instead looked at the document where it lay. "No. I've never seen this before."

I put the song back where it was and returned everything to the bag. "Gabe, I'm sorry we disturbed you. I really hope you feel better soon."

Laurel and I stood and left, leaving Gabe to his baseball game.

"Well? What do you think?" Laurel asked.

"I think Gabe's an addict, but that's about it. Come on, let's go find the sheriff."

Laurel and I jumped into the waiting car, and the driver took us to the sheriff's office. Laurel waited in the car while I stepped inside to visit Sheriff Cross.

The desk officer escorted me to Cross's office, which was open. I knocked on the door just to be polite, entered, and sat down in the leather guest chair in front of his desk without being asked.

The sheriff was in the middle of typing out a report when I entered, but he turned his attention from the computer to me.

"What can I do for you, Ms. Cassidy?"

"I have a few items here that Bozeman's attorney asked me to turn in."

I opened the bag and lined up the pill bottle, bag of capsules, the pad, and Bozeman's lyrics on his desk, then explained the significance of each.

He seemed especially interested in the drugs, but not so much in the notepad or Bozeman's song. To his credit, though, he put each of the items into its own evidence bag and labeled everything with Bozeman's case number.

Nothing more needed to be said, so I rejoined Laurel, and we rode together to the park. Once we were out of the car, Laurel came over and gave me a hug.

"I guess I'll be shoving off soon. It was such a pleasure to meet you, Codi. I hope Bozeman gets out of jail, and you two can get back to a normal life."

I smiled. "Thanks, Laurel. I appreciate it. I wish you well on whatever it is you do next."

Laurel let go of me, and I watched her walk away.

CHAPTER TWELVE

When Laurel left, I took a seat and placed my head in my hands. I wanted to cry, but I wouldn't. I wasn't about to descend into that pit of misery, although I was in the mood to feel sorry for myself. Here I was, sitting all alone, but then I remembered Bozeman sitting all alone in the slammer. At least I had my freedom.

I couldn't understand where I got it wrong. All signs pointed directly at Gabe as the killer, but those signs were mistaken. I considered what to do next. Clean the bus? Practice my guitar? Wallow in self-pity? None of the options seemed like good ones.

At that moment, I remembered Laurel's garish yellow raincoat that she'd left with me. Not wanting her to go without it, I stepped onto the bus to get it. When I leaned across the dinette to pick up the coat, something caught my eye outside the window, or rather, someone.

My eyes followed Tommy as he crept out of the tree line near my bus. He didn't even glance in my direction, and seemed interested in Toby's bus, not mine. He disappeared from view, so I quickly repositioned myself near the driver's seat. From there, I watched as he picked his way to the other bus.

Once at the bus, he crouched down and rolled under. As I watched, a bundle flew out from beneath the bus, and a second later, another followed. After a moment, Tommy's leg popped out, followed by the rest of him. He hesitated, took a tentative look around and picked up both bundles and scampered away. I noticed he followed the same path as the trash I picked up earlier. This piqued my interest, so I placed Laurel's rain jacket on the driver's seat and left the bus.

I sprinted to Toby's bus and flattened myself against the side so no one would spot me through any of the windows. Slowly, I made my way to the rear and peeked around the corner to ensure no one was by the outdoor kitchen. The coast seemed clear, so I ran to the woods where I'd seen Tommy enter.

Once in the trees, I stopped, looked around, and remembering Tommy's earlier threat, took Betty from the holster and clicked off the safety. I found a deer path that I followed for a few yards and soon came to a junction. I had a decision to make. Left or right. Since he'd come out of the woods near my bus, I turned right and walked along the trail. Off in the distance, I overheard voices, so I slowed my gait.

Fifty feet later, I walked around a bend and stopped. Up ahead, kneeling on the ground facing away from me, I found Tommy. The voices I'd picked up came from a small radio, and the two bundles he'd taken occupied Tommy's attention. I took a few silent steps forward, and I realized the bundles were pillowcases, and from one, Tommy was removing canned goods.

"You progressed from playing guitar to stealing food?" I asked. I hoped my voice didn't shake out loud like it did in my head.

Tommy turned so quickly he lost his balance and fell flat on his behind. He looked like he wanted to pounce but spotted my firearm and settled back in his seat.

I waved the gun at the food. "What's going on here?"

He looked at the can of soup he held in his hand and returned it to the pillowcase. "This isn't what you think."

"Not what I think? So, then I didn't just witness you sneak over to his bus and steal this stuff. What is all this, anyway? How did you get on the bus?"

"I didn't."

"Why lie to me? It's only going to make things worse for you."

Tommy brushed his hands on his pants. "There's a maintenance panel near the back. It opens up into Toby's bedroom."

That made me wonder about the security of my bus, and Tommy read me like we were sitting around playing poker.

"Don't worry about that. Your bus is too old. It doesn't have that same design."

"Why did you break into Toby's bus? For food? You expect me to accept that? I thought you live in L.A."

"I do. There are some things you don't understand," he said.

I thought I understood fine, but if he wanted to talk, I'd let him go. "Why don't you explain it all to me? What brought you here?"

I could tell he didn't want to talk to me, so I motioned with the gun to implore him to continue the story.

"Things haven't been going well for me, and I've been down on my luck. I used the last of my money to drive out here to see Toby."

"Where's your car? There's no one else in the parking lot."

"The old clunker broke down as I got into town. I kept it going until I got it to the garage, then I walked the rest of the way here."

"Why did you want to see Toby?"

"Because. I wanted to ask for a loan, you know, for old time's sake. I thought he'd do that for me, especially for the way he screwed me over by replacing me with Fran." Tommy shifted in his seat. He put his hand under his backside and tossed an uncomfortable rock into the trees.

"Interesting. Did you talk to him?" I asked.

Tommy took a sudden interest in the ground. He found a stick, picked it up, and started drawing patterns in the dirt.

"Tommy? Did you talk to Toby? Tell me the truth."

"Yes, I did. After the sound check, I followed him back to the bus."

"What happened?"

"I asked him to give me a loan. He seemed already angry, so he said no."

"Then you got mad and strangled him and shoved a song down his throat?" I asked. There was no way to cushion that question.

"No. Of course not, no" Tommy raised his stick, but because it was only the size of a magic wand, it seemed more cute than threatening. "I never touched him that way. I couldn't."

"But I'll bet you wanted to," I said.

Tommy dropped the stick. "Of course I wanted to. Ever since I was a young boy, I wanted to be in a band, so I worked hard to make that happen. Do you know what a distinguished career I had? How many albums I've been on? How many stars I've played with? I've toured with country music royalty, and Toby took all that away when he traded me in for that woman. I admit, I would've loved to kill him, but I didn't."

"Someone told me it was your own fault you got kicked out. Missing rehearsals, talk of you doing drugs, that sort of behavior."

I saw him getting agitated, but regardless of how much he got worked up, he didn't make a move toward me.

"Hey, I'm telling you, I did not murder Toby. I couldn't have."

"Are you sure?" He seemed sure, but I wanted to see it in his eyes when he denied it.

"Yes. I never even stepped on the bus. There's no way I could have strangled him on the ground and carried him on the bus. I'm not strong enough,"

"What do you mean?"

Tommy retrieved his stick and retraced the patterns he already drew in the dirt. "I'm ill. Chronically. I've only got a couple of months left to live."

His body language told me he spoke the truth.

"I'm sorry." His confession hit me in the heart, and I lowered Betty to my side. I kept the safety off. I can be sympathetic without being stupid.

He smiled. "Thanks. I appreciate it."

"Toby knew?"

"Of course. That's why I missed rehearsals. And the medications they had me on initially only made it worse. They kept me in a half-comatose state most of the time. Those first days were so hard on me. Physically and mentally."

"And your long-time friend turned his back on you, and rather than help, he cut you loose."

Tommy nodded.

"Nice guy," I said.

Tommy nodded again and threw his stick into the brush. "Yeah, tell me about it."

"So, why are you stealing?" I asked.

Tommy shrugged. "I'm hungry. And like I said, with my car in the shop, I can't get back to Los Angeles, anyway. Once Toby got killed, the bus stayed empty most of the time, so I dropped in when I noticed no one around and took whatever supplies I needed."

"Show me your treasure."

Tommy hesitated, then grabbed the first pillowcase and tipped it upside-down. I watched as canned goods, a head of lettuce, two bananas, and an orange tumbled out. The other pillowcase held a blue melamine plate, a steak knife, two spoons, and a fork.

I nodded, and Tommy gathered up the items and placed them back into the cases.

"Are you going to turn me in?" he asked.

"I should. You're a thief. But no. I don't think I will, as long as you answer one more question for me."

"Sure. What is it?"

"Do you do drugs?"

"Like I said, I'm terminal. I eat dinner with the Grim Reaper at the table every night. Of course I do drugs. Mostly pain killers."

"I meant illegals. Street stuff."

"No. I admit, I tried cocaine once, but I hated the way it made me feel afterward, and I never did it again. Also, I had the unpleasant opportunity to see firsthand what they did to a lot of good people. I always avoided illegal drugs like the plague."

"Ever sell them?"

"Nope. I never got into that, either. Hell, I never even got much into liquor."

I stared at him for a few moments, satisfied he was being honest with me.

"Do you need anything out here?" I asked.

Russell shook his head. "No. With this haul, I'm good for a few days."

"Where have you been sleeping?"

"I don't really sleep much, but when I need to, I either nap on the bench in the locker room or go over to the bleachers."

"Look, I'd like to invite you on the bus, but I'm all alone on there."

Tommy nodded. "Sure, I understand."

"You didn't let me finish. I have a lounge lawn chair I will put out next to the bus, and I'll put a blanket out there too, okay?"

"I'd appreciate that. Thank you."

I tucked Betty back into her holster and gave Tommy a tentative wave goodbye and turned to leave.

Tommy stopped me. "Hey."

I turned back around to face him.

"Take the first trail you find on your left. It'll take you right back to your bus."

"Thanks."

I left Tommy with his treasures and walked back to my bus. Once there, I trudged once more up the bus steps, and ran right into Laurel, who stood there waiting for me.

"Where have you been? Get in here."

I accepted Laurel's invitation to enter my personal domicile and threw myself into the first chair I came to.

"What's up? I thought you guys had an itching to leave," I said.

"We are soon, but I found something I need you to look at."

Parched, I rose from my chair, headed to the storage room, grabbed a couple of bottles of water, and headed back for my chair. On the way, I passed one bottle to Laurel. I opened mine and drank half the contents before I returned my attention to my visitor.

"What do you need to show me?"

Laurel thrust her phone at me, so I took it and looked at the screen.

"What is this?" I expanded the view on the screen to make it bigger and examined the picture. I had to keep moving the image on the screen to read it normally, but I got the gist quick. "Holy cow, is this a life insurance policy? Where did you find this?"

"Russell's room."

I read the page more. The insured was Toby Madden, and the

beneficiary was a trust, and I could only guess who headed that trust. The policy paid two million dollars. I read the fine print and discovered the double indemnity clause I assumed I'd find there.

I held up the phone. "Do you know what you found here?"

"I do if you mean a motive to kill off Toby?"

I nodded. "If what you say is true, and Toby wasn't the best of singers, maybe his act was over-inflated. What about this scenario? Russell knew that Toby's star had limited reach. Between his lacking vocal abilities and his over-bearing personality, Toby would end up playing at dirty bars and supermarket openings. So, rather than lose all the money, Russell kills him off."

"It sounds plausible to me, and four million bucks is an excellent motive. Of course, you don't know for sure who that trust is for. For all you know, all the money goes to homeless, hungry children," Laurel said.

I nodded. "That's fair. Point taken. Any chance you have more pictures in here that would show that?"

"I had little time, so I was lucky to grab these pictures."

"Where did you find this in Russell's room?"

"Well, I got to thinking about that false bottom in Gabe's room, and I wondered if everyone had those secret hiding spaces. Toby had a false bottom in his closet, but I found it empty."

"Wait, did it look like it was always empty, like Toby never knew it existed? Or did it look like he stored something there at one point, but someone removed whatever Russell had there?"

"I don't know. I didn't stay long enough to get into that kind of detail. Once I saw nothing in it, I moved on."

"Did you find other hidden compartments in Toby's room?"

"No, but that doesn't mean there aren't any. So back to where I found this, in a false bottom of his bottom dresser drawer."

"Did you spot anything else in there?"

"Actually, yes. He filled the drawer with documents, but I thought I heard someone coming, so I snapped this picture, closed it back up again, and left. Did I do okay?"

I grinned at her. "You did great. Now, do you think you can do me one more favor?"

It took about fifteen minutes to explain my plan, then Laurel grabbed her raincoat and left me. While I waited for Laurel to implement the secret plan, I headed outside and pulled the chaise from the compartment. I set it up near the front bumper on the passenger side, so it would hide Tommy from view as much as possible. Then I rummaged around inside until I found a blanket and a small travel pillow, then added a couple of bottles of water to the pile in my arms. I carried it all outside and set everything on the chair.

When that task was complete, I wanted to check on all the kids. It was getting close to dinnertime, so Willie and Waylon had already returned to their nest for the night. I closed the little chicken-wire gate we used to keep them safe at night and during travel times.

Next, I checked on Merle and Dolly. Merle must have had a busier day than usual because the little guy was in full nap-mode in his blanket. Dolly wasn't home. You would think I'd worry about my animals wandering free at night, but there was never a time when they weren't back by morning. I hoped that would always be the case.

Merle and Dolly share a water bottle, just like the type you'd find in a pet rabbit cage. I removed the bottle, noticed it was only half-full, and took it into the kitchen and filled it up. I made it halfway back to the cage when a van pulled up. Unwavering, I returned the water bottle to its place, and as I finished the task I saw Laurel, Fran, Steve, and Russell get off the bus and into the van. I waved as the van pulled away and left the park.

Once the van disappeared from the lot, I walked over to the bus and tried to open the door. The door was locked up tight, which I expected. Undeterred, I walked to the back wheels of the bus, then crawled underneath and rolled over onto my back. A third of the way under, I found the panel that Tommy had described.

I had brought no tools with me, but it turns out I didn't need any. There were two latches that reminded me of the ones on airplane doors, and I turned them to unlock, and the panel dropped open.

If ever there was a time when I was happy I was as small as I am, it was now. I sat up and put my arms into the hole, then easily stood. The floor level of the bus was above my waist, but not by much, so I could get into Toby's room with no trouble at all.

Now that I was inside, I went directly to Russell's room. There, I emptied the drawer and opened the false panel. The top document was the life insurance policy for Toby. I lifted it out and placed it face-down on the floor. To my surprise, the next three documents were also life insurance policies for Fran, Gabe, and Laurel. All were worth five-hundred thousand dollars, and each had the double indemnity clause for wrongful death. The beneficiary for each was the same trust listed in Toby's policy.

Just beneath the insurance policy documents were a pile of papers related to the business. They included boring things like expense reports and tax documents. I stood up and looked at the bookshelf beyond Russell's desk. There were several binders, two of which were labeled expense reports and tax documents. I grabbed the two binders, brought them back to the dresser, and sat back down on the floor. There, I compared the expense reports first, and although it took me a little while to figure out how to read the things, I determined that there were two reports. The official one in the binder had numbers that were thousands of dollars higher than the one in the drawer. I compared them, month after month, and the results were all the same. The expense reports were off.

Next, I checked the tax forms, and there were discrepancies in those as well. They had prepared the taxes in the binders in such a way to lessen the tax burden, or to ensure the largest refund possible. It proved to me that Russell was indeed playing fast and extremely loose with the accounts.

I saw everything I needed to see for now, so I returned everything to its rightful place, then went over and looked at Russell's closest. It wasn't a large closet, only about three feet wide, and I opened the door and peered inside. On the closet floor were six pairs of shoes. I removed the shoes, then rapped on the floorboard. It felt hollow for me. At the rear right corner, there was a small notch, and I put my index finger in there and popped out the floor.

"Holy cow," I said.

Beneath the floor were at least fifty pill bottles. I lifted one and saw it held the same label as the one Laurel had found in Gabe's room. Dozens of bags of pills took up the rest of the space. Most of them were gallon sized, but there were several each of quart, sandwich, and snack sized bags as well. The small ones I found were half the size of a credit card and contained only two pills each.

Although we'd only found two pills in Gabe's things, there were at least a dozen other colored tablets in Russell's stash. I pulled out a final baggie, and that one contained empty capsules. Capsules that matched Gabe's poisoned pills.

I had all the answers and proof that I needed to finger Russell for several crimes. Now what I needed to do was put everything back the way I found it and call out the calvary. I started by replacing the floorboard and putting back Russell's shoes where I found them.

Once I looked around to make sure everything was as it was before I arrived, I left the room and closed the door behind me. I was about to head for the door, but then I saw the shine of headlights pierce the windshield.

"Oh, no. They're back early."

I ducked back into the shadows until the light passed, then quickly made my way back to Toby's room. Plan A was to go out the main door, and lock it behind me, then go back and close the hatch, but I had to put Plan B into action instead. I rushed to Toby's room and closed the door behind me.

I heard voices as I sat on the floor and swung my legs into the hatch. The voices were getting louder, and I dropped through the floor and onto the hard ground below. I let out a small yelp as my knees hit the concrete, and I prayed it wasn't loud enough for anyone to hear.

Hinges connected the hatch on one side, so all I needed to do was swing it up and close the latches to lock it. I secured the final latch just in time to hear footsteps above my head. Frozen, I waited until it was silent above me, then I crawled the length of the bus. I waited near the front right tire, and when I thought the coast was clear, I rolled out from beneath the bus, then trotted over to mine.

By the time I got back, I was panting from the stress. I found the water I'd started earlier, then drained the bottle. My right knee hurt, so I pulled down my jeans and saw something had pierced through the fabric and cut my knee. It was bleeding. I grabbed the first aid kit, rinsed the blood away with some hydrogen peroxide, then determined all it needed was a strip of cloth first aid tape to cover it.

Once I had myself back together, it was time to put in a call to Sheriff Cross.

CHAPTER THIRTEEN

Once I got my pulse below that of a hummingbird's, I called the sheriff's station and asked to be put directly in contact with Sheriff Cross. In the movies and television shows I've seen, it was a matter of whoever simply transferring the call, but in real life, it was no easy feat. I had to explain myself and stress the importance of my call to the dispatcher and two deputies before the second deputy took my phone number and told me to sit tight.

Twenty minutes later, my phone played *On the Road Again,* so at last I got a call back.

"Hello?"

"Is this Codi?"

"Yes. Is this Sheriff Cross?"

"Make it quick, Codi. I'm at an accident scene here. What's so important?"

"I've got more evidence for you on the Toby Madden murder."

I caught a huff of exasperation over the line. "What is it this time? A soup spoon?"

"Don't be condescending. I found papers that prove that Toby's manager is embezzling money and selling drugs. He also has life insurance policies for not only Toby, but for everyone else in the band."

"So what? Lots of people have life insurance."

"Yeah, but most don't have policies that pay out for four million bucks."

"Okay, okay, I'll come over after I'm done at this scene."

"No, it can't wait. They'll be leaving soon, driving right on out of here, and you'll never get them."

"Hold on."

I could tell the sheriff took the phone from his ear, and I could hear him in the background barking out orders to other people.

"Okay. I'll be there in ten minutes."

He disconnected the call without saying goodbye. Afterward, I played the waiting game again. I started pacing, wearing a hole in the floor, like my mother used to say. To pass the time and dispel some of my nervous energy, I tracked down Gibson and gave him a cat treat. He wasn't happy I woke him from what appeared to be a delightful dream based on his tail twitches, but he appreciated the salmon-flavored treat I fed him. He started out defiant, but I got a fair share of purrs in the end.

I saw red and blue flashing lights approaching, so I set Gibson back where I found him and rushed outside. By the time I got there, the sheriff had parked and stepped from his truck.

"Okay, tell me what you got."

I was about to spill the complete story, but I stopped before I began. The problem slapped me right in the head. I slipped up. I had found Russell's dirt while in the process of committing a crime myself. The sheriff would consider it either trespassing or breaking and entering, and I imagined that would taint the evidence I gathered. I realized too late I should have called the lawyer before I called the sheriff.

"Well? I'm waiting," he said as he glared at me.

"Sheriff, I've come into some information about criminal activity on Toby's bus. I think Russell killed Toby for insurance money, and deliberately poisoned Gabe for the same. And I also believe Russell is a drug dealer."

"Sure. Anything else?" He seemed unimpressed.

"Um, potentially tax fraud and embezzlement," I said.

I saw the sheriff roll his eyes.

"Come on, Sheriff, I'm not kidding here," I said as I crossed my arms.

"How did you come about all this information?" he asked.

I looked out into the twilight night. "I can't tell you yet."

"Do you know if anyone appears hurt or in any physical danger over there?" he asked.

I didn't know how to answer that one, but I suspected not.

"I don't think so," I admitted.

"Okay. Wait here."

I planted my feet and watched as the sheriff walked to the bus. Instead of going directly to the door, he stopped at every window, looked in, and moved on to the next window. Once he'd made a complete loop around the vehicle, he approached the door. I closed the distance to about half so I could overhear what was going on while he knocked.

Russell opened the door and stepped from the bus.

"Sheriff Cross. What a surprise. What can I do for you?"

"Mr. Davidson, we've received a tip that someone has committed one or more crimes on this bus. Do you mind if I come aboard and check it out?"

I got a sense of vindication. It was almost over. Surely, the sheriff would uncover everything I did.

Russell and Sheriff Cross got into a staring contest, and Russell broke first. "Actually, we're getting ready to leave, so no. You may not come aboard."

"Mr. Davidson, if you cooperate, I'm sure we can clear everything up quickly and have you on your way in no time. I'm sure it won't take me more than five minutes of your time."

The sheriff stepped toward the stairs, but Russell was already there and got on the bottom step to block the way.

"Sheriff, I said no. I saw you walk around the bus, and I bet you have neither reasonable suspicion nor probable cause of any crime here. So, again, I ask you to step away and either produce a warrant to enter or let us be on our way."

Sheriff Cross stood still for a moment and tipped his hat at Russell. "Have a pleasant night, sir. Travel safe."

He turned and walked back in my direction. My internal anger thermometer was on the rise. "That's it? Have a pleasant night? You're going to let him get away?"

"Listen, there's nothing I can do right now. He's right. I can't get on the bus without an invitation or a warrant. If there is evidence of a crime and I break in to get it, anything I find wouldn't be admissible in court."

In my heart, I accepted that, because my dad had often said the same. "Based on what I told you, will you get a warrant?"

"I can try. I'll use the evidence that you found earlier to convince the judge to give me one."

"How long will that take?"

"Oh, I don't know. A couple of hours. Perhaps more."

"What about drug dogs? Bring those in. I'm sure they'd hit on something."

"We're too small a county to have our own dogs. We'd have to call them in from L.A., and that would take at least six hours before they got here."

"And what if they just drive away before that happens?"

Sheriff Cross looked at me, then at Toby's bus, then did a circle and looked around the park. He shot me a sly smile.

"I wouldn't worry about that. I'm going to go. You have a good night now."

To my surprise, the sheriff climbed into his truck, and I watched as he drove away. When he got to the park entrance, his taillights brightened, and I could tell he'd put the truck in park. He got out, walked a circle around the truck, then got back in and drove off.

I'd felt good before, but now I seemed deflated like a five-day-old birthday balloon.

I moved inside and got a jacket to protect myself from the chilly evening, then returned outside and sat in my chair. If I couldn't get the sheriff to investigate, I thought I'd get lucky and spot Russell dragging away a body. Hopefully not Laurel's.

An hour later, the engine on Toby's bus roared to life, and I knew it was over. I looked toward them and saw Steve in the driver's seat. The headlights came on, and the bus made a small lurch as Steve shifted it into Drive. He got about ten feet when the flashing lights of a police vehicle approached and stopped directly in front of Toby's bus. It lurched again as Steve slammed on the brakes and shifted back into Park.

This time, Deputy Marvin made an appearance and glanced over at me before he headed to Toby's door. Russell was down and off the bus before Deputy Marvin got within five feet.

"This is outrageous! What do you want?" Russell screamed.

"I'm sorry, sir, you can't leave."

"Why? Do you have a warrant?"

"No, sir, there's been an accident," Deputy Marvin said.

"Accident? Where?"

"At the park entrance. A drunk driver ran into the culvert just outside the entrance. Sorry, road's blocked until the investigation is over and we can get a tow truck in here to remove the vehicle."

"I don't believe you," Russell said.

"Whether you believe me doesn't change the facts, sir. You're welcome to walk down there and take a gander for yourself."

Russell did just that. As he stomped past me, I saw his furrowed brow and angry face. When he walked by, he huffed with every step, like an old steam-powered train engine trying to pick up speed. It was a bit of a walk to the park's entrance, and I waited for Russell to come back. Deputy Marvin stayed still where he was.

Minutes passed, and eventually Russell came huffing by on his return trip. His mood hadn't improved while he was away, and he seemed to be even angrier.

"How did you get in here?" he asked.

Deputy Marvin refocused his attention on Russell. "Well, sir, there was a deputy chasing the car headed southbound, and I was driving northbound. The alleged drunk driver attempted to play a game of chicken with me. I swerved into the park at the last second, and he drove right into the ditch."

It seemed like a logical explanation to me. Believable, almost. Russell didn't like it, though. He looked frustrated and threw his hands in the air.

"Well then. I guess we're just stuck here."

Russell got back on the bus and slammed the door in the deputy's face.

Deputy Marvin turned his attention to me next. "Ma'am, will you be okay?"

I smiled. "Sure. I'm good. I wasn't planning to go anywhere. It must have been quite the car chase with the crash and all."

Deputy Marvin shot me a sly smile. "Yes, it sure was."

"Any idea when it will get cleaned up?"

The deputy removed his hat and scratched his head. "If I had to guess, I'd say they won't have it cleaned up until mid-morning."

"I guess I'll head off to bed, then. What are you going to do, Deputy?"

"I'll be back down at the crash site to monitor things. I'll be around if you need me."

"Thank you, sir."

Deputy Marvin nodded at me, then drove away. I returned to my bus, collapsed into a chair, and when I did, I realized how tired I was. It had been a long, emotionally draining day. My body cried out for sleep, and I hoped I'd actually get some.

I passed through the bus and turned out all the lights and shut all the shades before I robotically went through my nighttime routine and slipped into my bed. I laid there on my back, staring at the dark ceiling, and listening to the quiet. It was too quiet for my taste, with not even a peep from an insect or frog to break the silence. I exhaled, knowing it was going to be a long, sleepless night.

I opened my eyes. I must have been more tired than I thought. I'd slept through the night without moving, and didn't even notice that at some point, Gibson had joined me. He was lying on my chest and was staring at me with his pretty green eyes.

"Good morning. Did you sleep well? Can I get up?"

Gibson licked my nose once, then stood, stretched, and jumped from the bed. I threw back the covers, put my feet on the floor, and looked at my phone. It was just after six-thirty in the morning, and it was time to rise.

After I visited the bathroom and brushed my teeth, I fed Gibson, then checked the fridge for something to feed Merle and Dolly. I knew they probably spent the night dining on whatever they could scavenge, but I still liked to give them their daily bread. Since I was running low on fruits and vegetables, I pulled a tofu-based hot dog from the freezer, cut it in half, and put it with the lettuce and carrots I had.

I reminded myself again that I needed to go out for groceries, and if I didn't do it soon, I'd have to rely on eating whatever Dolly and Merle could bring back for me.

I changed out of my pajama bottoms and into my jeans, then

rather than attend to my hair, I put on a baseball cap. Finally ready to face the world, I unlocked the door and stepped outside.

I half-expected Toby's bus to be gone, but it was right where Steve had parked the beast the night before. Deputy Marvin wasn't in sight, but I had a feeling he was around somewhere.

I checked on Merle and Dolly, who were both in for the day. Merle was napping, and Dolly was playing with a shiny rock she'd found somewhere. She was always bringing home treasures, and after I dropped the food into their bowls, I checked underneath her blanket to look for her secret stash. In it, she had another rock and an orange golf ball. I didn't feel the need to confiscate any of her booty, so I replaced the blanket, gave them both head scratches, and closed the door. If there was going to be trouble this morning, I didn't want my pets in the middle of it.

Next, I went to check on Tommy. I stepped around the bus, fully expecting to see him asleep on the chair, but I was wrong. Tommy was gone. He had been there. The blanket, which I had spread out for him the night before, appeared neatly folded, and one of the water bottles was empty. I wondered where he could be, either in the woods, or in the shower house, but in the end, it was his business, so I put him from my mind.

My stomach growled, so I got back on the bus to feed myself. I found a quarter-loaf of bread and was in the middle of preparing a gourmet peanut butter and jelly sandwich when I saw the sheriff's truck pull up and park. From the window, I watched as he got out of the truck, papers in hand, and walked over to Toby's bus.

He knocked on the door, and Steve answered. Steve took the paper, read it, and let the sheriff in. I finished making the sandwich, cut it in half, put it on a plate, and took it outside. It was a glorious morning for breakfast outdoors.

Deputy Marvin pulled up and nodded at me when he got out of his truck, then waited outside the bus. A few minutes later, Steve emerged, followed by Russell. Russell wasn't saying anything, but the way he displayed his body language told me he was angry about the early morning intrusion.

Next off the bus stepped Fran. She was dressed in a dark blue nightgown. Satin, I guessed, based on the way it reflected the morning sunlight. She also wore a long black robe but didn't bother to close it. Laurel was the last passenger to exit the bus. She was more modestly dressed in gray sweatpants and a plain charcoal-colored T-shirt. Laurel spotted me and came my way. She plopped down into Bozeman's chair.

"Good morning," she said.

I held out the plate, offering her the sandwich half I hadn't touched yet. "Morning. Peanut butter and jelly sandwich?"

"Sure." Laurel accepted the sandwich and took a bite. She chewed for a bit, and then swallowed it down. "That's good. I can't remember the last time I had a peanut butter sandwich."

I smiled. "We eat them all the time. What's going on over there?"

"For some strange reason, the sheriff showed up this morning with a warrant to check over the bus. Something about drugs. I didn't get all the details. I was just told to get off the bus while he conducted the search."

"Do you think he'll find what we need him to?" I asked.

Laurel winked at me. "Well, I may have accidentally let it slip that there are several secret compartments within the furniture and closets on board. He just smiled at me and asked me to leave the bus."

"Interesting. I hope he finds what he's looking for."

"Me, too," Laurel said.

Laurel and I ate our sandwiches and watched the activity near the other bus. Russell and Steve stood nearby the bus and waited. Fran had an animated conversation with Deputy Marvin about something. Finally, Fran took off her robe and spun in a circle. The deputy nodded. Fran replaced her robe, then took off for the shower house.

"What do you think that was about?"

"We're all supposed to stay within view of the good deputy. They want to make sure we smuggled nothing off the bus or that we get into any other trouble."

"I didn't see him try to stop you. Why was that?"

"Oh, the sheriff himself checked me over before I left the bus, so I got his blessing. Besides, the deputy can see me from there, so I'm good."

It took about an hour before Sheriff Cross emerged from the bus. Once he did, he waved me over.

Laurel seemed concerned by the gesture. "Uh, oh. What's that about?"

"I don't know. Wait here, and I'll go find out."
I walked over to the bus and gestured for me to join him onboard.

Before I could get my foot on the first step, Russell objected. "Hey, what's going on? Where's she going?"

The sheriff didn't even acknowledge him, but Deputy Marvin stepped in front of Russell to impede him from going any further. "Police business, sir. Please step back and relax."

Sheriff Cross came up behind me. "Go. Keep moving."

Once we were both aboard, I turned around. "What's going on?"

Cross moved ahead of me. "Ms. Preston let slip about potential hiding spots in here. Come with me."

Our first stop was Gabe's room. Someone had removed the panel. Gabe's nude magazine was still there, but there was nothing else in the drawer.

"So?" I asked.

"So porn isn't illegal in this state. There's nothing here," the sheriff said.

We passed Fran's room, and the sheriff pointed to it as we passed. "Nothing of interest in there."

The next stop was Toby's room. I could tell Cross had done a thorough search in there, as everything looked out of order. He guided me to the closet, and I looked in. He'd found the panel, but there was nothing beneath it.

"See? It's empty."

We left and walked right by Laurel's hovel without comment. I knew from being in there before there were no secrets, other than her classical music training and unorthodox violin.

To his credit, Cross had gone through Russell's room with a fine-toothed comb. He'd removed all the books from the shelves, all the dresser drawers were empty, the desk looked rummaged through, and the closet was open.

He led me to the dresser first. "Come over here and look."

I looked at the bottom drawer. He'd removed the false bottom, but the contents looked different. I bent over, went through the drawer, and found it filled with random things related to Toby. There were promotional flyers, old set lists, articles clipped from newspapers, and what looked to be fan mail.

"What? No, this isn't right!" I said.

I got up and rushed to the closet. The false bottom was leaning against the closet door. I looked in and saw several shoe boxes. I opened the lid of the first box and found a new pair of golf cleats. The second box contained the whitest pair of Converse I'd ever seen. I flipped open the covers of the other four pairs and found the same thing in each box. Shoes.

I picked up a sneaker, looked at it, and threw it back down. I felt frustrated and flustered. All the evidence that pointed to Russell's crimes was gone. "No, this isn't right. Drugs filled up this whole thing. And in the dresser were the insurance policies."

The sheriff leaned on the doorjamb and crossed his arms. "You want to explain to me how you knew that?"

"Because I…" My brain finally caught up with my tongue, so I stopped speaking. The last thing I needed was to be arrested. "Because I had it on good authority, that's how."

He dropped his arms and shook his head. "Look, I'm sorry. I found nothing. Not so much as an unpaid parking ticket shoved into the glove compartment."

"Wait. I'll bet if you brought in the dogs, they'd hit on something. They'd bust this case wide open."

"Codi, I know you're trying to help your friend out of a jam, but trying to get someone else in trouble isn't the way to do it. I'm sorry, but I found no evidence of any crime. Come on, let's go."

I didn't like to whine, but I started to and pleaded with him. "But wait, you're making a mistake!"

"No. Stop. You're wrong. I repeat, for the last time. There. Is. Zero. I. Can. Do. There's no evidence. I'm a cop, I work from evidence, and the only evidence I have points to Jesse James as a murderer."

Dejected, I turned and left Russell's room. I walked directly down the stairs, over to my bus, and entered my home without saying a word to anyone. That included Laurel, who wore a confused look as I passed by without comment. I sunk into a chair and put my head in my hands. I had failed. Failed myself, and failed Bozeman.

I heard a light knock at the door, but I didn't bother to get up and answer it.

"Go away."

I said the words so silently that I was the only one who could have heard them.

The knock repeated, and I said the words again, this time louder. I heard the door open, and a few seconds later, Laurel was by my side. She said nothing, but leaned over and gave me a warm hug.

"It's all gone. All the evidence I found. Cleared out. Gone, and there's nothing we can do about it," I said.

Laurel held the hug to comfort me, which I appreciated. Then, suddenly, she let go and pushed away.

"Hey, Codi? Why is Tommy outside your window waving at us like a madman?"

CHAPTER FOURTEEN

I looked out the window to where Laurel was pointing and indeed Tommy was outside, trying to get my attention.

"Stay here," I said.

"Are you going to be okay? I can come with you." Laurel asked.

"Of course. I'll be fine. He's harmless. Besides, I've got a gun."

I did a double check and made sure Betty was with me, then I stepped off the bus and around the back. Tommy was waiting for me, moving his weight from one leg to another like he was a toddler needing to use the bathroom.

"What's your deal?" I asked.

"What's going on? Are they here for me?" Tommy asked, looking around him as he spoke.

"No. They're not here for you. Why would they be? For a vagrancy charge?"

I heard a couple of doors slam, so I walked around the bus. The lawmen were driving away. Steve and Russell were nowhere in sight, so I guessed they'd returned to their bus. I returned to Tommy.

"The cops are gone. You've got nothing to worry about."

"But why were they even here?" he asked, still frightened.

I gave him a loud, extended exhale. "They were here because they were looking for drugs and other stuff. Yesterday I used that panel you told me about and broke into the bus. I found a whole stash of drugs and a bunch of paperwork that proves Russell is up to his eyebrows in questionable things, so I called the sheriff. He executed a search warrant this morning, but he came up empty. Everything I found yesterday afternoon was gone by this morning."

I looked at Tommy and he had an expression on his face that I didn't quite place. "What? Are you shocked I did what I did?"

Tommy shook it off. "No. It's not that. I watched them last night."

"Watched who?"

"I couldn't really tell who it was in the dark. They slipped off into the woods. They were gone for maybe twenty minutes and came back."

"You think you could show me where they went?" I asked.

Tommy thought for a moment. "I guess so."

"Okay, lead the way. I don't want to be seen by anyone, so let's stay out of view."

Tommy nodded and started off into the nearest clump of trees. I followed Tommy, and before long, we arrived at his makeshift camp. On a tree stump sat an open can of baked beans with a spoon sticking out of it.

"Last night I saw the weirdest thing. I was sitting right there on that stump having a snack when a raccoon walked right past me carrying a golf ball. It was orange. Can you imagine that?"

I chuckled. "Nope. Not in a million years. Where to next?"

Tommy led me along the deer trail I'd followed the previous day, and eventually we came to the junction I'd found. There, he stopped and looked around. I remembered the left path headed to the parking lot.

"Well, should we go straight ahead, or turn right? Which way?"

"Let's try right," he said.

I followed Tommy down the right trail. It started out about eight inches wide, but after a hundred yards, it narrowed down to nothing. The trail ended at a bramble of shrubs with long thorns I couldn't identify.

We turned around, found the junction, and took a right turn. We followed the trail for perhaps a quarter mile and the area opened up to a spot that contained several downed trees.

"Hey, Tommy, do you think whoever you saw was carrying anything?"

"Possibly, sure," he said.

"Okay. Let's spread out here and check around all these trees for anything they may have hidden, okay?"

"Like what?" he asked.

"Beats me. A garbage bag? A box? Perhaps a plastic tote? Who knows what they would have hidden? Look around, okay?"

We separated. I headed into the trees from where we were, while Tommy walked farther down the trail to examine another group of trees. I made my way through and checked both sides of every downed tree, and behind each one in the vicinity still standing. Several minutes of searching brought me no results, except a disturbed squirrel who chittered at me as I passed him.

I was about to give up and move on to a new location when Tommy whistled. I looked around and spotted him thirty yards away. Rather than pick my way through the trees, I backtracked to the deer path and headed in his direction from there. When I was fifteen feet from him, I saw the largest downed tree in the area complete with an exposed root ball.

"Back here. Go around to the left. The right is kind of thorny."

I took Tommy's directions, and soon I was next to him. Obscured by the roots and stacked branches were two small suitcases.

Tommy moved the branches and reached for the suitcase handle.

On impulse, I reached out and slapped his hand. The retort echoed in the trees. "Sorry about that. Don't touch the handle. In case there are fingerprints."

Tommy nodded. "Yeah, good idea."

Tommy reached again, this time for one of the suitcases' roller wheels. He grabbed the wheel, gave a tug, and dislodged the case. The suitcase was about the size of a small carry-on and looked zippered shut.

"Hold on." Slowly, I made my way to the other side of the tree, where there were indeed ground vines with thorns. I found a section where the vine was thin, and doing my best to avoid the prickers, broke the vine away in a section about five inches long. I returned to Tommy and fed the vine through the zipper's hole and looped it. Pulling on the vine, I moved the zipper and opened the case.

Tommy seemed impressed. "That's a smart move!"

After I unzipped the case, I used a stick to open it. I looked in and discovered it stuffed with paperwork, and right on top was the insurance policy on Fran.

"This is good. Pull out the other one."

As I closed the suitcase and zipped it up, Tommy struggled to get the other case.

"Heavy?"

Tommy nodded. "Yeah. Probably twice the weight."

That seemed logical, since the second suitcase was about twice the size of the previous one. Again, I applied the vine trick and unzipped and opened it.

"Oh, wow," Tommy said.

"Yeah, for sure," I answered.

The second case held all the drugs. The ones in plastic baggies sat on top, but I used the stick to move those aside and uncovered all the mislabeled vitamin bottles.

"Bingo," I said.

"Now what? Should we put them back?" Tommy asked.

I thought about it for a moment and decided against it. "No. I think that's a bad idea. Why don't we take them back to your camp? Can you handle that?"

"I think so."

"Can you carry the bigger one?"

Tommy nodded. "Sure. No problem. No handles, right?"

"Right." Since I was closest to the trail, I turned the smaller suitcase upside-down and lifted it by the wheels. I struggled to get it through the underbrush, but eventually I made it to the trail. There I stopped and looked for Tommy, but he was right behind me.

I took the lead and trudged on, struggling with the case as I walked. I plodded on for another ten yards when I received a quiet whistle from behind me. When I looked behind, Tommy had stopped. The suitcase was on the ground, and he was leaning against a tree, breathing hard. I put my case down and stepped back to him.

"Sorry. It's so heavy. I don't think I can do this," he said, his breathing turning to wheezing.

"Okay. Wait here. I'll be right back."

I returned to the smaller case, picked it up, and started walking as fast as I could manage while carrying the awkward load. After a couple of minutes, I passed the trail junction. Five minutes later, I spotted the pillowcases, and the bean can. I set the suitcase down and trotted down the trail back to Tommy. He didn't look well. He was still breathing hard and looked pale.

"I'll help you carry this one, okay?"

He nodded.

"If you can't do it, let me know, and I can find another way. I have a hand truck on the bus, but I'd probably attract attention getting it out, so I'd rather we carry it, okay?"

He nodded again. "You've given me enough rest. I can go on."

"Great. I'll lift the wheels and walk backwards. You grip it by the sides. Remember, don't touch the handle."

"Got it. You can count on me."

We bent over together, and I grabbed the wheels and lifted. Tommy picked up the other end. He couldn't get a good grip, so he rested the suitcase on his forearms. Slowly, we started moving.

"Tell me if I'm going to ram into a tree or something," I said.

"Sure. You're going good. Keep it slow, and we'll be fine."

We moved at a turtle's pace along the trail since I needed to check every footstep so I wouldn't trip over anything. The suitcase was too heavy for me, even with the help of another person, but I didn't want to drop it and give up. After fifteen minutes of struggling, we finally reached Tommy's camp, and we set the case down.

Tommy brushed the bean can from the tree stump and sat down.

"Are you okay?" I asked.

"I'm fine. I need a rest and to catch my breath. Give me a couple of minutes and I'll be okay."

"Can you watch this stuff while I get the sheriff back here?"

Tommy nodded. I could tell he was tired, and I hoped he

wouldn't doze off while I was gone. I hated to leave him that way, but I didn't have a choice.

From the campsite, I rushed back to my bus. As I turned the corner, I found Laurel out in the parking lot having an argument with Russell.

"You can't just leave us here!" Laurel yelled.

"So, get out of the way!" Russell screamed back.

I saw the bus inch forward. Steve was behind the wheel. I could tell he was looking at Laurel, who was certainly in the way, and I feared he would hit the gas and run her down.

I jumped onto my bus and checked my pockets for the keys. They weren't in there. I didn't have the time to search all over the bus for where I had left them last, so I ran directly to Bozeman's room. There, on the desk next to his wallet, were his keys. I grabbed them and rushed to the driver's seat.

"Oh, man," I said.

I looked out and saw Toby's bus inch closer to Laurel. While I appreciated her bravery, I questioned her sanity.

I shoved the key into the ignition and started the bus. Bozeman was the designated bus driver, so the way he positioned the seat was farther back than I could work with. I positioned my butt on the front edge of the driver's seat and pressed the brake pedal. Satisfied I was as ready as I was going to get, I put the bus in reverse and cranked the steering wheel all the way to the left.

I took my foot off the brake, and the bus swung backward. I laid on the horn to get Laurel's attention. She looked behind her and I saw the fear in her eyes when she realized she was in danger of getting sandwiched between sixty thousand pounds of steel.

Laurel made a quick decision and ran out of the way.

I saw Toby's bus speed up, and I tapped the gas to increase my momentum. The bus swung wildly around and before I knew it; there I was facing the woods instead of the other bus.

I felt a slight nudge when the buses kissed each other, and I put mine into Park and turned off the engine. I rushed to the door, opened it, and locked eyes with Steve, who was only a foot and a windshield away from me. With my hand, I motioned to him to back up his bus. He reversed it about four feet and parked.

From my bus, I ran directly to theirs and started my fake outrage the moment the door opened.

"You idiot! Steve, you hit me! You could have killed me! I'm calling the police."

Russell appeared, to his credit, equally antagonistic. "Screw you, Codi. You got in our way. We're leaving."

"Go ahead. Then the cops can arrest you for fleeing the scene of an accident, too."

Russell dismissed me with a wave. "Steve, let's go."

I'd had enough of the game. I pulled Betty from the holster, stepped in front of the door, and took a shooter's stance. "Steve. Turn off the bus."

Steve took one look at my gun and switched off the vehicle.

"Good boy. Now toss the keys down here."

Steve complied, and Laurel scampered over and picked them up.

"Now, both of you. Get off the bus."

Russell and Steve got off the bus with their hands in the air. Honestly, for an impromptu plan, the results pleased me so far, even though I was in the middle of committing a felony myself.

"Laurel, would you mind calling the sheriff for me?"

Laurel did as I asked and placed the call. As she finished up, Fran made an appearance from the shower house.

"What did I miss?"

Laurel chuckled. "Quite a lot, actually. The cops will be here momentarily."

Everyone stood where they were and waited. Off in the distance, I heard the peal of the siren, and soon after, the sheriff and two of his deputies rolled into the lot. As soon as Sheriff Cross stepped out of his truck, I placed my gun on the ground and put my hands in the air.

Before I could count to ten, I was face down on the pavement and I felt the cold steel of handcuffs on my wrists. It was an odd sensation, one I've never had before, and one I wanted to avoid in the future.

Sheriff Cross picked up my gun, removed the clip, and put it on his truck's hood. He lifted me to my feet.

"What's going on here now?" he asked.

Russell stepped forward first. "That nutty woman pulled a gun on us. I want her arrested for assault and unlawful restraint."

Cross turned to me. "Is this true?"

"Partially. Steve, the driver over there, tried to run over Laurel and hit my bus. And then, when I told him to stop, Russell ordered him to drive away. That's felony hit and run. I was justified in keeping him at the scene."

Sheriff Cross literally growled. "I'm so glad I have so many lawyers here. Boys, cuff these other two until we can figure this out."

The deputies moved with haste, and within two minutes, Russell and Steve had bracelets that looked just like mine.

The sheriff turned to Steve. "You have anything to say?"

Steve glanced at Russell, then shook his head. "No comment."

Cross spun around and addressed Laurel. "What about you?"

Laurel looked at him straight on. "It's just like Codi said. They were trying to leave without us, and I stepped in front of the bus to stop them, but they kept coming at me. Then Codi pulled her bus out, and Steve hit her, then Russell wanted him to just drive away."

"Who's us?" Sheriff Cross asked.

"What?"

"You said they were trying to leave without us."

"Oh. Me and Fran," Laurel said.

Fran was up next for questioning.

"What do you have to add?" the sheriff asked.

Fran smiled. "Actually, nothing. I was in the bathroom. I just got back here when you did, so I didn't see or hear anything."

"How convenient for you," Sheriff Cross said.

"Hey, am I interrupting anything?"

I looked over and saw Tommy holding the smaller suitcase by the wheels. I turned just in time to see the look that Russell and Steve passed between each other.

"Who are you?"

I stepped over. "Sheriff, that's Tommy Skye. Within that suitcase is all the documentation you were looking for yesterday."

Fran walked toward Tommy. "Hey, what are you doing with my suitcase? I was looking for that."

"Hold it there, ma'am," Deputy Marvin said. Fran stopped in her tracks.

"Bring that over here, Lee."

Deputy Marvin took the case from Tommy, set it on the ground next to the sheriff's truck, and opened it up. The sheriff looked inside, then grabbed a corner of the top document, removed it from the case, and glanced at the document below it.

"I've seen enough. Anyone want to explain these?"

No one said a word, then Tommy spoke up. "I've got another case, but I can't carry it myself. Can I take your deputy with me to get it?"

"You lead the way and keep your hands in sight, okay?"

Tommy walked off, followed by Deputy Marvin, and within three minutes, they were back. Deputy Marvin set the suitcase next to the first one and unzipped it. All three officers looked in disbelief at the drug-stuffed case.

A movement caught my eye. "Hey. Officer. Someone's making a break for it."

Sheriff Cross looked up from the case and saw Steve making a break for the woods. "Deputy, please bring that idiot back."

Deputy Marvin took off running. I heard him shout a couple of times, and then all was silent. Moments later, the deputy returned, walking with Steve ahead of him. Marvin's shirt was untucked, and Steve had a bloody nose.

"What happened?" Sheriff Cross asked.

"He resisted arrest, Sheriff. I had to tackle him."

"Why don't you put him in the back of your truck? Obviously, he's under arrest."

Deputy Marvin did as ordered, then rejoined the group.

"Do you have anything you want to say yet?" Sheriff Cross asked Russell.

Russell was getting nervous. "It was all him, Sheriff. He's a drug dealer. He's got contacts and makes sales all over the west coast."

"You're saying when I run fingerprints over all those drugs, I won't find yours anywhere?"

"No. Yes. Yes, you will, but he made me do it. Please understand. He's been threatening me my entire life. That guy is pure evil. He would have killed me if I didn't help him."

"Your entire life?"

"Yes, Sheriff. Steve's my cousin. He forced me to be a mule for him."

"Okay, fine. Now, what about all these documents? These life insurance policies? Are you involved in any of that?"

Russell had enough of answering questions and clammed up. I didn't blame him. It was actually a good idea to pin the drug stuff on his cousin. Dealing drugs was a lot worse than whatever white-collar nonsense Russell was involved in.

"I guess that's it then. Put him in my car," the sheriff said.

"Wait! There's something else. I'll be right back." Laurel ran onto the bus and returned with a laptop. She put it on the hood next to my gun and adjusted the screen so everyone could see it. She opened a video file and Fran's image came on the screen.

"You don't get it. I can destroy your career. It will all be over. Everyone in music will find out about your lack of talent and desire to sleep your way to the top."

I'd only talked to Toby a few times, but the disembodied voice on the video was his.

On the video, Fran smiled. "Oh sweetie, tell whoever you want. I don't really care, but I'm sure your wife will when it all comes out."

The video suddenly ended. "Sorry. I opened the wrong file. Let's try this one."

Laurel clicked on another file and let it play. The camera was in the same position, but it was Russell's face on the screen. It took a couple of seconds, but Toby's voice came through the speakers.

"Game's up, Russell. I know all about your cousin and his drug running."

The on-screen Russell hesitated, then spoke. "So, what are you going to do? Call the cops?"

"No. I'm going to take a cut. I'm sure that's the easiest thing for everyone around here. He keeps making money, you keep making money, and I make money. Money, money, money. Enough to go around, and everyone's happy. "

"I'll have to talk to Steve about it. Make sure he approves."

"Oh, he'll approve. Otherwise, he must just find himself buried in a hole in the desert. Get my drift?"

"Yeah. I got it." Russell turned away, but Toby's hand came into the frame and grabbed Russell's shoulder. "Wait. I'm not done with you yet."

"What?" Russell's tone was snarky.

"I also discovered that you've been playing with the numbers. Oh, you're good at it, but you almost got caught. An accountant from the record company called looking for you and asked about one of the expense reports. You were out somewhere that day, so I told her I'd look into it. She sent me a copy over the phone, and lo-and-behold, I stumbled across your secret stash."

"What's your point?"

"The point is, I want in on that too, or you'll be on your way to prison. And if you go, Steve goes. You're doing all the hard work, so I'll make it easy on you. Fifty-one, forty-nine split, and you get the higher percentage."

Russell looked dead on at the camera, so I assumed Toby had it positioned somewhere above and to the left of where Toby was sitting.

"Listen, you no-talent hack. Fine, you'll get the money, but you'd better watch your back from now on, because I know things about you, too. Like you're cheating on your wife, and I know you're cheating on your taxes. And I know you're stealing songs from other songwriters without compensating them. Remember that minor incident in Nashville? Do you think I don't know of the other dozen instances of intellectual property theft you've committed? You may think you have me over a barrel, but we're over the same barrel. We're done here."

The video played for a few more seconds, then faded to black.

"Who was the man not on camera?" the sheriff asked.

Laurel spoke up. "The murder victim. Toby Madden. That's

his voice."

Sheriff Cross closed the laptop. "I have to take this into evidence, too."

"That's fine. It belonged to Toby. He won't need it," Laurel said.

The two deputies transferred all the evidence into the third deputy's car. While they did, Sheriff Cross turned me around and unlocked my handcuffs. Then he handed Betty and the clip to me.

"You know, it was a nice bluff. They could have taken you down, even if you had shot someone. Rubber bullets do minor damage."

I smiled. "Yeah, but they didn't know that."

CHAPTER FIFTEEN

The next morning I woke with a horrible pain in my neck.

The night before, once the police left, I invited Laurel and Fran over for a beer. Laurel accepted, but Fran didn't. I imagined the loss of her meal ticket disturbed her and she was dreading going back into the real world.

Laurel had one of Bozeman's beers, and I drank a cola, and we stayed up and talked most of the night. Bozeman's beer turned out to be too much for Laurel, and she fell asleep in her chair. I covered her up with a blanket and I sat in the other chair. My intention was to stay there for only a few minutes before I continued off to bed, but Gibson jumped in my lap and got comfortable. He purred himself to sleep, and the next thing I realized, sunlight was streaming in through the window and my neck wouldn't cooperate.

I counted to three, held my breath, and twisted my neck from side to side. There was instant pain, and I could have sworn I heard something pop, but it immediately seemed better.

I fed Gibson, and wanted to wake Laurel, but she was sleeping soundly and snoring softly, so I didn't have the heart to do so. Instead, I gathered some things and went for a long, hot shower.

When I got back to the bus, Laurel was awake and nursing a bottle of water.

"I'm sorry. I can't believe I slept so long," Laurel said.

"Hey, it's not a problem, really. You want some breakfast?"

She smiled. "Peanut butter and jelly again?"

I opened the fridge and grabbed the strawberry preserves. I opened the jar and looked inside. "Well, we're out of jelly, so it'll only be peanut butter."

Laurel crinkled her nose. "You mean by itself? What kind of

psycho eats peanut butter by itself? I've got a better idea. How about some pancakes?"

It took me a fraction of a second to mull it over. "Sure. I love pancakes. Do you use real maple syrup or the fake stuff?"

"Oh, the real maple syrup. Direct from Vermont. It's the only way to go. We might be out of pecans though, so you'd have to choose between regular, blueberry, or chocolate chip pancakes." Laurel understood how to tease me.

I grinned. "I love blueberries."

"Me too. Let's go," Laurel said.

Laurel and I left my bus and stepped into hers. She led me into the kitchen, and she started gathering the ingredients for breakfast.

"Do you want sausage or bacon?" she asked.

That was a simple choice for me, too. "Bacon. The answer is always bacon, even when bacon isn't an option."

Laurel chuckled. "I get what you mean. I'm with you there. Um, I hate to do this, but can you start breakfast while I run for a quick shower? I'll be back in ten minutes, fifteen at the most."

"Yeah. Of course. I'll get things ready, and we'll save the pancakes until you get back. Oh, before you go though, do you like your bacon crispy or not so crispy?"

"I prefer it not so crispy, but I'll eat it any way it comes out."

Laurel disappeared into her space and came out a few seconds later with her backpack. As she rushed out of the door, I opened the cabinets, looking for a frying pan.

"It's the far cabinet on the right, down below."

I looked over, and Fran was standing in the hallway. She looked less like a supermodel and more like a woman who'd gone through the ringer.

"Thanks. Would you like to join us for breakfast?" I asked.

Fran shrugged. "Sure. Might as well. Do you want some coffee?"

"No. I don't drink it."

Fran laughed. "Neither does Laurel. I don't understand people who can actually wake up in the morning and be productive without coffee."

While Fran made a pot, I retrieved the largest frying pan I could, set it on the range top, and layered the bacon in the pan. By the time Fran was sipping her first cup, the smell of cooking bacon wafted through the bus.

"That smells so good." Laurel said as she returned, dropped her backpack on the floor next to the door and joined us in the kitchen. "Want some juice or some tea?"

"Juice would be good."

Laurel pulled out two glasses from the cabinet next to my head and poured glasses of orange juice for both of us. Then she grabbed a bowl and started making the pancake batter. It was an instant mix, but I didn't complain.

Fifteen minutes later, the three of us clustered around the dinette table. Laurel had opted for a short stack of chocolate chip pancakes. I went with three fresh blueberry ones, and Fran had a single plain pancake. The plate of bacon sat in the table's center, within reach of everyone.

"Now that this is over, what's next for you two?" I asked.

Unlike Laurel and me, Fran opted to eat her pancake without syrup. She also ate it without a fork. Instead, she tore pieces off with her fingers and ate it that way. She swallowed what she was chewing and took a sip from her third cup of coffee.

"I talked to a rep of the record company last night. They're sending another driver in from the city to take the bus. I imagine it'll pass on to the next up-and-coming star," Fran said.

"What about you, personally?" I asked.

Fran shrugged. "I don't have any idea. I'm kind of tired of music. The money's not as good as I imagined it would be, and I get bored easily. And I really miss the excitement of the city. I'm not worried though. I'll land on my feet somewhere."

"What about you, Laurel?" I asked.

"Like I said the other day, I'm not sure. I've been wanting to visit my grandmother, so perhaps I'll take a break and do that. After that, I'll be looking for another place to play. I love playing for people."

I nodded. "I understand that. Playing music for people is

even better than bacon."

"Hey," Fran said.

Laurel and I looked at her. Fran took the last strip of bacon and held it out before her. "There's nothing better than bacon."

Laurel and I laughed as Fran ate the slice, then Laurel got up and collected the plates. I pitched in and did the dishes while Laurel cleaned the rest of the kitchen.

After we were done, I said goodbye to them both and stepped off the bus. I was halfway back to mine when I saw the sheriff's truck approaching.

"Oh, no. Now what?" I asked no one.

I stopped and waited for him to get to me. "Hey there. I brought you a present."

The sheriff stepped around to the back seat and opened the door. Bozeman stepped out wearing the biggest smile I'd ever seen on his face. He came over and gave me a bear hug that almost squeezed the life from me.

"I need a beer, and a shower, and another beer."

"But it's only ten o'clock. Bozeman!" I was too late. He was already on the bus. I turned to Sheriff Cross. "Thanks for bringing him back."

"You gave me a murderer and a drug dealer, so I thought it was a good trade."

"Am I going to have to come back and testify at the trial?"

"I doubt it. There's enough in those suitcases to implicate the both of them without you. Besides, I've got your contact information. I'll call you if I need you."

Sheriff Cross extended his hand, and I took it. He let go, and I watched him drive away for the last time.

Later that afternoon, with Bozeman freshly showered, he and Tommy were enjoying the sunshine on the lawn chairs. I sat on the bus steps and listened to them trade stories of the people they used to know.

Bozeman got quiet, took a swig of his beer. "Hey, Tommy,

Codi told me about your condition. I'm really sorry, man. It really sucks."

Tommy slapped Bozeman's knee. "It's okay, really. I mentally prepared myself for the inevitable outcome of it a few months ago. All I want now is to get home to Los Angeles. I'd like to spend my remaining time down at Santa Monica Beach. Watch the water and the seabirds. Catch as many sunsets over the ocean as I can."

"That sounds like a lovely way to spend your time," I said. And I meant it. I was always a sucker for the ocean myself.

"Hey, Codi, when's our next gig?"

I checked the calendar on my phone. "Ten days."

"Is Los Angeles on the way?"

"It's up near Monterey, so it could be. Why?"

"I was hoping we could give Tommy a ride back to the city. Maybe see some sites, like the tar pits, or Rodeo Drive?"

"We can skip those. I've always wanted to see the Santa Monica Pier."

Bozeman smiled. "Sounds great. Done deal. Hey, are you okay, Tommy?"

"Sure, I'm just exhausted. I think I might go take a nap."

"Yeah, sure. Want me to wake you for dinner?" Bozeman asked.

"What are you having?"

"I have no clue," Bozeman said.

Tommy looked at the ground, then back at Bozeman. "Okay. It sounds delicious. I'm in."

Tommy started for his chaise, but I stopped him. "Hey Tommy, you can nap on the bus if you want to."

"No but thank you. I really like being outside. When I'm… when I'm done, I want to be outside. In the sunlight or covered in moonlight. Not cooped up in some whitewashed hospital room. Outside. In the fresh air."

Tommy dropped his head and used a slow shuffle to get

around the bus. He looked tired and a lot older than he did from even the day before.

"Thanks for that. He's been through a lot," Bozeman said.

"Don't mention it. I'm happy to help." I took Tommy's words to heart and turned my chair so it faced the sun. After I had the angle just right, I sat back down, closed my eyes, and felt the warmth on my face. I loved it and vowed to do it more often. Just sit, rest, and enjoy the sun. I felt the temperature drop and guessed a passing cloud blocked the heat.

"Are you sleeping?"

I opened my eyes and saw Laurel standing before me.

"No. I'm just enjoying the sun. Do you ever sit in the sun?"

"I'm a natural redhead. If I spend over three minutes out in it, I burn like a match head."

"So, what's up?" I asked.

"I just got off the phone with Gabe. I thought you'd like to know."

"Yeah, sure. How's he doing?"

"Much, much better. You were right about the rat poison. They gave him something to counteract it, so he's recovering faster than expected."

"That's excellent news," I said.

"I've got even better news. He wants to get clean. Once he gets out of the hospital, the company's going to get him into rehab."

I smiled. "Hey, that is great news. Good for him."

"He's young. I think once he gets past this hurdle, he'll be able to do anything he wants to."

"Including being a talented drummer?" I asked.

Laurel smiled. "Well, almost anything."

"Hey, Lauren."

I rolled my eyes because I knew Bozeman was messing with her. I readjusted my chair so I could face them both.

"It's Laurel," she said.

"I know. This isn't easy for me, but Codi told me everything you did to help her help me. I want to say thank you."

Bozeman held out his hand, and Laurel took it, then moved in closer and gave him a hug. "You're welcome."

Bozeman held the hug for a moment, then let her go.

"Codi told me you have a grandmother in Bakersfield you haven't seen in a while."

"Yeah, so?"

"Hey, Codi, that's kind of near Monterey, isn't it?"

"I think we'd go right by Bakersfield on the way," I confirmed.

"Do you think we can stop off and see Laurel's grandma?" he asked.

"Sure, we can do that. You know I'm always up for a good road trip," I said.

"Okay. We'll take you to see your grandmother. There's something you need to do for us, though."

"Sure. Anything. Name it," Laurel said.

"Well, Codi's been itching to add a fiddle player to the band, and we'd like you. Interested?"

Laurel's face beamed. "Am I interested? I'd love to."

"You'll have to sleep on the couch until we can figure out a more permanent arrangement," I said.

"That's fine with me," Laurel said.

I clapped with excitement. "All right then. I'll come over and help you pack. Then we're on the road again to our next big adventure!"

Codas
and
Calibers

CHAPTER ONE

I didn't think I could eat another piece of cherry pie, and to be honest, cherry pie isn't even my favorite type of pie, but I couldn't say no to Tammy. I don't think anyone in history ever said no to Tammy. She was too strong of a personality for that. But, instead of pushing myself away from the table like a sane person, I insisted on finishing the last of my lemonade. In the space of those twenty seconds, another slice appeared in front of me like the results of a magic trick.

"And that's when I caught her in the barn with the prom queen." Granny Tammy slammed a hand on the table hard enough to make the plates jump and started to laugh so heartily that she eventually broke into a coughing fit.

I glanced over at Laurel to see how she was handling the conversation, and although she was smiling, I noticed that not only was the grin fake, but she forced it as well. Her eyes darted around the room as if she was looking for a piece of furniture to hide behind.

To not seem rude, I ate a fork full of pie and smiled as I did so. Bozeman enjoyed the story, though, since his belly laugh seemed genuine.

I didn't remember if Laurel said her grandmother was in her early seventies or early eighties, but she looked decades younger than that. In fact, Granny Tammy had the same long red hair that topped Laurel's head. If it weren't for the silver streak of hair running right down the middle, someone might have mistaken them for sisters. Besides her youthful appearance, Granny Tammy was young, almost a teenager at heart. She loved to tell stories and jokes, and unprompted, would occasionally break into song.

"Is that story true, Laurel?" Bozeman asked.

If I were sitting within reach, I would have kicked him in the shin under the table to save Laurel from further embarrassment. But because I'm a couple inches short of five feet, my little legs wouldn't reach him. Unless I slid way down in my chair, which would certainly take the discretion away.

Laurel's attention turned to Bozeman for the briefest of moments before she looked Granny Tammy in the eyes. "Not entirely. Janie was the homecoming queen. Not the prom queen."

Everyone was silent for a moment. Surprisingly, it was Laurel who broke into the first bout of laughter, and the others followed suit.

I ate another bite of the pie, sighed, and pushed the plate away, not far, only enough to trigger the idea that I really didn't want or need any more.

Granny Tammy spotted the motion with her sharp eyes. "Don't you like the pie?"

I dabbed at my mouth with a napkin. "Oh, no, I love the pie. I'm so full I can't eat anymore."

Granny Tammy frowned. "You should really eat it. Codi, you look much too thin. You can't weigh more than a hundred pounds."

Bozeman finished his slice, and pushed his plate away, too. "She only breaks a hundred when she's wearing her heavy cowboy boots."

I shot a glare at Bozeman, the one I always did when I wasn't happy with him. "Thanks, Boze. Can I take the pie with me and finish it later?"

Without a word, Granny Tammy turned and walked to a cabinet next to the stove. When she opened the door, I could see there were dozens of different sized plastic containers in there. She rummaged around until she selected one, found a matching cover, and handed it to me. I took the container, which, based on the size and shape previously held sliced ham, and transferred my pie from the plate to the container. After I licked a bit of cherry filling from my finger, I snapped the red cover on top.

"Thanks, I appreciate it," I said.

"I'd give you the rest of the pie, but Maura Sanders is coming over later for tea, and I want to save her some. You don't have to return that. You wash that out and save it when you're finished with the pie. There's always a need for a good plastic container."

I nodded, and to an extent, I agreed. I've got plenty of them myself, holding everything from cat treats to guitar picks. Bozeman has one filled with random nuts, bolts, screws, and nails that appear from nowhere, and we don't know what they belong to. Of course, the little containers can be overkill. When you have so many in the fridge that you need to open a dozen of them before you find what you're looking for, you've gone too far.

"So, how did you meet?" Granny Tammy asked.

I glanced at Laurel, who looked at me, expecting I should answer.

"We were both on the same bill, going to play at the same concert," I explained.

"You were in the band with that Timmy singer, right dear?"

Since Granny Tammy had addressed Laurel directly, she fielded the question. "Toby, Granny. Toby Madden. He had… an accident, and the band disbanded. Codi and Bozeman were nice enough to take me on."

The simple statement impressed me. Laurel summarized nicely how at our last gig Toby Madden got murdered and Bozeman ended up accused of the crime. In the end, though, everything worked out okay.

"That was nice of them," Granny Tammy said.

"It was no problem, actually," I said. "We've been wanting to add a fiddle player to the band, so we're lucky to have her. Laurel's very talented."

Granny Tammy reached out for my hand, and when I offered it, she practically pulled me from the chair. "Come with me."

I followed her through the house to the front stairs and up the creaking steps to a bedroom at the back of the house. For the most part, it looked like any other guest bedroom I've ever seen. There was a twin bed positioned on the far wall, nestled between two windows, perfectly made with a dark blue comforter and pink throw pillows on top. In the corner sat a dresser topped with a vase of fake flowers. For a moment, I couldn't understand why Granny Tammy had brought me up here until she pointed to the largest wall. I stepped to the middle of the wall and gazed at the dozens of photographs, awards, and accolades of Laurel.

There were several closeups of her playing in a symphony, dressed to the nines in a tuxedo, and several of her standing alone, center stage, working the bow. Another shot caught my eye. Laurel with her foot on a hay bale, wearing overalls with one strap undone, a straw cowgirl hat on her head. She wore a smile on her face far more prominent than in any other photo on the wall. Then there were the awards, running from junior high school through college. Disbursed among them were several newspaper articles with grainy black-and-white photos of Laurel. I turned to ask Granny Tammy a question, but she had disappeared.

I retraced my steps back to the kitchen and found Granny Tammy back in her seat. When Laurel saw me, she rolled her eyes and looked like she wanted to turn into water and slip through the floorboards. "Oh no, she showed it to you, didn't she?"

I grinned. "Yep, she sure did."

"Showed her what?" Bozeman asked.

"Why, I call it Laurel's Wall of Fame," Granny Tammy answered.

Laurel rolled her eyes again. "More like a Wall of Shame," she muttered, just audibly.

"There's nothing to be ashamed of," I said. "It's amazing. I wish my parents had something like that. Granny Tammy, how did you feel when Laurel turned from being a classical violinist to being a fiddle player in a country band?"

Granny Sammy's head dropped. "I have to admit, I was a little disappointed."

Silence engulfed the room. After a beat, Granny Tammy raised her head, her gray eyes glinting. "Disappointed that I couldn't join her on the road and go to every concert."

Bozeman and I laughed, and Laurel finally cracked a smile.

"Well, there's plenty of room on the bus. You could always be our roadie," I offered.

Granny Tammy shook her head. "No, dear, that's quite all right. I'm too old now to go traipsing all over the country. Besides, I have a weekly bridge game that I host, and I volunteer at the community center, and there are a couple of ladies I take to appointments and for groceries."

"You're right, you're much too important here to come along with us," Laurel said.

"That doesn't mean I don't want to hear about your adventures, of course."

Laurel got to her feet and gave Granny Tammy a hug. "I promise to write you a letter every week."

Granny Tammy returned the hug and scoffed. "I don't want a letter. Text me or send me a video! I'm not old, you know."

Laurel gave Granny Tammy a kiss on the forehead and went to the sink to attend to the dishes. "Hey, one of you two come on over here. I'll wash, and you dry."

Bozeman rocked back in his chair for a second and got up and joined Laurel at the sink. He picked up a towel and stood ready to receive dishes.

Granny Tammy settled back in her chair. "Laurel hasn't told me much about you."

I could understand that. Laurel had only been with us for a little over a week, and we'd known her only a skosh longer than that.

"There's not much to tell. Bozeman and I travel the music circuit from the great plains to the Pacific Ocean, playing music and living life."

Granny Tammy turned in her chair and watched Bozeman for a moment. He stood over six feet, was under two hundred pounds, and had abs you could play xylophone on. He looked absolutely ridiculous crammed next to the sink, trying to dry a teacup with his large, athletic hands. "Is he your fella?"

I smiled. "No way. He's not really my type. We're merely business partners. He drives the bus, plays guitar, provides backup vocals. Partners."

"You live on that big bus? Only the two of you, traveling the country and you're only partners?"

"Yep. I assure you, there's nothing going on. You want a tour of the bus?"

Granny Tammy's eyes brightened. "I thought you'd never

ask!"

Granny Tammy was on her feet and halfway to the back door before I was even out of my chair. When I caught up to her, she was standing by the side of the bus, staring at the writing on the side.

"Well, look at that. Codi Cassidy. Your name's on the bus."

"Yes, ma'am. That way, I know which one is mine. Come on aboard."

I opened the door and held it while Granny Tammy climbed the steps, and I joined her in the living room and kitchen area. "Sorry, it's a little messy right now."

The kitchen was in its typically tidy order, but the dinette held Laurel's few bags and violin cases.

"Is this where Laurel sleeps?" Granny Tammy asked.

I was a little embarrassed, especially since the grand tour would show off the other areas of the bus, including the private rooms Bozeman and I both had.

"It's temporary. She's only been with us a week, and it will take a little time to get her settled. Don't worry, though, that dinette converts to a nice comfy bed. Come on, I'll show you the rest."

Granny Tammy followed me down a short corridor, and just past the kitchen, I opened the first door I came to. "This is Bozeman's room."

She stepped in and looked around. Bozeman was a neat freak. He made his bed with hospital corners. On his small desk was a mug filled with a half dozen pens, and next to that was a spiral notebook, laid open to the page of the latest song he was writing. Nothing was out of place, all his clothing and belongings tucked away into drawers, cabinets, and crannies. Granny Tammy nodded and followed me to the next door.

"This is our storage room. This is where we keep our equipment. The first chance we get, we're going to reconfigure this and turn it into Laurel's room."

Granny Tammy stepped into the space and found herself surrounded by totes of cables, guitar cases, amplifiers, and microphone stands. "Will she have room in here?"

"Oh yes. It was originally a bedroom, but since there were only two of us, we converted it to storage. It'll be easy enough to change it right back. Come on, I'll show you my room."

The next room was the small bathroom, just large enough for a toilet, small vanity, and a shower half the size of an old-fashioned phone booth.

My room was next. The door was halfway open, so Granny Tammy pushed it open and stepped in. Unlike Bozeman, I'm not a neat freak. I made my bed, but not neatly. There was a T-shirt on the bed, the one I'd slept in the night before. My small desk had the same Codi Cassidy branded coffee mug that Bozeman had. Instead of pens, I filled mine with hair ties, guitar picks, spare change, buttons, and anything else I picked up that fit in the mug. Instead of one notebook, my desk held my laptop, which was perched on top of three notebooks, and on top of the computer was a paperback that I was working my way through. The closet door was partially open, and there was one lone cowgirl boot on the floor at the foot of the bed.

"Oh, my lord," Granny Tammy exclaimed as she put her hands on her cheeks.

I thought she was freaking out about the mess, but then she made a beeline for the bed and reached for my tuxedo.

Gibson, my cat, saw her coming. As usual, he was napping atop a pile of pillows on the bed. He looked at her with one tired eye, then opened both wide when she swept him up, sat on the bed, put him on her lap, and started petting him.

"What's his name?"

"Gibson. I named him after my favorite guitar."

She leaned over as she petted him, and started speaking to him like he was a toddler. "Who's a good boy? Who's a wuzza, wuzza, wuzza?"

I wasn't quite sure what a wuzza was, but Gibson seemed to know and started purring loudly enough for me to hear him from where I stood by the door. I watched for a few minutes as she nuzzled with the cat. Then she stood and placed Gibson back where she'd found him. Gibson stretched out one back leg, then the other, then did a couple of slow circles and settled back to his nap like nothing had happened.

"I just love animals," Granny Tammy said as we headed back to the bus door. "Did I mention as a little girl I lived on a farm in Missouri?"

I shook my head. "No, you didn't."

"We had every animal imaginable. Cows, of course. Horses, goats, pigs, chickens, ducks. I even had a pet turtle. A turtle! Have you ever heard of having such a creature as a pet?"

I smiled, then motioned for her to follow me. We stepped off the bus, and I went to one of the storage compartments, crouched over, and invited Granny Tammy to do the same.

"Take a gander in here."

I moved over, and Granny Tammy filled my space. Beyond a makeshift chicken wire door were two creatures, each sleeping on their own blanket.

"Is that a raccoon?"

I nodded. "Yep. That's Dolly, the world-famous three-legged raccoon."

Out of habit, I opened the door and ran my hand under her blanket. I found a marble, removed my hand, and closed the door. I held up the marble for Granny Tammy to see, then dropped it into her palm.

"She's always collecting trinkets on her nightly adventures. If I didn't confiscate them, her little home would be full of junk in a month."

Granny Tammy stared at the marble. A perfect cat's eye. "What do you do with it all?"

"It depends. If it belongs in nature, like sticks, rocks, leaves, stuff like that, I send it back to nature. Trash goes in the trash, coins go into the pet food budget bucket, and some things I keep for her. I've got half a gallon-sized ice cream bucket filled with things she's collected. Now and then, I open the bucket for her, and she likes to rummage through it and rediscover things. She's almost like a kid cleaning out the toy box and finding things to play with that they forgot they had."

Granny Tammy nodded. She handed me back the marble, and I shoved it in my pocket. She looked into the cage at Dolly's roommate. "Is that a cat? It looks like Gibson."

"Nope. That is Merle. He's a skunk."

Granny Tammy took a tentative step back, but since she was crouched over, she almost fell on her butt. I reached out and steadied her.

"Don't worry. He's de-scented, playful, and extremely friendly."

"How in the world did you get a raccoon and a skunk?"

I got up, then started walking to the rear of the bus. "Those two I rescued from a vet. Neither one would make it out in the wild, and he couldn't find a home for them, so they came to live with me. Then there's these two guys."

In the back of the bus was a brick-sized hole, and behind the chicken wire were two chipmunks. They were in the middle of running circles around each other, and when they saw me, they stopped and came to the cage front.

"This is Willie and Waylon." I dipped my hand into my pocket and pulled out four whole peanuts. I passed them through the wire, and Willie and Waylon gathered them up and took them further into their domain. "They just showed up one day and made a nest in this rusted-out hole. I cleaned it up a little, and made them a home, too."

Granny Tammy passed me a stern, unhappy look. "Are they happy living on a bus, caged up like this?"

"Oh, no. It's not usually like this. When we're in a location for more than a few hours, they get a full run of the world. Willie and Waylon usually go out during the day, climb trees, look for food, run around and do whatever they do to occupy their time. Dolly and Merle are mostly nocturnal and prefer to wander around at night. Then, like magic, they all come back to the bus."

"That doesn't sound too bad, I guess."

"Of course not. They have all the freedom they want. More than we humans, sometimes."

"But you won't let them out tonight?"

"Nope. Not until tomorrow when we get to our next gig in Monterey."

CHAPTER TWO

I must admit that the road trip from Bakersfield to Monterey isn't one of my favorites. I'm more of a mountain view girl, and the trip up I-5 presents nothing but rolling hills and farmland. Fortunately for me, I now have Laurel as a traveling companion, because when Bozeman is driving, he's not much on conversation. Every hundred miles or so he'll say something, but it's always something uninspiring like 'there's a rest stop coming up', or 'I'm going to stop soon for gas'. On past adventures, I'd have to spend my time napping or reading, and although I love Gibson with all my heart, he's not a skilled conversationalist.

Instead of watching the mile markers pass by, Laurel and I were hard at work on the set list for tomorrow's gig.

Working from an email I received, I read off the list of special requests and Laurel jotted them down on a sheet of paper.

"*Celebration*? The Kool & The Gang song? Seriously?" she said.

I smiled. "Yep, that's the one. It would amaze you some of the strange requests we get when people book a gig. Granted, we'll usually throw in a few, and sometimes a lot of the songs are ones we rotate in and out of the set list anyway, but a lot of times people will send in requests that are either too ambitious or too outrageous for the two of us to handle. Let me see that."

Laurel moved the paper so I could see it more clearly. I took a pen from the table and crossed a line through *Celebration* and three other songs, circled three others, and put dots next to the remaining four.

"What's the shorthand mean?" Laurel asked.

"The crossed off ones are hard passes. Either we don't know them, or we'd never play them. Circles mean that they're already on the set list. Dots mean they're in limbo at this point, neither in nor out. Bozeman and I, and now you, usually decide together which of those we'd include."

"You don't simply put them in?"

I shook my head. "Not usually. The way we typically set up the list is a few of my original songs, a few of Bozeman's original songs, and then the rest we fill with covers."

"How long is a typical show?"

"Between an hour and ninety minutes. Sometimes longer. We got booked for a wedding once and played for almost three and a half hours. I love to perform, but even for me that was stretching it, especially for a two-person band."

"Okay, so what's next?" Laurel asked.

I got up and retrieved a bottle of water for myself and one for Laurel and returned to the dinette.

"Now we get to the fun part. We use computerized backing tracks to provide a more full-band sound, including bass, drums, and, of course, fiddle. We need to figure out where to remove the fiddle parts so you can take their place."

Laurel uncapped the bottle and took a drink of water. Some dribbled out onto her chin, but she wiped it away with a nonchalance that made me think it happened all the time.

"It sounds hard," she said.

I shook my head. "Sounds worse than it actually is. All I need to do is go into the sound file of the song and uncheck the box that says 'fiddle'."

"That sounds easy," Laurel admitted.

"Here's the plan. We'll go through all the songs we have in our library, see if they have a fiddle in them, and see if you can play the song. If you can't, we'll either remove it from the list if it's a cover, or we'll take a note if it's an original, so you can learn it."

Laurel agreed, so I pulled my laptop from the seat next to me, put it on the table, and brought up my music library.

We'd gotten about halfway through the list when I sensed the bus decelerate. I looked out the window and saw that we were pulling into a rest area. Before long, the bus shifted into Park between two semi-trucks that were also headed northbound.

"Let's go," I said as I stood. "The general rule is, one goes, all goes. Bozeman hates cleaning out the bus toilet, so we make use of public facilities whenever we can. Besides, it's good to stretch the legs."

Bozeman waited while Laurel and I got off the bus and followed behind and locked the doors. He stretched his arms in the air, touched his toes a couple of times and headed off for the men's room without a word.

"He doesn't talk much, does he?" Laurel asked as we followed the sidewalk to the toilets.

"Not really. Sometimes he gets on a roll and will talk your ears off, but generally, he's pretty quiet. You were thinking maybe it was you?"

I glanced over at Laurel, and she nodded. "Well, don't worry about it. Quiet is his nature. If he has something to say, he'll say it, and he'll always answer questions when you ask them."

Laurel nodded again. Then we finished our walk and parted ways when we moved to separate stalls. Five minutes later, I was back outside in the sunshine. I found a bench, sat down, closed my eyes, and lifted my face to the sun. I heard it said that it's bad for my skin to do that, but at the moment, I didn't care since I loved the warmth on my face and the quiet moment I had for myself.

"Hey, little lady, you need a ride?"

The voice shattered my silence, so I opened my eyes and looked at the road warrior who was speaking to me. Overalls hid a body that was at least double the weight it should have been, and a greased-stained trucker hat covered a head of hair that hadn't seen a barber in months. He clearly needed a bath, since he smelled like a mix of corn chips and hot dogs.

"No thanks. I have my own ride."

He stepped closer. "Come on, baby. I know you want me."

I wondered if the guy was a card-carrying member of the sleaze-of-the-month club based on that awful line. But I figured it was time to leave, which wasn't a problem because I had my own keys to the bus. The only thing I worried about was if the jerk was idiotic enough to follow me.

I got up from the bench and took a few steps toward the parking lot. Behind me, I heard him grunt, and I could tell by the shifting shadow on the sidewalk that he did indeed intend to follow me.

"Hey." He grabbed my shoulder, trying to spin me around.

That was all the encouragement I needed. Many people, when they deal with me, assume that I'm not powerful. That bad assumption is because I'm short and skinny. I swung around, and as I did, I performed a perfect uppercut that connected square on with the trucker's private parts. That took the fight and bravado right out of him, and both of his hands went right to his groin before he groaned and dropped to his knees. I took two steps back to make sure his gumption was truly gone. I was about to turn back around and head to the bus when I spotted a small crowd of people watching the entire encounter. Laurel and Bozeman among them.

A few seconds later, Bozeman appeared at my side. "You need any help here?" He looked down at the trucker, who at that moment rolled over from his knees onto his side.

I smiled and locked arms with him. "Oh, my hero! No. I think I'll be okay." We waited for Laurel to catch up to us and climbed back on the bus.

"Does that sort of thing happen a lot?" Laurel asked as we settled back into our seats.

"Not as much as it used to. Early in our touring career, we played a lot of bars and honkytonks. I'm sure you know the places. Long wood bar, sawdust on the floor, chicken wire in front of the stage. It got to where if I didn't have drunken cowboys attempt to pick me up at least three times over the course of the night, I started feeling bad about myself."

"So, what happened?"

"I decided to stop playing shows in those places. Now we do mostly private events, theme parks, festivals, county fairs, places like that. Bar gigs are rare for us now, but occasionally we'll pick one up."

"Sounds nice. See this?"

Laurel turned to her left and pointed to her right arm, an inch above the elbow. I moved in close and saw a half-inch scar she was pointing to.

"Let me guess, flying beer bottle shard?" I asked.

"How did you guess that?" Laurel said as she rubbed the spot.

I smiled, stood, and turned around. I pushed down the back of my jeans a couple of inches and pointed to my own scar. "Because I have one exactly like it."

Laurel grinned. "We're twins."

I laughed with her and retook my seat. "Come on, let's finish going through the songs."

Laurel and I hunkered down and concentrated on the task while Bozeman kept us rolling down the road. The timing was good because we finished our task and I had just shut down the laptop when Bozeman pulled into the parking lot of a diner. I looked out the window and saw the four lanes of California Highway 1, and beyond that, sand that led into the waters of Monterey Bay.

"Is this the place?" I asked as Bozeman appeared from the front. "It's a lot less fancy than I would have figured."

Bozeman smiled at me. "It's not the place. It's where—"

A knock at the door interrupted Bozeman, and since he was the one closest to it, he opened it. I heard him express his greetings, then he stepped backward to let someone else aboard. The black man who stepped onto the bus was large enough to make the bus sway as he climbed the stairs. I guessed he was at least three times my weight, and from what I could tell, he was all muscle. Dark blue jeans obscured his legs, but based on the arms and torso definition beneath his T-shirt, I guessed he had a lot lower body fat percentage than I did. I think I could have played xylophone on his abs. Seeing the man would have been intimidating under different circumstances. However, the enormous smile on his face and the way he swept Bozeman into his giant arms for a bear hug told me all I needed to know about the man.

"This is my old friend, Loren Mullen," Bozeman said, once he escaped the clutches of his buddy. "Loren, this is Codi Cassidy, and Laurel Preston."

Loren greeted us both with a hug, and I literally felt like a letter being stuffed into an envelope when he grabbed me.

"I'm honored to meet you both," he said, the smile never

leaving his face.

"You look like you lost weight, Loren. Have you been feeling okay?" Bozeman asked.

"Oh, come on now, Boze. Don't tease me like that. You know it ain't right."

"Want to sit down?" I asked.

"No ma'am, I'm fine standing, and we'll only be here for but a minute."

I was grateful for the answer since I honestly didn't know if we had a piece of furniture on board that would hold him.

"Where are we going?" Laurel asked.

The grin reappeared on Loren's face. "For pie, of course."

The way he said it made me think that going for pie was the only logical answer, but I was always up for pie, so I didn't mind. Even though I still had a slice in the fridge to work through.

"If y'all are ready, you can follow me."

Whether we were ready or not, Loren backtracked to the stairs and stepped back off the bus, rocking the boat as he did. Bozeman, who was ready, followed him right off. Laurel and I both took a minute to slip on our shoes, and Laurel grabbed a light jacket from the chair.

Loren crossed the parking lot with his long legs in what seemed like six strides, while I had to do triple-steps to keep up with him. To his credit, he waited at the door and held it open for the rest of us. Once inside, he guided us to the back corner to the largest booth in the place. The booth was in a shape of a U, and although two sides were the standard booths found in thousands of diners across the country. The third side was a wood pew that looked like someone had liberated from a church.

Loren took his place in the center of the pew, and the rest of us slid into the booths.

"You have your own seat at the table?" Bozeman asked.

Loren lifted an arm and waved his hand in the air.

"Seat at the table? I own this place."

Bozeman shook his head. "No way. Sign out front says Lulu's."

Loren grinned. "Yes, it's mine. I had to do something with my time and my money after my playing days were over. And Lulu is my mom. I named the place after her. After all, it's her recipes I use for the pies."

As if on cue, two servers appeared. One was carrying plates and silverware, the other had a large tray with a variety of pie slices on it. Once they spread the pies across the table, the server took drink orders, then disappeared.

"Dig in. There's apple, cherry, French silk, pecan, peach, mixed berry, and Key lime. Or, if there's something else you'd rather have, just say the word and I can make it happen."

I didn't want to offend Loren, so I reached out for the slice of French silk and at the same time Laurel went for the Key lime. I grabbed a spoon and dug in. The chocolate goodness exploded my taste buds. I thought for a moment that I'd die happy right then, and based on the moan coming from Laurel, the lime was just as wonderful.

"This is amazing," I said between bites.

Loren leaned back and grinned. "Thank you. I'll tell mama you liked them."

Bozeman had polished off a slice of apple before I'd even made it partway through my slice, then pointed his fork at Loren. "You sell a lot of these? You must."

Loren grinned even wider than he had before. "Enough to keep this entire business afloat. Besides the pies I sell here, I get special orders like mad. I have three delivery people on staff that do nothing but drive around all day transporting pies. I cover all over the region, including up to San Francisco."

"That many pies? Every day?" Laurel asked.

"Yep," Loren said with a look of pride on his face.

"Why go through the trouble of having a diner instead of just a bakery?" Bozeman asked.

"I make the pies off-site. The diner I keep open to please the locals and the travelers who whiz on by at fifty miles an hour. It also helps keep a bunch of people in town employed. I couldn't close down the diner. These folks are my family, not just my employees."

Laurel giggled and rolled her eyes. "Isn't that what the boss always says?"

"Usually, but in this case, it's true. Everyone makes more than a living wage and has a full benefits package, including health care and paid time off. There's even a retirement plan match I do."

Bozeman grinned in between bites, which made him look silly considering there was a small pecan attached to his chin. "I don't even have one of those. Can I have a job here?"

It was Loren's turn to grin, and he grinned widely, his white teeth looking like two rows of perfectly set tombstones.

"Sorry, man, I'm actually over-staffed at the moment. Besides, knowing you, you'd get bored out of your skull by the end of the first day."

Bozeman shrugged, licked his fork clean, and pushed the plate aside. He didn't say another word, just leaned back in his chair and folded his arms over his chest, looking satisfied, like a cat just finishing a hearty meal.

Although I wanted to keep going, I didn't want to embarrass myself by opening the top button on my jeans. I pushed my plate aside as well without bothering to lick the fork clean, even though I wanted to.

"Bozeman tells me we've got you to thank for the gig tomorrow," I said. I took a drink of water, set the glass down, and wiped my mouth.

Loren looked at me, and although there was nothing aggressive about his gaze, it seemed like there was something he wanted to say.

"Yeah, that was me. When Mr. Harris' secretary called to order desserts for the party, she let it slip that they were having problems booking entertainment. I knew Bozeman was in the business, so I simply connected the dots."

"You're providing the pie?" Laurel asked.

Loren leaned back in his seat, which creaked under his mass. "I'm also invited to the party, since I'm considered an upstanding member of the business community."

"Well, we appreciate it. We're always looking for gigs to play." I smiled a genuine smile, and when he saw it, Loren's face drooped a bit. He looked around to see if anyone was listening in, then leaned forward into his booth.

"Did you get paid?" he asked, his voice low.

At first, I didn't understand what he was asking, but then it clicked.

"Forty percent upfront. Our standing booking fee," I said, telling him the truth.

Loren nodded, then moved in even closer, and his voice dropped to just above a whisper. "Listen, I don't want to tell you how to do your business, but make sure you get that other sixty percent before the show starts."

"Why?" I asked.

"This doesn't leave the diner. Hawthorne Harris has a bad habit of forgetting to pay his bills."

"Isn't he like a millionaire?" Bozeman asked.

Loren glanced in Bozeman's direction. "Multi-millionaire is more like it. Unfortunately, he has that annoying problem that some rich people seem to have where he thinks because he's rich, everything should be free for him. And even when people push him to pay, he still tries to cheat them out of what he owes them."

"Then why do you do business with him?" Bozeman asked.

"Like I said, we're part of the same small-town business community. Doesn't look right if I don't play along. Besides, the bakery has a pay-on-order policy, so I always get the money up front. You should take care to do the same."

Loren's attention strayed when an older gentleman approached the booth, took Loren's massive hand in his frail one, and started making small talk.

I looked over at Bozeman. His eyes met mine, and I knew we were both thinking the same thing.

CHAPTER THREE

Are you sure we have the right place?" I asked as Bozeman pulled the bus up a driveway and stopped at a gated entry, rolled down his window, and pressed an intercom button.

Bozeman shot me a glance and pointed out the front windshield. I looked and noticed a giant letter H on the iron gate blocking our way.

The intercom let out a squelch of static, then came to life. "Yes? Can I help you?"

Bozeman turned his head to face the voice. "If this is the home of Hawthorne Harris, my name is Bozeman James. I'm here with Codi Cassidy, and we're the entertainment for tonight."

There was a pause and got no response for half a minute and the squelch returned. "Go ahead. Stop at the guard shack."

Before the last syllable cleared the air, the gate clicked and slowly opened inward. Bozeman pulled ahead at a snail's pace. Two hundred yards later, he stopped at the guard shack where a guard dressed like a U.S. Army commando stood in the center of the driveway, blocking the way. As we got closer, he held a hand up in front of him, like he was going to stop the bus with mental powers. The brakes squealed as we came to a halt, and Bozeman stuck his head through the window and said hello. The no-nonsense guard requested to come aboard, so Laurel unlocked the door and let him in.

"Can I see some identification, please?" the guard said without so much as a grunt of greeting.

Bozeman and I got up from the seats in the front and each of us headed off to our respective rooms for our wallets. Since we lived life on the bus, neither of us carried our wallets on our physical person unless we were going somewhere. Like anywhere we needed money or an ID, and even then, I often forgot mine.

When I returned with my driver's license, the guard was already scrutinizing Laurel's passport. When he spotted me, I handed him the license, and he took it, compared me against the picture.

"Your hair is different," he said.

He had me there. The photo of me he held in his left hand showed a prematurely graying woman in her mid-thirties. The real-life version of me standing in front of him was sporting a hair color of deep purple, almost raven colored. I hoped it would lighten as a little time passed.

In response to his non-question, I shrugged. "Women, am I right?"

He stared me down, then checked my name off a list on the clipboard he carried and handed the license back to me. By the time he finished that task, Bozeman had appeared and passed over his license. The guard looked at it for half a second, then found an issue with Bozeman's credentials as well.

"The picture's the same, but the name isn't. Your license says your name is Jesse, not Bozeman."

Bozeman gave him his signature grin. "Bozeman's my stage name. I really don't want to be known as Jesse James."

The guard didn't laugh, but checked Bozeman off the sheet and handed the license back. He pointed his pencil in Laurel's direction. "You're not on the list at all."

Laurel opened her mouth to say something, but I held up my hand to stop her and jumped in instead. "Laurel's only been with the band for a couple of weeks. It's my fault. I should have called ahead and let you know she needed to be added to the list, but I didn't do it."

"What does she do?" the grumpy guard asked.

"I play the fiddle," Laurel answered for herself.

The guard looked back at me. I shrugged. "She's right. She plays the fiddle."

The guard turned around and pulled a phone from his pocket. Although he pretended to be discrete, we could all hear him talking to someone about Laurel. After almost five full minutes, he clicked off and put the phone back where it came from.

"Okay, she's good to go." The guard copied her name from

the passport to the clipboard, then passed the booklet back to Laurel. "Follow the road down to the left. It'll curve around to the back of the property, and you can park the bus on the basketball court. The caterer's van is already there, so pull in next to that."

Bozeman returned to his place behind the steering wheel, and I got back into the passenger seat. Once we all strapped in, Bozeman put the bus in Drive, waved to the guard, and headed down the driveway. We traveled for a quarter mile before we climbed a hill, and once we crested that, the house finally came into view. House was actually an understatement, because it looked more like a hotel resort than a private residence.

As we descended the hill toward the main building, we saw a private golf course on our right. Beyond that, we saw the edge of an Olympic-sized, in-ground swimming pool. The main building was impressive, especially with the large Doric columns that lined the front entrance. But the view beyond the building, which included a drop into Monterey Bay, and the expanse of the Pacific Ocean beyond, was unbelievable. By my estimate, there were just under a million different shades of blues and greens underneath the whitecaps that gently lapped their way toward shore. As Bozeman dipped down the hill, we passed three giant oak trees that obscured my view of the ocean enough to snap my thoughts away. Then, before I realized it, Bozeman parked the bus next to a caterer's truck that looked more like a high-end restaurant on wheels than the typical van I was used to seeing. When I stepped off my bus, I noticed a flurry of activity in the caterer's truck. A third of the side opened up, like a food truck. Through the window I saw several people in chef's whites busy at work while several other workers transported goods from the truck into the house.

"You're the band?"

I turned around to look for the owner of the question and saw a man in a dark gray pinstriped suit standing before me with a clipboard.

"Howdy. Yes. We're the band. I'm Codi Cassidy." I stuck out my hand for a shake, and the man inspected it for a moment until he finally accepted it and gave me the shortest shake I'd ever received. He stood straight, shoulders back, heels together. He was six feet tall, wore his light brown hair high and tight.

"I'm Brantley Wilson. I'm Mr. Harris' assistant. Please, follow me." He spun in place without another word, and then, with military precision, walked off toward the main house.

I followed, double-time, in order to keep up with him, and Bozeman and Laurel fell into step beside me. We entered the house through a double-door that led from the basketball court into a home gym that was larger than most apartments I'd lived in. Past the gym, we walked down a long corridor past several closed doors, and finally, Brantley led us into the first ballroom I'd ever seen inside of a house. The center of a ballroom featured a long table at which a man in a black suit and white gloves was busy setting a service for twelve. At the room's far end was a riser, which was where I assumed we'd be setting up. Sure enough, Brantley led us to the riser.

"You'll be here. I assume this space will be large enough?" he asked.

Bozeman stepped up onto the riser and did a quick loop around the area. I knew from experience that he was stepping off the space and also looking to make sure there were ample places to plug in our equipment. He stopped in the center of the riser, looked over at the rest of us, and smiled.

"This'll do fine," Bozeman said.

"Good, good. I'm glad you approve. I'm Hawthorne Harris." The voice boomed through the room, and when the group turned, they saw a short, portly man striding toward them. He wore a dark blue jogging suit that appeared to be more everyday wear for the man rather than athletic apparel.

"I'm Codi," I said, as I stepped forward and met the man halfway. He took my hand in his meaty paw and gave it a single shake before releasing it. His palm was moist, and when he let me go, I had to resist the urge to wipe my hand on my jeans while he was watching me.

"I assumed so. Are they the rest of the band?" he asked without looking at them, but rather just tipping his head in their general direction.

"Bozeman James and Laurel Preston. Two of the finest

working musicians on the road today," I answered.

He smiled. "I'm looking forward to your performance. You come highly recommended. You need anything, you tell Brantley, and he'll take care of it." He turned to leave.

"Sir, excuse me, before you go."

Harris stopped and hesitated, and I could tell at that moment he wasn't used to people calling for his attention. To my surprise, he turned to face me rather than just walking away, even though the smile that stretched across his pudgy cheeks looked fake.

"Yes?" he asked.

"There's a matter of the band's fee. I hate to mention it now, but it's our policy to be paid on arrival. I'm sure you read it in the contract?"

Harris hesitated. "Sure, yes. Remind me the amount due?"

I told him, and to his credit, he didn't flinch when I gave him the number.

"Would cash be okay?" he asked.

"Sure. That would work," I said in a tone that suggested handling American greenbacks would be beneath me.

Harris fished a phone from his pocket and sent a text. "No problem. Jackie will be here in a couple of minutes with the money. Anything else?"

I didn't answer in the few seconds he allotted me, so he turned away and headed toward the door. He paused briefly, waved without looking back, then disappeared.

"Interesting man," I said.

"Mmm," Brantley answered.

The cell phone clipped into a case on his belt dinged, and he checked the message before returning his attention to me.

"I need to go. Please be set up by four. The caterer will make sure you're fed tonight and be ready to play at seven-thirty. Any questions?"

I didn't have any, so I shook my head.

"If you need anything, I'll be around somewhere." Like his boss, Brantley left the room.

"Friendly people," Laurel said, although I could hear a twinge of sarcasm in her voice.

"Can't always get the genuine fans when we do gigs like this. Hey, at least it's a nice place, right?" I said.

"That's true. I'm going to help Bozeman with the gear," Laurel said.

"I'll wait here for whoever Jackie is, and then I'll be there," I promised.

Unencumbered by activity, I stood where I was and watched the man setting the table. Even from where I was, I could tell it was a fancy affair based on the way the silverware shined. Another man joined the first and paid particular attention to any spots on the glassware before he set it on the table. In a way, I was glad I didn't get invited to dinner since not only did small talk before a show leave me feeling off my game, but also, I never learned which forks, spoons, and knives to use at the fancy feast. Give me a good old-fashioned barbecue picnic any day of the week. I much preferred the joy of eating corn off the cob rather than snails out of their shell.

A woman entered the room, and at first I assumed she was Jackie, but then I noticed she dressed the same as the men at the table. They looked up from their work as she approached and greeted her warmly, and she folded the napkins into fancy shapes and set them atop each plate.

Another woman glided into the room, and I could tell this one wasn't part of the hired help. She was five-seven, just over a hundred pounds, and had a pair of designer sunglasses on top of her perfectly quaffed platinum blond hair. Her eyes were blue, as was the over-application of eye shadow, as were the tennis shorts she wore. Her teeth were the same white shade as her shirt, and her arms and legs were so tan it made me question her genealogical background. To her credit, as soon as she spotted me, a wide, genuine grin crossed her face, and she made a quick beeline to me.

"Codi Cassidy as I live and breathe! I'm Jackie May, and I'm so happy to make your acquaintance."

I extended my hand for a shake, but before I could even blink, she had wrapped both her arms around me in a hug that I doubted I could escape from on my own. Finally, I exhaled, and somehow, she drew me in closer.

"I'm such a big fan," she said when she finally released me.

"Thank you. It's always nice to meet a fan."

"When Hawth said he'd booked you for tonight, I got so excited. I listened to your CD over and over again. Are you going to play the whole thing for us?"

"About half," I answered. "My partner will play some of his songs too, and, of course, we'll play a bunch of covers. You have us booked for over three hours. That's a lot of time to fill."

"It sounds like it. I've been to lots of concerts where bands play for over three hours."

"Probably, but there were probably other bands on the bill too, right? Hardly anyone plays alone for three hours, unless it's the Boss. Don't worry. We'll give you a good show tonight. And if you have any requests, simply get my attention, and I'll see if we can work it onto the set list."

Jackie's grin got even wider. "Really? You'll do that for me?"

"Yep. Sure will."

I smiled, although I wasn't offering anything special to her. We took requests at all our shows, and usually we honored them since they were often the same requests from venue to venue. They were usually the classics by Willie, Dolly, Reba, Garth, and other mainstream country artists. Some requests would often venture into classic rock selections as well. Of course, there was always the one smart guy who would request *Free Bird*, which we more often than not honored. That one was always a showstopper.

"Oh, silly me, I forgot about your money," Jackie said as she slapped her palm against her head. "Hawth says I'd forget my own brain if God didn't cage it in my head."

"That's not a nice thing for your boss to say," I answered.

Jackie let loose with a laugh that was half hysterical and half donkey bray. She kept at it until she got a stitch in her stomach and had to stop and bend over to catch her breath.

"What did I say?" I asked.

Jackie straightened up and inhaled. "Oh, sugar, Hawth isn't my boss, he's my fiancé."

That one took me by surprise. I felt my cheeks redden in

embarrassment. "I'm so sorry. You see, I thought…"

"The same thing most people think when they see us together. It's okay. I'm used to it. And now you're probably thinking what someone like me would see in someone like him, other than the obvious big bank account, right?"

I didn't say anything, but I'm pretty sure my facial reaction gave it away. "No, that's not what I was thinking at all."

Jackie's grin returned. "You're the cutest little liar I've ever seen. I may be a blond, but I'm not an idiot. I know what people say about me, especially behind my back. Sure, I get I don't look like I would belong with someone like Hawth, but believe me, if you knew him like I know him, you'd fall madly in love with him, too."

I doubted it, since he was far beyond what I considered as my type, but I nodded and smiled, anyway.

"You're right. You can't really know about falling in love until you really get to know someone. I should have remembered that, since I've written about two dozen songs about it."

"Exactly. Now, about your fee for tonight." Jackie reached around to her back, and when her hand came back into view, there was an envelope in it, like a magician making an elephant appear from thin air. She held it out, and I hesitated for a second, then took it and went to shove it into my back pocket.

"Aren't you going to count it?" Jackie asked as her brow furrowed and for the first time, a frown appeared.

"I trust you. I don't need to."

Her shoulders slumped, and although it didn't seem possible, her frown deepened. I got the message, retrieved the envelope, opened it, and pulled out the stack of hundreds. In a dramatic display, I fanned through them, pretending I was counting, then felt something was off. I put the stack back together and paid closer attention when I actually did count them off the second time until I discovered there was indeed an error.

"Wait, there's a mistake here. There's twice as much as there should be." I went through the pile a third time, took from the top what the contract said they owed me, then held out the rest of the bills.

The grin returned to Jackie's mouth, and her eyes brightened again. "Gotcha!" She waved both hands in front of her. "I'm not taking that back. It's yours."

"It's too much. I can't take this."

Jackie looked offended. "Let me ask you this. Do you ever take tips? Or put out a hat or open your guitar case for passersby to toss pocket change into?"

I wondered if she realized that I was well past the point of my career where I had to play on random street corners, but I let it go.

"Rarely, and never when we have contracted gigs such as this," I said.

"What about T-shirts? Do you ever sell stuff like I've seen at other concerts? T-shirts and hats and stickers and whatever else?"

She had me there. "Yes. That we do. Except in cases like this. There's a difference between playing a private party, which we don't sell merch at, and playing a county fair where we do."

"Well, I'll make you a deal. You give me a T-shirt, autographed, and you consider that money payment for both. Come on. You're not going to win this argument. No one ever denies me of what I want."

I wanted to argue, and give the extra money back, but then I spotted Bozeman and Laurel lugging gear and I needed to jump in and help them. Besides, with the extra money, I knew we could afford to skip out on a gig or two if we wanted to.

"All right. You win. What size shirt do you want?"

CHAPTER FOUR

I placed the money back into the envelope and shoved it back into my pocket. I waved to Laurel, who was busy unpacking her fiddles and setting up her microphones, and I made my way through the corridors and back to the bus. When I finally arrived, I found Bozeman hauling amplifiers from the storage compartment under the bus and loading them onto a small cart.

"Everything go okay?" he asked when he sensed my approach.

"Why wouldn't it? I got the rest of the payment, so we're ready for tonight. Even got a bonus."

Bozeman raised an eyebrow at me. "Really? How much?"

"Over double the contract price," I said.

He smiled. "You're an excellent negotiator." Bozeman set an amp on the cart, but was unhappy with the placement, so he adjusted it to fit better.

"It was nothing to do with my skills. She says she's a fan, and she certainly enjoys throwing her man's money around. I'm going to drop this into the safe and I'll be right back out."

I boarded the bus and made my way to the equipment storage room. It was where we kept everything we didn't want to store under the bus. We were in the slow process of weeding through the room in order to convert it into a bedroom, since we wanted Laurel to have a place of her own other than the couch every night. Just inside the room was a built-in wall safe, not unlike the kind you'd find in a fancy hotel room, although ours was twice the size. I punched in the code, opened the safe, stowed the cash, and locked everything back up tight. A fleeting thought ran through my head, and I hesitated, trying to capture it again. Something was nagging at me, but I couldn't quite put a finger on what it was.

"Everything okay?"

The voice from nowhere startled me, and I backed right into the shelf behind me.

"Sorry. I didn't mean to scare you. Are you all right?" Bozeman asked.

"Of course. I thought you were outside," I said. I reached behind me and rubbed my lower back, where I'd caught the corner of something when I hit the shelf.

"Until I came in for the cable box, I was," Bozeman explained.

Since I was already standing where he needed to be, I turned around and grabbed the blue plastic milk crate that contained a variety of audio cables.

"Do you want all of them, or only a couple?"

"Hand me the box. I'd like to dig out some of the longer ones. Are you sure you're okay?"

"Yeah. I was just thinking about what to do with the kids tonight. I'm not sure I want them running around in the wild in this place. We certainly don't want them digging up the fairways or getting into the landscaping. I doubt Mr. Hawthorne Harris would be appreciative if Merle ate his prize roses."

"Probably not. Let them run free on the bus while we're gone. Once we get to the campground tonight, we can let them get some fresh air."

I nodded as I handed Bozeman the crate. "Good idea. Let's finish the load in and I'll come back and take care of them."

Bozeman turned left out of the room to head for the bus exit, but I turned right and stepped into my bedroom. For the gig, I needed my guitar, which was in its case, lying on my bed waiting for me. On top of the hardshell case was Gibson, who passed me the evil eye the second I entered the room.

"Hey, buddy, what's up with you?" I asked as I swept him up in my arms and sat down on the bed. "Are you trying to get me to stay home tonight? You know I can't do that. Mommy has to play the show so she can keep you in kibble."

I turned Gibson onto his back and gently scratched his belly. Before I'd even touched him, he purred, and the sound only increased the more I scratched him.

"Who's a good boy?" I asked as I watched a tiny puff of

detached fur float into the air like a dandelion seed. After I gave Gibson a final scratch, I placed him on his usual spot, the tower of pillows at the head of my bed, and he did a slow circle and laid down. I reached for my guitar case, then stopped when I saw Gibson had left me a gift of enough cat fur on the front of my shirt to make another cat. Undaunted, I replaced the black T-shirt I was wearing with a clean black T-shirt exactly like the one I tossed on the floor. Satisfied I was ready to face the world again, I grabbed the case and left the room.

When I got outside, I saw Bozeman had the cart loaded up and was ready for another trip.

"Can you grab my guitar?" Bozeman asked. He grunted once, then started pushing the heavy equipment-ladened cart toward the door.

I didn't answer, but I grabbed his road-worn guitar case and followed him with both our guitars in tow. It wasn't long before we reached the ballroom, and I set both guitars off to the side, then observed the stage setup. "We ready to go?"

Bozeman was rummaging through the crate of cables, looking for the specific one he needed, and didn't bother to turn around when he answered. "I've got everything except the laptop."

I looked around the area, and sure enough, the laptop wasn't present. "I'll go back and get it. We need anything else?"

"I'm good," Bozeman answered.

"Laurel?"

Laurel was busy rosining up her bow, and shook her head, so I began the trudge back to the bus. I was almost past the catering truck when someone bounded down the stairs, bumped into me with a tray of salads, and knocked me onto my backside. Besides the jolt of my butt encountering the basketball court, I also jarred both wrists as I landed on my hands, and felt a cold liquid run down the front of my shirt.

"Oh, twiddle, I'm so sorry."

I looked up and saw a chef from the food truck standing over me with half a tray of salads. The other three plates had shattered around me. The greens, assorted vegetables, and what smelled like

Italian dressing became a part of my wardrobe.

She set the tray on the truck stairs, leaned over, and offered a hand. "Are you okay? I'm so sorry."

I took her hand, and she pulled me to my feet. My tail bone hurt, and my hands stung, but I didn't mention it. I hoped I could shake it off before the show started. "I'm fine, Heather," I said as I brushed off my shirt the best I could.

"How'd you know my name?" Heather asked as she pushed her plastic turquoise eyeglass frames up farther on her nose.

"Your name tag gave you away."

She giggled, then ran a hand through her pixie-cut light brown hair. "I guess so."

"You mind if I have the salad on the ground?" I asked.

"Odd question, but sure. I'm certainly not going to use it."

I smiled. "I've got a couple pets on board, and they love fresh veggies."

Heather's face brightened. She grabbed one of the salad plates from the tray and started adding the salad remnants that she picked up from the ground.

"I can get that," I offered.

"No. It's my fault. I'll do it. You might want to give this all a rinse before you give it to them. Get the dirt off and such."

I nodded in agreement as I helped by picking up the larger pieces of the broken plates. Together we worked in silence, and in a few minutes, the basketball court was back to mostly good playing condition. Heather handed me the plate of greens, and I handed her the broken plates.

"Again, I'm sorry. If I can make it up to you, please let me know how," she said.

I answered with another smile, turned, and returned to the bus. My first stop was in the kitchen, where I set a colander in the sink and thoroughly rinsed the vegetables. After the washing, I picked through them carefully to make sure there wasn't any unnatural debris in them. I kept them in the sink while I stripped off my shirt and went into the bathroom. There, I checked my image in the mirror, and it didn't surprise me when I saw my skin glistening where I got smeared with salad dressing. I sighed, fished a washcloth from the cabinet, and gave myself a quick wipe down. Once I felt cleaner, I returned to my bedroom, reapplied deodorant, and donned my third black T-shirt in less than an hour. I took a moment and grabbed my favorite long sleeved blue chambray shirt from my closet, then left the room. I found the laptop, which was on the dining table, then put my shirt on top of it so I wouldn't forget either item.

In the tiny kitchen there is a small metal grate inset into the floor, and I bent over and undid the clasp and opened the grate. I looked down into the hole and saw Dolly looking up at me.

"You two can have the run of the house for a while, okay? Be good, and don't bug Gibson too much, okay?"

I filled a plastic dish with water and placed it on the floor, and next to it I placed the rinsed vegetables on a plastic plate. As a last chore, I gathered up Gibson's dry food dish and locked it away in an upper cabinet.

Ready to leave the bus, I hesitated for a moment when I heard people speaking outside my bus.

"I'm telling you, I've had enough of him and his deals."

"Shh, someone will hear you."

I couldn't tell who was speaking, as their voices were low and were coming in through the cracked kitchen window.

"No one will hear me. There's no one else around. I'm telling you, Hawthorne Harris has screwed me over for the last time."

Curious, I wanted to see who was beneath my window, so I silently pulled over my step stool and set it into place next to the sink. I climbed the first step and leaned over to look out the window, but I wasn't high enough to see who was out there. Undaunted, I stepped on the second step. When I did, I leaned over a little too far and came into contact with the bottle of lemon scented dish washing soap that was right there. I realized I had contacted the bottle, and I looked down and watched it tip. Although I thought it was going to right itself, it continued moving and fell into the aluminum sink and made a sound like a gong.

"What was that?" a voice said.

"I don't know. Let's get back in there."

I jumped down from the stool and ran to the bus door, but by the time I made it outside, there was no one there.

Frustrated, I returned to the bus and passed through, shutting all the doors except my own, then gathered up my shirt and the laptop and left the bus, locking it behind me. I was already past the catering bus when I remembered the T-shirt for Jackie and backtracked to the bus. Once again, I fished the keys from my pocket and opened a storage compartment. I pulled out one of the plastic bins where we kept our merchandise, and I rummaged around in it until I found the correct size shirt. Quarry in hand, I closed everything up again and rejoined my friends.

"Took you long enough," Bozeman said as he looked up from his guitar. He plucked the D string, adjusted the tuning, then plucked it again to make sure it sounded pure.

"Sorry. I bumped into the caterer. I also had to change my shirt and feed the kids. Did I miss anything exciting?" I explained.

"Just Bozeman tuning that guitar for about an hour," Laurel said.

"And Red there has been playing Mozart stuff since you left. Good waste of a fiddle if you ask me," Bozeman teased.

"Come on, you two, play nice," I said as I made my way to a small table Bozeman had placed on the stage. I unfolded my laptop, booted it up, and called up the musical program I put together for the upcoming set. Most of the music was live, including my guitar, Bozeman's guitar, and Laurel's fiddle. When things really got popping, the computer added backing tracks for drums, bass, piano, and other assorted instruments. The vocals were live, and I found Laurel complimented my lead perfectly.

Once I had the program up and running, I connected the computer to the soundboard, and as simple as that, we were ready to go. At least we would be once I tuned my guitar. I opened the case and pulled out my Gibson. Although I could usually tune it by ear alone, I turned on the built-in tuner to move things along a little faster. Once I'd tightened the high E string, I plugged my guitar into my amplifier and set it on the stand, ready to go for the first number.

"Everyone else ready?" I asked.

Bozeman and Laurel nodded, almost in unison.

"Great. Any worries about the set?"

"Is there a set list?" Laurel asked.

I looked at the floor next to Laurel's microphone stand and noticed there was no paper taped to the floor. "Oh, I'm sorry. I forgot to lay it down. I'll do that now."

Bozeman and I had played together for so long that we hadn't used a written set list in years. Since Laurel was new to the band, I promised I wouldn't leave her hanging in the dark wondering what song was next up. I went back to the laptop bag and pulled out several sheets. I found the three with today's date on them.

"Do you want these taped down, or do you want them loose?" I asked.

Laurel extended her hand. "I'll just take them and keep them on the stool next to my water. Thanks."

"Hey, listen. Can you guys do me a favor and keep your eyes open for me tonight?" I asked.

"What does that mean?" Laurel asked.

Bozeman moved over closer to us, leaned in, and whispered. "That means she's going to get us into trouble."

"Trouble? What kind of trouble?" Laurel asked, confused.

"Let's just say for someone so small, she can get into really large situations."

I was losing my cool, which was unusual for me. "Like last time, when you got accused of murder? That kind of trouble? Look, I overheard some people talking by the bus, and it sounded like they were unhappy with Hawthorne Harris."

"Unhappy how?" Bozeman asked.

"One of them mentioned how Harris had screwed them over on some deal," I said.

"Isn't he a real estate magnate? I'm sure he makes all kinds of deals that people are unhappy with," Bozeman said.

"Sardines," Laurel interjected.

"What?" I asked.

"Sardines," Laurel reported. "He's the great-grandson and only heir to the HH Sardine Company."

"How in the world do you know that?" I asked.

Laurel dug out her phone, opened the photos, and showed

me a picture of the historical marker. I took the phone from her hand, blew up the picture, and read it aloud.

"HH Sardine Company established near this site in 1890 and quickly became the largest fishery and one of the largest companies in Northern California. Okay, but how did you tie that back to Hawthorne Harris?"

Laurel smiled. "It took me all of perhaps thirty seconds to bring up the HH Sardine Company website and see that Hawthorne Harris is the current CEO of the company. He's the fourth generation to run the company."

"What kind of dirty deal is there in the sardine business?" Bozeman asked.

It was a good question, and I didn't know. I shrugged.

"That's exactly what I thought," Bozeman said. "So why don't we just eat dinner, then play our gig, then pack up and go? Whatever his business is, it's not our business, so we should keep it that way."

"I agree with Bozeman," Laurel said. She stepped away from the group and placed the set list underneath the water bottle she kept on the wooden stool next to her station.

I took a moment, realized there was nothing at work except my overactive imagination. I smiled.

"That's fine by me. I don't like sardines, anyway."

CHAPTER FIVE

I gave a last look around at our setup and ran through the pre-concert checklist I always kept in my brain. It helped me to make sure everything was perfect. It also helped calm the jitters I always felt before every show. I heard someone approach, and I turned around and saw Brantley Wilson standing before me in the most outlandish getup I'd ever seen. The first thing I noticed were the knee-high leather boots, followed by the olive pants, green and brown tunic, and a green felt hat with a long red feather stuck on his head. Over his shoulder he carried a quiver, and in his left hand, he clutched a longbow.

I giggled. "Who are you supposed to be?"

Brantley rolled his eyes. "Robin Hood. No one mentioned that this is a costume party?"

"No. Had someone told me, I dress up like a spot-on Janis Joplin," I said.

"Doesn't matter. You won't be interacting with the guests much. If you and your compatriots would follow me to the main dining room. The caterer will feed you there, and you should stay there until it's time for the show."

We followed Brantley from the room and within two minutes he stepped aside and waved us into the dining room. Compared to the ballroom, the dining room seemed tiny, but it still held a table large enough to seat sixteen without touching elbows. At one end of the table, three place settings were waiting for us. Laurel and Bozeman took the seats across from each other, which left the head of the table for me. Since I was uncomfortable in that position, I gathered the dishes, silverware, and glasses, and moved them to the spot next to Laurel. I had just finished resetting the table when Heather entered, pushing a cart.

"Hello, again," Heather said to me as she stopped the cart

near the table. She removed domes from the plates on the top shelf of the cart and placed salads before each of us.

"It looks much better on a plate," I said.

Heather slid me a sly smile. Since neither Laurel nor Bozeman knew the context, neither reacted to the comment.

"What would you like to drink with dinner? The other diners are having a specific wine with each course, but I can offer you about anything you'd like."

Although the wine sounded nice, all three of us opted for water. Heather had a pitcher on the cart's second shelf, and she filled Bozeman and Laurel's glass. She was filling mine when a loud gong reverberated throughout the room. Heather, startled, overfilled my glass, spilling the liquid on my lap.

"Oh my. I'm so sorry, again. I can't believe I did that," Heather said as she put down the pitcher and retrieved a towel from the cart. She started patting at my lap, but I took the towel from her.

"It's okay," I said while I sopped up the liquid. "It's only water. Hopefully, my pants will dry off before we hit the stage. What was that, by the way?"

"The gong? It's Hawthorne's way of letting everyone in the state of California know that he's ready for the next course."

"How many courses are they having that they need a gong?" Laurel asked.

"Six. Hors d'oeuvre, soup, appetizer, salad, main course, and dessert," Heather said without thinking about it.

"How many are we having?" Bozeman asked as he picked up his fork.

"Three. Salad, main course, and dessert. Sorry about not giving you all six. Hawthorne likes to cut corners where he can."

"Not a problem," I said. "I never like to eat a lot before a show."

Heather smiled. "In that case, I'll make sure you have plenty to eat afterward. Would you like some fresh baked bread?"

That got Bozeman's attention. "How is that a question that anyone ever says no to?"

"This is California, honey. It would astonish you the things that people turn down. The one nice thing about Hawthorne Harris is that he always decides the menu, and it's always things that he likes. There are no special options for vegan, or gluten-free, or low-carb, or anything else. If a guest doesn't like what's being served, they either eat it anyway, or they're not invited back to any future parties. I have to go and supervise the service, and afterward I'll be right back with the bread. Again, I'm sorry about the water."

I smiled. "I'm just happy there's no soup course for us." Everyone laughed at that line, and Heather's cheeks turned pink with embarrassment. She dipped her head as she pushed the cart from the room.

Left alone, Laurel and I dug into our salads, even though Bozeman was already most of the way through his plate.

"Not a fan of olives?" I asked as I watched Laurel pick them from her salad.

"Not especially. As a kid I used to love them, and would eat them right out of the can, but one time I got a bad batch and got sick from them and haven't touched them since."

"That's fair," I said. "Do you mind if I take them?"

Laurel slid her plate over so it touched mine, and I used my fork to push the little pile onto the edge of my plate. When Laurel retracted her plate, I added my olives to her pile, and as I did, she watched with interest.

"What are you doing?" Laurel asked as I moved the last of them to the stack.

"I don't like olives either, but Dolly loves them."

Laurel and I both looked over at Bozeman, who was just putting his fork down on his clean plate.

"What? I like olives, too," he said as he wiped away a spot of dressing from his chin.

I heard the door open, and I looked over, expecting Heather with the bread, but it was Brantley.

"Mr. Harris has requested that you come and meet the guests," he said as he approached.

I wiped my mouth with the napkin and pushed my chair away from the table. "Okay. Let's go, gang."

Brantley cleared his throat, then leaned in toward me. "I'm sorry, he requested only you come and meet the guests."

I made a move to sit back down again, but Laurel stopped me by putting her hand on my arm. "Go ahead. I'm not big on schmoozing, and we both know how Bozeman feels about it."

I glanced over at Bozeman, who hadn't moved a muscle, other than to place his salad plate to the side to prepare for the next course.

"All right," I said, "let's go."

I followed Brantley back to the ballroom, and I had to stop for a moment when we entered the space so I could gather my thoughts and take in the sight. There were ten people seated around the giant table, and three steps behind them were what I assumed were servers, but they all seemed to be the same person. Each of them was female, had brown hair worn in a ponytail, and wore tuxedo pants, a stark white shirt, a purple cummerbund, and white gloves.

As I took another step toward the table, the gong rang out. It resounded even louder in the ballroom than it had in the dining room. With military precision, the servers stepped forward and cleared the hors d'oeuvre plates and silverware and left the room, silently, in a single file line.

"Hold up here for a moment," Brantley said to me. "Mr. Harris is particular about the service."

As requested, I stayed where I was and waited without speaking. Within three minutes, the server army returned, each carrying a large bowl of soup. I caught a glance at one of the bowls, and to me, it didn't even look appetizing. I always believed a soup needs either be hearty, like a nice stew, or needs to invoke memories, like the tomato with grilled cheese I got when I was a kid. The plain looking consommé looked like only the base of what a soup should be. The servers approached the diners, placed the soup before them, and stepped back to their original positions. To my amazement, concurrently, like they shared a hive mind. I noticed they changed the cummerbunds as well, from purple to a deep pink.

Once the sound of spoons contacting the bowls started up,

Brantley took his seat at the table. I approached Hawthorne Harris, who sat at the head of the table. He dressed, of all things, like Julius Caesar. When he saw me coming, he stood, and I observed the full regalia he was wearing, from the laurel crown on his head, to the toga, to the leather sandals on his feet.

"Everyone. Everyone, your attention please. I'd like to introduce you to our entertainer for tonight, Codi Cassidy. She's a famous country star."

I heard one person applauding, and when I looked at the opposite end, I saw it was Jackie, who wore the outfit of Cleopatra. Right down to a rubber snake that she attached to her right shoulder. Hawthorne sent her a glare, so Jackie stopped the clapping and picked her spoon back up.

"Would you mind going around the table and saying hello to my guests?" Hawthorne asked.

He took his seat without waiting for an answer, and I knew then he was one of those people who just expected people to do whatever was requested of them.

I slipped into performer mode, as easy as putting on a pair of shoes, and started making my way around the table.

Seated directly next to Hawthorne was someone I recognized right away. He wore a black Victorian high collar coat, black pants, red vest, and a black cape with a red border. It was the black slicked-back hair, pointy ears, and pointy teeth that gave it away.

"Count Dracula, I presume?" I said as I presented my hand.

The count stood, snapped the heels of his dress shoes together, took my hand, and kissed the top of it. "It's a pleasure to meet you Ms. Cassidy," he said in his best Bela Lugosi impression that, to be honest, wasn't that good. "My name is Claude Garrison. And may I present my friend, Amelia Brown?"

Amelia was in conversation with the person to her left, so Claude bent over and nibbled on her bare neck. That got her attention.

"Hey!" Amelia turned and slapped Claude playfully across the cheek. "Would you please stop doing that? It's getting annoying."

Dracula took his seat. "I just wanted to introduce you to Codi

Cassidy."

"Charmed, I'm sure," Amelia said as she redirected her attention back to the man sitting next to her. Based on the pigtails, blue gingham dress, and the picnic basket at her feet with a toy cairn terrier sticking its head out, I assumed she was Dorothy Gale from *The Wizard of Oz*. Although upon first meeting she lacked any of the warmth that I associated with the character.

I moved on to the person she was talking to, who dressed as Frankenstein's monster. The monster, Danny Ewing, introduced me to his wife, Amy, who dressed as the Bride of Frankenstein. Based on the way he looked at me and paid more attention to Amelia than to Amy, I could tell he was a player. I made a mental note to not get involved in his game, which wasn't hard since I didn't care for men with green skin and rubber bolts attached to their necks. I found Amy to be more interested in the alcohol that surrounded her place setting than she was in me. Based on her pout and glare, she wasn't happy with her husband, either so I moved toward the other end, where Jackie was excitedly waiting for me.

She took both my hands in hers and gave me the air kisses that the Europeans prefer, and when she did, the snake on her shoulder nuzzled my cheek.

"Thank you for coming to say hello. My outfit is out there, isn't it? Can you guess who I am?" Jackie said giddily.

"Yeah. You look great. Just like the real Cleopatra. I'd better say hello to the others so I can get back to my band. I'll talk to you later, okay?"

Jackie let me loose from her grip, so I moved onto the next person, who, out of everyone, looked the least like she was at a costume party. She wore a long white dress, and a white shawl covered her shoulders.

"Hello, I'm Codi Cassidy," I said as I offered my hand.

"Helen Troy," the woman said as she put down her soup spoon and gave me a quick shake.

"Helen of Troy? That's a pretty obscure costume, I might say."

The redhead laughed, then dabbed her mouth with a napkin.

"No. My parents, Deana and Armond Troy, were both history buffs and thought it would be hilarious to name their only daughter Helen. I hate costume parties, so I just throw on a nice dress and go as my namesake. Saves me a lot of effort."

I nodded, and Helen returned her attention to the soup, so I assumed the conversation between us was over. I said a brief hello to Brantley, who was next in line, then I moved to the woman seated to his left. Before I got there, she stood.

"Codi. It's so good to see you again. It's been a long time. You don't recognize me, do you?"

She was a black woman and was a good six inches taller than me. Since she wore dark blue sorcerer's robes adorned with stitched silver stars, a tall, pointed hat to match, and a long white beard, I couldn't pinpoint if I'd met her before.

"You're a wizard?" I asked.

"Merlin. It was Loren's idea." She pointed a thumb at Loren, who, I guessed, had decked out like King Arthur. The woman took off the hat, then removed the beard. I saw she was a pretty woman, but other than that, I didn't recognize her.

"Viola. Viola Park. I was your dad's partner in Denver for a couple of years. Don't you remember me?"

I reached back into the recesses of my mind, trapped a memory, and grinned.

"You used to sneak me chocolate bars all the time."

Viola nodded, then pulled me into a hug. "It's so good to see you again. How are you?"

"I'm good. What are you doing out here? Are you not with the Denver Police Department anymore?"

"No. Once I got my detective's shield, I hit the glass ceiling, so I went searching for other positions. I'm the head dog out here."

"No kidding?"

"That's right. Police chief," she said.

"That's amazing," I admitted.

"How is your dad?"

"Good. He retired from the force a few years ago." I was about to expand on the small talk when the gong rang. Without a word, Viola retook her seat.

"You can go."

I turned around and saw it was Brantley speaking to me.

"Go. Back to your friends. We don't want to keep you any longer."

I hesitated for a moment, then stepped back from the table. The servers had waited for me to leave, and as soon as I headed toward the door, they progressed through the act of clearing away the soup bowls. By the time I got to the door, the servers were only a step behind me, so I moved to the side and let them pass. I didn't want to impede whatever the next course was.

I backtracked my way back to the dining room, where I found Laurel and Bozeman in the middle of their main courses. At my place was a stainless-steel dome, under which I assumed my dinner was.

"There you are," Laurel said. "We didn't know when you were coming back, so we dug in. Hope you don't mind."

"Of course not." I lifted the dome. Underneath was a Cornish game hen, a bed of wild rice, and two roasted carrots. "Did Heather ever bring the bread?"

Bozeman grunted and passed the plate on which sat three dinner rolls. I took one, found the butter, and lathered up the roll. Then I went to work on picking apart the miniature chicken.

"What's it like in there?" Laurel asked as she scooped up a forkful of rice.

"Just your average costume party for rich people," I answered.

Daintily, I removed a leg from the hen and took a bite. I wasn't normally one for fancy food, but I had to admit, it was delicious.

"I've never been to a costume party," Laurel said. She was only half finished with her meal but pushed her plate away. "I don't know why people think these mini chickens are so great. I think they're way more trouble than they're worth."

"Bozeman didn't have any trouble with it."

Laurel and I looked at Bozeman, who was nibbling away the last of the meat on a tiny wing. On his plate was a small pile of bones. He looked at us, then added the wing to the pile, wiped his mouth, and drank some water.

"They're all right by me," Bozeman said. "Although I'd prefer it fried."

The gong sounded before anyone could say another word.

"That's a little much," Laurel said.

"You should see what it triggers. The servers have this well-coordinated dance they do to remove the plates and bring in the next course. It's quite fascinating to see, like they're all programmed robots. Although, it's also a bit disconcerting. Trust me, though, I'd rather have dinner with the two of you."

I finished half of my meal and pushed it aside. Although everything was delicious, I didn't want to fill up too much before the gig.

"I wonder how much longer we'll be stuck in here," I said.

Neither Laurel nor Bozeman answered me, but fifteen minutes later, the gong sounded. I had lost track and didn't know if it was the fifth course or sixth, but I was certain someone would come to tell us at some point or another.

CHAPTER SIX

Forty-five minutes later, after we'd each eaten a slice of Loren's excellent pie, Brantley stepped halfway into the room and motioned for us to follow him.

"Now is the time for your sound check. I want you to make sure that everything is perfect for your performance. Mr. Harris is very particular and won't stand for any problems during the concert."

"Okay," I said. What I didn't say that there were problems all the time during performances. There were a few dozen things that could go wrong during a show. A guitar string might break, a light bulb in the lighting rig may pop, an amplifier could decide to whine and emit some feedback. Once I forgot to plug in the laptop, and I ran out of battery right in the middle of a Reba McEntire medley. The most likely thing to happen would be that Bozeman would drop several guitar picks over the course of the night. I asked him once why he dropped so many during a show, and he said he played with them until they didn't feel right anymore. The odd thing is, he'll pick them up from the floor after the concert and use them for the next gig, almost as if the act of falling to the floor returns the original mojo to them.

Brantley escorted us to the ballroom. The servers, now in dark green cummerbunds that matched Brantley's tights, were busy clearing the table. On the far side of the room, two women in tuxedos were setting up a portable bar.

"You have a half an hour to get ready. All the guests are in the drawing room," Brantley said, bored with us. He gave us a dismissing wave, then let us be.

"Drawing room? I don't even know what that is," Bozeman said as he stepped onto the riser and started turning on the sound equipment.

"It's something we don't have room for on the bus," I said as I took my place behind the microphone.

I picked up my guitar, gave it a couple of strums to check the tuning, then started playing the first song that jumped into my head, which happened to be an old Willie Nelson classic. As I worked my way through *Angels Flying to Close to the Ground*, Bozeman left the stage and walked to different spots in the room to check on the acoustics. Twice he came back and adjusted the soundboard, then he settled into a chair along the farthest wall from us next to a row of floor to ceiling windows.

When I finished, I received a smattering of applause, and looked over and learned it was the bartenders giving me love.

"Thank you," I said. I waved to them and removed my guitar from my shoulder.

"Laurel, play something for us," Bozeman called out without moving from his chair.

Laurel stepped forward, and after a quick mic check, launched into a short classical piece on her fiddle. It wasn't anything that would fit into our normal set, but I have to admit, I loved to listen to her play anything. She was so talented; I felt lucky to have her as a part of the band. When she finished, she got more of an ovation from the bartenders than I had gotten, and I joined in as well.

"Do a mic check on mine," Bozeman requested.

I picked up Bozeman's guitar and from his setup started the song I'd just finished, but I only made it through half of the song before Bozeman stood and waved me off.

When I returned Bozeman's guitar to the stand, and I turned back around, a large sonic boom rocked the room. I looked over at Bozeman, but he was staring out of the window. Laurel and I crossed the room and joined him.

The large windows faced west, and beyond a hundred yards of well-manicured lawn, the property ended at the cliff side. Out in the Pacific, there were large black clouds forming, blotting out the setting sun. Although dark was falling, I noted the raging whitecaps on the waves.

"Storm moving in," Bozeman said.

Just as the words left his mouth, a bolt of lightning appeared over the ocean and a few seconds later, another peal of thunder rumbled through the house.

"I guess so," Laurel said.

I saw Brantley walk toward us in the window's reflection, and he stopped by my side and looked out the window just as another flash lit up the sky.

"Are you ready to go?" Brantley asked.

"Yep. We're all set," I answered. "Are we going to be okay here? Seems like a terrible storm coming."

Brantley smiled to assure me. "We'll all be fine. They built this house like a fortress, and if we lost power, the emergency generator would kick on so fast you wouldn't notice the disruption."

Brantley left us and I watched his reflection in the mirror as he walked to the bar and ordered a drink. By the time I'd turned around, he'd already downed it, and was holding his glass out to the bartender for a refill.

"I guess it's going to be one of those nights." I shook my head as I walked in his direction.

By the time I'd reached the bar, Brantley had retreated with his drink.

"What can I do for you?" the bartender asked.

"Do you have any bottled water for us? Preferably room temperature?" I asked.

"Not back here, but Stacy can get you some. How many do you need?"

"Six will do for now."

The bartender turned and addressed her counterpart, and Stacy hustled from the room. "I like that song you played before. I've always been a Willie fan," the bartender said.

"Thank you, um," I hesitated as I looked for a name tag, since I always liked to address people properly. I didn't see one, though.

"Ashley," the bartender filled in as she smiled at me.

"Thank you, Ashley." I smiled back.

Ashley looked over my shoulder and her eyes got brighter, and I knew what that meant. Bozeman was right behind me.

"Think I might get a beer from you?" he asked, putting down a southern drawl like a thick blanket.

"Sure thing. We have a bottle or tap, depending on what you'd like," Ashley started.

As Ashley ran through the options with Bozeman, I turned away and headed back to the stage.

"Does that always happen?" Laurel asked. "He steps into the picture and every female eye around gets diverted his way?"

"Usually. You'll get used to it, though. And to be honest, sometimes it's nice that the attention goes to him."

Stacy came back, wheeling in an entire case of water on a small hand truck. She parked it by the stage, ripped through the plastic, and pulled out two bottles. "Here you go."

I took the two bottles and put them on Bozeman's stool, then grabbed a couple more and handed them to Laurel. Finally, I took two more, cracked the seals, and put them next to my station.

"I can leave the rest of these here, but I'll have to find a tablecloth or something to cover them," Stacy said. "Mr. Harris doesn't like any trash sitting about."

"I can put it behind our gear back here. No one will notice," I offered.

Stacy smiled, lifted the rest of the case, and put it on the stage. "Thanks," she said, then she turned and wheeled the dolly from the room.

"You need help with that?" Laurel asked, pointing to the bottles.

I smirked at her. "No, but thank you."

I picked up the remaining six bottles in the case and moved the whole thing to the back of the stage, where we'd stacked up our cases and other gear. I dropped it behind Bozeman's guitar case and stepped back to my position.

"Oh, boy," Laurel said. "Live one coming in hot."

I looked up and saw Jackie coming toward us. Her dress tapered inward the farther down it went, so she had to do a quick shuffle to get to us.

"Are you ready to go? I'm so excited!" she screeched.

"I can tell," I said. "Oh, here's something I promised you." I moved back to the gear and found the shirt I'd pulled out for her. "Would you still like me to sign it?"

"Of course!" she blurted, as if it were even a question.

Laurel did a half eye roll and handed me a marker. I set the shirt flat on my stool, removed the cap, and signed the shirt. "To Jackie, with love, Codi Cassidy," I said aloud as I wrote.

I returned the pen to Laurel as I gave the ink a few seconds to dry, then I handed the shirt to Jackie.

Jackie opened the shirt and stared for a moment at the signature, as if she hadn't believed her eyes when I'd signed it a few seconds ago. She squealed with joy.

"I'm going to go put this on right now."

"I don't think it will fit over your snake," I said. "And it doesn't go with your pretty dress. You should save it for another time."

She pouted for a couple of seconds, then her smile returned. "Okay. I'll go put it in my room, so it doesn't get lost or dirty."

"Good idea," I said. She didn't need my permission, but she seemed to appreciate it, and shuffled away with her prize in her hand.

"You sure made her day," Laurel said. "Can I have your autograph, too?"

I thought about giving Laurel a punch to the shoulder, but then the doors opened wide, and the costumed guests started filling the room. Bozeman noticed it as well, so he stopped flirting with the bartender and joined us on stage. Bozeman and I donned our guitars, and we both put on our hats to complete our stage personas.

The guests filed in and half of them headed to the bar. The other half took seats at two-person tables that replaced the main table, which the staff had disassembled and turned into side tables that lined the walls.

Once everyone had drinks in their hands and seemed to be settled in, we prepared to jump right into our set. I began a rhythm count and got as far as two before Hawthorne Harris scrambled to his feet and started waving his hands at me.

"Wait! Wait! I want to say a few words!"

Since he was the one footing the bill, I moved back from the mic and made way for him. As he stepped onto the riser, his sandaled foot caught the lip and he fell forward. I thought he would slam right into my Gibson, but Bozeman caught him before he did a face plant. Harris approached the mic like it didn't even happen.

"Thank you again everyone for coming to the party tonight, and thanks for playing along with the costume theme. There's a prize for the best costume, and I'll announce who the winner is later."

As Harris spoke, I looked around the room to catch the reaction of those listening. Brantley was finishing yet another cocktail, and based on the way he eyed the bar, I assumed he wanted a refill. Danny Ewing stood directly behind Helen Troy, and I noticed by his line of sight that he was more interested in her backside than Harris' speech. Meanwhile, his wife was clearly watching Danny watching Helen. If it were physically possible for steam to come from someone's head, Amy would be hot enough to power a locomotive. The rest of the room, except for Jackie, was watching the speech, mostly with disinterest.

The guests clapped, so I brought my attention back to Hawthorne, who was holding a hand toward me. I gave him my stage smile, shook his hand, and thanked him. He left the stage and took his seat. When he did, three servers appeared from nowhere, each with a tray of champagne flutes. Once each of the guests had a glass, Hawthorne gave a toast, and everyone drank. Then he waved at me, and I took that as a sign to start the show.

I turned around to face the band. "Ready? Again?"

Laurel and Bozeman both nodded, so I faced the audience, began the rhythm count again, then swung into the set. As usual, we started with a couple of songs from my first album, and then Bozeman performed one of his. The first few songs we always played acoustically so that the audience knew it was really us behind the guitars and the vocals. After that, I kicked on the computer to use the backing tracks.

We were halfway through our fifth song. Bozeman was crooning about having *Friends in Low Places*, when I spotted a flash of lighting that cracked loud enough to be heard over our music.

"Holy crap," someone exclaimed. Although it was a male voice, I couldn't tell where it came from.

Our speakers lost sound, and the lights in the room flickered, then dropped out. A woman screamed. Another bolt of lightning flashed outside the window, and a few seconds later, a rumble of thunder shook the house.

"Don't worry folks. The lights will be on in a second," Hawthorne said. As if on cue, two counts later, the lights popped back on as bright as before. "Nothing to worry about. That's why we have a generator. Let's get back to the party. Bring back the music!"

I looked out into the crowd and caught lots of expectant eyes staring back at me. When I did a mic check, I discovered my first problem when I heard nothing from my amp. I stepped from mine to Bozeman to apologize. "I'm sorry, but it's going to take us a couple of minutes to get back to the show. We need to do a quick equipment check to make sure everything is good. I promise, it will only be a brief break."

Several from the crowd moaned at the announcement, and I could tell from the daggers Hawthorne Harris was shooting at me from his eyes that he wasn't happy. But what could I do? Electronics and power snafus have never gone together well.

"Let's get back up and running, as fast as we can, okay?" I said to Laurel and Bozeman.

I did a fast check of my amp and guitar, and determined my problem was the power strip I used popped a fuse. After I reset it, I moved over and checked the computer. Something had happened to it, since the screen displayed a black screen with a blue circle spinning around. Since my hardware technical knowledge only spanned as far as rebooting the machine, I pressed the power button until the display darkened. I counted to ten in my head before I turned on the laptop. I waited with bated breath until the screen popped up and informed me that something terrible had happened, but it asked if I wanted to continue as normal. If only such things occurred in real life, I opted for booting up as usual, then checked on how the others were doing.

"How's everything?" I asked Laurel first since she was the closest one to me.

"All good," she answered. "It looks like Boze has a problem, though."

I looked over at Bozeman, and he displayed the red ears he got every time he was getting frustrated. I joined him to see if I could help.

"What's going on?" I asked.

"Amp is dead," he answered.

"Did you check the fuse?"

"I was about to."

Bozeman bent over and popped the fuse out and passed it to me. I held it up to the light and determined it had fried.

"Yep. It's dead. Got a spare?" I asked.

"On the bus," Bozeman answered.

I looked out the window in time to see another flash of lightning, and it was raining hard.

"I don't suppose you brought a spare amp?"

Bozeman smiled at me. "Of course. It's also on the bus."

I handed him the fuse. "Looks like you're going to get wet, my friend. You have the keys? I locked it when I left."

Bozeman checked his pocket, nodded, and rushed from the room. I turned around to find Brantley waiting for me.

"What's the delay?" he asked. I could tell by the way he slurred his speech that he'd been drinking too much.

"We're almost ready to go. We've got a blown fuse, and a couple of other things to check. Give us ten minutes, and we'll be back at it."

Brantley glared at me for a second. "Okay, but you need to know that Mr. Harris isn't happy."

He left without waiting for a response. That was probably for the best because I could feel the snark monster that lives in my brain wanting to take over the conversation for me. Instead, I returned to the computer, saw everything had booted up as normal, so I called up the program. Once I did a quick check to see it was working fine, I returned to my stool and had a seat while I waited for Bozeman. He appeared five minutes later, dripping wet, with a new fuse in hand. A couple of minutes later, we were back in business.

"Sorry for the delay, everyone. We're back. Bozeman here is going to take the last song from the top."

Bozeman started playing the opening riff of the song, inhaled a breath to start the lyrics, and the dinner gong sounded. It was a distraction, sure, but we were seasoned musicians used to distractions, so we kept on playing. Out in the audience, I saw Hawthorne call Claude Garrison over, and based on the body language and the flying arm gestures, I could tell Claude was getting a reaming. Near the beginning of the first chorus, the gong sounded again, and Hawthorne seemed to get even angrier. I could hear an argument brewing, but since I was singing backup in the chorus, I couldn't make out the words. He pointed at Claude, pointed at the door, and a millisecond later, Claude the vampire headed for the exit.

Things settled down, and when Bozeman finished the song, he got a nice round of applause.

I stepped up to my mic. "I'm going to take things back, and here's a nice slow dance number, so if you want to grab a partner and hit the floor, do so."

I took a moment to swallow a mouthful of water while people paired up, then I stepped up to the microphone. Bozeman started the opening riff, and I had barely opened my mouth to sing the first word when the lights went out again.

The woman who had screamed the first time screamed again. Clearly, she wasn't a fan of surprises, summer storms, or the dark. The dinner gong sounded five times in a row, and thirty seconds later, the lights came on again.

There was another scream, this time from a different woman. When I looked out at the audience, I saw Hawthorne Harris face down on the floor, with a bright red spot widening on the back of his white emperor robes.

CHAPTER SEVEN

The lights stayed on for a scant fifteen seconds before they dropped out again. The scream returned.

"Stop that," a woman ordered. Even in the dark, I recognized Viola's authoritative tone. "Nobody move, stay exactly where you are," she said, loud enough for everyone in the room to pick up over the oncoming peal of thunder.

The voices stopped. All I noticed were a couple of echoing footsteps, and then nothing but a loud sob. The lightning flashed again, and for the briefest of seconds I saw the people in the room standing still, as if they were statues.

"Everyone hold where you are," Viola said.

Without thinking about it, I counted the passing seconds in my head, and when I reached forty-nine, the lights flickered twice and came on. Although I expected them to pop off again, this time, they brightened and remained. I looked around the room and detected that most people had complied with the order to stay where they were. Even so, I noticed Danny had taken a seat, and Helen had sprawled out on the floor as if she'd fainted.

Viola took off her pointed hat and fake beard. With haste, she rushed to Hawthorne's side. She kneeled down and felt for a pulse. When she didn't find one, she shook her head and unzipped her robes in search of her cell phone. She dialed a number, held the phone to her ear, and waited. After a moment, she looked at the phone and shoved the phone back into the pocket of her black jeans.

Brantley stepped over to her, and without looking at the body, he asked the pertinent question we all wanted the answer to. "Is he alive?" Brantley asked.

"No," Viola answered. "I need to call this in, but my cell isn't going through."

"911?" Brantley asked.

"That will do," Viola said.

She moved away from the scene and stripped off the wizard's robes. Along with the black jeans, she wore a black shirt as well. On her belt I spotted her badge and gun and assumed, like my dad, she never considered herself off duty.

Brantley retrieved his phone and tried to make the call, then gave up and put it away. "I can't get through to anyone, either."

From my vantage point, I saw a couple of other people try to call for help, but like Viola and Brantley, no one got through to anywhere.

"Is there a land line?" Viola asked.

Brantley led her in my direction, and they stopped at a wall phone right next to the stage. Odd that I hadn't noticed it before, since I was usually aware of my environment like that.

Viola picked up the receiver, placed it to her ear and hung up right away. "It's dead, too." She gave a weak smile. "Sorry. Bad choice of words, considering the circumstances."

"Trying to call for help?" I asked.

Viola nodded at me. "Cell service and land lines are both out."

"Bozeman can drive into town and get help," I offered.

I looked over at Bozeman, who was giving me the impression that he didn't appreciate me volunteering him for things, especially during heavy rain.

"Don't bother," Brantley said. "Once we lost power, the compound would have gone into automatic shutdown, and the gates would have closed and locked. Someone would have to walk to the guard shack and perhaps they would get help in here."

"You up for a stroll, Bozeman?" I offered.

Much to Bozeman's delight, Viola answered the question. "I don't want anyone leaving the building at this point."

She turned her attention back to Brantley. "So, you're saying we're stuck here?" Viola asked.

"Well, only until the power gets fully restored and security clears the compound," Brantley answered.

"How long will be that be?" Viola asked. As the last syllable left her lips, the lights flickered again, but fortunately, they didn't go out.

Brantley's gaze focused on the crystal chandelier in the middle of the room, and when it flickered again, his eyes shifted back to Viola. "I'd say at least until this storm passes. Maybe longer if there are any lines down or any other disruptions to the power grid."

"I guess we're here for the duration," Viola said. "Can you grab me a notebook and a pen from somewhere?"

Brantley looked at her for a moment, then averted his eyes. "No problem. I'll be right back."

Viola didn't move as Brantley left the room. She turned to me.

"What did you observe?" she asked as she took a step closer to me.

"Not really much of anything," I answered.

Viola smiled at me. "You? Codi Cassidy? There was a reason your dad always called you eagle eye. You never missed a thing. Remember the game we used to play when you'd come over to my place?"

"I remember." I wasn't lying. Every time my dad and I visited Viola's place, she moved items around in her living room for me to notice. It was never anything major, like rearranging all the furniture, but rather something minor, like moving a ceramic figurine from one shelf to another, or exchanging pictures on a wall. At the end of the visit, she'd asked if anything seemed different, and I listed off what changes I caught and for each one I got correct, she'd give me a cookie. I always enjoyed those well-earned treats on the way home.

"You've always had a better eye for detail than anyone I've ever known. Now tell me, what did you notice?"

"There's not much to tell. We were just starting a new song, the dinner gong rang, the lights went out, the lights came back on again, and Hawthorne was lying dead on the dance floor."

"Did you see anything else?" she asked.

I smiled. "I know I have excellent observation skills, but even I can't see in the dark. You know I'm not a wolf, right?"

Viola sighed at the response. "What about before the room

went dark? Can you tell me if you spotted anything unusual?"

"Not really. Danny Ewing seemed to be getting sloppy drunk, which, to me, isn't unusual. I always spot a few people in the crowd who have had too many. Oh, and Jackie wasn't back yet."

Viola looked around the room. Jackie was still nowhere in sight. "How long has she been gone?"

I tried to give it my best estimate. Since I had focused on the show, she could have returned and left again. "Twenty or thirty minutes?"

Voila jotted the information into the notebook. "You know where she had gone to?"

"I gave her one of my T-shirts and autographed it for her. She told me she was going to run it to her room so nothing would happen to it."

Viola nodded. "Can either of you tell me anything more?"

Laurel and Bozeman were both standing within four feet of us and had overheard the entire conversation.

"I didn't. I was paying more attention to Codi than anything else," Laurel explained. "Since I'm relatively new to the band, and this is my first performance with them."

"I got nothing, either. I had my eyes closed most of the time," Bozeman said.

Viola gave him a look I remembered from my childhood when I said anything she didn't believe. "Seriously?"

"Probably," I jumped in. "He goes into this kind of Zen state when he's playing and it's so automatic that he often literally keeps his eyes closed while he's playing. Especially if he's only playing guitar and not singing."

"Craziest thing I've ever heard," Viola said.

Bozeman shrugged. "It's normal for me. Guitar is mostly muscle memory since I've been playing so long."

"You've got company headed your way," I said.

Viola turned around and saw Brantley rushing toward us, carrying the supplies she'd asked for. Without a word, he handed her three notebooks and a handful of pens, then turned and headed toward the bar.

Viola took a notebook, then handed it to me. "Look, I have a concern that since we can't get outside help that this crime scene will turn into a contaminated mess. I need to start documenting everything and get a jump on what happened here. Can you help me out? Maybe interview the staff? And Bozeman, could you find a way to seal off the perimeter around the body to make sure no one messes with it?"

"Why not just seal off this room?" I asked. "Keep everyone out. That would keep the body from being disturbed."

"It would also mean I'd have suspects running free all over the house. No way. I want everyone in this room where I can keep an eye on them until I get reinforcements."

"Suspects?" Laurel asked. "We're all suspects?"

Viola looked at Laurel like she'd just said the silliest thing ever. "I wouldn't be as concerned if Hawthorne had dropped dead of a heart attack or even got struck by lightning, but he didn't. Someone shot him in the back. And yes, everyone is a suspect, except, I believe, you three."

I'd heard that before. Being on stage performing in front of a crowd always provided an excellent alibi for any crime. Except, occasionally, messing up the lyrics to a George Strait song.

"Okay. Is everyone in and willing to help me?" Viola asked.

I agreed, as did Bozeman.

"What should I do with the body?" Bozeman asked.

"Cover it up with something, like a blanket, and somehow cordon it off so no one will mess with it," Viola said. "Then keep a close eye on it, so no one goes near it."

"What about footprints and fingerprints?" he asked.

Viola smiled. "You've watched one too many television shows. Don't worry about the footprints, unless you see a bloody one. All of us in here have been tromping all over the place all night. So has the staff."

Bozeman glanced over at Laurel. "Can you give me a hand?"

"Sure. What do you want me to do?" she asked.

"Find something to cover the body with, and I'll take care of the perimeter."

"Wait until I give you the word to cover it. I want to get some pictures first," Viola ordered.

Bozeman nodded in understanding. Voila and I stood aside as Bozeman grabbed the cable crate and headed toward the body. Laurel made her way to the side of the room, where the staff had shoved a table against the wall. She removed a giant candelabra from the center, placed it on the floor, and stripped the tablecloth from it.

Bozeman arranged four chairs, one at each corner of Hawthorne's body. Then he used the microphone and amplifier cables to block off the body. When he finished, the area looked like a homemade wrestling ring.

"Okay. Let's get to work," Viola said. "Like I said, you take the staff, like the servers and the bartenders, and I'll handle the guests at the party. Take pictures of everything you think is pertinent and get witness statements and contact information for everyone you talk to."

Without waiting for an answer, she turned to leave, but I knew I had to stop her. "Viola, wait."

She pirouetted and waited. "Earlier today, I heard a couple of people talking outside my bus."

"About what?"

"I couldn't tell for sure. The voices were quiet, but I overheard them talking about some poor deals that they'd been through with Hawthorne."

Viola subconsciously scratched her temple with a pen. "Bad business usually makes for likely motives."

I smiled. "My dad always said love and money were behind ninety percent of the crimes he'd investigated."

"That percentage sounds about right. Do you know who was talking?"

I shook my head. "No. Sorry. Other than the sentence that caught my attention, and the loud shush that quieted everything down, I couldn't tell."

"Could you at least give me a clue? Man? Woman? Accent? Speech impediment?"

I hesitated for a moment before answering so I could think for a moment to see if anything came to mind. "No."

"Okay. Hopefully, we'll figure that out. Grab your phone and let's go to work."

We stepped from the stage, and I followed Viola to Hawthorne's body. Once there, Viola retrieved her phone and snapped pictures from every angle. I thought she'd want to roll Hawthorne over, and I was there, ready to volunteer Bozeman's services again. But when she finished, she nodded at Laurel.

"Okay, cover him," Viola said.

Laurel grabbed the tablecloth and passed one end to me. Bozeman disconnected a cable to give us access to the body, and we stepped in and gave Hawthorne a shroud. We stepped away, Bozeman reconnected a cable, then pulled up a chair and sat down, ready to do the next part of his duty.

I turned to ask Viola a question and saw she'd stepped away and was busy taking photos of the room, including all the people in it. I did a quick scan for all the people I'd remembered meeting, and everyone, including Ashley and Stacy were at the bar, which had suddenly turned into a popular place. Except Jackie. Jackie remained missing from the room, and I wondered where she'd been all that time. I also wondered how she'd react when she learned her meal ticket was gone forever. Then my thoughts passed to his will, and I wondered who would be inheriting the estate and whatever fortune he had. I let that one pass and assumed it had crept into Viola's mind already. This certainly wasn't her first rodeo.

"What should I do?" Laurel asked when she noticed Viola seemed too busy to answer the question.

I thought about it for a second. "Can you lend me your phone? I left mine on the bus and she wants me to take pictures of people I talk to."

"Where's yours?" Laurel asked as she pulled her phone from her back pocket.

"On the desk in my bedroom," I answered, even though I'd just told her where it was. I remained horrible about always carrying it with me, even though Bozeman continued to stress the importance of having it on my person at all times. Even so, I liked to disconnect from the world, so it spent more time in my bedroom than in my pocket.

Laurel fidgeted with the phone for a moment, then passed it to me. "I've turned off the lock screen, so you have access to anything you need."

Since her phone was different from mine, I pushed a button to check it, and the screen lit up immediately, displaying her apps. I saw the camera icon, pressed it, and it opened fine.

"You're not worried about me finding all your secrets in here?" I asked.

"I would be if I had any," she answered right away. "What do you need me to do?" she repeated.

I glanced around the room. Someone had revived Helen and gotten her into a chair where she currently nursed a drink. Everyone had clustered into small groups of two or three, and Viola had Loren off to the side and I could tell the interrogation had begun.

"I think you should keep alert and help Bozeman guard the scene."

"He can't handle that himself?" Laurel asked.

I shook my head and pointed behind her. Laurel turned around and looked at Bozeman. He had found a second chair to put his feet on, then pulled his hat down and seemed to be in the midst of a nap.

"Seriously?" Laurel asked.

I smiled. "We could be in the middle of a zombie apocalypse, and he would probably ask someone to wake him when things got really bad and head off to slumberland. Don't worry, if there's trouble, he'll wake in an instant and will stand ready to deal with anything."

"Is there anything else I should do?" Laurel asked. She moved a few feet away, retrieved a chair for herself, pulled it close to me, and sat.

"Yeah. Sit with your back to the wall and remember, someone in here is a murderer," I answered.

A look of realization flashed into her eyes, a look that told me she grasped finally what was happening. She opened her mouth to ask a question, closed it, rose, and moved her chair next to the wall where she'd retrieved the tablecloth. She sat literally with her back to the wall, and I don't think a gallon of black coffee would make her more awake and intense than she looked at the moment.

I returned to her and grabbed her hand. "It'll be okay. Just stay where there are lots of people around, and you'll be fine."

Laurel pointed toward Hawthorne. "The group didn't prevent that from happening."

She had a valid point there.

"Okay. Then also hope the lights stay on," I said.

She gave me another smile, one I suspected she flashed to convince herself that all would turn out well. I gave her hand another squeeze.

"You'll be fine," I said. A final squeeze, and I let her go. I turned to leave.

"Hey, Codi?"

I turned back around. "Yeah?"

"Be safe."

It was my turn to smile. "Of course. What's the worst that can happen?"

Laurel didn't answer. Instead, she rolled her eyes at me. In response, I shrugged, made sure I had everything I needed, and left the ballroom.

CHAPTER EIGHT

When I stepped from the ballroom, my intention was to find the staff and conduct interviews, just as Viola requested. I realized I had three issues to overcome with the task.

First, I didn't know who all the staff were. From earlier, I learned of at least ten servers, and Heather, the caterer, but I didn't know if there was anyone else. I should have asked for a list from Brantley of who else might be around. For all I guessed, Hawthorne dedicated one entire wing of the house to cooks, butlers, drivers, caretakers, or whoever else Hawthorne Harris had on staff.

My second problem occurred to me right after the first one did. That one was I didn't know where to find anyone except Heather, whom I assumed had returned to her food truck. What was I supposed to do? Wander the halls like a ghost until I ran into people?

My third issue was my biggest hurdle. I had no actual authority. I'm a musician, not a cop, so although I could request that people speak to me, they had the complete right to tell me to bug off. Granted, when I talked to fans, they were always more than willing to talk to me, and would do so for as long as I let them. The staff may have never heard of me, so chances were I couldn't use my fourth-tier celebrity status to coax conversation from them. Still, Viola asked for my help, so I wanted to help. Even if half the people I encountered wouldn't say a word, that was that many fewer people she'd have to interview later.

My initial priority was to locate people to talk to, so I backtracked through the rooms I'd actually been in to see if anyone was around. I hit pay dirt on my first stop when I entered the room I'd eaten dinner in. Around the massive table sat Heather and the service crew.

"Codi Cassidy, come in and join us! I promise not to spill anything on you. Well, I'll try not to, anyway," Heather said when she noticed me standing in the doorway like I was waiting for an invitation to join the party.

As I stepped into the room, Heather used her foot to push out the chair next to her, and I took that as a sign to sit down and join her. I set the notebook on the table and placed the pen on it.

"Would you like something to drink?" Heather asked. "Carolina, pass the bubbly."

Carolina, who sat three people from Heather, picked up the bottle before her without breaking the conversation with the person next to her. From there, I watched as the bottle transferred from hand to hand until Heather grabbed it. She held it up to the light to check how much volume remained, then topped off her glass.

"No, thank you. I'm not big on wine," I said.

"What's your pleasure, then? Whiskey, probably, or perhaps a beer? I can give you whatever you want."

"A bottle of water would be perfect," I said.

"Liz, throw a bottle of water down here, will you?" Heather yelled across the table.

I looked down to see which one was Liz and spotted her at the opposite end of the table. She reached down and came up with a bottle from somewhere beneath the table. I saw her raise it above her head, then before I might utter a word to stop it, Liz tossed it into the air. To her credit, Liz had a great arm and Heather caught it in midair without hesitation. She handed it to me without comment.

"That was impressive," I admitted as I opened the bottle and took a drink.

Heather laughed. "Not really. We're on a baseball team together. So, what's up, buttercup?"

I moved my chair close enough to Heather for our knees to touch, then leaned in.

"Did you hear about Hawthorne Harris?" I asked.

Heather turned her champagne flute in her fingers, then drained the glass without pause.

"I did. We all did."

I didn't recall seeing either Heather or any of the service staff in the minutes leading up to the big event, but that meant nothing. Distracted by the performance, I might well have missed someone popping in and out.

"Is it true he's dead?" Heather asked as she refilled her flute.

"It's true." I paused for a moment to watch her drink, hoping I could catch any visual clues from her, but I didn't. "Do you have any information about it?"

"I don't have much to tell you. I was in my truck cleaning things up. Dinner was done, therefore, so was I."

"Why didn't you leave?" I asked, curious since I usually liked to bail out myself the second the contract obligation ended.

Heather tilted her glass toward the rest of the women at the table. As she did so, she spilled some drink over the glass's edge, and it plopped onto the table. She didn't seem to notice. I did, and since there was an unused napkin within reach, I dropped it over the mess. Instinctively, Heather took the napkin, wiped up the wine, and threw the napkin onto a used laundry pile near the wall. The pile was already tall with napkins, tablecloths, shirts, and cummerbunds.

"These ladies are in my employ for the evening. Every single one. They're some of my regular subcontractors I use for servers, bartenders, valets. Whatever is needed for a party human resource-wise, I usually provide. For a price, of course."

"Of course," I agreed.

"Anyway," Heather continued, "after they're done, I like to make sure they're fed, paid, and have a ride home."

The payment comment struck a chord that I needed to explore further.

"I received a rumor that Mr. Harris had a bad habit of not paying his bills. Did you get paid for tonight?" I thought about the cash I'd squirreled away into my safe and reminded myself to thank Loren later for the tip to get the money up front.

Heather emptied her glass. Was that the third or fourth she'd downed since I'd been in the room? I couldn't remember. She coaxed the last of the liquid from the bottle and collected another three-quarters of a glass. She drank, then smiled.

"Oh, yeah. I got paid. I ask for one hundred percent upfront. For Hawthorne Harris, I also included the costs of the people I brought with me. I inflated prices to boot since I knew the tightwad wouldn't tip anyone at the end of the night."

"And he was good with that arrangement?" I asked.

"He had to be. I'm the only caterer who'll work with him now, other than Loren, for the pies. Every contract I have for other clients is fifty percent up front, balance due the day of the event. The first time I worked with Harris, he conveniently forgot to pay the rest of the bill. He blamed it on a bookkeeping error, and although he said he'd get the money to me right away, it took me almost eight months to get paid."

"But he finally paid?" I asked.

"He had to. Summer rolled around and he was looking for a caterer for a picnic, and he called every caterer within a hundred-mile radius, and everyone was busy. Then my phone rang, and he agreed to not only to pay the back balance but also agreed to the new terms."

"It's a good thing for you then that everyone else was booked."

Heather laughed and waved away my comment. "Oh, posh. Any one of two dozen caterers had open calendars then. They simply didn't want to deal with his nonsense. It's not like I was the first one he screwed over, and we caterers do talk to each other."

"Were you alone in the truck while you were cleaning up? Can anyone vouch for you?" I asked.

"You're asking me for an alibi?" Heather responded.

I could tell right then she was a straight shooter, so I returned the favor. "Yes."

"Liz," Heather yelled across the table. "Can you tell Codi here where I was over the last hour?"

Without hesitation, Liz answered. "On the truck, cleaning."

"How do you know?" Heather asked.

"Because I helped. Don't you remember me standing right beside you? Cut back on the booze, Heather," Liz answered.

A lady near the middle of the table raised her hand. I hadn't caught her name. "I can vouch for both of them. Thanks to drawing the short straw, I got to run equipment and food back and forth from the truck to inside."

There were eleven women at the table, and I had alibis for three of them. I looked from person to person at the table.

"You're wondering about the rest of them?" Heather asked.

I nodded. "Yes, I am."

"After they finished their duties, they were all in here, eating, drinking, making conversation."

"You're certain?" I asked.

"One hundred percent," Heather said.

"There's no one who slipped out of the room, then came back after someone killed Harris?"

"It's plausible, but doubtful."

"Why?" I asked.

"No motive. So far as I believe, no one in here has even talked to Hawthorne outside of their duties. And since I'm the one who pays them, there's no need for them to worry about anything except spilling soup on someone."

Heather made a convincing argument. Despite that, I needed to verify things for myself.

"Do you mind if I ask around? Take statements and contact information for the chief?" I asked out of politeness, since I was going to do it regardless of the answer.

"Be my guest," Heather said. "Listen up, everyone. Codi here is going to go around and ask you some questions. Please give her all the answers she needs, and make them the truth."

The women at the table took in the advice, then went back to their conversations.

"They'll play ball. Do your thing."

"Thanks for your cooperation," I said.

I spent the next hour taking statements and photographs, and each story I gathered fit like a clean puzzle piece. Everyone collaborated on everyone else's whereabouts. Heather, Liz, and the other woman, who turned out to be named Malorie, all had airtight alibis.

In the end, I was no closer to getting any farther than I was before. When I finished taking the last statement, I returned to the seat next to Heather and reviewed all my notes to make sure my work didn't contain any major holes. Finally, I closed the notebook, and pushed it away from me.

"Well?" Heather asked.

"Well, I think your entire group is in the clear."

"Except Stacy and Ashley," Heather said.

"Who?" I asked.

"The bartenders. They should have been in the ballroom all night working at the bar."

I slapped myself on the forehead. "Ashley and Stacy."

I'd spoken with them both earlier in the evening, and remembered how helpful they'd been, then completely forgot about them.

"They're probably innocent, too," Heather said.

In my mind, I agreed, but I still needed to get statements from them, provided Viola hadn't already. "I'll have to talk to them. Can you think of anyone else, maybe someone from Hawthorne's staff, who might have been here tonight? Drivers, butlers, those sorts of people?"

Heather leaned back in her chair and considered the question for a moment. "You'd best ask that question to Brantley Wilson. Since he's Hawthorne's assistant, he would have the list. I assume there are gardeners on staff, as well as a regular chef and a driver, but I didn't see any of them around today. I don't know who else might work here, and it wouldn't surprise me if Harris had the same issue with other workers as he did hiring caterers. After all, there's no shortage of rich people around here who have yards to maintain and meals they need cooked. And they generally pay their people with a modicum of respect, unlike how I imagine the staff around here gets treated."

I wracked my brain for another question to ask when the gong sounded. Heather rolled her eyes.

"What?"

"It's that damn gong. Gets on my nerves every time. Is that the pinnacle of entitlement, or what? Does Hawthorne think he's a king or something?"

"Not anymore," I said. "Where does the gong come from? What sets it off?"

"I don't have the faintest. I imagined he had some button or something to push that rings it, but I'm not totally sure about that. All I know is when it sounds during dinner service, the next course should be served. Stupid gong. Do I look like one of Pavlov's dogs to you?"

Heather drained her glass, picked up the bottle, realized it was finally empty, and slammed it back down on the table. The bottle tipped over, rolled a few inches, and fell from the table. I heard the thump as it connected with the wood floor, but fortunately, it didn't break. Heather didn't move a muscle to check on it.

I decided I had all I needed from this group, so I excused myself and left the room.

Rather than return right away to the ballroom, I thought I'd explore the house a little. I made my way back to the home gym. Through the large windows, I saw the rain pelt the ground in fat drops and the lightning continued to strike as the storm continued. During a brief flash of light, I saw Heather's truck and my bus just beyond it, both sitting still in the rain. I hoped the kids were all okay. Since four out of five were technically wild animals, I suspected they fared fine. As a bit of thunder pealed, I pictured Gibson searching out a hiding spot on the bus, probably under my desk, or in my closet if I left the door open.

I left the gym, and instead of turning right, I walked straight ahead down a corridor. It wasn't a long corridor, but it certainly stretched farther than the length of my bus, and I thought, the length of most houses I'd been in.

The half-dozen doors before me were closed, but that didn't bother me since I knew how to solve that problem. I turned the knob of the first one I came to and pushed it open. I turned on the light and discovered I'd found a bathroom. It was only a half-bath, and had only a toilet and a sink, but it was still more impressive than most. To my surprise, the toilet was a standard porcelain one, and not made of solid gold like I expected. The pedestal sink appeared made of marble, and its fixtures were solid brass. There was a lone towel hanging on a rack, monogrammed with Hawthorne's initials. I rubbed a corner between my fingers and determined it was thicker and plusher than some carpets I've stood on.

I left the room and returned to the corridor. There, I crossed the hall and tried the door. Locked. I wandered up the hallway and found each door locked. I considered returning to the bus for my lock picks, but then I heard the peal of thunder and I remembered the rain and elected to stay warm and dry in the house. Instead, I backtracked to where I'd come from and eventually made it back into the ballroom.

"How's it going in here?" I asked Laurel, who was sitting just inside the room where I'd left her.

"Well, no one else got shot in your absence, so I consider that a win," Laurel said.

I looked toward Bozeman's way. He was right where I'd left him, and it didn't look like he'd moved a muscle. "He's taking his job seriously," I said.

"He sure is. Although he did one of those jerk awake things about twenty minutes ago, looked around to see if anyone noticed, then went right back to his nap," Laurel said.

I smiled; sorry I had missed it. It was a classic Bozeman move that I'd experienced several times. The look on his face was always hilarious when he woke, not knowing where he was.

"What's Viola been up to?"

"She's been slowly making her way around the room. And I mean slowly. I think that's only the second person she's talked to since you left."

I scanned the room. Viola was currently talking to Danny Ewing. Everyone else was still clustered in small groups, and to my surprise, the bar was still open and serving drinks. I returned my attention to Laurel.

"Two people? I've been gone for over an hour."

"Yep. She talked to Brantley for most of that time. She's only been with that guy for about ten minutes now."

"How are you holding up?" I didn't need to ask, because I could tell simply by looking at Laurel that she was tired, stressed, and ready to leave.

"I'm good. A little bored, but I'm still hanging in there."

"You look exhausted," I said, perhaps a little more bluntly than I intended.

Laurel looked at me for a moment. "Okay, maybe I could use a quick nap. And perhaps a slice of Loren's pie."

The mention of the pie caused my stomach to growl. I wouldn't mind one myself.

"Why don't you take a break, and I'll check with Viola and see when we can get out of here."

"Thanks. I could use something to drink," Laurel said. She stood, stretched, and headed for the bar. I wanted to call after her and ask her to avoid alcohol, but she was an adult, so if she needed something to take the edge from a wayward night, she could have it.

From my spot, I watched as Viola talked to Danny, and I waited. I didn't want to interrupt since it wasn't like we were at a cocktail party, and I wanted to insert myself into a conversation. As I watched, I noticed the conversation must have taken an unexpected turn. Danny started flailing his arms around and now looked like a monster trying to fend off a swarm of wasps. In response, Viola took three steps backward to give him room.

"What do you think is going on there?" Laurel asked as she handed me a glass.

I was so intent on watching Viola and Danny, I never sensed Laurel's return, and I accepted the glass and drank without even checking the contents. I drained the Diet Coke from the glass and placed the empty vessel on the nearest table. To Laurel's credit, it was without a hint of alcohol.

"You're thinking of going over there, aren't you?" Laurel asked.

I passed Laurel a glance that should have said everything that needed to be said, but I answered. "Of course. What's the worst that could happen?"

Laurel winced. "I hate it when you ask that question."

CHAPTER NINE

I waited for a few seconds more, then finally, Viola dismissed Danny. While Danny walked toward the bar, Viola dipped her head and reviewed the notes she'd taken. The thunder rumbled; the lights flickered. My eyes instinctively focused on the chandelier overhead, as did Viola's. When I brought my gaze back down, I caught sight of Viola as she dropped the pen she held. As she bent to pick it up, once again, the lights dropped out, and darkness shrouded the room. I expected them to come back on within a few seconds, but they didn't.

Around me, the silence broke as a few murmurs erupted, and as the lights failed to come on, I heard an uncomfortable laugh. A moment later, I caught a sound that didn't belong, like someone had dropped a Santa sack filled with laundry onto a table. Fifteen seconds later, the lights returned, and I noticed right away I had another problem to contend with.

"Viola!" I screamed as I rushed toward her. She was lying on the floor on her side, her back to me. Next to her prone body was one of the giant candlesticks from a side table. Even with a cursory glance, I noticed the fresh blood along the bottom edge. I dropped to my knees next to Viola and reached for her neck.

"Thank goodness," I said as I detected a pulse. I moved my hand from her neck to her chest and felt it rise. Viola and I both exhaled at the same time.

"What happened?" Laurel asked as she kneeled beside me.

"Whacked in the head," I answered.

I leaned over Viola's body, intending to turn her onto her back.

"Wait, stop," Laurel said.

I froze while Laurel did the same things I did, checking Viola's pulse and then her breathing.

"Leave her the way it is. You there, get something I can put under her head, and get me some water and a compress."

I thought Laurel was giving me directions, but when I looked up, I spotted Helen Troy rushing away.

"What do you want me to do?" I asked.

"Nothing, I got this."

I stayed out of the way as Laurel checked Viola's pulse again, then moved her top arm farther out, like Viola was reaching for something in front of her body.

"I don't want her to throw up and choke," she explained.

We waited another minute, and Helen returned carrying a bottle of water, a napkin, and a tablecloth.

Laurel opened the bottle, dumped some on the napkin, and checked out Viola's wound.

"You still have my phone?" she asked.

Without a word, I handed it over. Laurel took it, turned on the flashlight, and pointed it at Viola's head. "Hold it right there."

I did as I was told and watched as Laurel dabbed at the wound. "I don't think this is too bad. It looks like it already stopped bleeding, but I'm going to apply some pressure to make sure."

"Is she going to be okay?" I asked.

"Beats me. I'm a fiddle player, not an EMT."

"Where'd you learn to do this? Girl Scouts? Medical training?" I asked, genuinely curious.

Laurel smiled. "Mostly television." She removed the napkin from Viola's head and showed it to me. Even with my limited experience, I could tell the wound wasn't serious.

"When she wakes up, I imagine she's going to have one nasty headache. And hopefully not a severe concussion."

"Can you keep an eye on her?" I asked.

"Certainly," Laurel responded without hesitation.

Satisfied Viola would come through fine, I stood. Around me, I studied the faces of the rest of the people in the room, every eye following every move I made. My eyes dropped to the floor and saw Viola's pen laying on the ornate Italian marble. I picked it up and did a quick search until I spotted the corner of the cover of the notebook she'd been using under her right heel. With care, I lifted her leg, pulled out the book, and gently set her back down.

I righted myself and looked around. Brantley Wilson had moved to within two feet of me. His hat was askew, as was his quiver, and his left knee, bony and pale, had broken through his tights. Instead of saying anything, he stood staring at me, and after a moment, his foot started tapping out a Morse code message I couldn't decipher. Eventually, my impatience got the best of me.

"What?" I asked.

Brantley put his hands on his hips and leaned forward, nose turned slightly upward. "What are you going to do?"

The question confused me. "About?"

His right hand broke free, and he swirled his hand at Viola, and then in the general direction of Hawthorne's covered body. "All this. What do you intend to do about all this?"

"I don't really understand."

"I know you were helping her, so now what?"

"You don't get it. She only wanted me to take names and pictures of the staff, so she didn't miss anyone. I'm not a police officer, I'm a musician. You saw me up there doing my thing, didn't you?" I pointed toward the stage for effect.

"But you seem to have experience with what you're doing. Keep doing it."

I turned and discovered the speaker was the woman dressed as Dorothy, whose name I had already forgotten. Somewhere she'd misplaced her basket, so I imagined she lost poor Toto somewhere.

"Look, um, Dorothy, I don't know what you've learned, but there's nothing I can do here."

It was Loren's turn, so he stepped forward and spoke. "Bozeman told me the story about how you got him out of a bunch of trouble. He's told me you've solved mysteries before."

"It's not like that. This is a police matter, not mine. I'm sure backup is already on the way and will be here in no time."

Brantley shook his head. "How? No one got a call out. There's no reason for anyone in the outside world to speculate that anything out of the ordinary has gone on here tonight."

"I hate to jump in, Codi, but you're also missing the bigger picture."

That voice I recognized. A quick turn of my head verified that Bozeman had not only woken from his nap but had placed his feet firmly on the floor and tipped his hat back. He didn't speak much, but when he did, he commanded attention.

I sighed. "What's that, Boze?"

Bozeman lifted his arm and swept his finger across everyone in the room. "One of these fine people here is a murderer. Almost two-times over, I reckon."

I followed the direction of Bozeman's finger as he did another pass. As I did, I looked each person in the eyes. Then I glanced over at Laurel, who still tended to Viola, and across the room at the shrouded body. Bozeman was right. Someone had not only killed, but attempted to do so a second time. If the power remained shaky all night, chances are there might be more prone bodies on the ballroom floor.

At last, I relented. "Okay. I'll do it. I'll keep looking into this. With conditions."

"Okay. Name them," Brantley said.

"First. No one leaves or enters this room. Everyone finds a seat and stays put."

"What about the restroom? I need to go now, in fact," Frankenstein's bride said. I'd forgotten her name too, although I was confident it began with an A. Annie, maybe.

She had a good point, so I considered the question for a moment. "Okay. Bathroom breaks excepted, but only one person at a time, and with an escort. Either myself, Laurel, or Bozeman will take you to the bathroom and back."

"How do we know you weren't involved?" Danny stepped forward and asked.

To my surprise, Loren fielded the question for me. "Come on, man. You really think that when the lights darkened, one of those musicians, who have met none of you before, put down their instrument, crept across the room in the dark, killed Hawthorne Harris, and then took their place back on stage?"

Danny's shoulders slumped, followed by his eyes. "Okay,

yeah. That seems improbable."

"More like impossible," Helen interjected.

"Okay, escorts to the bathroom," Brantley said. "What else?"

"No more alcohol comes out of the bar tonight. Only sodas and water from here on out. Coffee, if they have it."

Danny raised his glass and was about to protest when Loren wagged a finger at him in a distinctive no gesture. Danny closed his mouth and set his empty glass on the ground.

"Done," Brantley said. "And?"

"And everyone stays seated and cooperates. No one refuses to answer my questions."

"What is all this really going to buy us?" Dracula asked.

One of my first points of business needed to be relearning everyone's name.

Brantley turned. "Maybe she'll be able to finger the perpetrator. Is that not good enough?"

"So what?" Dracula's fake fangs impeded his speech, so he ripped them from his mouth and tossed them on the floor. "So what?" he repeated. "It's not like anything she gets will be admissible in court, even if she figures out who did it."

Loren stepped forward. "The benefit is, Claude, if she figures it out, we can hold that person for the authorities so no one else ends up like Viola, or worse, Harris."

I don't know if it was Loren's logic or his impressive size that convinced Claude the vampire to back down, but he did.

"Anything else?" Brantley asked.

I didn't think of anything at the moment. "That's it for now. Why doesn't everyone grab a seat and get comfortable? I'm sure it's going to be a long night."

The crowd disbursed, and as a group, they wandered around until each one found a chair. Instead of conversations in small groups like before, everyone seemed fine to be on their own for the moment.

I took a few steps over to Bozeman.

"What's your plan?" he asked.

"I carry on where Viola left off. Talk to the group, see what I can figure out."

"What do you want me to do?"

"Start by escorting that one woman to the bathroom, and then watch my back for me."

Bozeman tipped his hat and stood. "You got it."

"Oh, and Bozeman? Don't get yourself killed."

Bozeman shot me a smile that told me not to worry, and he headed toward the bride.

I sat down in Bozeman's seat and opened the notebook. I expected it to be filled with names, descriptions, random thoughts, or other information I remembered seeing scribbled in my dad's books. Instead, the notebook was empty except for the first three pages. She'd filled the first page with swirls. I'd seen plenty of swirls like that in my lifetime since I created the same ones when I tested to see if a pen was out of ink.

The second page didn't contain swirls, but rather squares. I almost pictured the design being made. A large square placed in the center, then two lines dividing it into fourths. Then she'd added more and more squares until it grew to the size of a chessboard, and then, for good measure, she'd penned in even more squares.

The third page, rather than the murderer's name written in bold letters in the center with arrows pointing to it, contained triangles. I could tell the page started off like the square page did, but she inked in diagonal lines to bisect the squares into triangles. Viola hadn't completely finished the project, as there were still several squares that were still squares.

"What in the world?" I whispered. "What was this all about?"

It tempted me to tear the pages from the book, but I thought that might give the wrong impression to anyone watching me. I flipped to the fourth page, grabbed my pens, and stood. I knew who I wanted to talk to first.

It didn't take me long to traverse the ballroom to the bar. Ashley was still manning her post, but Stacy was in a chair a few feet away, looking at something on her phone.

"Would you like a drink?" Ashley asked as I approached. "I can offer you a variety of soft drinks and water." She lowered her voice so only I could hear her. "I also have a pitcher of iced tea, but honestly, most of the ice in it has melted, so it's probably pretty diluted by now."

"I'll take a bottle of water," I said.

Ashley handed it over, and I opened the top and drank. I hadn't realized until that moment how thirsty I was. As I drank, I gave Ashley the once over. Like the servers, she had flowing brown hair, clinched into a ponytail. Unlike the others, it suited her. I could easily picture that ponytail trailing through the back of a baseball cap as she biked or hiked the endless trails in the area. She tugged at the black vest she wore like it constricted her like a python. Even though she looked uncomfortable, she kept her professionalism.

"Lemme guess, you're here for information, not just the water, correct?" Ashley said as she picked up a bar rag and ran it over the top of the bar, even though I couldn't see a drop of liquid or stain upon it.

I took another swallow, then nodded. "Can I start by getting your full name, your phone number, and your picture?"

She smiled and asked for the notebook. I complied, and she took a pen from behind her ear, then jotted down her personal details in block letters which were easily readable. I appreciated that. Even with my own writing, I was often sloppy enough that I couldn't read my own notes. After I snapped her picture, I took the notebook back, added the date and time, and began.

"Where were you when everything happened?" I asked, getting right to the point.

"Right here."

"The entire night?"

"Yep."

"You didn't leave? Go to the bathroom? Run for supplies?"

Ashley smiled and shook her head. "Nope. Stacy is my runner, and I used the facilities before my shift started."

I didn't do the math, but it had been several hours since the night began.

"You haven't moved? You must have really comfortable shoes."

"It's all about the mat," Ashley said.

I was about to ask when she invited me behind the bar. There, underneath Ashley's feet, was a thick cushioned mat.

"That looks comfortable. You mind if I give it a try?" I asked.

Ashley moved aside, and I took her place behind the bar. Climbing onto the mat was like stepping onto a cloud.

"This is amazing," I admitted as I moved to my proper side of the bar.

"It is. Heather provided it for us. She's always watching out for our comfort. I can stand on this thing for an entire shift and not feel any worse for wear by the end of the night."

"If you didn't go anywhere, what did you see or hear?" I asked.

"A couple of the girls came around to serve the champagne at the beginning, and after that was gone, the guests started coming to me for drinks."

"Is it an open or cash bar?"

"Open, with limitations. Hawthorne Harris provided the alcohol I used tonight."

"He gave it to you himself?"

"No. His assistant did. But I can tell you it's not the good stuff."

"What do you mean?"

Ashley reached behind the bar and pulled out four bottles of liquor. She turned the labels so I could read them. Before me, were whiskey, vodka, cognac, and a rum bottle.

"See these? They are all top shelf all the way. This bottle of vodka would normally go for three hundred bucks. The rum, eighteen hundred. The others are also so top shelf I wouldn't be able to reach them."

"Okay, so he serves the best booze."

Ashley shook her head. "No. He doesn't. These bottles have been married."

She saw the look of confusion on my face and continued her explanation. She held up the whiskey bottle. "Someone has emptied this bottle of whiskey of the good stuff and replaced it with a brand us commoners would drink."

"You're sure?" I asked.

"Definitely. I've been tending bar a long time, and I know my booze."

"Has anyone else noticed?" I asked.

"If they did, no one has said anything about it."

"Has anyone drinking too much tonight?"

"Frankenstein has been by several times. If it wasn't a private party, I would have cut him off a long time ago."

"Has he been a problem?"

"Not as much as Dracula has."

"What do you mean?"

"He's only been over twice, but he was gross both times. The first time he asked for my number, the second he pinched Stacy on the bottom. What is it about men? Put them into capes and they turn into Neanderthals."

"I don't know the answer to that one, but it isn't just capes. It's also blue jeans, cowboy hats, boots, and a million other things. It probably all comes down to the drink, though."

Ashley nodded. "I'd agree with that."

"Have you noticed anything else out of the ordinary?"

"Not really. I've gone through more wine than anything. Most parties are like that."

"What about when the lights went out? Did you see anything or anyone?"

"No. The lights went out, gong sounded, lights came on, and you know what happened from there."

"You saw no one moving around? Anyone who might have approached Hawthorne, or even Viola?"

"No. I wish I could be more help. To be honest, I have horrible night vision, anyway. Once the lights grow dim, I can't see a thing."

I had no more questions for her, so I moved on to Stacy. As I got closer, I noticed she was still fiddling with her phone.

"Do you have a cell signal?" I asked.

Stacy looked up at me, back at her phone, then up at me. "Oh. No. I don't. I'm doing a crossword puzzle offline."

"Too bad. I was hoping you had contacted the outside world somehow."

Stacy turned off the phone and shoved it into her pocket. She, too, had long brown hair and wore the same tuxedo as Ashley, although her shirt tails had pulled free and peeked out beneath her vest. Over the course of the night, she'd worked up enough of a sweat to turn the shirt under her arms translucent. Now that I took a good look at her, she looked younger than all the other women I'd talked to that night.

Stacy confirmed my suspicions when she told me she was only nineteen. She had been busy all night running all over the place to keep the bar stocked with booze, beer, wine, and ice. I got Stacy's contact information and photo and asked her the same questions I'd asked Ashley. She gave me a detailed version of her encounter with Dracula, but other than that, she provided no more information than I'd gotten from Ashley.

Satisfied all of Heather's people were in the clear, it was time to turn my attention to the big fish in the room.

CHAPTER TEN

I tried to decide who to talk to first and that decision became easy for me when I spotted, of all people, the missing Jackie May. She was sitting alone in the far corner of the room, wedged between a wall and a window. I hadn't seen her come in, and did not have a clue when she'd arrived. Clearly, my powers of perception were a bit off.

I headed right toward her. Once I got to within ten feet, I grabbed a chair and dragged it with me across the floor. I placed it right in front of Jackie and sat. I leaned forward, my expression a mix of concern and minor annoyance.

"Hey, Jackie. Where have you been?" I asked, my tone gentle.

She looked at me, but at first, I didn't think she recognized me, even though she was the reason I was here in the first place.

"Codi, I..." she trailed off. She'd learned what happened. Crying had turned her eyes red-rimmed, and her mascara had run, giving her the same look my pet raccoon generally had. She sat with her hands folded tightly in her lap, and she subconsciously fiddled with her engagement ring.

"Jackie? Can you hear me, honey?"

She blinked twice and sniffed. I looked around for a tissue, and not finding one, I gave up on the search.

"Where were you all night?" I waited.

After almost a full minute, tears welled up in Jackie's eyes, and she took a deep breath before responding. "You gave me that shirt, and I wanted to put it away so it wouldn't get ruined. I took it to my room. Hung it in my closet."

"That happened several hours ago. What happened next?" I asked.

Jackie stared at the floor for a bit. If her head were transparent, I probably would have been able to see the gears turning.

"Well, the storm. Lots of thunder and lightning. Then the power died. Hawthorne always said if the power died to go into the room and stay there until he came for me. I went in, but he never came. I fell asleep waiting, and when I woke up, he still wasn't with me, so I came back here."

"What room?"

"The room. There's a room in the back of Hawthorne's closet. It isn't big like his bedroom. There's only enough room for a small bed, one of those mini fridges, a microwave, and a bunch of computer monitors."

"Is there a thick door? With a lock of some sort?" I asked.

"How did you guess?" Jackie asked, amazed by my powers.

The answer was simple. I'd seen safe rooms in several movies and television shows.

"Are you okay if I ask you a few questions?" I asked.

Jackie nodded.

"Did anything unusual happen during dinner or afterward?" I asked.

Jackie shook her head. A strand of her hair fell from behind her ear and across her face. "No, nothing unusual. Just the typical dinner party chitchat. You were there, so I don't need to tell you how it happened."

"I wasn't there the entire time," I corrected. "I only stopped by for a quick meet and greet."

Jackie nodded. "That's right. I remember now."

"Did Hawthorne mention any conflicts or trouble with anyone at the party?"

Jackie hesitated, her gaze dropping to her hands. She seemed to fixate on the diamond on her finger, and as she touched the ring, she started to cry again. "No. He didn't have any problems with anyone here."

Based on my conversations with Heather and Loren's insistence that I get my cash in advance, I detected a lie, assuming she knew how Hawthorne did business.

"Okay. If everyone at the party was okay, did he ever mention any enemies? Anyone at all who might have wanted to harm him?" I asked.

Jackie's head shook back and forth. "No. Of course not. Everyone loved him. He got along with everyone. No one would want to hurt a single hair on his head."

Again, I imagined that was stretching the truth by a bit. I figured she didn't want to speak ill of the dead. Or perhaps she preferred to wear the rose-colored glasses that prevented her from thinking anything bad about him.

"Did he have any secrets? Anything he might have kept from you?"

"No! Of course not. We were open with each other. We trusted each other with our deepest secrets."

I had trouble believing that one as well, as I jotted down a few notes to keep everything straight.

"You say you took a nap in the safe room? Why? I assumed you were excited to see my show."

Jackie looked at me in the eyes, then rubbed her forehead. "I'm not sure. I remember walking all the way to my room. The lights dimmed, and I rushed to the room. Then, from out of nowhere, I felt really sleepy. I couldn't keep my eyes open. I think I fell asleep before I hit the pillow."

"And when you woke, you came right back here? You didn't go anywhere else?"

"That's right," she said.

"Did you see or talk to anyone in the hallway? Or when you got back here?"

She shook her head again. "No. When I got back here, I looked around for Hawthorne, and I knew that he was under there. I came here and haven't moved since."

Jackie took a moment, wiped away a tear and a good bit of mascara as well.

I looked around again for a tissue and spotted a napkin on a table nearby. Once I retrieved it, I handed it to Jackie, and she wiped her eyes and blew her nose.

"I realize this has been hard for you. If you can think of anything else, no matter how insignificant it may seem, let me know."

Jackie nodded, blew her nose again, and shut down.

I scanned the room, wondering who to talk to next, and decided on Brantley Wilson. In my mind, he was not only the most logical person to speak to as Hawthorne's assistant, but he was also the person physically closest to me. I reviewed my notes a final time, made one correction. Afterward, I made my way over to where Brantley was sitting at the edge of a table, one leg propped over the other, fingers drumming on the table. I slid into an empty chair next to him and placed the notebook on the table. I opened it to a blank page, added the date, time, and his name to the top. His gaze as he scrutinized me had an apprehensive expression on it.

"So, Brantley, how did you get that hole in your tights?"
His eyes dipped from my notebook to his legs. He spotted the exposed knee. "I don't know. I think I must have run into something in the dark."

"It looks like you're bleeding there. You must have run into something sharp," I noted.

He bent at the waist and took a closer look. There, almost in the exact center of his patella, was a drop of blood. He licked his thumb and rubbed it away. As I watched, I noticed it came off cleanly. It didn't start bleeding again, and there didn't appear to be a spot of it left. I concluded the blood wasn't his. I also realized I made a mistake by pointing it out. Since he removed it, that evidence was now gone.

"Did you notice anything strange tonight?" I asked.

"You mean other than the two bodies lying on the floor?" he asked, with a side of snark.

I nodded.

"Not really. Just another Hawthorne Harris party."

"What's that mean?"

Before he could answer, the large feather on his felt cap drooped right over his eyes. In a flourish, he removed the hat and tossed it on the table. "He loved having these parties once or twice a month. Bring in his friends. Show off."

"You didn't seem to enjoy yourself tonight," I noted.

"That's because I was on the clock. You don't think he organized these things himself, do you? Nope. That's me. I have to take care of everything. Catering, entertainment, menu, seating arrangements. Everything. It's a hassle to do all that on top of my day job."

"What is your day job?" I asked.

"Anything Hawthorne tells me to do." Brantley took a moment and glanced across the room at the body on the floor. "Told me to do. Correspondence, post office runs, meeting setups, driving. Anything and everything."

"It sounds like he trusted and relied on you."

Brantley scoffed. "Trusted? Right. He didn't trust anyone. No one."

"What about her?" I asked, pointing my pen in Jackie's direction. "Did he trust her?"

Brantley's brow furrowed, and he shifted uncomfortably in his seat. He leaned in closer and lowered his voice. "Not her, either."

That surprised me. "Then why would they get married?"

Brantley shrugged. "I don't think he ever intended on actually marrying her. After they got together, she was always pushing for that rock on her hand, and ever since, she's been pushing him to set a date for the wedding. He's been avoiding that topic for months."

"Why would he keep her around?" I asked.

"Eye candy. Nothing more. Older man of his status is always looking for a beautiful woman to hang around. To him, she was a symbol, like the Bentley in the garage."

I wanted to direct the conversation in a direction away from Jackie. "How's the pay?"

Brantley's hesitation to answer was clear. He grabbed his hat and fiddled with the feather, like a preening bird. "It's fine."

"Did you get paid on time?" I asked.

I could tell he didn't like the question, because he didn't answer.

"You agreed to cooperate with me, Brantley. Come on. Did you get paid?"

After a long pause, he answered. "Eventually."

I made a few notes in the book.

"Did Mr. Harris mention anything concerning, or out of the ordinary recently? Get any threats? Any hate mails?" I asked.

Brantley smiled. "Any rocks with notes attached thrown through the window? Mr. Harris is… was a powerful, rich man. People were always giving him threats of lawsuits, or threats against his person. Especially the environmentalists. We hear from different groups at least six times a week blathering on about over-fishing and saving the planet and whatever."

"Did he have any enemies?" I asked.

"He's put more than a few people out of business as he's consolidated operations in the area, so probably. I don't have any names in my head offhand, but I'm sure I could get you a list."

"Is there anyone here who'd like to do him any harm?"

Brantley took a moment to scan the room. Based on his demeanor, I sensed his reluctance to divulge more information. He seemed to hold something back, but he didn't say. Finally, his eyes came back to mine. "You'd have to ask them."

I wrote a few more notes, then thanked Brantley and left him alone. Thirsty again, I returned to the bar and got another bottle of water from Ashley. I still had another half-dozen people to talk to, and as I drank, I considered who to approach next. Then I caught the echoing clack of ruby slippers against the marble floor and noticed Dorothy headed my way. She stopped at the bar, asked for a Diet Coke, and once she had a glass in hand, she stepped toward me.

"What's up, buttercup?" she asked.

"Can we talk?" I asked.

"That's why I came over. I'd like to get the interrogation over with."

I laughed. "It's hardly an interrogation. Just a few questions. Let's have a seat."

Dorothy followed me to the nearest table, and we sat. I turned the page in the notebook and added the date and time to the top of the page and asked for her full name.

"Amelia, with an A. Last name Brown, like the color."

As I took down the name, Amelia adjusted the blue gingham dress she was wearing. The light from the chandelier reflected off the sequins sewn into the fabric. As she waited for questions from me, she fidgeted with the hem of her skirt, then folded her hands on top of the table.

"Can you tell me how you knew Hawthorne?"

Amelia took a drink before she answered. "I'm his chief accountant. He's been a client of mine for several years."

"Is it true he had trouble with paying people?" I blurted out. Not where I wanted to start, but I couldn't stop now.

As Amelia stared at me, I noticed one of her irises was a deeper brown shade than the other.

"He paid all his bills within the limits of accepted accounting principles," she said.

That was the longest yes or no answer I'd ever gotten to a question. "What does that mean?"

"That means he paid all his bills within the limits of accepted accounting principles."

My inside voice screamed at dippy Dorothy that repeating the same answer word for word didn't provide any additional context. My outside persona smiled and recorded the quote verbatim.

"Did he pay you on time?" I hoped a simple question would generate an equally similar answer.

"Yes." Amelia crossed her arms and sat back in her chair. She started to pull away from me, and I'd barely begun the questioning.

"Did you witness anything when the murder occurred?"

"The lights went out, that gong sounded, and that was all I can tell you."

"Who were you near at the time?"

Amelia didn't answer right away, but I can tell she was working on coming up with one. "Danny Ewing? I don't know for sure, but he's been chatting me up all night. I can't shake the guy. Oh, and Claude. He's been equally creepy. Keeps saying he wants to suck my blood or some such nonsense. Apparently, he really got into character."

"Did Hawthorne get along with everyone here?"

Amelia shrugged. "I guess. They were all invited to the party, right? And everyone showed up rather than make other plans."

I leaned in a little closer. "Did Hawthorne ever mention anything unusual or seem concerned about someone or something?"

Amelia's brow furrowed, and she tapped her chin thoughtfully. "Not to me, he didn't. You should ask Jackie or Brantley that question."

"Did he have any enemies or conflicts that you were aware of?"

Amelia shook her head. "Not that I know of. From my perspective, his business dealings were usually…smooth."

I smiled. "And he paid all of his bills on time?"

I got no response.

"Within the limits of accepted accounting principles?" I added.

Amelia hesitated for a second, then smiled and nodded. "That's right."

"What happens with you now that your biggest client is gone?"

Amelia smiled a half-smile. "He wasn't my only client. I'll be fine. And someone will have to take over his estate, and of course, they may choose to keep me on as their accountant."

Her comment sparked a thought, so on my pad I scratched down two words in block letters. I drew three boxes around the words and set the pen down.

"Is anyone else here your client?"

Although her words hesitated, I followed her eyes and her gaze passed beyond me to the crowd behind. I imagined she balanced somewhere between the truth and a lie and didn't want to answer the question.

Finally, she answered. "I'm not sure that question has anything to do with the incident. I doubt it would make a difference one way or another if someone here was a client of mine or not, and professional ethics wouldn't allow me to say, anyway."

"You're not going to say?"

"No." The word spoken with a hint of harshness to it.

"I was told I would have everyone's cooperation if I agreed to do this," I said.

Amelia spotted a stray speck of lint on her dress, just above her left breast. She picked at it indifferently at first, then actively worked at setting it free. At last, she pulled the offending element from her, held it in the air for a moment to get a closer look at it, then let it fall to the floor. We both watched the white fuzz as it descended to the ground like a December snowflake.

"That was Brantley's deal, not mine," she said. "I'll answer any questions regarding tonight you may have, but I've got no interest in telling you about my business dealings or personal life unrelated to what happened here."

"Fair enough," I agreed. "Can you tell me anything about the attack on Viola Park?"

That question Amelia answered right away. "No more than I can tell you about the attack on Hawthorne. I saw you just before it happened, and since I can't see in the dark, I doubt I got any more knowledge about it than you do."

I couldn't dispute that. Whoever attacked Viola and Hawthorne had set it up perfectly to correspond with the cuts to the power. I made a note of that and hoped Brantley could shed a little light on it. Pun intended.

"Do you remember seeing Jackie come back into the room?"

Again, there was an extended pause, but I didn't think this one was one of evasion, but more one of recall.

"If I'm not mistaken, I was chatting with Loren at the time. Do you know him? Dressed as King Arthur? He's the pie king of central California. As we talked, I noticed Jackie staggering into the room. She looked around, probably for Hawthorne, and then she spotted the body on the floor. She stepped toward it, then walked backward until she fell right into the chair she's been sitting in since she got back."

"Do you know what time that was?"

"I can't tell you. I don't have a watch, and my phone is in my picnic basket."

When I glanced at her feet, I noticed she still didn't have it with her. "Where is it?"

Amelia shrugged. "If you have time for another mystery, I'd appreciate it if you solved that problem for me. You need anything else from me?"

I said no, and Amelia rose without fanfare, and after a stop at the bar for a Diet Coke refill, she returned to the group at the far end of the ballroom. I still had a few people to talk to, and as I moved to stand, I glanced back at the words I'd written earlier. A question that I needed to answer. Who inherits?

CHAPTER ELEVEN

The next person I wanted to talk to was Loren, and I spotted him easily because he stood out in the crowd. He was facing away from me and seemed deep in conversation with Bozeman. When I had been in the room earlier, I had bypassed him at the meet and greet because we'd already broken bread, or rather, pie, together. As I stepped closer, I marveled at how detailed his costume was. From the back, the first thing I noticed was his rich, velvet cloak attached to his broad shoulders. The cloak bore images of heraldry, and contained the emblematic dragon of Camelot, its scales shimmering with shades of gold. A ruby made up its eye.

Atop his head sat a well-crafted crown, adorned with glass jewels that caught the light and cast a kaleidoscopic effect around him.

I stepped up and stood off to the side, so not to interrupt Bozeman in mid-sentence.

"So that's when Sonny turned to me and said I should have warned him there was a quilting bee going on," Bozeman said.

I didn't see the humor in it since I'd missed most of the story, but Bozeman and Loren seemed amused by it. They both laughed, Bozeman so hard he let a snort loose that made me giggle.

"Aw, man, that's great. Whatever happened to old Sonny?" Loren asked as he regained his composure.

"Last I learned, his wife left with the kids, and he started hanging with the wrong people. Ended up in the state penitentiary. That was about ten years ago," Bozeman said.

"That's too bad. He had everything going for him. Goes to show that you just never know. You looking for me?"

I didn't realize Loren had addressed me, so I missed the question at first. It took me a moment to catch up.

"Sure. Do you mind if I pry you away for a minute or two?"

I asked.

"Lead me away, my dear."

Loren turned toward me, giving me a full view of the rest of his costume. He wore a leather belt, embellished with intricate designs and fastened with a gleaming brass buckle. The belt held a scabbard that housed a sword. I had no doubt it was a replica of Excalibur. Although the scabbard covered the blade, I appreciated the mythical patterns that adorned the hilt.

When I first met Loren at the diner, he seemed like a giant, and the King Arthur getup made him even more imposing. As we walked to a nearby table, he carried himself as if he was the embodiment of the storied hero. Chivalry wasn't dead, as he waited to sit until I did.

"What can I do for you, milady?" Loren asked.

I smiled at him. "You can start by calling me Codi, and not milady."

Loren took the crown from his head and set it on the table. "Sorry. Sometimes I get too wrapped up in the role when I dress up."

"You do this often? Do you play King Arthur at the Renaissance fair?"

He smiled. I liked him and hoped he wasn't a murderer.

"No. But I do perform in the local theater productions when I can, and every December I always dress up like Santa and visit the local schools and shelters."

I could picture him dressed in a Santa suit. Because of his massive size and appearance, I wondered how many yuletide nightmares he gave children.

"What would you like to know, Codi?" Loren asked as he clasped his hands, threw one massive leg over the other, and leaned back in his chair.

"Anything you can tell me about tonight? Let's start with anything you know about the murder."

"I'm afraid I can't be much help there, Codi. Everything faded to black, and when the lights came back, I was just as shocked and surprised as anyone to see Hawthorne like that."

That answer seemed to be the outright winner, and to be honest, if someone asked me, it would be my reply as well. But I needed to ask that same question to everyone on the off chance someone noticed even the smallest of details.

"When the lights failed, you didn't see anything. That I get. I didn't either. Did you overhear anything? Like shoes squeaking on the floor? Or smell anything, like a passing cologne or perfume? Or sense anything, like a slight breeze as someone passed you?"

I hated the leading questions, but I'd gotten nowhere with the open-ended ones.

Loren dipped into silence. I couldn't hear him breathing, but I watched as his chest rhythmically rose and fell.

"No. Nothing. The only thing I got was a jab in the ribs."

"Where did that come from?"

Loren smiled. "From Viola. When the lights first dropped out, she got startled. She elbowed me right in the ribs."

"And you're sure it was her?"

He nodded. "Yep. She whispered an apology to me right after she hit me. Not that she needed to. I barely felt it."

"She whispered in your ear?"

Loren smiled. "More like in my upper arm. But it was her voice."

"Does anyone here have a problem with Hawthorne?" I asked.

Loren made a raspberry with his lips, then rolled his eyes. "Would be shorter if I told you who didn't."

"Okay, we can run with that."

"Did you get your money for tonight like I suggested?"

I nodded.

"So, then. You. Everyone else, excluding me and Viola, I'd be suspicious of," Loren said.

"Why should I let you off the list?" I asked.

"Remember how we talked in the diner? When he buys the

pies, I have my system to get the bread. As long as he shoots straight with me, I got no problem with him."

"And why not Viola?"

Loren didn't answer. He pointed to where Viola lay still on the floor, Laurel still by her side.

"I doubt that she'd shoot Hawthorne in a room full of witnesses and then knock herself out to throw everyone off the scent," Loren said.

He had a valid point.

"What about when Viola got hit? Did you witness anything, then?"

I saw a flash of anger run through Loren's eyes. Then, just as quick, it transformed into a tinge of sadness.

"Again, I didn't see anything. But I can tell you that when I figure out who did it, that man is done."

I reached out and put my hand over his. "I'm sorry. Were you and Viola dating?"

Loren nodded. "We've been seeing each other on and off since she first moved here. It didn't mean to start out romantic, but..."

Loren trailed off, and I nodded. I understood since I've written more than my fair share of songs about friends that have become more over the passage of time. I felt the overwhelming need to change the subject.

"Tell me, are you a client of Amelia Brown?"

Loren leaned in and as he did, his shadow passed over me like a solar eclipse. "Did she tell you I was?" he whispered.

"No, but she eluded someone here is. Since you're a business owner, you are the most logical person."

Loren shook his head furiously. I suspected the crown would have flown from his head had it not been already on the table.

"Do not trust that woman," he growled. "I have it on good authority that she's a cheat and encourages her clients to cheat. And not only on their taxes."

"Has she ever approached you to be a client?"

"Oh, yes. She came to the diner once. All flash and no substance. Tried to talk her way right into being a business partner."

"What happened?" I asked.

"I tossed her out without fanfare and banned her from the place."

"If you're not working with her, does anyone here?"

Loren stood, turned, and started reviewing faces. As he did, he pointed at people, which told me that subtlety wasn't his strong suit. After a minute, he sat down again. "Maybe the Ewings. Maybe Claude. Hawthorne was for sure, but anyone else is simply a guess on my part."

"Based on what you told me before, you think everyone besides you and I potentially have a grievance with Hawthorne?"

Loren smiled. "I'd probably rule out Bozeman too. He wouldn't hurt a fly. Unless it was drunk and obnoxious. Oh, and the fiddle girl."

"Laurel," I provided.

"Right. Laurel."

"Why?" It was meant to be an internal question, but it slipped out.

"Money, sweetheart. The answer is always money. You think Jackie over there is attracted to a man almost three times her age because they have great conversations? Amelia's been cooking his books for years. Brantley's been the inside man for forever. Claude's his attorney. Money connects everyone here. It makes the world go around."

"What about the Ewings?" I asked. "Or Helen?"

"Good question. I've never met them before."

"Sorry. I just assumed you did," I said.

"I would have made the same mistake. But I would bet that the reason they're here is so Hawthorne could get something out of them."

I sighed. "Okay, I guess you can go on back to Bozeman.   I know where to find you if I need additional information."

Loren stood, put his crown back on his head, and bowed at me. "Yes, milady."

I laughed, and Loren walked away.

Since I had a moment alone, I took a few notes about things Loren had said, then quickly reviewed them. I looked around at who to talk to next. By my count, I was down to only four, and the first of those headed my way.

"Mind if I sit down?" Helen asked, taking the chair before I responded.

"Go ahead," I said.

"I noticed you standing alone over here and thought I'd come over instead of waiting for you to come to me. You were intending on coming to me, right?"

"Yep. Just about to come to you, in fact," I said, although I hadn't actually decided on who to pester next.

"I saw nothing happen. It was dark. Too dark. You remember, right? Boom! Lights gone out."

Helen was a bundle of energy, which, to me, didn't match the mood of everyone else in the room. Circumstances had trapped us in here together. Over several hours, with nothing to do except make awkward conversations with people we'd love to get away from, anyway. Not to mention the emotional drain of being witness to a murder and an assault.

"What about when Viola got attacked? Did you notice anything at all?" I asked.

Helen took a deep breath, like she was preparing to fill a balloon. "Nope. No. Not a single thing. Again. Lights out, lights on."

She stopped speaking, and I hesitated to ask another question. She seemed wired to me. I'd been around the music scene long enough to know when people were doing special substances. Although I'd always been clean, and expected

Bozeman to remain the same, I'd seen enough people in a manic state like the one Helen currently displayed.

I hoped to tune down the volume a little and calm the situation.

"So, Helen, what do you do?"

"Do?" she asked.

"Yes. Like for work." I didn't think it was a hard question, but apparently, I was wrong.

"I'm…"

Helen trailed off like she'd fallen asleep, but she wasn't. Her eyes were wide open and darting back and forth, unable to focus on anything.

"Helen? Hello? Can you hear me?" I asked.

Whatever vacation she just went on ended, and her eyes settled back to mine.

"What do you do for work?" I repeated.

"I'm a personal trainer. Diet and fitness coach," she finally said.

In my mind, that would explain her excellent figure. Well, working out and the drugs I imagined she was on.

"Was Hawthorne one of your clients?" I asked.

She grinned. "Oh, yes. We had sessions almost every day. He was insistent about it. Said he wanted to pay… special attention to his physical fitness."

I felt the urge to give up an eye roll, but I fought it and won.

"Did he pay you?"

Her grin grew wider. "Oh, yes. He paid me very well."

"Did you work out with Jackie, too, or just Hawthorne?"

Her smile disappeared like I'd erased her face.

"No. Never her. Just him."

"And when everything went down tonight, you didn't notice something unusual?" I clarified.

"Nope," Helen answered.

"You didn't hear or smell anything?"

"Nope. Not a single thing. Can I go now? I need to use the

restroom again."

"Again? How many times have you gone?"

Helen shrugged. "I don't know. You'd have to ask the cowboy." The right strap of her dress fell off her shoulder. She made a half-hearted attempt to fix it, but when it fell again, she gave up on the exercise.

I gathered up the notebook, wrapped my arm around Helen's, and led her away from the table.

When we got to within four feet of Bozeman, she pulled away from me and raced to him.

"Hey, cowboy. Can you escort me to the restroom?" Helen cooed.

"I can take you," I offered.

She waved me off. "Oh, no, that's fine. He knows the way. Don't you, cowboy?"

Bozeman exhaled through his nose, which was a telltale sign she irritated him. "Yes, ma'am. It's no trouble at all."

Bozeman got to his feet and Helen slipped under his arm like they were long-time lovers. Together, they walked off into the proverbial sunset, leaving Loren and me behind.

"She's an interesting one," I said.

"No doubt. She's bad news," Loren said.

I turned to face him. "Wait. I thought you said you've never met her."

"And that's true. But I know of her. She's been in the diner a few times. Usually trying to drum up business for whatever it is she's doing. What was it? Some kind of gym thing?"

"She told me she does personal training. Diet and fitness."

Loren scoffed. "Well, my staff tells me she likes to drum up other business. Usually down at the beach when the surfers come to town. I understand she likes to peddle the white powder, and I'm not talking about confectioner's sugar. You catch that drift?"

I nodded. "That would certainly explain her odd behavior. How many times has she gone to the bathroom?"

Loren scratched his chin. "I think three since Boze and I have been talking. Although I'm not sure if she's been using that as an excuse to talk to your man."

I considered the point for a second. Helen wouldn't be the first woman who tried to get Bozeman's attention. There were plenty of times where after gigs we'd find a woman hanging around the bus waiting for him. One time, an entire bridal party had approached him. They hoped the cowboy would wrangle the bride into one last rodeo before she walked down the aisle the next morning. He never took anyone up on their kind offers. At least on the bus. If Bozeman was interested in a woman, he'd typically make sure his business happened away from the bus. I think that was partially out of respect for me, and partially out of his desire to keep his private life private.

"It's not my business, but I don't think she's really his type if she is trying to get some action," Loren said.

I remembered back to all the women I'd seen Bozeman take an interest in. He'd dated blonds, brunettes, and redheads. Tall women and short, skinny and heavier set. The thing that attracted him the most was personality, a good sense of humor, and sobriety.

"I agree. She's got no shot if she's playing that game."

"Did you get any information out of her?" Loren asked.

If I had him on the top of my suspect list, I would have avoided the question, assuming he was trying to get me off his trail, but at this point, I had other people in mind, so I took his question merely as a way to make small talk.

I shook my head. "Not really. In the condition she's in, I'm surprised she didn't answer a question about what her name is with a recipe for a peanut butter and jelly sandwich. One missing the jelly. And bread. And peanut butter. She was pretty much useless to me. I'll have to pass her back to Viola when she wakes up."

At the mention of Viola, Loren looked over to where she still lay quietly on the floor. I looked as well. Laurel was no longer sitting on the floor with her, but she had pulled a chair close and settled into it. She'd also taken the time to cover Viola with a folded over tablecloth. Although I wanted Viola to jump up and take control of the room, it pleased me to see Laurel was taking good care of her.

"Don't worry. She'll be okay," I said.

"How can you tell for sure?" Loren asked.

"Look at Laurel's face. Does she look worried?"

Loren's eyes went from the floor to Laurel. In silence, he studied her countenance for almost a full minute. "No. She looks tired and bored. And uncomfortable from sitting in that chair. But she doesn't look worried."

I put my hand on his shoulder. "Then you shouldn't either. Trust me. Viola will be fine."

"They're coming back," Loren said.

I shifted in my seat and watched as Bozeman escorted Helen into the room. Rather than bring her back in our direction, Bozeman guided her to the opposite side of the room and sat her down in a chair near where Amelia and Brantley were deep in conversation. Once he got her settled, Bozeman came back to us and took his seat. He removed his hat, put it on his lap, and ran his fingers through his hair.

"I reckon she needs some serious help."

"And let me guess, you're just the man to give it to her?" I prodded.

Bozeman, rather than speak, growled at me.

I smiled. "I take it no wedding bells are on the horizon then."

CHAPTER TWELVE

"Hi there," I said as I slid into the chair next to Danny Ewing.

From somewhere he'd appropriated not one or two, but three bottles of wine.

Initially, he'd had the bottles of Sauvignon Blanc clustered in a little triangle, but one had tipped over at one point. Part of me wanted to pick it up and place it back where it belonged, complete with the labels lined up to the front, but I let the bottle lie where it was.

He stared at me for a moment before answering. I noticed the synapses were slow to fire, I suspected, because of the wine and whatever else he'd imbibed during the night. Finally, he found his focus.

"You're the band," he slurred.

"Part of it, anyway. What's your name?" I asked.

He smiled and sat straighter in his chair. I suspected he thought I was hitting on him. If that made him more willing to answer my questions, I was all for it.

"Danny. Danny Ewing."

"You're here with your wife, right?" I asked.

At the mention of the wife, Danny got a little rattled, and his eyes began to dart around the room, and he almost fell from his chair when he shifted to peek behind him.

"You see her anywhere?" he asked.

"Nope," I lied. She was sitting fifteen feet away and staring at me. I passed her a tentative wave. She waved back, but with only one finger. I was looking forward to my conversation with her.

"So, sugar, what's your phone number?"

He grinned like a jack-o'-lantern as he leaned toward me and told me the digits. He teetered for a moment, and I imagined gravity would eventually take hold and he'd tumble into my lap. I reached out for his shoulder and pushed him back into his chair.

"Do you like me? I look good, don't I?" he asked.

I stopped for a moment to glance at him.

On his feet, he wore square-toed platformed boots I suspected added a good three inches to his height. He wore a tattered, dark-colored suit, stitched together with different fabrics. Large, oversized patches adorned the clothing, creating a patchwork effect that reminded me of the creature's pieced-together appearance.

On his head, he wore a flat-topped wig of dark hair, but over the course of the night it had become dislodged and sat atop his dome at a slight angle like he was wearing a jaunty hat instead of a wig. I fought another urge, this one from ripping the thing from his head completely and tossing it across the room.

On the right side of his neck, he had a plastic bolt attached. He'd lost the one on the left somewhere, and I made a mental note to see if I might locate it. If I found it beneath either Hawthorne's or Viola's body, I thought that would take me a far way to finding the perpetrator. Of course, his face, neck, and the tops of his hands he painted in greenish-gray tones to resemble closely the movie monster, but like the bolt and the wig, the paint was wearing away, especially at his neck where I assume he'd been rubbing himself. I made another mental note to see if I could spot any speck of body paint on either of the bodies, or on the candlestick someone had clobbered Viola with.

I wasn't much for lies, but I told a second fib over the course of as many minutes. "Sure. You look great."

He grinned again. It disturbed me.

"What do you do for work?" I asked.

"What word?"

"Work," I repeated. I slowed my speech and over-enunciated the word to offset the brain fog he was hearing through.

"Right. Where I work. Realty." He extracted a business card from a pocket. I took it by the edges to not smudge the fingerprints he'd just given me and looked at it. Based on the card, he not only worked in real estate, but was the president of his own company. Carefully, I placed the card between the sheets of the notebook near the spine so it wouldn't slip out. I would have preferred to drop it into an evidence bag, but not only would that seem suspicious, I didn't have one on me.

"Do you do a lot of business with Hawthorne?" I asked.

He sat in silence. For a moment, I thought the drink had taken him to dreamland. Eventually, he glanced around to see who might overhear us, then leaned forward again. This time, he leaned so far forward, the back legs of the chair lifted from the ground. Once again, I pushed him backward so he wouldn't fall. I didn't want that to happen. At least, not until I'd left the general area.

He leaned forward again, not as far, then dropped his voice. "Want to learn a secret?"

I nodded. "Of course. I love secrets."

"We were about to close a deal that will transform this town completely," he whispered.

"How? To me, he looks like he already has the most impressive property in the county."

Of course, I didn't know that for sure. I'd only seen part of the outside of the compound, and the few rooms I had permission to enter.

"No. I'm not talking about this place. I'm talking about the gold mine along the highway. There are lots of opportunities to tear down many of the ramshackle buildings and put up shiny new ones. A new bank, new office complexes, new restaurants, parking lots, and the like. Revitalize this town completely." He grinned yet again as he sat back. I began to hate that disgusting expression on his face.

"Wouldn't the town have anything to say about one person owning so much property?"

Danny picked at a nail, then flicked the dirt to the floor. "Not a word. Especially since there's a new town hall and a public library in the plans, too. Get the picture?"

I got it in color and in 3-D. Loren was right. It was all about the money.

"What about Loren's little diner?" I asked.

Danny started to snicker, then full-out laughed. "That diner will become a paid municipal parking lot with trails down to the beach. It will add at least a million dollars of revenue to the town coffers every year."

Loren hadn't mentioned anything about anyone buying the diner from him. I wondered if he even knew, or if the town was going to play the eminent domain card.

I took a moment to jot down some notes. As I did, I asked my next question. "Can you tell me anything about what happened to Hawthorne or Viola tonight?"

I waited for the answer, as I read what I'd just written. I looked up and realized I wouldn't get a reply. Danny had leaned back in his chair, chin on his chest, softly snoring.

"Great," I said to him, expecting nothing back.

"He never could hold his liquor," Frankenstein's bride said.

I looked at the woman whose name I still couldn't remember. She wore a long, flowing white gown, which contained random rips and frayed edges. Along the neck was an intricate tulle pattern, but that too looked in disarray. Her hair was the most striking feature. She had it styled in a high, wild beehive, teased and sprayed with a gray streak in an homage to the movie classic. Like her husband, she, too, wore makeup. Unlike Danny's green pallor, the bride went with a pale, almost luminescent, with a greenish undertone. She wore dark, exaggerated eye makeup, including heavy eyeliner and mascara, which gave the impression of deep-set and haunting eyes.

"If he really took out three bottles of wine by himself, he gave it a good fight," I responded.

"I'm Cody Cassidy," I said as I held out my hand, hoping she would take the bait.

She fell for my ruse. "Amy Ewing."

I quickly wrote her name on the next page. Amy. I at least had the first letter correct when I'd guessed before.

"Did you actually get any information out of him, or did he try to pick you up?" Amy asked bluntly.

"What?" Her question surprised me and dropped me into a

defensive posture. Not that this was the first time I've had to deal with a jealous spouse.

"What did he give you? I saw him pass you something."

"Just his business card," I said, regaining my footing.

"The one with his private number?" Amy said, barely giving me time to answer before launching into the next question.

"Beats me," I honestly said. "I only glanced at it before I tucked it away. Don't worry though, I have no intention of contacting him."

Amy locked eyes with mine for a moment, then gave me a curt nod. "You have to understand, he has this annoying habit of trying to pick up women, especially when he drinks."

It wasn't my business. I only wanted to finish questioning her so I could move on to the lawyer.

"How long have you been married?" I asked. It wasn't pertinent, but I asked anyway, to regain my role as the questioner.

"Six years," Amy said. She picked up the two standing wine bottles, and as she discovered each was empty, she set them back where they were. She spotted Danny's full glass near his hand, took that, and drank down the contents. "You really should open the bar back up. It's not like Hawthorne's going to need to drink anymore."

"Can you run through what you experienced tonight with Hawthorne?" I asked.

She glanced at her husband, saw he was still out, and spoke.

"I don't understand what help I can give you. I'm sure you've heard the same story a dozen times tonight already. You were playing. The thunderstorm started going crazy, the lights went out, and all of a sudden, Hawthorne was down. You know when we can get out of here? I'd really like to go home."

With some effort, I threw her a half-hearted smile. "I get you. I'd love to leave too, but we're stuck here for a while yet."
"Do you work with Danny at his realty company?" I asked.

Amy exhaled, then leaned over and undid her high heels and kicked them off. She draped her right leg over her left and began to massage her foot.

"No. I'm the bank president," Amy answered without

looking back at me. "I should have worn my Nike shoes instead of these stupid things. No one ever looks at a person's feet, anyway."

"Right," I agreed. "Dress shoes can be annoying and uncomfortable. I can't stand them myself."

Of course, I found them annoying to where I didn't even own a pair. I only owned sneakers, cowboy boots, and flip-flops. One of the benefits I found of being a country singer was high-end designer shoes weren't an expectation.

"Did you know about the real estate deal that Danny and Hawthorne were putting together?" I asked.

Amy let her foot drop to the floor and shook her head. "He told you about that?"

I nodded.

"He's such an idiot. There's no way he should discuss that project with a stranger."

"So, you did. Is it as big as he laid it out?"

Amy shrugged her shoulders and clammed up. "I'm not at liberty to say."

I put my notebook aside. "Brantley said y'all would cooperate with me."

"Brantley is another idiot. He and Danny could have dressed as twins tonight. Look, I don't know anything about Hawthorne's murder other than it's tragic."

"What about what happened to Viola? She didn't hit herself on the back of the head."

"No clue. It wasn't me, though. And it couldn't have been Danny."

"You're vouching for him? You've been together the entire night?" I asked.

"No. But I've kept him in sight. You know who would be his perfect alibi if he were to admit to it? Her."

Amy pointed across the room, where I saw Dracula speaking to Dorothy.

"Amelia? Why her?"

"I have no clue. But he's been talking her up all night. Surely, you've seen it."

I had. I remembered the look of irritation on Amy's face at

dinner.

"What are you talking about?" Danny asked. Neither one of us noticed he'd woken and was ready to get into the conversation.

"About that tail you're always chasing," Amy said to him, a sharp edge in her voice.

Danny sat back in his chair, closed his eyes, and exhaled. "I'm not chasing any tail. Again, for the billionth time, you're my favorite and only tail."

"Then what about her? You're always talking about her." Amy raised her voice and changed her pitch on the last half of the sentence that I recognized as a beginning of an argument. I did the best thing I could at the moment, which was to grab the notebook, leave the lovers to their quarrel, and seek out Dracula.

When she saw me approach, Amelia stopped speaking in mid-sentence and scurried away. Dracula, who had his back to me, seemed uncertain about what to do, and took a step to follow her when I tugged at his cape and stopped him.   He turned, spotted me, and his shoulders slumped.

"Ms. Cassidy," he said, not even trying to give me the traditional Bela Lugosi accent.

"Mr...."

"Garrison. Claude Garrison."

"Can we talk for a few moments?" I asked.

"That depends. I understand you think you're doing a favor to Viola by getting statements, especially since she's unable to do the work herself at the moment, but you've got no proper authority here. Any statement you've gotten here tonight, any mediocre lawyer could get thrown out during a trial."

"Can I ask what you do, Claude?"

"I'm Hawthorne Harris' attorney."

"Interesting. I assume you don't know what happened here tonight?"

He nodded.

"Can you tell me who will inherit the estate and the business, and everything else?"

"I can't say," he said. "Before you ask, I can't say because I've never seen his will."

"Do you know if he has one?" I asked.

"I believe so, but until it's brought forth and read, I can't really say for sure."

"What kind of cases do you represent him on?"

"Mostly lawsuits and contracts."

"What sort of lawsuits?" I asked.

Claude moved to a chair nearby and sat. "Oh, the usual. Frivolous lawsuits that always came out of the woodwork. Everything from employee lawsuits from his business to trip and fall claims from his properties. He once had a gardener try to sue him because the gardener was allergic to the flowers Hawthorne wanted planted. Can you imagine that? Why would you even choose to be a gardener if you're allergic to gardens? That one got thrown out of court pretty fast. My services were probably overkill. A good paralegal or even someone who has watched more than an hour's worth of a courtroom drama could have handled it."

"Are there any pending from anyone here tonight?"

"Nope," Claude answered immediately.

"How can you be so certain?" I asked.

"If it was one thing Hawthorne was excellent at, it was holding grudges. He wouldn't have anyone near here who had a lawsuit against him."

I took a brief note, then I put down my pen. "What about the contract side? Can you share anything about those?"

"That I cannot do. Most of those pending contracts are not in the public domain yet, so they'll stay a secret."

"What about the one where Hawthorne was attempting to buy up half the town?"

"Where did you hear about that? That one is under the strongest lock and key we have."

"Danny Ewing is currently under a stronger influence, and according to my sources, he's a bit of a tattletale."

Claude smiled at me. "So, he drank too much, and him and Amy spilled the beans."

"You got it. According to them, Hawthorne was in a position to revamp the town, at the expense of a lot of the people who live here. Is that true? New bank? Library? Some businesses razed to the ground and turned into parking lots while he adds another billion to his portfolio?"

"No comment." Claude shifted in his seat, and I guessed right then every word was as true as the sky was blue.

"Well, someone else should expect to make a ton of money. What about the construction of all these new buildings? Who would do that?" I asked.

Claude mumbled something that I didn't quite hear, so I asked him to repeat what he said.

"Hawthorne Construction won the bid for any construction regarding the project you're talking about," Claude answered.

"Hawthorne Construction? I thought he was in the sardine business."

Claude chuckled. "Have you never heard of diversification? Hawthorne was into much more than sardine canning. He owns a fleet of boats to catch them. And a printing firm to print the labels, along with magazines, and anything else a client needs. Along with sardines, his plant also cans fruits and vegetables. He also owns a car dealership through another name, two restaurants, and a large construction firm that can handle everything from putting in roads to erecting an outhouse."

"He brokered a deal to buy all the land, then got the contract to rebuild the town? Sounds like he was double dipping in the deal."

Claude waved a hand at me. "Doesn't matter. It is all above board, and perfectly legal."

"Can you think of anyone in a competitor's construction company who might have not been so happy with the deal?"

Claude thought for a moment. "I'm sure there were several. There are winners and losers in any bid. As I recall, there were a dozen firms who submitted bids, but Hawthorne's company beat them all."

"I'm sure they did," I said. "Is there anyone in this room who will either benefit greatly or get destroyed by any deal Hawthorne was involved in?"

Claude winked. "You're the singer and amateur detective.

You figure it out."

CHAPTER THIRTEEN

After Claude left, I found myself alone in a room full of people. Rather than seek someone else to talk to, I immersed myself in my thoughts as I reviewed the notes I'd taken.

The lights blinked out again. Rather than return right away, they stayed out. Someone moaned, and someone else muttered the words 'not again'. I'd always found solace in the quiet moments, and normally didn't mind the darkness, but this was different. Bad things happened every time the lights went out here, and I instinctively pressed into my chair that I hoped would protect me from a potential attacker.

As I waited, my heart thudded in my chest as I strained my ears, trying to catch any hint of movement or sound. The silence was as pressing as the darkness. In my mind, I counted the seconds off as I sat uncomfortably waiting for the lights to return.

Off in the distance, I picked up a loud thud, as if something had fallen. With my luck, it was a chandelier toppling from the ceiling, creating yet another mystery I couldn't solve. I overheard whispers but couldn't make out any words. A flicker of panic surged within me. My mind raced through all the possibilities of the lights failing so consistently. I didn't think it was the storm causing it. I'd remembered someone saying something about a backup generator, and if that kicked on, I didn't expect the power would still be so shaky. There had to be something else, and I wanted the lights to return.

Then I remembered I had a light in the back pocket of my jeans. I leaned forward and found Laurel's phone. It took me only a few seconds to turn on the built-in flashlight, and with that on, I at least saw my feet. I considered heading over Bozeman's way, but then it dawned on me that if I could see using the little light, the perpetrator could also see me. That thought overwhelmed my mind, so I turned the light off and shoved the phone back in my pocket. At that moment, I realized I had seen no other lights during the outages. Phones were so prevalent I couldn't do a single show without seeing at least a dozen pointing in my direction, but tonight, except for the bar-back, no one else seemed to have one. I wondered why.

I considered my next move as I internally counted off the seconds of darkness. Funny how the seconds seemed to stretch when one couldn't see. Then, with a sudden click, the darkness shattered as the room was once again flooded with light. Since the light had been out for an extended time, I blinked against the brightness, squinting as my eyes adjusted to the sudden change. I glanced around the room and noticed that everyone else seemed to be no worse for the wear.

I wanted to figure out what the sound was, and to do that, I wanted to get a little help, so I approached Bozeman and Laurel, who were still sitting together.

"How is Viola?" I asked.

Laurel looked down at her patient. "She seems to be sleeping. Breathing is fine, and I've checked her pulse periodically, and that's remained steady. She'll need a scan to determine if she has a concussion, but that will have to wait until we can get her to a hospital."

"You've done a good job with her. Thank you," I said.

Laurel smiled, but didn't respond.

"Did either of you hear that noise when the lights were out just now?" I asked.

"Sounded to me like a chair fell over," Laurel said.

Bozeman disagreed. "I don't imagine it was a chair. It sounded smaller, with not as much heft to it."

I considered it for a moment, trying to replay the sound in my mind, and I tried to determine the direction from which it came. Finally, it hit me.

"Come with me," I instructed Bozeman. I headed toward the stage with Bozeman right on my heels, and before we'd even gotten there, I saw what had happened. My microphone stand was lying on its side. I stepped onto the riser and picked it up.

Concerned that my favorite Shure microphone had taken some damage, I examined it carefully, looking for dents or other issues.

"Codi," Bozeman said.

"I guess it's okay," I answered. "I can hook it up to one of the small amps and give it a quick test."

"Codi," Bozeman repeated. This time, something in his tone told me I should forget about the microphone for a moment.

I turned to face him. "What?"

He didn't speak, he simply pointed at my old wooden stool on which I usually kept my water, and an extra guitar pick or two if I dropped mine during a show. When I wanted to get down-homey with the audience, I would sit on the stool and play an acoustic number.

I glanced at the stool. My water bottle was on the floor, leaning against the stool's leg. Next, I saw the guitar picks scattered across the floor.

"Codi. Please, look," Bozeman insisted.

Finally, my eyes focused on the top of the stool. And there, lying innocuously on the round seat, was a single sheet of paper, folded in half. My heart raced with a mixture of curiosity and apprehension as I leaned to take a closer look. The paper was part of the set list I'd printed for Laurel, and someone had folded it so the song list showed on the outside. I unfolded the note cautiously, and my eyes widened as I read the stark message scrawled across the paper in bold, menacing letters: BACK OFF.

The words sent a chill down my spine, and my skin prickled with unease. I showed the note to Bozeman and set it back on the stool. I turned around and faced the room, like I was ready to give a performance, but instead, I studied the room and tried to notice if anyone was watching with interest, or if I could pick up any tell of who might have left me the love letter.

Someone tried to intimidate me, but that was a mistake. Because of my size, people had been trying to intimidate me for my entire life, but it wasn't going to work. Over the years, I'd grown a spine and an unstoppable spirit, both of which I was more than ready to use. I refused to be intimidated, refused to let fear dictate my actions. The note was simple, for me to back off. That meant to me I needed to double down and figure this thing out before I was the next person receiving a candlestick at the back of my head.

I took a deep breath, and I felt my resolve harden. More than ever, I was determined to uncover the truth. And I knew just where to start.

I left Bozeman on the stage, and I headed right for Brantley. He locked eyes with me when I was still several strides away. He attempted to step backward, but since he was at the edge of a table, he had nowhere to escape to.

"What's up, Brantley?" I asked when I'd got close enough for the tips of my shoes to touch his green boots.

"What… what do you mean?"

"I'm really curious about a few things, and the first of which is why the lights keep going out."

"It's a power fluctuation. We get them all the time when storms roll through. All the time," Brantley answered.

"We all live and work around here, and have gone through severe storms before, and we've never had a problem with the power grid," Loren said.

During my brief bout of tunnel vision, as I wanted to question Brantley, I hadn't noticed the group that had gathered. Loren was standing just to the left of me, and Amelia, Helen, Amy, and Claude gathered in a small semi-circle around Brantley and me. Perhaps they were expecting a good old-fashioned schoolyard fight. The thought crossed my mind as well, and I had to admit, I was ready if it came to that.

"No. I don't mean the grid itself," Brantley said. "I think I explained before that when there's even a second of power disruption, the automatic systems pop into place. The generator turns on, and the house locks down."

"Why?" I asked.

"Why?" Brantley repeated. Apparently, he was having trouble understanding my questions all of a sudden. He made me question if I had to slow things down for him and enunciate better, or if I had to get closer to his face.

"Why," I repeated. "Why does the house go into a full fortress mode at the loss of an amp of power?"

Brantley tried to move back, but encountered the table again. Instead, he boosted himself up and sat, trying to look nonchalant in the process. "I shouldn't say. Mr. Harris wouldn't like it."

I threw a thumb over my shoulder toward the body. "Honestly, I don't think he's going to object at all."

Brantley sighed. "Okay, okay. Several years ago, there was an incident here. A small group of thieves waited until the early morning hours, then cut the power at the main line. After they broke in, they held Mr. Harris at gunpoint until he opened his safe. They got away with money, jewelry that had been in the family for generations, and a couple of paintings. A Rembrandt and a Van Gogh, if I'm not mistaken."

"So that prompted the power to cut over?" I asked.

Brantley nodded. "And more. He hired a security company to do an assessment of the property. On their recommendation, Mr. Harris added the guard out front, along with a roaming night patrol. And the generator, along with an electrified fence. Rumor has it there are multiple safe rooms in the house now, but I know of only one myself. I also heard he added a huge walk-in safe behind a wall somewhere, but I've seen no evidence of that."

"After the robbery he became a paranoid recluse?" Loren asked.

"A recluse, no. Paranoid? Certainly. I think he would have added a moat filled with crocodiles if it wouldn't have been a potential eyesore."

"What about the thieves? They get caught?" Amelia asked.

"Almost immediately. And only because of their bad luck. A local cop had pulled over a speeder, who had turned into the driveway to get off the road. The thieves, in their hurry to escape, plowed right into the unlucky speeder's car."

"I didn't know about that," Claude said.

"No one did. Hawthorne feared if people knew, he'd be even more of a target. So, he buried it deep. He even managed to keep it out of the papers," Brantley said.

"To get back to my original question, what's the deal with the lights?" I asked. "Even if the generator didn't get wired correctly,

I wouldn't expect that the power would fail so much. And it's doubly suspicious that every time the lights go out, something bad happens."

"Unless there's someone standing over there by the switch." I looked at the doorway where I expected the light switches to be, just like every other building on the planet. There weren't any. It was the only entry into the room, so I didn't bother looking elsewhere other than where they should be. "Where are the light switches?"

"There aren't any in this room," Brantley said, like it was a logical answer.

I rolled my eyes. I was growing tired of having to ask questions to people like I was interrogating a group of five-year-olds who didn't speak English.

"Look, Brantley. Stop with the word play. If there aren't any light switches in this room, how are the lights controlled? I can't imagine they just stay on until all the bulbs burn out."

"There's an app for the lights in this room that Mr. Harris uses."

I stared at him, hoping he'd get the hint that he should expand on his answer, and eventually he did. "When Mr. Harris made the security improvements to the house, he also added technology to turn it into a smart house. Cameras, an app to control the lights and temperature, that sort of thing. Surely, you've seen those commercials where people turn on the lights before they even get home? Or have those doorbells they can answer remotely?"

I was well on my way to frustration. "I don't watch a lot of television. Who has access to the app?"

Brantley stewed on it for a while. "Mr. Harris, of course. I have it. The security chief, and I believe the head maid."

"That's it?" I asked.

He nodded.

"Is that annoying dinner gong controlled the same way? Through an app?"

"Yes. The same one. It's quite remarkable. It can dim the lights, play audio, all kinds of things."

"Fascinating. Can I see your phone, Brantley?"

"No. I don't have it with me," he said.

"I find that hard to believe."

"No, it's true. Mr. Harris didn't like people having phones at his dinner party."

"Paranoia again?"

"No. He simply thought that people should live in the moment and enjoy each other's company without doing so behind a phone."

"Laurel had a phone on her. So did the bar-back. So did Viola."

"He wasn't as concerned about the band. We should have checked the bartender, and we wouldn't have allowed the phone in had we found it. Heather has worked with us before. She knows all the rules quite well. They're all spelled out right there in the contract."

"And Viola?" I asked.

"Why, she's the police chief," Brantley answered. "She wouldn't have parted with it even if we'd asked her to. A call could come in for her at any time, and there have been events here where she's been called away on police matters."

That tracked with me. My dad was the same way. He always said he was a cop twenty-four hours a day, eight days a week, three hundred and sixty-six days a year. Even when on vacation out of state, he carried his badge and gun, just in case. Fortunately for the family, he never got pressed into service when he was enjoying his well-needed time off.

"What about the patrol?" I asked.

Brantley didn't answer at first. Once again, he looked at me as if he hadn't heard the question.

"You said before at night there were roaming night patrols. Why hasn't anyone come in to our rescue?" I pushed.

"The gate closed and locked. No one will get in until it's unlocked." Brantley said.

"What about the guard at the shack? That was inside the gate, wasn't it? I seem to remember driving through the pillars, then down the road for a spell before we got to the guard. He was well within the gate. What happened to him, Brantley?"

"I don't have an answer to that question. You're right. The guardhouse is always manned, and as soon as the compound went into lockdown, he should have been in here."

"Where is he, then?" Helen asked.

I glanced at Helen when she asked the question. She looked like she'd come down some since I'd last talked to her, but her eyes had reddened, and her complexion seemed a little off. I assumed she was in the middle of a crash.

"Good question, Helen," Amy added. "Where is the guard if there's someone always on duty? We've been stuck in here for literal hours now and no one has come to get us."

Brantley shook his head. "I'm sorry, I can't tell you. I've been here with you. All night. I don't have knowledge about anything going on outside of this room."

"And you've got no way to contact the guard?" Claude asked.

"We could try the land line again," Brantley said, pointing to the phone he'd try to use earlier.

"What's the number?" I asked.

"It's on speed dial. 8911."

I turned around and yelled to Bozeman across the room. "Boze, see if that phone works, will you? Try to get the guardhouse." I gave him the number and watched as he ambled to the phone and picked up the receiver. He put it to his ear and jiggled the hook switch a few times. He replaced the receiver and shook his head at me.

"I guess we're still cut off from the outside world."

"Unless we leave here," Amy said. "Why can't we just leave? Get in our cars and go?"

That was an excellent, simple solution to the problem.

"What about it?" I asked. "Could I send Bozeman out to get help?"

Brantley frowned, then shook his head. "I wouldn't advise it. He electrified the fences. The best we can do at this point is wait until daybreak and have someone stand by the gate and see if they can flag down a passing car."

It wasn't the news I wanted, but was the news I got, so for

now I had to live with it.

Some of the others had additional questions for Brantley, but I stepped away, my brain processing what I'd recently learned. As I headed back to the stage to talk to Bozeman, I surveyed the rest of the room. Laurel still sat next to Viola, diligently watching over her. Danny appeared to be sleeping off his wine, and based on the way he slumped in his chair, he would wake with the backache of a century. Jackie wasn't in the corner I'd left her in. She'd moved to another seat farther down the wall, between where she'd sequestered herself in the corner and the stage. Hawthorne still lay where he'd fallen, which, I thought, was a good thing. The last thing I needed to deal with was a zombie running amok.

I took another three steps forward, then stopped in my tracks. A question popped into my head. Why had Jackie switched seats?

CHAPTER FOURTEEN

Rather than heading right to Jackie and start up with my questions, I took a seat at a table nearby, and adjusted my chair so I could study her while I pretended to review my notes.

I started at the beginning of the notebook and turned the pages, stopped at each one for close to a minute before turning the next page. Although my head tilted down as if reading, I focused my eyes on Jackie.

To me, she looked like she fully recovered from the trauma of finding her fiancé dead on the floor. She no longer sobbed and appeared to be in complete control of herself. In fact, she looked downright bored, as if she were sitting in a bus station waiting for the eight-fifteen to Albuquerque. Her eyes no longer glistened with tears, and they occasionally darted around the room to take in everything else going on around her.

Jackie crossed her arms and uncrossed them again. She gave the impression that she couldn't decide how her body language would look to anyone else in the building. Like she tried a little bit too hard to play the role that she found herself in.

As to the other people in the room, she showed disinterest, if not disregard for each of us, and showed no initiative to interact with anyone.

"What's going on? Are you checking her out?" Bozeman said as he pulled up a chair and joined me.

"Am I being too obvious about it?" I asked.

"No. Not really. I love the way you use the notebook as cover. Super discrete move," he teased.

I chuckled. I would always count on Bozeman to break the tension.

"What's the deal, Codi?" he asked.

"I finished talking to Brantley a moment ago."

"I noticed. So now what?"

"Something is bugging me about her. Can you see where she's sitting?" I asked.

"Of course. She's right over by the wall. I would point at her, but that might break your cover." Bozeman grinned at me. He enjoyed getting my goat occasionally.

"When I came back from interviewing the catering crew, I found her in the back corner. She looked like her world had ended, and I imagined for sure she would have an emotional breakdown. But now she's over in that chair as composed as can be."

"That's all? You're suspicious of her because she calmed down?"

"No," I said, a little louder than I intended. Jackie looked at us for a moment and suddenly took an interest in her fingernail. I dropped my tone. "I'm also a little suspicious because she switched seats. She spent most of the night in the corner, and now she's almost on the stage."

Bozeman rubbed his chin, finally getting my gist. "You think when the lights left, she planted that note and didn't make it back to her original seat before they returned?"

I nodded. "Something like that, sure. But plausible?"

"I'd say so. You going to ask her about her movements?"

"I certainly am," I said.

"Before you do, I'd go check out her first chair."

"Why?" I asked.

Bozeman smiled. "I assumed you were the one with the super observation skills."

Calming myself, I took a moment, and before I spoke. When I looked over to where Jackie had been. I didn't notice anything unusual at first glance.

"What am I looking for?" I asked, no longer desiring to figure the mystery out on my own.

"Does anything seem different to you about the table compared to the one next to it?" Bozeman asked.

I looked again. This time, instead of the chair alone, I expanded my view to the tables next to the chair. The table farthest away from the chair looked normal. I observed two candlesticks on either end, and its surface held two empty wineglasses. The black tablecloth draped over the table dropped halfway down to the floor. In contrast, the table next to the first contained a tablecloth that dropped to within an inch of the floor and looked askew from where I sat.

"I think I'm going to go for a stroll," I said.

Leaving Bozeman at the table, I headed for Jackie's chair. When I arrived, I sat down. I looked around the room to see if anything had noticed my trip, and when I saw no one looking at me, including Jackie, I took a peek under the table.

"Well, I'll be a daughter of a gun," I said to myself.

Obscured by the tablecloth was a picnic basket, with a stuffed terrier sticking out of the top. I reached in and extracted my find. I set the basket on the table, removed the dog, and looked inside. At the bottom of the basket was a cell phone, and I had a good idea of who owned it. I put the puppy under my arm, picked up the basket, and sought Amelia.

"Hey, I found something you lost," I said as I approached Amelia.

She looked at me, at the basket, then at the stuffed dog under my arm. "Toto! Where did you find him?"

"He was in the picnic basket, just like when I saw him earlier this evening," I said. "I also found something else."

I opened the basket and extracted the phone. "Is this yours?"

Amelia opened her palm, expecting me to hand the phone to her, but I didn't.

"You didn't confirm that this is yours. Is it?"

"Open up the front. My driver's license is in there."

I opened the front cover of the light purple case and checked. From a slot, I extracted the license and confirmed it was Amelia's.

"Can I have it back now?" she asked.

"Can we check one thing on it first?"

"What?" she said.

"If that app is on there to control the lights," I answered.

"I don't even know what the app is, so there's no way it's going to be on there," she said.

She offered a good point. I didn't know what the app was

either, so I wouldn't recognize it if I were staring right at it.

"You mind if Brantley takes a look?" I asked.

Amelia shrugged indifferently. "I don't care. Knock yourself out."

I waved at Brantley from across the room, got his attention, and motioned for him to join us.

"What?" Brantley said in a huff when he got to us.

I handed him the phone. "Can you see if the app Hawthorne uses on the lights is on this phone?"

He took the phone from me and swiped a finger across it. "It's locked. How did you get this in here in the first place? You understand you can't have phones here."

Amelia shot him a coy smile, but didn't answer.

I grabbed the phone from him and handed it to Amelia. "Do you mind?"

Amelia took the phone, entered her security code, then passed it back to Brantley. He accepted it, accessed the apps, and scrolled for a while.

"Yep, here it is," he said as he handed the phone back to me.

I didn't use a lot of apps, but this one wasn't one I recognized as being in the mainstream. "Are you sure? I've never heard of this before."

Brantley rolled his eyes at me. "Open it up and try it. Mr. Harris had it created specifically for this house. It's not on the open market."

I touched the icon that resembled a castle, and the app opened. Once it did, a little map opened up, and I spotted a blinking blue dot. I zoomed in on the dot and as I did; I saw the layout of the ballroom on the screen. Several icons appeared on the screen. I pushed on a light bulb icon, and when I did, a sliding scale appeared, with a bar all the way at the top. When I touched the bar and moved it down, the lights above dimmed. I pushed it back to full. I touched the icon next to it, and the gong sounded. Satisfied, I closed the app.

"This leads to my next question. Why is this on your phone?"

Amelia held out her hand, expecting the phone. "Beats me. Never seen it before. I didn't even realize it was on there. You caught what Brantley said. It wasn't something on the open market, so whoever put it on there needed knowledge of it. Knowledge that I don't have. Besides, if I was involved in all this, do you think I'd be stupid enough to leave the app on there, then put my phone where anyone might find it? "

She had a valid point. But, then again, she might be playing me for a fool.

"Okay. Then how did it get there?" I asked.

"I can't tell you. Like I said, I lost it earlier tonight."

"Do you mind if I hold on to it?" I asked it as a question, but I didn't intend to give it back to her.

"Sure, but you have to do something for me. Try to call for help."

It wasn't an unreasonable request, so I activated the phone and attempted to dial 911. The call never connected.

"No luck," I said.

"Fine. Can you lock it again? I have information on there I'd prefer people not have access to."

I didn't think that was an unreasonable request, either, so I locked the screen, then shoved Amelia's phone into my pocket.

"Can I have Toto back now?" Amelia asked.

I hadn't realized I still had the toy under my arm in a death grip. Without comment, I handed her the dog and the basket.

"Thank you," Amelia said.

I wanted to keep my focus on Jackie, turned and took two steps before I stopped and turned back to Amelia.

"When did you lose your basket?" I asked.

Amelia thought about it for almost a full minute. "Actually, I can't quite put a finger on it."

"Did you have it at dinner?" I asked, already knowing the answer, since I'd seen it when I first met her.

"Yes. I'm one hundred percent sure of it."

"And then?"

Amelia considered it for another thirty seconds before answering. "I had it with me when we headed for drinks in the other room. I remember now. When we first came back here, just before your show, someone handed me a glass of champagne. I already had a glass, so I set the basket down next to me to take the glass."

"Why'd you set the basket down?"

"I had to put it down to take the other glass."

"Who gave it to you?" I asked, really wanting to learn the answer.

For the third time, Amelia thought it over. This time, the pause was unbearably long. "It was a man. Might have been Brantley or Danny, but I'm pretty certain Claude gave it to me."

"How certain are you? Eighty percent? Ninety?"

"Fifty? Forty?" Amelia said.

Those weren't the percentages I wanted. "Okay, thank you."

At last, I left Amelia and strolled across the ballroom to where Jackie was sitting. She saw me coming, and I confirmed she was indeed playing me since, by the time I got to her, the tears started flowing again.

"Hey, you. How are you holding up?" I asked as I dragged a chair over and sat in front of her, knees to knees.

Jackie sniffed once, then again for effect. She didn't fool me, but I let her think she had.

"I'm doing the best that I can considering… everything."

"Why did you move to here?" I asked, getting right to the point.

"What?"

"When I last talked to you, you were sitting in the corner over by the window," I said. I pointed in the general direction where I'd seen her last.

"I moved."

"Yes, I saw that. Why?"

Jackie's eyes moved from mine and appeared to focus on my right shoulder instead. I don't know what she was thinking, but I guessed it wasn't the truth.

"The storm," she said finally. "Every time the thunder pealed, the window shook, and I got scared. I moved here instead."

It was a possible truth, but her answer didn't totally win me over. "Why didn't you go sit with someone? There's an entire group of people here who I'm sure would love to keep you company. And offer you support, of course."

"No. These are all Hawthorne's friends and associates. I wanted to invite a couple of girlfriends of mine. Emily, from the gym I attend. She's my best friend. We talk every day. But Hawthorne said I couldn't invite anyone because he had only a certain number of seats available at the table."

"That's too bad," I said. I meant it. I'd seen people in that position several times over the course of my career. You put me on stage in any small venue where a group of people assembled, and I would always tell who the third wheel is, or who got a pity invite to the party. At the moment, Jackie was my number one suspect, but yet I felt empathy for her.

"That's true. I wish Emily was here with me now. I could really use her hug. She gives great hugs. You ever have a friend who gives great hugs?"

I nodded. Gibson will always be my go-to person for hugs, followed closely by Dolly, with Merle bringing up the rear. Gibson never failed to purr the second I picked him up. I could always count on Dolly to wrap her cute humanoid hands around my index finger. Merle loved to nuzzle my neck and occasionally mistook my ear for a grub. Fortunately, he only ever gave me playful nibbles.

"But Hawthorne said no. Emily couldn't come to the party."

"Did that make you angry?" I asked, looking for a motive.

"At first. But then, when he said you would be here tonight, that made up for it. After all, I'll see Emily at the gym tomorrow, right?" Jackie explained.

Unless she landed in jail.

"Did you have any other problems with Hawthorne? Any fights about marriage, or money, or living arrangements, or anything at all?" I asked.

"We argue sometimes," she admitted. "Every couple does. Usually just about little things about what to have for dinner, or what dress he wanted me to wear to whatever event we went to. It's always easy for a man, you know. They just have to put on a tuxedo and shiny shoes. We women have to worry about the right dress, and shoes, and jewelry. And perfect hair, and fancy nails, and smelling good. All that stuff, you know?"

I didn't really know since I always had my performance persona to slip into and it never involved a dress. In my closet, pushed all the way to the side, stuffed in a garment bag, was my one dress. Knee length, and black of course, so I could wear it to one of the two events I had it for, either a wedding or a funeral. No fancy shoes, though. That's why I had short black boots.

"Do you think I did this?" Jackie whispered.

"I'll give it to you straight. You're certainly a suspect. And near the top of the list."

"You know, there's someone in here who had a big grudge against Hawthorne."

"Who?" I asked.

"Amelia Brown."

That name surprised me. "Really? Why her?"

Jackie leaned forward. "I was supposed to be Hawthorne's first wife, but I wasn't his first fiancé."

You're telling me he was engaged to Amelia before you two got together?"

"Yes."

Now I seemed speechless.

"Amelia never mentioned that to me." I admitted.

"I'm not surprised," Jackie said.

"Were they together long?"

Jackie smoothed the dress over her knees and removed a piece of black lint before she answered. "Three or four years."

"She was his fiancé? Not just a girlfriend?"

"Nope. She had an enormous ring on her finger from him."

"You're sure?" I asked.

Jackie smiled, then wriggled the ring finger of her left hand. She wore at least two carets on that finger. "I'm sure. It looked exactly like this one."

"No way," I said. "That's the same ring? He took it off her finger and put it on yours?"

"Yes. It was his mother's. Or maybe his grandmother's. I forget which."

"Do you know what happened between them that caused the

breakup?"

Jackie shook her head. "Not entirely, but I have my suspicions."

I waited a beat for her to fill in more information, but she didn't get the hint.

"What were they? Your suspicions? Did they have something to do with her being his accountant?"

"No. Amelia is a strong, independent, capable woman. Hawthorne is one of those old-fashioned men. And by old-fashioned, I meant it in the Biblical sense. Women should stay seen and not heard. Should be happy in the kitchen and be a baby incubator. I think Amelia bit off more than she could chew when they got together. I've heard she tried her best to play that role, but in the end, she wouldn't do it. Amelia is too much of a modern woman to put up with his mindset for too long."

"She broke off the engagement? Not him?" I asked.

"That's what the rumor was around town. And since it's such a small town, that rumor spread around like a wildfire."

"How did he take that?"

"He tried to destroy her career for making him look bad. Threatened to take his business to other firms, and trust me, that would have sent her firm from riding high on the hog to right into the toilet."

"But yet she's still his accountant?" I asked. "And through all that, he still invited her to this party tonight?"

A small smile traversed Jackie's face. "That's where I came in. We met when he was still with her, and it didn't take long to get this ring onto my finger."

"He invited her here to make her jealous?" I asked.

Jackie nodded. "He had a mean streak that way."

"Why did he keep her on then?"

"Because I think he's still sleeping with her."

That comment caused me to do a double-take. "What? Do you know that for sure?"

"They worked a lot of long nights together, and usually when they did, they met at his office. Anyone else, they came here. He needed something from Danny, Loren, or even Helen, and they came here. To his office upstairs. But Amelia? Her, Hawthorne left the house for. That doesn't quite add up, does it?"

It did not to me, and I wanted to go back and ask Amelia a few follow-up questions. I got up and made my way halfway across the room. Just as I hit the exact center of the room, the lights went out. Again. This time, I reacted and pulled Amelia's phone from my pocket, intending to use the app to turn the lights back on. I opened the phone, encountered the lock screen, then shoved the phone back in my pocket. Before I could pull Laurel's phone out and activate the flashlight, I heard a crash behind me, and a muffled squeak that sounded like a large mouse.

I moved back toward where I left Jackie, misjudged my steps, and ran right into a table, knocking the wind out of me.

It took me a couple of minutes to regain my composure, and when I was ready to resume my march, the lights suddenly lit and I could see again.

Jackie's chair sat empty.

CHAPTER FIFTEEN

I figured Jackie must have gone somewhere, so I turned in a complete circle while searching for her. Unless she had squirreled herself away under a table or magically turned into a chair, Jackie wasn't in the room.

"Where in the world?" I said to myself. I spun in a circle a second time, just to make sure I hadn't missed her.

"What's going on?" Bozeman asked. "Is there a reason you're spinning like a top?"

"Do you see Jackie anywhere?" I asked.

Bozeman took a moment and spun in a circle himself.

"Nope. Perhaps she's over by the stage."

I nodded. The stage had a half-wall built on either side. Each wall only measured three feet wide by four feet high, but that still left plenty of room for someone to hide over there if they wanted to. I did the due diligence and headed for the stage.

I explored the left wing first. There, I discovered a stack of three cheap, vinyl-backed chairs. The kind I'd seen in conference rooms dozens of times. The chair on top had a slit through the seat, exposing the thin yellow foam beneath the brown vinyl. I suspected the other two also had damage of some sort.

When I moved to the right wing, my interest peaked when I noticed a black tablecloth covering something. I reached out and grabbed a hunk of cloth. I pulled with all my might, intending it to float free, like that trick where someone removes a tablecloth from a full set table and doesn't disturb a thing. That's the way it worked in my head. In reality, it didn't come free.

I yanked again and got the same results. Clearly, it snagged on something. I took a less impressive approach, found an edge, and worked the tablecloth free. When I finally had it released, I discovered the treasures beneath. Three crates of items. The top crate held a box of light bulbs for the chandeliers in the ballroom. I didn't bother to check what the other two contained since they were too small to hold Jackie. I dropped the tablecloth without covering the crates and returned to Bozeman.

"Well?" he asked.

"No luck. Did you spot her?"

He shook his head. "Neither hide nor hair."

"Okay. I'm going to go check the other rooms."

"You want me to go with you?" Bozeman asked.

"No. I'd like you to stay here in case she reappears. And keep your eyes on Amelia, too, since I want to have a friendly chat with her when I get back."

"Which one is Amelia?" he asked.

"The one dressed as Dorothy."

Bozeman nodded without speaking, and I left the room. The first place I checked was the room Heather and her crew were hanging out in. I stuck my head in the door, not wanting to get engaged in any conversation. Someone had brought decks of cards because they had broken into two groups and were playing a card game I didn't recognize. It didn't take me long to notice Jackie wasn't among them.

I did a lap around the area I was familiar with. The gym was devoid of people. I checked the doors leading to the outside and found them locked. I thought that might be a fresh development, but I didn't remember if I'd checked them before to tell if they opened or not. They had at some point, since Bozeman ran out to the bus for fuses, and Heather accessed her truck. Since I didn't know if the door locks were automatic on shutdown, I made a mental note to ask Brantley.

I left the gym, and my next stop was the bathroom. Although I expected the room to be occupied, when I turned the knob, it freely rotated and I pushed the door open, turned on the light, and found it empty. I noticed the towel was crooked, so I reached out, touched it, and found it still damp from someone who had recently washed their hands. Another mental note, this one to ask Bozeman who he'd brought recently, passed into my brain. I righted the towel, shut off the light, and left the room.

The only thing left for me to do was take another trip down the hallway, and I did. I made my way up the left side, checking each knob as I walked. None of them turned. I got the same result with the door at the far end of the hallway and most of the doors on the way back. Until I reached the last one. To my surprise, that knob turned.

I took a deep breath, then pushed the door open. To my satisfaction, it didn't squeak like in old horror movies, and it opened all the way until the door encountered the stop. I brushed my hand along the wall next to me, hoping to encounter a standard switch, and when I hit it, I turned on the overhead lights. Where the chandelier lights were classic and comforting in the ballroom, what I turned on was anything but. Overhead, bright lights shone through plastic panels, giving the room an ambiance impression like that of a clinic or a warehouse.

I'd stumbled into a storeroom. The room was approximately thirty-feet square, and each wall held floor-to-ceiling wood shelving units. I couldn't identify the wood, but I recognized the scent as cedar. To my left were shelves packed with everything needed for a fancy dinner service, like the one I'd witnessed.

I stepped to the shelf and saw rows of water and wine glasses. In addition to the wineglasses, beer mugs, and rocks glasses sat among the shelves. Next to the massive display of glassware sat the china. I counted six unique patterns of dinner plates, salad plates and bowls, soup bowls, coffee saucers and cups, and those little plates people were supposed to use as bread-and-butter plates. I picked up a dinner plate and grunted at the heft. Personally, I preferred melamine since it was light and didn't break whenever we forgot to secure the cabinet and Bozeman made a sharp turn. Granted, it wasn't made for the microwave, but that's why we owned various containers made for that job. So what if they were all spaghetti stained?

Past the china, I came to several large boxes. I opened one and found the silverware. Based on the box, I guessed it was the good stuff, and when I picked up a fork, the weight confirmed it. What was the rule? The heavier the fork, the tastier the food? Perhaps I made that up. I inspected several boxes. All held silverware, again in distinct patterns and alloys. One box held nothing but serving utensils such as fancy meat forks, actual metal ladles, and tongs in several sizes. Not a speck of plastic anywhere. Clearly, Hawthorne Harris would have detested a meal served on my bus.

The back wall, although covered with shelves, contained only cloth napkins. I counted six shelves from bottom to top, and each shelf contained napkins in a separate color. I picked one up at random, Burgundy red, twelve inches square, in a thickness that seemed wasted on a napkin. Nothing unusual about it, so I refolded it the best I could and returned it to its place.

The shelves on the third wall contained all things decor. Candlesticks of various sizes, vases, trinkets, and do-dads galore. Chinese lanterns stood lined up next to foot-high crystal Christmas trees and a variety of wooden soldier nutcrackers. I seemed surrounded by something for every holiday. Glass shamrocks, red crystal hearts, even a porcelain Easter bunny that looked like an antique to me.

The center of the room held two wooden tea carts, one twice as large as the other. It was large enough to contain an interior compartment, so I opened the double doors and discovered nothing except what a mouse had left behind. It seemed even the rich had to deal with vermin occasionally. Smiling, I shut the doors. I moved to the door, turned, and looked around a final time. I'd found some interesting things, but not Jackie. Another mental note for Brantley passed into my head, this one to see if he had keys to the remainder of the house so I could snoop around a bit more.

As I sighed, I turned off the lights and closed the door before me. I tried the knob again, and it turned easily. Someone had unlocked the door and left it that way. It added another question to my growing list.

My search for Jackie had failed in underwhelming fashion, so I returned to the ballroom to have a chat with Brantley about the keys and Amelia about her supposed affair.

I spotted Brantley first, standing at the bar and having an animated discussion with Ashley, whose arms-crossed posture told me she wasn't having anything he was ranting about.

"What's going on?" I asked.

"I'll tell you what. She's refusing to serve me a glass of wine," Brantley snorted. He didn't seem happy. I didn't feel sorry for him.

"You agreed to that. No more alcohol tonight. Remember?"

He scoffed. "It's only wine. That's barely alcohol. It's Californian, for grape's sake."

I wasn't sure how those things connected in his head, but at the moment, I wasn't interested.

"Do you have keys for this place? I can't find Jackie, and she's nowhere that I can actually access. I'd like to check the entire house for her."

Brantley shook his head. "No way. Mr. Harris wouldn't like that at all. No unauthorized person in restricted areas. That's the rule."

"Is this a secret government facility? You talk like it is. Besides, Mr. Harris won't care because he's too busy waiting for the coroner to arrive. You promised that you'd cooperate with me, and frankly, it's a promise that several people have broken several times tonight. I'm getting tired of it. You going to give them to me, or not?"

Brantley looked at me, then at the prone body, then back at me.

"I'll tell you what. I'll make it easy for you."

With purpose, I stepped around to the back of the bar, and as Ashley stepped aside, I saw what I wanted. From the wine fridge beneath the bar, I extracted an opened bottle of what I assumed was a cheap California wine. I placed the bottle on the bar top and pointed at it.

"A barter. A trade. The house keys for the bottle. The whole thing, all to yourself. What do you say?"

He thought about it for a good, long minute. Apparently, it gave him some trouble because I noticed several beads of sweat appear on his forehead.

"Fine," Brantley said at last. He rooted around in his tunic for the keys and slammed them on the bar. In one motion, he grabbed the bottle, gave us a sneer, and stomped away like a pouting toddler carrying a cookie.

"You know, he'll be right back," Ashley said.

"Why?" I asked.

Ashley held up the tool in her right hand. "That bottle has a cork in it."

I couldn't help but smile, and I did so. I even managed to laugh. It was only a short one, but it felt good. A simple chuckle had knocked away some of the tension I'd let build up over the course of the last few hours.

I was about to respond when the lights dropped out.

"Amelia, what's the password to your phone?" I called out in the darkness. She replied without hesitation.

As I reached for her phone in my pocket, I took a step to my left, caught the edge of Ashley's mat, lost my balance and fell. At that moment, I heard the loud report of a firearm, followed by several screams. I had dropped Amelia's phone in the fall and flailed my arms around on the floor until I finally found it. I punched in the code, opened the lights app, and ended the darkness.

"Are you okay?" Ashley asked as she leaned over me.

"I think so. Can you help me up?"

With her assistance, I got to my feet and took a second to regain my balance.

"Holy cow," Ashley said. "Look at this."

I turned and looked at where she had pointed. It was a small, round hole in the plaster, directly in line with where I'd been standing a second before the lights failed. My neck and ears got warm, which meant only a single thing. I transformed from happy-go-lucky Codi to overwhelmed and angry Codi.

Play time was over.

There was a new sheriff in town, so I strode to the middle of the room, and in my most commanding voice, issued an order. "Everyone come here and line up. Now."

"Why should we?" Claude asked.

"Because someone took a shot at me, so do it."

Loren stepped forward first. "Come on, folks. Let's go."

Reluctantly, everyone lined up, including Stacy and Ashley, who stood in line but a step away from those in costume. Except

Danny Ewing.

"Bozeman, can you go search him? See if he's really asleep or if he's pulling a con. Oh, and if he's armed."

Bozeman nodded and headed for Danny, who remained in the same position I'd seen him in for at least two hours. I watched as Bozeman did a quick search of Danny's person, and finding nothing, let Danny sleep and returned to the line.

"Here's what's going to happen. If you have pockets, empty them, then you'll get a pat down search."

"No way, I don't want him touching me," Amy said, pointing at Bozeman.

"Fine. Bozeman, you take the men. Laurel, please take the women. Start with Ashley and Stacy."

"Why them?" Helen protested.

I shrugged. In my mind, they were both innocent, so I knew I could exclude them immediately. I also knew it would irritate the rest of the group if the hired help got to go first for a change.

Laurel walked in front of the line and got to Ashley first. When she emptied her pockets, Ashley produced a bottle opener and two corks. Laurel did her TSA impression, patted her down, and said she was good. I nodded, and Ashley returned to the bar.

Stacy, next in line, had nothing in her pockets, and the pat down revealed nothing.

"Where's your phone?" I asked, noticing she didn't have it on her.

Stacy gestured to the wall where she'd been sitting most of the night. There, on the floor and plugged into an outlet, was her phone. I nodded, and she left the line.

"I'm next since I've got nothing to hide," Loren said as he stepped out of line and approached Bozeman. Loren removed from his pockets a wallet and a set of car keys, got patted down, then received the green light to sit down.

"This is ridiculous," Claude said.

"Think so? Then you can be next," Bozeman said.

Claude made a noise similar to a growl, but he stopped with the theatrics the second Bozeman got close to him. Like Loren, Claude carried keys and a wallet. He also carried a pocketknife, which Bozeman slipped into his own pocket, vowing to return it when the night's festivities were complete.

Brantley was the easiest of the men to search. He had a single empty pocket and had nothing on him.

Laurel found Helen and Amy to be equally easy to search. Neither had pockets, nor anything on them. That only left Amelia, who, I finally noticed, was missing from the line.

"Okay, did anyone see where Amelia disappeared to?"

No one had an answer to the question.

"All right then, does anyone remember seeing her before this latest round of lights out?"

Claude tentatively raised his hand. "I did. I was talking to her right before."

"About what?"

Claude shrugged. "Not much, really. Small talk. Weather. Business. That kind of thing."

"Did anything seem unusual about the conversation? Was she distracted, or anything?"

"Unusual, like holding a handgun while we talked about the storm?" Claude chuckled. "No. She seemed fine. Maybe a little bored, but I can't blame her there. I am too. Given my druthers, I'd have been out of here right after the pie was served."

"What happened next?" I asked.

Claude rubbed his chin. "Well, both of us grew bored with the talk. I could tell. It was like a bad first date. Ever have one like that? Things go okay at first, but then you get that knot in your stomach and things go downhill from there? Become awkward? That's what it felt like to me. So, I left to find someone else to talk to."

"As simple as that?" I asked.

"Yep."

"You see anything when the power failed?"

Claude gave an extended exhale before he answered. "No. When things went dark, I was probably five or six feet away from her already. When it went dark, I stopped in my tracks, and didn't move until the lights came on."

He stopped speaking but looked at me for an extended few

seconds without dropping eye contact.

"Is there anything else?" I asked.

He moved closer to me. "I think I saw the gun fired."

Those were words I wasn't expecting.

"You saw the shooter? Who was it?"

"No, I don't know who the shooter was. It was way too dark. I think I saw the muzzle flash when it fired. Just a blip and it was gone."

"I don't understand."

"If I had my guess, I'd say something covered it, like a napkin, maybe?"

I thought about it for a second. I only carried a small firearm myself, and rarely fired it, but my dad would often take me to the range and practice with all sorts of weapons. Depending on the gun, it had a muzzle flash ranging from a sparkler to barely visible. Unless I dug the round from the wall, I couldn't tell what I was dealing with, but I liked where Claude headed with the napkin idea.

"Did you take the keys?"

I turned around. Ashley was there in front of me, asking the question.

"What keys?" I asked.

"The ones Brantley gave you. It didn't dawn on me until after I got back to my station after your lineup. Those keys were gone. Unless you took them, they're missing."

CHAPTER SIXTEEN

I sat down at a table and ran my fingers through my hair. Once again, I felt like I was missing something, or, in this case, several things, including two witnesses and a gun. I crossed my arms on the table and laid my head down on my arms, intending to rest my eyes for just a moment.

It wasn't long before I received a nudge. I lifted my head and noticed Laurel standing over me.

"Hey," I said.

"Have a nice nap?" Laurel asked.

"No nap. I only closed my eyes for a few seconds."

Laurel grinned at me. "How many seconds are in a half hour?"

"No? Really?" I took Laurel's phone from my pocket and checked the time. She was right. I dozed off. Clearly, I was more tired than I'd imagined.

"How's Viola doing?" I asked.

"There's some good news on that front. She regained consciousness for about ten minutes."

"Is she okay?"

"I think she'll be fine. Someone rang her bell pretty good. I asked her a few questions, and she knew her name, the current year, who the president is, stuff like that."

"Can I talk to her?"

"Sure. That's why I came over. She wants to see you."

I nodded, then stood. I guessed I'd really napped based on the way my back cracked the second I straightened my spine. After I stretched my arms over my head and flexed my legs, I was ready to go.

"Lead the way," I said.

I followed Laurel over to the table that Jackie had first used when I found her the first time. Viola was sitting up straight in a chair, a tablecloth draped over her shoulders like a blanket, and she held a plastic bag of ice to the back of her head. She smiled weakly at me when she saw me coming.

"Codi."

"Viola. How are you feeling?" I asked. I wanted to hug her, but she already looked uncomfortable, and I didn't want to add to it by squeezing her too hard.

"Like Humpty Dumpty. Like my head cracked open." She removed the pack and looked at the towel someone had wrapped the ice in. "At least, thanks to your friend, I'm not bleeding."

"Do you remember what happened in here tonight? About what happened to you?"

Viola returned the icepack to her head. "Just bits and pieces, and most of those are foggy. I remember several power outages, and that Hawthorne got killed. Did I ask you to get statements for me, or did I dream that?"

"It's real. You asked me to get statements from the service staff, which I did. When you… got assaulted, I expanded that and talked to everyone here."

Viola slowly nodded. "How did that work out for you?"

"Some people seemed helpful; others bordered on evasive."

Viola cracked a slight smile. "That sounds about right. Have any trouble or any primary suspects?"

"I had two people as my front runners, but they're both currently unaccounted for."

"You lost two people in a locked down house?" Viola asked.

I felt my cheeks redden. "Yes, I did."

"That's a first for me. What else do you have?"

I found a chair and spent the next several minutes recounting the events of the evening. Afterward, I retrieved my notebook and reviewed my notes with Viola.

When I finished, she nodded. "Not too shabby, actually. I'm surprised you got as far as you did. Clearly, you're your father's daughter. What's next?"

"My intention was to look for anything that may have gunpowder residue on it."

"Good plan. Perhaps I'll come along and help."

"No, Viola. You should stay right here," Laurel interjected.

Despite Laurel's advice, Viola dropped the icepack on the table and struggled to stand. To my surprise, she staggered three short paces before she almost fell. Laurel and I reached out almost as one and grabbed Viola's upper arms and guided her backward to the chair.

"I'm a bit dizzier than I expected," Viola admitted. "I'll wait here. You find anything. Bring it to me right away, okay?"

I nodded. "Will do, Chief. Laurel, would you mind staying here?"

"Of course," she said without a second of hesitation. "Go. Do what you need to do."

"You need any help? I've got a pretty good nose," Bozeman said.

"You know what I'd really love for you to do? Take a spin around the rooms you can actually enter and see if you can locate Amelia or Jackie. It shouldn't take you long, then you can come and join me."

"Consider it done. I'll be back in two shakes of a lamb chop," Bozeman said. He had his assigned mission, so he hurried from the room to accomplish it.

I scanned the area, deciding where to start. I returned to the bar and asked Ashley to move aside for a moment. Using my best guess, I stood with my back to the bullet hole in the wall and attempted to find out where the shooter stood. I figured they had done one of two things, either dropped the covering where they'd taken the shot, or carried it with them and disposed of it later. Mentally, I flipped a coin and chose to check the site straight ahead and work my way around the room counterclockwise.

The table directly across from me had a tablecloth, but it didn't look disturbed, and contained the requisite candlesticks and a wineglass. Nothing looked displaced, and I doubted in the time it took to take a shot at me, someone might have discretely removed the items, taken the shot, and reset the table. I realized at that moment, I only needed to check the settings that looked disrupted, much like how Bozeman pointed out the tablecloth that hid Amelia's basket. I followed the rabbit hole. If Amelia's basket held her phone, might it contain the missing gun as well?

Although the tablecloth looked undisturbed, I checked under the table. Nothing. I checked several tables, for both the scent of gunshot residue, and for Amelia's basket, but I found the same. Nothing.

When I arrived at the ballroom's corner opposite, I found two piles of napkins. The first pile was on the floor, hidden behind the table. I assumed people had discarded them after use. The second pile held a half dozen, still folded into neat rectangles. I took a seat behind the table, tried to be as discrete as possible in a room filled with people, and inspected the top napkin on the pile. It smelled like a tropical breeze, so I set it aside and worked my way through the pile. No luck.

I sighed, then looked at the floor, at the mess next to my seat. In my mind, I tried to justify the process of picking up each of those napkins and giving them the sniff test. Since they were dirty, I caught all kinds of scenarios in my mind. From the innocuous, someone picked up a napkin, wiped off the tips of their fingers and discarded it, to more uncomfortable scenarios. Spilled drinks, food remnants, sneezes. I didn't dive in with both feet, as I normally would with a task, instead, I moved the pile with my foot to make sure nothing hid beneath it, then, satisfied it held no secret treasure, I moved my chair and placed it over the pile. The police forensics lab could deal with it instead.

I sat for a moment, both to rest for a moment, and consider my next move, and it came to me in three quick bullet points. The missing keys. The gun. Amelia's basket. The thought of the gun reminded me to ask Viola if she carried a weapon, and if so, was hers still on her person somewhere. The shot at me and the assault of her would tie to a single perpetrator, if that was the case.

Break over, I resolved to do the easiest task and talk to Viola first, when I saw Loren and Claude talking to each other. It dawned on me that I'd seen them in various areas of the ballroom, and as I watched them, they looked like they were doing circles around the room's perimeter, like mall walkers getting their daily steps in. They rounded a corner and strolled in my direction. My intention was to wait until they passed before I got up so I wouldn't have to interrupt their walk, but they stopped just before they got to me when Loren grabbed Claude's forearm and stopped him.

"Seriously, man?" Loren said. His words came out as a low growl, like the way I'd expect a grizzly bear to sound if they would talk. "You mean we could still lose everything?"

Claude hesitated and looked to his left to see if anyone was within earshot. Since he didn't bother to turn around, he didn't see me sitting there as obvious as a bright yellow dot painted on a black canvas.

"Yes. It all depends on what the heirs to the estate decide to do," Claude answered.

"All of this nonsense tonight could be all for naught?"

"Look, Loren, you had a chance to go before the city planners to express your concerns, just like every other citizen in town at the open meeting we had."

Loren gave Claude a backhanded wave. "You mean the city planners who all have an individual stake in the plan? There wasn't a person on the committee who wouldn't benefit from these stupid plans. Revitalize the town! Ha! More like enrich the already rich."

"You're forgetting about all the additional tourists we'll get. People will stop here from all over. This won't be just a drive-through town on the way to anywhere else. Every business here will benefit," Claude said.

"Come on, man. Stop with the bull. I don't understand where you're getting all these additional tourists from. All the better surfing beaches are to the south, and all the great attractions are in either direction. You think people are going to flock here for the summer productions of Shakespeare plays they put on down at the Playhouse Theater?"

"Think of the new diner. You'll have lots of opportunities to make more money."

"How? By forcing me to move to the opposite end of town? I'm right on the main drag now, where I've made a name for myself for years. Do you think the tourists are going to want to inconvenience themselves by heading to the opposite side of town, which, by the way, won't receive a single fancy upgrade in buildings or services?"

"Concessions had to be made," Claude said.

"What about the people that work in my diner? Some of them live within a few blocks away and need to walk to work. They don't have the resources to buy a car to get to another location."

Claude shrugged indifferently. "Not my problem. That's yours. Perhaps you should pay them better."

From where I sat, I saw Loren clench and unclench his fists.

"I already have the best paying restaurant in town."

Claude shrugged again. "So, you'll have to hire new people. So what? It's the cost of doing business, and every business needs to deal with staffing issues. You're not alone here."

"This is going to ruin the diner," Loren said.

Claude laughed. "Hey, at least you still have the pies. You do most of your sales outside the diner. Pivot, Loren. Get a website. Go for expanded distribution. Find a way to reach out beyond your current delivery zone. You've got a great product, there's no reason you couldn't spread out to include of all of California. Or go regional. Or national, even. I'm sure there's a way. If they can get those New York cheesecakes all the way here, I'm sure you can discover a way to get a pie out there."

"I don't think you're understanding me, Claude. We're not talking pies. I'm talking about lives. There are people at the diner who depend on me for those jobs. And locals who have no other place to go for an inexpensive meal out."

"That won't be the case soon."

"Wait. What does that mean?"

Claude dropped his voice to just above a whisper, but I could still hear him. "When they build the new off ramps from the interstate, several new fast-food places are going in. People will have all kinds of choices. Burgers, pizza, fried chicken, sub sandwiches."

"I didn't know that," Loren said.

"Few people did. Hawthorne did, of course, and me, and the planners. Beyond that, no one. But again, it's a benefit to the community."

"Those new joints wouldn't happen to be fast-food franchises, would they?" Loren asked.

"Nothing unusual about that," Claude answered. "Most fast-food places are."

"Let me guess. Those franchises coming in are owned by H.H. Holdings, Limited?" Loren said.

Claude didn't answer right away, and I couldn't see his facial expression since his back was toward me, but I could tell based on Loren's body language that he wasn't happy with whatever was on Claude's face.

"So, more truth finally comes out. That greedy pig cost me my prime location and was going to take away my employees and my customers." Loren growled.

Claude placed his hand on Loren's shoulder. "Look toward the future, Loren. What's past is past, and there's nothing we can do about it. Trust me, focus on your pies and you'll be fine."

Loren brushed Claude's hand away and leaned in toward him. "I've had enough of you, Claude, just like I had enough of your boss. Watch your step or you may end up just like him."

Without another word, Loren walked away toward the bar. Claude shrugged like he received threats like that every day, noticed Helen beckoning for him, and headed in her direction.

Alone again, I quickly rose and rushed back to Viola and Laurel. Bozeman was also there.

"I thought you were coming to help," I said to him.

"Well, I saw you over there not doing anything, so I figured you were done and didn't need me after all."

"I just overheard an interesting conversation between Loren and Claude," I said.

"About what?" Laurel asked.

"I'll tell you, but before I do, Viola, do you carry a sidearm?"

"Of course," she said.

"Do you have it on you?" I asked.

For a response, I expected her to whip it out of her side holster, but instead, she shook her head at me.

"It's locked in the glove compartment of my car. I didn't expect a shootout at a costume party."

She made a valid point; I thought. My dad often did the same thing when he entered places where he didn't expect to need a gun, which was usually smaller private events like backyard barbecues or Christmas parties.

"Could anyone have gotten it from there?" I asked.

Viola rooted around in her pockets and found her car keys. "Not without these."

That told me it most likely wasn't Viola's gun, which made things easier. Find the gun, find the owner, find the solution.

"Codi, what about Loren?" Bozeman asked.

"Apparently he may lose that diner of his," I said. "The way Hawthorne structured the land deal, Loren has to move to the other side of town, away from all the new developments."

"Why would he shut down because of that?" Bozeman asked.

"There are a bunch of new fast-food places moving in when they build the new interchange. You'll never guess who those new restaurants will be owned by."

"Hawthorne?" Laurel answered.

"Excellent guess. His entire plan included pushing Loren's diner to the other side of the tracks, quite literally. Viola, did you know about any of this?"

Viola shook her head. "I knew Loren was searching for other locations for his business, but he never told me why."

"Do you think he could have been the shooter?" I asked.

"Loren? No. I doubt it. It's not in his nature," Viola answered. "I've never even seen him with a gun."

"I have," Bozeman said. "Did you know he was a sharpshooter in the Army?"

"No. I knew he served, but he never went into much detail about it whenever I asked him. I got the impression it wasn't a good time for him," Viola said.

"It wasn't. But he loved to shoot. Earned several ribbons for it. When he got out, he did competitive shooting. I went to one once. Me, I consider myself no slouch around a rifle, but he impressed me that day. I don't think he missed a single bullseye during the entire competition."

"We should go talk to him," I said.

Bozeman frowned. "I assume by we you mean the two of us? You want me to go over and ask an old friend if he shot someone in cold blood?"

"Sure. What's the worst that can happen?" I asked. I smiled, but I guessed my charm wouldn't help. "He wouldn't shoot us, too, would he?" I was kidding, but it was a horrible joke that I regretted the second it passed my lips.

Bozeman looked hesitant based on his body language, but in the end, he relented. "Okay, let's go get this over with."

CHAPTER SEVENTEEN

We wandered over to Loren, Bozeman lingering a step behind. Normally he'd be right on my tail, but in this case, his stride matched his enthusiasm.

Loren, just finishing getting a glass of Coke from the bar, noticed us coming and headed for the nearest table. He sat and waited for us to join him.

"Bozeman. Codi. How's it going?" Loren asked. He drank from the glass and set it aside.

"Good, Loren," Bozeman said.

We both shifted into chairs and got comfortable.

"You have additional questions for me?" Loren asked.

"Tell us about your restaurant, Loren," Bozeman said, taking the lead.

He stared at Bozeman for an eon before, finally; he answered. "You know the full story?"

Bozeman felt his nod was enough of a clarification, but I wanted to make an addition. "We'd like to learn about it directly from you."

Loren took another drink, put down the glass, and turned it between his fingers. The glass created a wet ring on the tablecloth, so Loren picked up the glass and set it in the ring.

"I overheard you speaking to Claude," I said. "Care to share the truth with us?"

Loren fell silent once more. After another drink, he began speaking. "It was all true. What you heard. The town is using eminent domain to take the diner from me. The plan is to build something new and shiny on my lot, like a parking garage or some such nonsense."

"They're going to pay you fair value for your property, aren't they?" I asked.

Loren shot me an expression that implied I was an idiot. "The bank was in charge of determining the value, so they took great liberty of determining what 'fair' actually meant."

"You're losing the diner for real?" Bozeman said.

Loren nodded. "Yes. In ninety days, I have to be cleared out. I found another location, but it's on the south side of town. Far away from the highway that remains the lifeblood for this city. It's also in an abandoned industrial area, so as you can imagine, there's not a lot of call for morning pancakes there."

"Will your clientele follow you?" I asked.

Loren's caramel-colored eyes met mine. "Not likely. Some will, but the retirees that don't drive? They'll find a more convenient place to eat."

"And it's unlikely that the tourists will go to your diner since it's far from anything else?" I asked.

"That's a fair assessment."

"Codi, let's skip right to the brass tacks, shall we?" Bozeman said. "Loren, did you shoot Hawthorne Harris and later take a shot at Codi?"

"No." Loren denied.

"No? Sounds to me like you had a good reason to hate Harris. And I know you tend to hold a grudge."

Loren jumped to his feet. The chair he sat on fell back and crashed to the floor. He pointed a finger directly into Bozeman's face. "I didn't do it!" he yelled.

Bozeman, not one to be intimidated, took his feet as well, and headed into a stare down with Loren. I looked around the room and saw every face staring in our direction, so I realized I needed to deescalate things before the big boys got physical.

I stepped between the two men and held out a hand to each of them. "Come on, fellas, we had a nice civil conversation going. Why don't we head back to that?"

Bozeman glanced at me, and I gave him a light nod. In response, he took his seat. I leaned over and righted Loren's chair and invited him to sit. He did, took a drink, and regained his composure.

"I didn't do it. I couldn't have shot anyone," Loren said,

dropping his voice to a notch under a normal level.

"Why not?" I asked, cutting off Bozeman, who appeared poised to ask a question.

"Because. Look at this." Loren held both hands out and attempted to make fists with each. I noticed as he did so, the pointer and ring fingers on each hand didn't fold into the balls with the other three fingers.

"What are you showing us?" I asked.

"I've got severe arthritis problems in four fingers. Halfway is as far as I can close any of them. I couldn't pull a trigger if I wanted to."

I stared at his hands as he continued to hold them out.

"You think I'm faking?" he asked. "Try to push them closed. I won't resist. Go on."

I moved closed and took the index finger of his right hand and tried to push it in toward the palm. "I'm not hurting you, am I?"

Loren shook his head. "Not really. I feel tightness, nothing more. Those joints are swollen, so you won't get any farther than that."

I applied more pressure and attempted to close the other three fingers with no better results.

Giving up, I turned to Bozeman. "I can't do it. You want to give it a try?"

Bozeman shook his head. "Not necessary. Loren, I'm sorry I accused you of this. I should have known you didn't do it." Bozeman held out his hand for Loren to shake, but Loren didn't extend his in return. Instead, Loren stood, moved around the table, and took Bozeman into a bear hug.

While the brothers reconciled, I returned to Laurel and Viola.

"That didn't seem like it went too well," Viola said.

I shrugged. "Ended up fine, and we can scratch another suspect off the list. I don't think Loren did it."

"Who did?" Laurel asked.

"Honestly? My money is on either Jackie or Amelia, and now that they've both disappeared, possibly both."

"Why them?" Viola asked.

"Jackie dropped on my radar first since she disappeared when Hawthorne got shot, and she stayed missing for an extended period. She didn't show up again until much later, and she switched seats when the power dropped and someone left me this love letter." I opened the notebook and paged toward the back, where I'd stuck the note between pages. "She also headed into some interesting emotional dispositions. When I spent time with her, or talked to her, she seemed to play the part of the grieving girlfriend, complete with plenty of tears and heartfelt sobbing. But when I wasn't with her, she took on the demeanor of someone waiting for a plane to board."

Viola listened, thought for a moment, and spoke. "That all seems thin. And circumstantial."

I didn't disagree, but since I wasn't a trained detective, I would only go with my gut.

"What about Amelia?" Viola asked.

"If you thought my case against Jackie was thin, you're going to love what I have on Amelia. I figured out that a phone app controlled the dinner gong and the lights. That app showed up on Amelia's phone."

"And she claimed she didn't know about it?" Viola asked.

"Of course. In fact, she claimed her phone was missing for most of the night. I found it under this table right here. Where Jackie hung out for most of the night."

"Anything else about her?"

"Jackie said she was involved with Hawthorne."

"You mean like in a personal relationship?" Laurel asked.

"That's what she told me."

"If that were truly the case, why kill Hawthorne? Why wouldn't Jackie or Amelia go after each other?" Viola asked. "Typically, in situations where a man is stepping out on a woman, the women will generally go after each other and leave the man out of the fight."

I'd read that somewhere. "That factoid never made sense to me. Why not band together and go after the man instead of each other? He was usually the instigator of the whole thing."

"Perhaps that's what happened here," Laurel said. "Maybe

they decided to join forces and rub out the bad guy."

I considered it for a moment, and it certainly fell within the realm of possibilities.

"Is there anyone else you're thinking about?" Viola asked.

"No, not really," I said.

"Why not? You need to have reasons to exclude someone as a suspect just as much as you need reasons to include someone."

I smiled at the memory. "You got that from my dad, didn't you?"

"Yes. One of the first things I learned from him when we became partners."

"Okay. Let's run through them. I don't think Brantley is involved. No motive, and it's hard to be a personal assistant to someone six feet underground. I believe Amy and Claude are somewhat in the same boat as Brantley. They have too much to gain with Hawthorne being around, and now that he's not, I imagine they could both potentially take a financial hit."

I scrunched my nose, trying to remember who I left out. "Oh, I almost forgot about Helen. Personally, I think you ought to put Helen on your list as a probable drug dealer. I've heard from a couple of people tonight that she's been pushing things other than her personal training program."

Viola leaned toward and whispered. "She's already on my list. A person she's been selling to works for me. I'm hoping she'll lead us to her supplier, or anyone else higher up the ladder. Let's keep that between us though, I don't want her skipping town until I've had a chance to host her down at the jail."

Laurel and I both agreed to keep the secret.

"Okay," Viola said. "That only leaves Danny and the caterer's staff."

"I'd say you can ninety-nine and a half percent discount anyone involved with the caterer. Heather seems to have an excellent rein on her people, and I couldn't find one all night that had anything that resembled a motive. Danny, well, he's been on such a bender tonight. I'm sure he didn't do anything. I'm also sure he won't remember tomorrow he was here."

"That doesn't surprise me. He has visited me down at the jail.

He has a tendency to close the bars and stumble around on the street until one of my officers picks him up. Danny needs serious therapy and needs to get himself into a program before it's too late, but I'd agree that he's probably in the clear."

The three of us floated in silence for a few minutes. Laurel broke it. "Now what?"

I ruminated on the question. "I'd love to find the gun. Especially since I know now that it's not Viola's. I'd also like to track down Brantley's missing keys, and of course I'd love to find out where Amelia and Jackie disappeared to."

"I couldn't find them," Bozeman said.

Surprised to hear his voice, I turned in my chair, and there he stood behind me off to my right side. "Just now?"

"Yep. You sent me on that quest, remember?"

"Did you check everywhere?" I asked.

"Everywhere I could, which wasn't much."

I nodded. "Then I guess finding the keys should be our top priority."

"Where did you find them last time?" Laurel asked.

"Brantley had them. I set them on the bar, then all of a sudden, I found myself under fire. I didn't even realize I'd lost them until Ashley said something."

"Maybe he took them back," Bozeman said.

That seemed logical to me, so I wanted to find out.

"Can I have your keys?" I asked when I got to within three feet of Brantley and his almost empty bottle of wine.

"You already have them," he slurred. He picked up a bottle and waved it in my face. "Even trade, remember?"

"You didn't take them back after I got shot at?"

"Nope. Except for your round up, I've been here the entire time. Although, I'll help you look for them, provided you secure me another bottle of wine."

I decided against it and returned to my group.

"He doesn't have them," I said.

"Let's go search then. Should we check people too, or just places?" Laurel asked.

"Start with things. Don't bother them until you've exhausted everything else. It could be they just fell on the floor by the bar, or someone noticed them and set them down somewhere," Viola said.

"All right, so that's our plan, then. Laurel, you go left. Bozeman, you go right. I'll head back to the bar. Viola, you stay here and check under the table next to you. Everyone got it? Good. Go."

We disbursed, and I headed to the bar. Viola seemed right to me, and the most logical thing was they fell to the floor where I'd last seen them.

"Hey Ashley, how's it going?"

"I wish I were home."

"Me too. Did you see those keys?"

Ashley shook her head. "Nope. I checked everywhere back here, too, just in case I picked them up on accident to clear the bar."

"Did you check underneath?"

"No. Let's do it."

Ashley released the brakes of the bar and gave it a light push forward. It moved with ease, and when it was a few feet away from its original position, she stopped.

I glanced at the floor and spotted a black straw, a wine cork and the screw top from a bottle of some sort.

"So that's where that went," Ashley said as she scooped up the top. Then she grabbed the straw and the cork and dumped them all into a trash can. "Satisfied?"

I nodded. It was a long shot, and it didn't pan out. I sighed, then helped Ashley push the bar back into place, even though Ashley could handle it herself. Once back in place, I moved on, checking random tables as I passed them to make sure they weren't hiding any secrets.

Eventually, I made my way to the stage area. I did a quick visual inspection. Everything looked the same except Bozeman's acoustic guitar looked slanted in its stand. I did a quick check of the wings, discovered nothing, and intended to rejoin Laurel and Bozeman.

I stopped. Bozeman never left his guitar slanted. Well, he did once when we played at a county fair gig several years before.

He'd reached for it in the dark before a new song, and because he hadn't seated it correctly in the stand, he pushed it over onto the floor instead of grabbing it. When the lights returned, it took us a minute to get back on track while he performed a quick inspection to ensure everything worked fine. Since that day, he lined that guitar up in the stand as if it were a compass needle pointing north.

I picked up Bozeman's guitar and noticed right away something was off about it. I turned it flat and picked up a simultaneous jingle and thump inside. Then I shook it for good measure, and that action confirmed my suspicions when I saw the tip of a key over the sound hole. Not wanting to damage the guitar, I turned the tuning pegs to loosen the strings, then fished the keys from the hiding spot. I returned the guitar to the stand and myself to the group.

"I found them," I announced after Laurel and Bozeman rejoined Viola and me.

"Where?" Laurel asked.

"Over by the stage. By the way. Bozeman, you're going to need to check the tuning on your Martin."

He gave me a confused look, which I expected.

"You can do that if we ever get back on the bus. In the meantime, let's you and I go for a walk."

CHAPTER EIGHTEEN

Armed with the keys, I had a renewed sense of purpose and a hope that I'd finally get some of the answers I'd been searching for.

With Bozeman on my tail, I headed to the corridor near the bathroom, stopping long enough to check if Amelia or Jackie were involved in the poker game. They weren't.

"Why don't we look in here, first," Bozeman said when we neared the bathroom. He opened the door, slipped in, and I heard a click behind him. He wasn't keeping secrets, and I knew exactly what he was doing in there.

While I waited for him to relieve himself, I opened the door to the storeroom opposite. Upon first glance, nothing had changed. All the plates, glasses, and silverware sat right where I'd left them. The napkins looked all neatly aligned, except for the one I'd messed with and didn't fold exactly the way the others were. The decor stood all in place, waiting for holidays that would no longer come for Hawthorne. For a brief moment, I wondered if all these tacky treasures would remain with the house and the new owner, or if they'd end up in the discount bin at the local thrift shop.

That thought triggered another, and I pondered if Hawthorne himself had ever been in this room. I'd read somewhere a bunch of anecdotes of people who worked for rich folks and how the wealthy couldn't do the simplest of things, like operate a vacuum cleaner or make an omelet. Of course, the way it got spun in the article was those lucky, wealthy people did nothing that didn't add value to the bottom line, which, to me, made little sense. I hoped I never got so wealthy that I didn't want to butter my own toast.

I left the room and found Bozeman waiting in the hallway for me.

He grinned. "Sorry. Business called."

"That's fine, Boze. You didn't see anyone else in there with you?"

"Nope, sure didn't."

"Your hands are wet," I noticed.

He lifted them and looked in time to see a drop of water fall from the right one. "Yeah. I washed my hands, as usual, and as I was about to grab that towel in there, I noticed it seemed a bit gross, so I didn't take it."

"Such a rough and tumble cowboy you are," I teased. "Wait here."

I returned to the storeroom, grabbed the napkin I'd already mis-folded, and handed it to Bozeman. He wiped his hands, gave the napkin to me, and without thinking, I took it. A natural response to accept something that someone hands you. But now, I had the hot potato, and I didn't know what to do with it. I considered returning it to the pile in the storeroom, but instead took the more adult route of putting it in the bathroom on the rack next to the single hand towel. I'd let whoever attended to the bathroom figure it out.

"You ready?" I asked Bozeman as I stepped back into the hall.

"Just waiting for you."

Keys in hand, I found one to unlock the door next to the bathroom.

Bozeman turned the brass knob and swung the door open. Darkness seeped out, so he flipped the switch and lit up the room.

"What in the actual world?" Bozeman said as he stepped into the room and off to the left so I could enter behind him.

As I entered, I inhaled and held it, stunned by the sight. Instead of regular lights, flickering electric torches ensconced in ornate holders illuminated the room. The torches cast shadows across walls adorned with suits of armor. The suits stood four along each wall, a total of sixteen in all, each on a two-foot-high platform made of stone.

"Rich people and their toys, huh?" I said as I stepped into the room's depths.

Since I was neither an expert nor student of medieval Europe, I couldn't identify which countries the suits represented, or when in history someone wore them. But to my amateur eyes, they looked authentic. Some gleamed, the polished steel reflecting the dim lights. Others carried the weathered patina of age. I could only dream about the owners and the bygone battles and valorous deeds the wearers had lived through.

"It seems a little ostentatious to me, to be honest," Bozeman answered. "Why would anyone spend their money on all this... stuff?"

"I don't know. Any chance anyone could be in these?" I asked. "Like Amelia or Jackie?"

"I doubt it, but you want us to check, so let's do it. You take that half of the room," Bozeman said.

I looked at the row closest to me, and there before me stood a mixture of suits. Among them were towering full suits adorned with embellished helmets and imposing breastplates to smaller, agile pieces from plate mail to chain mail. The first two suits I encountered progressed quickly as the pieces didn't contain a helmet, and the way they sat on the mounts allowed me to see no bodies were hidden inside. The third was a full suit. I stepped onto the riser, and lifted the helmet, revealing nothing but empty space. The fourth stood empty as well.

In the corner was a large oak barrel, and within the barrel stood a variety of medieval weapons, from lances to spears, to a single quarterstaff. Leaning against the barrel was a mace, complete with an aged leather strap. On the wall above the barrel, three swords hung. One looked like the type I expected Loren to carry as King Arthur, but I didn't recognize the others.

I checked the remaining suits, found nothing of consequence, and joined Bozeman back at the door where he leaned against the jamb, waiting for me.

"Should we get one? I'd could be a statement piece during our shows," he said.

"Put a cowboy hat and jeans on a tall shiny object that won't budge for an entire set? Nah, the crowd would get it confused with you."

Bozeman stuck out his lower lip and pretended I'd broken his heart by the comment, and playfully punched my shoulder as I left the room.

"Come on. Let's see what else we can find," I said as I approached the next door. I found the correct key on the third try. The lock clicked open, and once again, Bozeman took the lead, stepped over the threshold, and turned on the light.

"Holy cow," Bozeman said.

"Now what?" I asked, following close on his tail.

"There's no way you have a key for that," he said.

I didn't bother checking. We'd only walked three feet into the room when we encountered another door. This door was one I'd always associated with either banks or movies that featured break-ins of a government installation.

The vault door stood a few inches over Bozeman's head, and a good four feet wide. Instead of an old-fashioned combination lock, a digital alphanumeric keyboard displayed on a screen inset to the door. I pressed buttons at random, counting as I went.

"A potential forty-character password? How long would it take to break that?" I asked.

"That would still be easier than these," Bozeman answered, pointing out two additional boxes on the wall beside the door.

"What are those?"

Bozeman sighed. "For fingerprints and a retinal scan."

"Holy cow seemed right on the mark. He must have something amazing in here."

"Probably the usual. Priceless artwork, hundreds of gold bars, and millions of dollars' worth of bearer bonds."

"Bearer bonds? What are those?" I asked.

Bozeman shrugged. "Don't rightly know. Saw it in a movie once. Are we moving on?"

"Might as well. Not getting in here unless Hawthorne has the password in his pocket, and he wouldn't mind us removing body parts to gain entry."

The door at the end of the hall was the one I was looking forward to the most. In my mind, it would open up to something fantastic, and whatever we found inside would magically bring all the pieces together and solve the night's mysteries. For good measure, I pictured a console with a big green button labeled 'END

LOCKDOWN' so we could leave this irritating place for good.

I put the first key on the ring into the lock, turned it, and tried again. It didn't unlock. I tried the second key with the same result. Wanting to move it along, I glanced at the ring and jiggled them in my hand. I attempted to unlock the door with one key after another until I tried all twelve keys, then I cycled through them all a second time to make sure I hadn't missed one.

"I don't have the right key," I said.

"Yeah, I noticed. Maybe Brantley doesn't have access to this part of the house." Bozeman said.

"I guess not. Think we can get through, like if you do some Bozeman magic?"

I stepped aside to give him room, and Bozeman stepped forward. He rapped on the door a couple of times.

"Step back a little," he said.

He watched as I complied, then encircled the doorknob with his right paw, and slammed his shoulder into the door. During the impact, he made a noise I didn't recognize as a good one, and before I could suggest he stop, he shouldered the door again. After achieving the same result, Bozeman stepped back.

"Sorry. I'm not getting through there without an ax."

"Is there another way? Could we pick the lock, or take the door off the hinges, or slide a credit card into the thing like in the movies?"

Bozeman pointed to the door side opposite the knob. "Hinges are on the other side. We don't have access to your lock picks, and if you have a credit card on you, I'd be happy to try, but I can guess where it is."

I gave him a half-smile. "Would your guess be that my credit card is in my wallet on top of the desk two feet above the drawer where I keep my lock picks?" I asked.

"It would," he answered.

"Then your guess would be a winner. I guess we will move on. We can ask Brantley about this door when we return to the ballroom."

Together we walked to the next door, and this time the lock yielded to the power of the seventh key I tried.

Bozeman, ever chivalrous, stepped into the dark void first.

"There's no light switch," he said. "It's dark in here."

"Don't worry, I'll save you." I retrieved Laurel's phone from my pocket, found the flashlight function, and after illuminating the small space for thirty seconds, I realized where we were. "Stay here. I'll be right back."

Using the light, I spotted a bit of reflective tape and followed it up three steps. I located a console, and after a few seconds, found the controls for the lights. After getting acquainted with the machine, I slid the controls up, and as I did, the canned lights in the room lit up. I stepped from the booth and rejoined Bozeman.

"Of course, he has his own theater," Bozeman said as he stepped farther into the room.

Before us was a three-level theater. For seats, we had a choice of a single seat, or a two-person love seat. Bozeman sat down in the chair closest to him.

"This is nice. Full leather." He fiddled with the buttons on the side, and I watched his feet go up and his back recline. "Oh, these have heating and cooling as well. And to think we've been sitting in those uncomfortable ballroom chairs all night. How did you know this was a theater?"

"I worked in one briefly while in high school. Of course, it wasn't as nice as this one."

"I can just imagine you in a little tuxedo with a red bow tie," Bozeman said. "Put on a film. Got any popcorn?"

I shook my head at him and looked around the rest of the room. "I'm going to check if anyone is here. Don't move."

"Don't worry about that."

I let him be and walked down to the front. I intended to check behind the screen, but the entire back wall, painted a reflective light gray, made up the screen with no place to hide behind. I moved to the center and looked up toward Bozeman, scanning each of the dark leather seats as I did. I saw no one other than my musical partner.

Just beneath the projectionist's booth, I spotted a popcorn cart against the wall. I breathed deep, and either picked up or imagined the scent of fresh popped popcorn with an artificial buttery topping and an unhealthy portion of salt. Next to the cart was a portable bar, a duplicate of the one currently in service in the ballroom. I took a couple of steps to my right and enjoyed the deep pile carpet under my feet. Based on the luxurious feel of the place, I knew wouldn't find a single dropped kernel or soda-sticky spot in this theater, and I suspected no seats had wads of chewed gum beneath them. I trudged up the steps and whacked Bozeman's boots as I passed him.

"Wake up, big fella, let's go."

Together, we left the theater. I sighed and let my shoulders drop. I'd hoped to find Amelia and Jackie, or at least one of them, but I'd failed in my quest.

"Where to next?" Bozeman asked.

"Back in the ballroom, I guess. We can ask Brantley if he has the key to the other door," I answered.

Bozeman cocked a thumb at the last room as we stepped past. "What's in there?"

I looked toward the door that stood ajar. "Just a storeroom."

"Did you check in there?"

"Yeah, twice. No one's in there."

"Can we take another look? Just to be thorough?"

I shrugged. "Why not? After you."

Bozeman swung open the door and turned on the light. He entered, and I followed. While he stepped in to examine the first set of shelves, I leaned against the clinically white wall, a mistake I found, since the light switch jabbed into my back. I moved over an inch and removed the irritant. I followed Bozeman with my eyes as he made a slow loop around the room. He even stopped at the same large teacart and checked the interior, just like I had done.

"Satisfied?" I asked.

"Sure. What was behind the other door?"

I looked at Bozeman like he had an aardvark on his head. "What other door?"

"Come with me."

I followed Bozeman to the far wall, to the shelves with the napkins. "Here."

"Here where?"

Bozeman crouched low and pointed at a set of scratches on the tile. As he moved his finger, I finally caught sight of the faint arc that opened into the room.

"Son of a gun. I missed that. How did you find it?" I asked.

"Dropped a napkin and picked it up. Spotted it then."

"I didn't see it. How does it open?" I asked.

Bozeman stood straight. "Well, I figure if it arcs out that way, the hinge is on the left side somewhere."

He grabbed the middle of the five shelves on the right side and pulled. Bozeman grunted, but other than that, nothing happened. He reached for the shelf above, then the shelf below, tugged with all his might, and again, nothing moved.

"Are you sure about there being a door here? Perhaps there was something else in the room, like a crate or something, and it scratched the floor?" I asked.

Bozeman crouched again, then got down on his hands and knees. He leaned over so his ear almost touched the floor. From his prone position, Bozeman reached out and touched the scratch with his fingertips, then traced it all the way to the shelving unit's feet.

"You're right. This doesn't match up completely. The scratches start about three inches from the feet, so whatever made these was out this way, and not flush with the shelves. Unless…"

I watched as Bozeman fondled the tiles around the unit's gray rubber feet. After he did it a first time, he did it a second.

"Bozeman? What are you doing?" I asked.

"Hold on a sec."

Bozeman got up and crawled on his hands and knees to the feet on the opposite side, went back to his belly, and ran his fingers along the surface of the tile. He stopped, got to his feet, and returned to the other side of the shelving unit.

"I think this unit moves out toward the center of the room and then slides open," he said.

"How can that be? You tried moving it and it didn't budge."

"There must be a switch or latch or something to open it."

I smiled. "Again, just like in the movies?"

Bozeman grunted at me like an unhappy gorilla. "Just look for something, will you? Along the inside edges of the shelves.

Probably close to the wall."

"Okay, okay."

I headed to the side of the shelving unit and wrapped my hand around the front vertical support. I ran my hand from shelf to shelf, and besides the cool stainless steel, I sensed nothing else. Moving on, I did the same with the next support, and the next, and found nothing. In frustration, I sighed and gave up on trying to find the secret by touch. Instead, I selected the third shelf to start with, and removed all the napkins from my half of the shelf and leaned over and pushed my way in until I felt my head touch the back wall.

From there, I visually inspected not only the vertical supports but also the horizontal ones on the shelf above and below me. I spotted nothing, so I slithered out from the shelves and repeated the process with the shelf above. No longer worried about keeping the creases neat, I threw the napkins aside, then used the bottom shelf to boost myself up to the fourth. I checked the vertical supports first, failed, then looked at the shelf above me. There I saw a small button, no larger than a pea.

"I think I got it," I said.

I pushed the button and waited breathlessly.

Inside the wall, I picked up the sound of a light click. I pushed away from the wall and felt the shelf move with me.

"Whoa, hold on," Bozeman said behind me.

Bozeman held the shelves while I freed myself from its clutches. I stepped backward until I contacted the teacart and told Bozeman to go ahead. He pulled the middle shelf and the entire unit moved forward a few inches. He grabbed the right side, pulled, and we both watched as the unit came away from the wall. I had wrongly assumed that the shelves backed up against the wall, but it turned out that a portion of the wall was connected to the shelves. When Bozeman pulled it open, he revealed a wooden door.

"Think it's locked?" I asked.

"I hope not. There's no keyhole. Let's give it a pull."

I stepped up, wrapped my hand around the knob, and gave it a yank. I expected a bunch of resistance that wasn't there, so the door flew open. The tiny room contained no light source of its own, but the storeroom provided all the light I needed.

At last, we'd found Jackie and Amelia.

CHAPTER NINETEEN

One would think the sight of two women bound and gagged would leave me stunned and frightened, but instead a sense of relief fell over me like a warm sunrise on a winter's morning. Someone had trussed the women up like calves at the local rodeo, except instead of rope, they were bound by black duct tape around their ankles and wrists. A short length of tape wrapped around their heads prevented them from speaking, not that they would, since they were both unconscious.

"Are they alive?" Bozeman asked.

The women laid sprawled on the floor facing each other. I saw Amelia's chest rise and fall like she'd just run a mile, and after a second, Jackie took a breath as well. "Yes, but I think Amelia is having trouble. Help me get them out of here."

I moved farther into the room, careful not to step on anyone, and bent over to lift Amelia's shoulders while Bozeman stepped in and attended to her feet.

"Let me know when you're ready," he said when he got into position.

"Okay, go," I said. I grunted, lifted Amelia an inch, then dropped her. "Sorry about that."

"You want to switch positions?" Bozeman asked.

"Not necessary. I lost my grip. Let's go again."

I counted to three this time, and since that magical spell always worked, I managed to lift Amelia's torso and together, Bozeman and I shuffled her out into the more spacious storeroom.

Bozeman searched for the edge of tape around Amelia's legs but didn't find it. "You have anything sharp on you?"

"Usually only my wit," I responded as I dug around in my pocket for Brantley's keys. My hand closed around them, and I tossed them to Bozeman. "Try these."

While Bozeman tried to free Amelia's legs, I worked at the tape covering her mouth. Someone had wrapped it around her head three times, so it extended from just below her nose to just above her chin. With a delicate touch, I started with her face. I pushed on her cheek to give me some slack and got a fingernail under the tape's edge. I lifted it and followed it around her head until I found where it had ripped from the roll near her left ear.

"Give me a hand here, Boze," I said.

Bozeman set the keys down and joined me.

"Sit her up," I said.

Bozeman grabbed Amelia's shoulders and gently got her to a sitting position. Once she was up, I at last loosened the tape edge and began to unwrap her. With the speed of a running sloth, I peeled the tape away, careful to take as little skin and hair with it as I could. On the second loop around her head, I discovered her abductor had covered her mouth with a dark red napkin. After I completed the third loop, I tossed the tape to the side and removed the napkin that had not only covered her mouth but was half in it as well.

As Bozeman watched, I gently removed the napkin from Amelia's throat. She took in a large gasp of air, and then her breathing returned to normal.

"Lay her down," I said.

Bozeman did and made a move to free her feet when I stopped him.

"Hold off on that. Let's go get Jackie first," I said.

He nodded, and we returned to the little room where we found Jackie still sleeping. This time, I let Bozeman take her top half, and together we wrestled her from the tiny spot and into the main room. I repeated the process to remove the tape from around her mouth and found she had a dark blue napkin shoved into her throat. Once I removed the obstruction from her mouth, Bozeman returned to undo Amelia's bindings as I worked on Jackie's.

I glanced over and saw Bozeman was still sawing away at Amelia's tape with the keys, and I guessed maybe that wasn't the best way to go about it. I ran a fingernail around Jackie's taped legs until I found the edge, picked at it until I got enough to grip, and pulled at it. The satisfying sound of the tape releasing filled my ears as I pulled, and after a half dozen loops around Jackie's legs, I released the last of the tape and placed it on the floor.

"Do you think they're going to want fingerprints from that?" Bozeman asked.

"I don't know," I said. "Nor do I really care at this point."

After I freed Jackie's legs, I started to work on her bound wrists. Fortunately, her assailant had ducted taped them together in front of her, so I didn't need to roll her over. I repeated the method I used on her legs, and soon I had her arms free and resting at her sides.

"Jackie?" I yelled. "Can you hear me? Jackie?"

I received no response at all, so I shook her shoulders.

"Jackie? Hey! Are you there? Hello?"

I still got no response. Whatever they had drugged her with was effective. As a last resort, I picked up her left arm and cradled it in my lap. I took her hand and pinched the tip of her index finger as hard as I dared. Finally, I got a response from her as she moaned and instinctively pulled her hand away.

"What are they on?" Bozeman asked.

I shook my head. "No clue, but it has to be something powerful. I can't bring her around at all. How are you doing over there?"

I glanced over, and saw Bozeman had Amelia's tape removed, and he had no better luck at reviving her than I did Jackie.

"Should we splash some water on them?" Bozeman asked.

I considered it for a moment. "No. Then they'd be unconscious and wet. I think the best we can do here is let them sleep it off until they either come to themselves, or we can get them some proper medical attention."

"So now what?"

"I'll be back in a jiffy." I rose and left Jackie lying by herself on the floor. With haste, I returned to the secret room and looked around, even though there wasn't much to see.

The room itself was only four feet square. Its spartan walls were unfinished, and whoever had created the room hadn't even bothered with drywall. The prominent feature was the vertical wooden studs that went from floor to ceiling every sixteen inches. Besides the studs, I saw cables in various colors, mostly in white and black. In the far corner, a small-diameter copper pipe came out of the wall, did a ninety-degree turn, and disappeared into the unfinished wood floor.

I crouched low to look for clues, but spotted nothing. No telltale torn buttons, no hair samples, no wayward threads, no confession notes. Nothing but dust, so far as I could tell. Dejected, I left the little room and rejoined Bozeman.

"Find anything?" he asked when I joined him.

"Not a thing. I couldn't even guess what that room is supposed to be used for."

"What's in there?"

"Conduit mostly, and I think a gas pipe."

Bozeman shrugged. "Now what?"

I shook my head, trying to produce a plan out of thin air. After all, I didn't have many items remaining on my list of things to do. I'd found the missing keys, and the missing women. All I needed to do was figure out the last missing piece of who the culprit was. Oh, and find the missing gun.

"Well, I'd really like to figure out who caused this entire mess and pass the baton back to Viola. And I'd love a nap and a shower. And maybe a peanut butter and jelly sandwich."

Bozeman chuckled. "I know what you mean. I've run out of gas and patience for this night. And I like your idea about the sandwich."

I sighed out of weariness more than anything. "We'll have to get Laurel to make them for us when we get back to the bus."

Bozeman got up, stretched, and took a seat on top of the large teacart. "There's something I don't understand."

"Just one?" I teased.

"Exactly one. How is it that of the three of us, Laurel makes the best sandwiches? I mean, it's the same ingredients, same counter, same knife, same everything. Yet somehow, they're on another level than what either of us make."

I hadn't thought about it, but now the question pushed into

my already crowded head. He was correct. Laurel's sandwiches were far superior to the ones Bozeman or I made. It must have had something to do with the peanut butter to jelly ratio she used.

I got poised to offer my opinion when I got interrupted.

"Codi?" My name was but a whisper, but it shot right into my ears and caught my attention as easily as a firework exploding in the sky.

I looked down and saw Jackie's bright blue eyes staring at me.

"Hey, you," I answered. I found Jackie's hand and gave it a squeeze. "How are you feeling?"

She blinked a couple of times. "Tired. My head hurts. What happened?"

"I'm hoping you can tell me. Do know where you are? Or remember how you got here?"

Jackie closed her eyes. I waited, and after half a minute I thought she'd gone back to sleep. Then she opened them. They seemed a bit more alert than a minute before.

"I was in the ballroom. I felt a pinch on my shoulder, then I overheard some voices, then I think I fell asleep."

"Which shoulder? And whose voice was it?"

"Left. It really hurt."

I looked at her left shoulder and spotted a small dot of red. I lifted the fabric of her sleeve and looked closer. There on her arm right above a freckle was the spot where someone had injected her with something.

"Hey, Bozeman, can you come down here and see if Amelia's got any needle marks on her?"

Bozeman did as I asked while I returned Jackie's dress to normal.

"Someone has drugged you with something. Do you understand?"

Jackie's eyes never left mine, and she blinked a few times before my words finally sunk into her head and she nodded.

"Do you remember the voice? Who did you hear?"

"I'm thirsty. Can I have something to drink?" Jackie asked.

"Bozeman, can you get her some water?" I asked, without breaking eye contact.

"Hold on, let me finish this first."

I waited, unaware I'd been holding my breath until my lungs started to burn. I exhaled and drew in a fresh breath.

"Found it, Codi. There's a blood spot on her right thigh. I'll assume that's where she got hit, because that's the only mark I found. Stay here and I'll go get that water."

I looked up and watched as Bozeman selected a glass from a shelf and headed for the bathroom. I returned my attention to Jackie. She'd closed her eyes again.

"Jackie? You with me?"

"Yes."

"Who did you hear?"

"Here." The words I heard got combined with the glass that floated into my visual field.

"Bozeman has water for you. Let's sit you up."

I struggled to lift Jackie's shoulders, but eventually got her to a sitting position. I repositioned myself so I kneeled behind her, and I wrapped my arms around her.

"Jackie. Have some water."

Jackie shook her head twice, like she'd just walked face first into a spiderweb. Bozeman held the glass steady to her lips, and when the water touched them, Jackie slowly raised her arm and took the glass from him. She drank deeply and finished three quarters of the water before I had a chance to tell her to take it easy. Jackie smiled and passed the glass back to Bozeman.

She found words, and they came out stronger than before. "Thank you. I needed that."

"Jackie, please. Can you tell us who did this to you?"

Jackie took a deep breath, exhaled, and finally gave me the answer I'd been waiting for.

"Brantley. He did it."

"You're sure?" I asked.

"One hundred percent. He did this to me, and I'm sure he's behind everything else that's happened tonight."

"Brantley? But why?"

Jackie shrugged. "That would be a question for him, wouldn't it?"

She was correct. "I guess I'll need to go ask him. Would you do me a favor and stay here and watch over Amelia?"

"I will," Jackie said.

I let her go and clambered to my feet. "Bozeman, would you care to join me?"

He didn't answer but based on his clenched fists and the look in his eye, he didn't need to.

From the storeroom, we hustled directly to the ballroom. Bozeman had stepped in front of me, and I struggled to keep up with him. Even moving into a light jog, I could barely match his lengthy gait. He stopped briefly just inside the ballroom door, and since I hadn't expected it, I almost ran right into his back. Bozeman paused for just a moment, spotted Brantley across the room, deep in conversation with Claude, and resumed his journey.

"Bozeman!" I shouted, trying to get him to stop, but he didn't. I'd seen Bozeman in a rage before, and although he wasn't anywhere near his worst, I still couldn't stop him.

Everyone in the room reacted to my yell, and every head turned in our direction. Brantley turned just in time for Bozeman to get close enough to grab him by the shoulders and bend him backwards over the table Brantley stood next to.

Without a word, Bozeman made a fist and drew his arm back, and I knew if I didn't do something quick, Bozeman would end up on the wrong end of a murder charge. Especially with the police chief watching.

I took the only action I could. I jumped and grabbed Bozeman's right arm. Normally, he'd have no problems lifting me, even with a single arm, but since he didn't realize I was there, I threw him off balance with my weight. He stumbled backward, tripped over the leg of a chair, and fell. Since I was still dangling from his arm like a Christmas ornament, I hit the deck as well. Lucky for me, I didn't get his full weight on top of me. Instead, I only received his elbow in my gut. I lost my breath, then heaved when I couldn't catch it back. I felt like his one blow had snapped several ribs, ruptured my spleen, and destroyed my soul.

Bozeman rolled over onto his side, and when he did, I sat up. I managed a couple of deep breaths, deduced I wasn't dead, and got to my feet. By the time I returned to Brantley, Claude had peeled him off the table like the sticker from a banana.

It was my turn, and I got toe to toe with Brantley and shoved my finger at his chest.

"You tried to kill me!" I screamed in his face.

Brantley raised his hands to protect his face. "I didn't do anything."

Claude stepped in front of me and forced me to back up a few feet. He put a hand lightly on my shoulder to restrain me. "What's going on here?" he asked.

"Brantley murdered Hawthorne, assaulted Viola, and shot at me," I said.

My comment drew some interest, and the circle of people around us grew. Helen, Loren, Laurel, and Viola had joined the party.

Bozeman hadn't found his feet yet, so Loren stepped next to me and wrapped his paw around Claude's wrist.

"You should let her be," Loren whispered.

Claude hesitated for a moment, then dropped his arm. "I only want to know what's going on."

"Boze and I found Jackie and Amelia in a secret room. He drugged and bound them up with duct tape. When Jackie came to, she told us that Brantley drugged her. It's not a far leap from kidnapping to think he did the murder as well."

"This all true, Brantley?" Viola asked.

"Of course not. Only pure speculation on her part."

"You had all the access, Brantley," I said. "And you had the keys to enter the locked areas, and you had the app. You controlled the gong and the lights when Hawthorne got shot. And the lights when you struck Viola. I'll bet your fingerprints are all over the note you left me, and the candlestick that struck Viola."

In a feeble attempt to regain his composure, Brantley took a moment to smooth out his tunic. I noticed the hole in his tights had expanded and ran all the way up his thigh.

"It's all circumstantial," he argued. "Should I remind you that you found no gun on me? Or that I stood almost right next to you when you got shot at? Or that it was Amelia with the app on her phone? Did you even see me with a phone tonight? No, you didn't. Because I don't have it with me, because I follow the rules."

"Is that it?" I prodded. "Did you get tired of following the rules? Sick of being underpaid and taken advantage of? Did you want a bigger piece of the pie?"

Brantley shook his head. "You have no clue what you're talking about. You've got nothing on me. No motive, no opportunity, no evidence."

"You mean no evidence except for Jackie's eyewitness account," I said.

"Don't forget about Amelia's," Bozeman added as he stepped to my side.

Brantley opened his mouth, but only a single unrecognizable syllable slipped out before he shut it again.

Viola put something cold in my hands. I looked down and saw her handcuffs.

"Do the honors, Codi," she said.

I lifted the cuffs and dangled them in front of Brantley's face. "Bozeman, Loren, could y'all help me get him turned around?"

Before the men could move, a gunshot rang out. As one, we turned around and faced the direction of the ballroom door. There, Amy Ewing had a gun pointed at the group. The muzzle smoked, and my eyes went to the ceiling, where I spotted a hole in the plaster above her.

"I told you she'd figure it out somehow. Come on. Let's go. No one else move."

Brantley pushed his way through the crowd and strode to Amy's side. He leaned toward her and she took her eyes off of us long enough to give him a kiss. When they finished, Amy raised the gun and shot another round into the ceiling. Almost everyone in the group instinctively ducked, and during the distraction, Amy and Brantley disappeared from the ballroom.

CHAPTER TWENTY

I looked at Bozeman, and he gave me a single nod before taking off at a dead-on sprint. Although I started my run only a second behind him, he disappeared out the door before I'd taken only three steps. Laurel chased me out the door, and someone followed her, but in the excitement, I couldn't tell who it was.

"Bozeman, wait up!" I screamed as I ran as fast as my short legs would carry me. Once I left the ballroom, I noticed he'd slowed to a walk, and when he got to the junction of the corridor, he stopped in his tracks. I got near and was about to pass him when he grabbed my shoulder and moved me back behind him.

"Whoa, there filly," he said as he slammed me into the wall. "Sorry about that."

I wanted to submit a protest when I overheard a report, and a bullet struck the wall to my left. Had I gone out into the hallway, I would have caught that round right in the chest.

"Thanks," I whispered.

"No problem," Bozeman said. "Now stay there a second."

I had no trouble complying with his order. As I stayed flat against the wall, Bozeman peeked around the corner. His head snapped back, and another bullet came whizzing by.

"I don't think she likes you," I said.

"There's hope for us yet. Don't give up."

I sensed someone brush against my left shoulder, and a turn of my head confirmed Laurel had arrived. Loren was right next to her.

"Hey," she said.

"Hey yourself. Loren, I don't suppose that armor you're wearing is bulletproof?" I asked.

He shook his head. "Nope, sorry."

I shrugged and turned my attention back to Bozeman. I

wanted to ask what plan he had in mind, but before I could speak, he took off in a full run once again. Slowly, I moved up and looked around the corner. I saw the door at the far end of the hall closing, and Bozeman was in a full sprint to catch it before it locked. He arrived in the nick of time, and I saw him reach out and grab the knob just before the door slammed closed.

He started to struggle when someone on the other side attempted to pull the door closed. Bozeman took the knob in both hands and leaned back. "I could use some help here," he called out.

Loren answered the call and ran down the hallway. He wrapped his arms around Bozeman's waist and pulled. He must have caught him tight because Bozeman began to hiss like a balloon losing air.

"This isn't going to work. I'm losing my grip," Bozeman shouted.

I took that as my clue to jump in. After a quick assessment of the situation, I ran to Loren, but rather than give him a bear hug, I unsheathed Excalibur, turned it around, and shoved the hilt into the door. I let go of the blade just as Bozeman's hands slipped off the knob. Since Loren was still tugging on him, he and Bozeman toppled like dominoes. The door banged against the hilt, and I saw someone trying to push it away. On impulse, I kicked the tip forward, then stood on the blade. The person on the other end of the hilt tried to pull the sword toward them instead of pushing it out, but the sword's guard caught against the jamb and effectively locked it in place. We were in a stalemate, and I felt the sword go slack, so I assumed they had given up.

I put my ear to the door and listened. "I think they left," I said.

Loren scolded me. "Come away from there before you get your ear pierced by a bullet."

Undaunted, I swung the door open and looked. The room beyond was empty, so I threw the door open wide and stepped inside with Loren, Bozeman, and Laurel right on my heels. The room looked like a large parlor dominated by a wide, winding staircase. Opposite from where I stood was another door, this one ajar.

"Now what?" Bozeman asked.

"Now we break into groups. You and Loren take the room across from here, Laurel and I will check upstairs."

Bozeman frowned at me. "You sure that's a good idea? Me or Loren could come with you."

"Oh, please. Just go. The bad guys are getting away."

Loren wanted to protest, but I cut that off by pointing in the direction I wanted them to go. After a moment, they took the hint and rushed across the room.

"You ready to save the day?" I asked.

Laurel nodded. Together, we approached the stairs and started our climb. At the top, we found two closed doors at the top, and we each took one.

"This one is locked," Laurel said.

This was supposed to be someone's house, so I couldn't imagine why someone would have so many locked doors. I figured Hawthorne either had too many secrets or not enough trust.

"This one isn't," I said when I pushed the large double doors open. I suspected that this way would lead to the bedrooms, and when I ducked into the first room I saw, I realized I was right. The room contained a queen-sized poster bed, a chest of drawers, and a matching nightstand. A coat tree stood sentry in one corner, and that was it for furniture.

"Must be a guest room," Laurel said.

"Check under the bed. I'll check out the closet," I said.

I moved across the room with purpose, not wanting to dally, and opened what I assumed was the closet door. It turned out to be a short hallway with doors on either side. To the left I found an empty walk-in closet, to the right I found an equally empty bathroom.

"No one here," I said as I passed Laurel and moved on to the next room. The next three rooms were exactly the same as the first, right down to the bedspreads. In the fifth room, we struck pay dirt. The room looked like a pack of wild dingoes had come through.

The bed was the same, a queen-sized poster bed, but instead of a clean, white bedspread, this bed contained one in a soft pink.

Only a corner of the bed was empty and based on the found pairs of shoes scattered on the floor, I got the impression that's where the owner changed her shoes. The rest of the bed had piles of clutter with all kinds of things, mostly clothing. In one look, I spotted several shirts, three pairs of jeans, two discarded dresses, and a pink sweatshirt with a picture of a unicorn giving me the finger.

I moved to the drawers. Again, they were the same as the others we'd seen, but this one the owner had topped with bottles of perfumes, body lotions, creams, and things I didn't recognize. Overcome by the combinations of so many flowery odors, I coughed and stepped away.

"Whose room is this?" Laurel asked as she stood after looking under the bed. "There's no room under there for anything but a dust bunny. Books, unpaired shoes, a couple of shirts, and a couple of small boxes."

"It's Jackie's room," I said.

"How can you tell?"

I pointed toward the dresser. The only organized thing in the room was the autographed shirt I'd given her, hung neatly on a hanger, the hanger clinging to the knob of the top drawer.

"Anyone in the closet or bathroom?" I asked.

Laurel disappeared for a moment, then returned with the report. "I've never seen a closet so full. It's stuffed with clothing and other things. The bathroom is a mix of beauty supplies and used towels all over the floor."

"Let's go then," I said.

The next room we entered belonged to Hawthorne. I stopped the second I entered the room to take it all in. The room looked at least three times the size of the other bedrooms we'd explored. The centerpiece was a massive king-sized canopy bed, complete with the curtains I'd always associated with Ebenezer Scrooge in the movies. Unlike Jackie's, someone had made his bed with military precision, and his deep brown bedspread had not a crease to be seen. I walked across the deep pile carpet to the bed, which came up to just above my hip. If I wanted a nap, I'd need a ladder to get in.

I dropped to the floor and looked under the bed and spotted nothing at all, not even a random piece of fuzz. I stood and visually inspected the remainder of the room. He had two dressers and a nightstand on each side of the bed, both holding ornate table lamps. One wall held three bookcases, although only one held books. The other contained knick-knacks and photographs framed in silver.

"I'll check the closet and bathroom," Laurel said.

While she explored the interior of the suite, I leaned against the bed and stared at the bookcases. Something wasn't quite right about them, but I couldn't put a finger on what.

Laurel reappeared. "Nothing in the closet except a thousand suits and two thousand pairs of shoes, all in boxes, I might add. I don't think he owned a pair of jeans."

"What about the bathroom?" I asked.

"We could live in there. Walk-in rain shower, Jacuzzi tub. There's even a fridge in there. Seriously, Codi, who has a fridge in the bathroom?"

"Rich people," I answered without thinking. "You notice anything off about those bookcases?"

Laurel joined me against the bed and stared at them for a minute.

"Other than the picture on the floor, no."

My eyes passed from the bookcase to the floor and noticed the picture sitting on the carpet. It was a small one, like a photograph you'd get out of a photo booth at a county fair. Even with the ornate silver frame, it had almost disappeared into the deep carpet. I retrieved it, then tried to figure out where it called home. At last, I decided on a spot and set it on the shelf. Once I placed it back, I began to run my fingers on the bookcase sides and beneath the shelves.

"What are you doing?" Laurel asked.

"Searching for this." I pushed a button, heard a familiar click, then pulled out the bookcase. It swung open and I spotted another door. I expected it to be locked tight, but it opened right away. There, on the safe room bunk, sat a startled Brantley.

When I opened the door, Brantley jumped to his feet like a

jittery deer, slammed me into the safe room door, and ran. I thought Laurel was going to let him pass, but just as he got to her, she shot out a foot and tripped him. He hit her foot, took another two awkward strides forward, then fell. I heard a sickening thud when his head hit a dresser, and he was still.

To make sure he wasn't faking, I moved to him and assessed his condition. He was down for the count. With Laurel's help, I got Viola's handcuffs around his wrists. To me, the sound of the handcuffs tightening was the most satisfying thing I'd heard all night.

"Now what?" Laurel asked.

"We have to wait for the boys to find us, or for him to wake up. I'm in no mood to carry him."

"Screw that. I'm sick of waiting. I've been waiting all night."

Laurel left my side and returned a minute later with a liter-sized bottle of water. "Want a drink?"

I nodded, took the bottle, and drank. The cold water felt refreshing, and I didn't realize how thirsty I was. I handed the bottle back to Laurel, who also drank.

"You want more?" she asked.

I shook my head. I thought she intended to cap the bottle and save the rest for later, but instead she inverted the bottle and dumped the rest of the contents on Brantley's head.

Brantley came too in a flash. He sputtered, realized where he was, and tried to escape. I put a foot on him and held him down.

"Now where are you trying to run off to?"

With Laurel's help, I got Brantley to his feet, and together we escorted him back to the ballroom. To my surprise, we received a round of applause as we entered, our prey out in front of us, doing his own personal walk of shame. I spotted Loren and Bozeman, then saw Amy tied to a chair. We moved Brantley over to Amy and plopped him down next to her.

"Everything go okay?" I asked.

Bozeman nodded. "Just fine. Caught up to her in Hawthorne's office. All we had to do was wait until she ran out of bullets, then we went in and got her."

After I gave him a hug, I moved away from the gathered

crowd. I stepped back to the stage, my sanctuary. I took a seat on the riser and leaned my back against Bozeman's amplifier. After a few cleansing breaths, I closed my eyes, ready to rest.

*

Two days later, Laurel, Bozeman, and I stepped off the bus and headed into Loren's diner. The hostess greeted us and led us directly to Loren's booth. I grinned when I got there, and Viola stood up and gave me a big hug.

"How are you feeling?" I asked once she released me from her clutches.

"Sit down. I'm good. I spent a night in the hospital for observation and had to undergo a few scans and a day of boredom, but I'm good now. Codi, I have to give you credit. You did a great job. Your dad would be proud of the way you handled yourself under such extreme circumstances."

I slid into the booth, followed by Laurel. Bozeman took a seat on Loren's bench. I wasn't sure how to move forward with the small talk, but I got saved when Loren appeared from the kitchen, carrying a large plate. He set it on the table and my mouth drooled the second I saw the steaming cinnamon rolls with the white frosting dripping down the side. The smell of the cinnamon took me back to helping my grandma in her kitchen.

Loren grinned and sat down next to Bozeman. He took a moment to serve a cinnamon roll to everyone at the table, passed out the forks, and ordered us to dig in.

"So, Viola, give us the scoop," I said as I dug into my roll. I cut off a bite and put it into my mouth, where it practically melted with one flavor after another.

Viola threw me a cross look and chided me. "You know I can't talk about an ongoing investigation."

I dropped my eyes to my breakfast and silently cut off another chunk.

"If I did," Viola started. "I'd tell you it was Amy, not Brantley controlling the lights and the gong using his phone."

"Then Brantley shot Hawthorne," Laurel said.

Viola nodded. "He also whacked me with the candlestick in the ballroom."

"And the shot at me?" I asked.

"That was Amy," Viola said. "Good thing, too. I think had it been Brantley, you wouldn't be here today getting frosting on your chin."

I hoped she was kidding, but when I touched my chin, my fingers came away with a dollop of sugary goodness on them.

"How did we manage to get trapped in there all night?" Bozeman asked.

"That was Brantley too. When my people went through the ballroom, we found a blocker he activated to block any phone calls from getting in or out. He also called off security, too, which is why no one came to our rescue."

"Did you find out how Jackie and Amelia are doing?" I asked.

Viola finished the bite in her mouth and washed it down with some orange juice before she answered. "They will both be fine. Like me, they stayed in the hospital for a few hours until the doctors discovered what Brantley and Amy drugged them with. They got released about the same time, and even shared a cab ride home."

"That part I don't get. Why abduct the women?" I asked.

Viola sighed. "Brantley and Amy thought it would deflect attention away from them. It would have been easy to say they slipped out of the house, and no one would have been the wiser."

"You know anything about the business? Is Loren going to lose this place?" Bozeman asked.

Loren gave us a grin wide enough to count every bright, white tooth in his mouth. "Nope. I'm good. Hawthorne was the only person in town with enough capital to carry the project forward. I heard this morning the entire deal is off."

"I guess I'll have to wait a little longer to get my bigger office in a nice new building," Viola said. "But that's okay with me. It turns out Hawthorne had a bigger heart than anyone realized. According to Claude, the estate and all the personal property will get sold off, and the proceeds divided up among the many local charities in town."

"What about the businesses?" I asked.

Voila laughed. She wiped her mouth and set her napkin on

the table. "You'll never believe this one. Claude told me Hawthorne's heir apparent will run the businesses."

"I didn't know he had one," Loren said.

"He does, and you met her. Helen Troy."

Based on the gasps, Viola's words shocked everyone at the table, except Loren.

"What?" I asked. "How did that happen?"

"Yep, it turns out that Helen is Hawthorne's half-sister."

"She wasn't just hanging around the office giving Hawthorne personal training services," I said.

"Nope. Turns out he was looking to retire soon, and they were using her ruse as a cover story, so no one would be the wiser."

"One last thing I need to know," I said. "Why? Why did Brantley and Amy do it?"

Viola drained her glass before she answered. "Well, it turns out that Brantley was the wiser and knew that Hawthorne wanted to step down. From what he gathered, Helen wasn't as fond of rebuilding the entire town as Hawthorne was and wanted to scale way back. She also wasn't fond of Brantley, so he knew he'd be out the door soon. So, he thought if he could get rid of them both, he could somehow control his own fate."

"Okay," I said. "That explains Brantley. What about Amy?"

"That one comes down to a combination of convenience and greed. She wanted to escape Danny's problem with the bottle, and she'd also invested heavily in several of the companies that would benefit from the construction projects. From what my investigators have revealed so far, she positioned herself to make millions. She saw Brantley as a way to get out of her marriage and into the life of a millionaire. Turns out the end result is bad for both of them."

I finished the last of the cinnamon roll and licked the fork clean of frosting. "That was delicious, Loren. Thank you."

"No. Thank you, Codi. And Bozeman and Laurel as well. We don't know what would have gone down had you not been there. And trust me, you've got another batch of rolls and a couple of pies going with you when you leave here."

I patted my stomach. "Sounds good to me."

"Speaking of leaving, where are you headed next?" Viola asked.

I shrugged. I had the destination written on a calendar on the bus, but I hadn't looked at it in a bit. The location didn't matter. I knew there would be music and adventure regardless of where the bus took us.

ABOUT THE AUTHOR

Dan DeKoning was born and raised in Milwaukee, Wisconsin, and currently lives in Knoxville, Tennessee with his wife and their cats.

He is a storyteller and poet who loves to write in a variety of genres and themes. He is also a voracious reader who loves to read anything he can get his hands on.

When he's not writing, you can find him hunting for treasures in used bookstores, or out exploring the planet, or geocaching, or searching for adventures and stories to tell.

ALSO BY DAN DEKONING

This is Dan DeKoning's complete library at the time of publication, but Dan has new books coming out all the time. Sign up for his newsletter at DanDeKoning.com to stay up to date on new releases.

<u>Fiction</u>
Déjà Vu
The Haunting of Hyacinth House
How Deep the Darkness

<u>Geocaching Mystery Series</u>
The Cacheland Conspiracy
The Quincy Bay Quandary
The Secret of the Seven Valleys
The Geocaching Mystery Omnibus – Volume 1

<u>Codi Cassidy Cozy Mystery Series</u>
Acoustics and Alibis
Ballads and Bloodshed
Codas and Calibers
Codi Cassidy Cozy Omnibus – Volume 1

<u>Poetry Collections</u>
Lost and Found
Random Thoughts